A Gift from the Sea

Ann E Brockbank

To Irene

Best wishes and happy reading

Ann x

A E Brockbank

First published in Great Britain as a paperback in 2019

Front cover by © R W Floyd, from an original oil painting

ISBN: 9781689110228

To Sarah

I am blessed to have you in my life.
Your friendship lights up my world.

Also by Ann E Brockbank

Historical Novels

A Gift from the Sea – 1901 - 1902

The Glittering Sea – 1912 - 1919

Mr de Sousa's Legacy – 1939 – 1960

Contemporary Novels

The Blue Bay Café

On a Distant Shore

Prologue

The warm, sour aroma of milk and dung in the Bochym Manor milking parlour has left a lasting memory - I can still smell it now, all these years later. I stand in the shadows, watching my fifteen-year-old self lean my forehead against the cow, my fingers squeezing the milk from her teat. I stare transfixed into the pail of milk, lost in my private despair.

The beast shudders suddenly, disturbed by an unwelcome intrusion in the parlour. My fingers hesitate. I know without looking who is standing beside me. Tears well as I catch sight of his highly polished shoes. I have to fight the urge to spit at them, for I know why he's there.

His knee nudges me. I straighten up and face him. He splays ten fingers while mouthing the words, 'ten-o-clock tonight.' My fate is sealed.

Derek the dairyman asks him, "What's your business here?"

'None of yours,' he replies curtly as he walks away..

Derek. Dear, kind man, how I wish I'd made it his business, but only my friend Ruby Sanders knew.

I return to my work as unfathomable tears salt my pail of milk.

In a vaporous swirl, the scene before me evaporates - though I know I shall continue to revisit this, my last day of innocence.

Without help, I am charged to watch this scene, and others, continually unfold, incapable of stopping it. For who will tell my tragic story? Who will seek out the truth, now everyone has gone?

1

It was the last day of June 1901. Elise Rosevear, Ellie to her friends, stood on the veranda of the Poldhu Tea Rooms, inhaling a deep breath of warm, salty air. With the tables ready, places set, cakes baked, and the veranda swept clean of sand, Ellie felt that familiar pull, an unmistakable bubble in the pit of her stomach that drew her to the sea.

Quickly discarding her apron, she kicked off her shoes and ran like the wind down the beach, marvelling at the warm sand between her toes. Though the day was warm, a strong south-westerly blew, pulling her long auburn hair from its pins. High above, the Sand Martins nesting in the soft cliffs were busy feeding their young. Their acrobatic feats and glorious twitters were the sight and sound of summer to Ellie.

Tucking her skirts into her belt, she picked her way carefully along the black ragged rocks at the south side of the cove. Pausing for a moment, she tipped her head back to let the sun warm her face. These few, precious, stolen moments from her busy life in the Tea Rooms, were hers to savour.

The tide had turned, but the rocks, jet black and slippery with kelp, were still exposed. With her feet, tanned by the Cornish sunshine, straddling the rocks, Ellie searched for the glint of sea glass, 'mermaid tears.'

Legend had it, that a mermaid fell in love with a captain and calmed the storm that would have wrecked his ship. Neptune, angry that she'd used her powers thus, banished her to the depths of the sea, and her tears wash ashore as sea glass. Ellie felt it was a sad story surrounding these special gifts from the sea. Reaching her slender fingers into the coolness of a rock pool, she retrieved a piece glinting in the sand - turquoise sea glass, her favourite colour. She held her treasure aloft as droplets of water streamed down her arm. Satisfied with her find, she placed it in her skirt pocket. Ellie never lost the excitement of finding a piece, smooth and rubbed shiny by the tumble of the surf. She found no use for them other to collect them in a jar to admire!

As the roar of the surf intensified, the offshore breeze had blown the waves out, so the tide had crept in faster than she'd estimated. It was clear Ellie needed to return to the beach before she found herself out of her depth in sea water and late for work. Saturday was their busiest day now. The ascension of King Edward VII to the throne after Queen Victoria's mighty sixty-three years, seven months and two days reign, had brought a period of happy optimism to his subjects - none more so than the wealthy clientele visiting the newly constructed Poldhu Hotel this glorious summer.

The influx of visitors to the beautiful sandy cove, beneath the hotel, brought a boom in profits for the Tea Rooms. Before that, the Tea Room had enjoyed a more sedate function, where regular customers visited daily and the well-to-do families of the surrounding areas came most weekends in the summer, to take in the sea air. Now visitors would stake out a spot on the beach, the ladies would take shade under umbrellas and canopies to shield their alabaster skin from the sun's rays, and those here for the benefits of sea-bathing, would make for the newly commissioned Poldhu Hotel bathing huts.

One or two people were beginning to arrive on the beach now, including Tobias Williams, a rotund but strong man, with little humour, who had been put in charge of the bathing huts. Ellie grinned to herself, Tobias certainly had no penchant to partake in sea-bathing himself and grumbled constantly whenever he had to trundle a hut down to the water's edge. With her treasures in her pocket it was time to make her way back, but as Ellie manoeuvred back over the high rocky outcrop, away from the rising tide, a sudden wave broke, showering her from head to foot. Whilst brushing her skirt clean, a gleeful shout from further up the beach alerted her to two young men approaching the water. Ellie quickly stepped back. Gathering her skirts higher into her arms, she bit her lip to suppress a smile when she saw that the first man was shedding his clothing as he ran. She recognised him as the Thatcher, Guy Blackthorn - a dark-haired, handsome, shy young fellow. Further up the beach, undressing more sedately, was his friend, Philip Goldsworthy, son of the wealthy Gweek Corn Mill merchant. Philip was equally handsome, though fairer in features and far more gregarious. Ellie marvelled at their friendship - neither man found the class difference a problem. They were no strangers to this cove, though for decency sake, Ellie knew she should not witness their state of undress.

The sea beyond the rocks where she stood was deep now and great foamy bubbles began to swirl across her feet. In her haste to make for the safety of the beach, a split-second, misjudged step on slimy kelp caused Ellie to fall heavily into the swirling water. A searing pain shot up her arm as she caught her elbow on a jagged stone. Unable to decipher which way was up, she tumbled helplessly in the surf, scooping great handfuls of sand as she grasped for a hold. Flailing frantically, blinded with salt water and hair, panic struck on realising the ungainly weight of her skirt and petticoats restricted her ability to swim free. Her lungs burned, fit to burst, as she pulled at the water. She finally surfaced, gasping and sucking great gulps of air. Relief preceded panic when a rip pulled her legs sideways. Down she plunged fighting the grasp of the waves. *I'm going to drown,* were Ellie's thoughts, the moment before her head hit a protruding rock. The blow shot an intense pain through her temple and the foam and turquoise water disappeared as her world turned black.

*

Betty Trerise, owner of the Tea Room, checked the tea urn, and warmed the teapots beside it, tutting as she glanced at the clock. *Where was that girl?* It was almost time to open. Customers would arrive at ten and Ellie was nowhere to be seen. She walked out onto the veranda, shaded her old eyes from the sun and peered down the beach. Betty did not relish the increased workload the hotel had brought to her small business. She'd managed 'very nicely, thank you' these last twenty-five years, but with her rheumatic knees worse than ever nowadays, she was unsure how much longer she could carry on.

*

Having been first to the sea edge, it was by sheer chance that Guy Blackthorn caught sight of Ellie falling. His heart lurched. Already shirtless, he struggled to shed his trousers and plunged into the waves in his underwear. Guy frantically battled against the oncoming waves. *Oh god, how long had she been under now? Ten seconds? Twenty?* Intent on his mission, Guy dived through the clear, green, massive waves to avoid being battered backwards. Eyes stinging, lungs on fire, spitting salt water he surfaced. 'Ellie! I'm coming!' he yelled.

*

After folding his clothes neatly on the beach, Philip Goldsworthy was unaware of the incident unfolding in the sea. Instead he was more intent on gazing up at the newly constructed 200ft aerials, which the young Italian, Guglielmo Marconi had constructed beyond the Poldhu Hotel.

'Bloody eyesore on the landscape if ever there was one,' Tobias Williams grumbled, as he shuffled to stand beside Philip.

Philip looked disdainfully askance. 'If what Mr Marconi is doing works, Mr Williams, we'll soon be able to communicate with people overseas. It's called progression!'

'Humph! I tell you, it's a bloody eyesore. They won't last you know,' Tobias said, in his Cornish drawl. 'First storm that blows in, they'll be down like a ton-o-bricks, you mark my words.'

Philip sighed impatiently.

''ere.' Tobias grabbed Philip's sleeve. 'What's happening down there then?'

Philip shrugged Tobias's hand from his sleeve before following his gaze seaward.

'Isn't that your friend, the Thatcher?'

Philip threw a puzzled frown at Guy powering through the surf towards the rocks.

*

Grabbing the mass of skirt swirling by the rocks, Guy fought with the material until he found Ellie's arms and yanked her upwards. She was open-mouthed, pale and motionless, but easy to move. Hooking his arm around her middle, helped and hindered in equal measure by her clothes and the mighty waves, he fought desperately to get her back to shore. Overwhelming relief engulfed him when he finally felt sand beneath his feet. He stumbled and fell as the waves undermined his footing, but a moment later they landed on the beach in an ungainly tangle.

*

Philip, dressed only in his black bathing suit, had paced the shore line with bated breath as Guy struggled back to shore. When eventually they beached, Philip grabbed Ellie as a wave dragged Guy helplessly back into the swirling foam.

Philip shook Ellie's limp body violently. 'Oh Christ, Ellie!' Blood glistened from her hairline as he pushed sand and kelp from her face.

'Philip. Turn her on her side!' Guy yelled from the battering surf.

Philip did as instructed, grimacing as Ellie coughed and spewed sea water everywhere. He knelt anxiously by her side until the vomiting subsided, before scooping her into his arms and carrying her up the beach.

*

When Guy finally struggled free from the waves, he knelt on all fours, panting with exhaustion. The muscles in his arms, normally so strong being used to heavy work, burned intensely. He lifted his head. Dark curls hung in wet, sandy clumps against his tanned face and he watched through bloodshot eyes as Philip carried Ellie away. He feared she must have swallowed a great deal of water. *Damn Philip! He should have left her on her side for longer, she could still drown.* Guy closed his eyes in secret prayer. *I hope I reached her in time.*

*

Philip's knees buckled on reaching the Tea Room veranda, very nearly dropping Ellie.

Betty met him at the door, glanced down at Ellie and felt her chest tighten. 'Oh lordy me! What's happened?' She pushed Philip aside to kneel beside Ellie.

Totally disorientated, Ellie groaned pitifully, her head swam and white stars danced behind her gritty eyelids. Feeling her stomach convulse she heaved and vomited sea water across the veranda. Despite her initial predicament, Ellie was conscious that her wet skirts had twisted up around her legs and tried desperately to reach down to cover them.

Betty's eyes narrowed angrily, on seeing Philip's gaze rest on Ellie's exposed thighs. As she helped Ellie to cover her legs from his view, she noted he gave an unabashed ghost of a smile.

'Oh sweetheart, look at the state you're in,' Betty cooed, as her work-worn fingers gently pulled the strands of sand-encrusted hair from her face.

Ellie's eyes flickered open, relieved to see Betty – though her face was etched with concern. She knew she was in a safe pair of hands now - Betty had looked after her as though she were her own, since Ellie's mother had died seven years ago.

'What on earth happened, Ellie?' Betty asked.

'Well, quite evidently, she fell from the rocks into the sea,' Philip declared, not waiting for Ellie to answer. 'You need to send for a doctor, Mrs Trerise. That's a bad cut to her forehead.'

'I'm well aware that she needs a doctor! You'll have to go,' Betty answered frantically, seeing the pony-traps descending down Poldhu Hill. 'My customers are arriving.'

'I'm not leaving her,' Philip answered adamantly.

'Can I be of assistance?'

They both turned as James Blackwell, a regular customer to the Tea Room whenever he was down from London, approached them.

'Goodness, is that Ellie?' James dropped to his knees.

'Apparently, she fell in the sea,' Betty answered tersely, looking narrowly at Philip.

Despite just being rescued from drowning, Ellie's more immediate embarrassment was being found prostrate and in disarray by her important customers.

'Betty, please just help me up,' Ellie whispered. As she struggled to move, the pain from the wound made her head swim. 'Ouch!' Her fingers probed her sandy forehead and she lay back defeated.

'Ellie, stay still for a moment,' Betty urged. 'Please Philip, *go* and fetch help.'

'Don't worry, I'll fetch the doctor from Mullion, Betty,' James offered. 'I've the pony-trap with me.' He turned to leave, just as the newly married Lady Sarah Dunstan, Countess de Bochym, came up the terrace steps.

Betty dropped a small curtsy, immediately regretting the action as it jarred her rheumatic knees.

Since her marriage in February to Lord Peter Dunstan, the fifth Earl de Bochym, Lady Dunstan frequented the Tea Rooms regularly and was one of Betty's most valued customers. A delicate beauty, Sarah bestowed warmth and kindness on all who came into contact with her. As she proceeded forward, a waft of sweet perfume filled the air. She was dressed in a mint-green, silk skirt and matching jacket, open at the neck to reveal a cream lace blouse. Her blonde hair curled down the side of her neck from under her mint coloured straw hat.

'Goodness Mrs Trerise, whatever has happened here?' Sarah lifted her skirts clear of the puddle of sea water. 'And pray, Philip, why are you dressed in swimwear?'

Philip swelled in readiness to tell of his heroic tale, but Betty butted in before Philip could speak. 'Begging your pardon for the mess, my lady, *and* for Mr Goldsworthy's *inappropriate* attire, but Ellie's had an accident in the sea. James is going for help.'

Sarah dismissed Betty's concern. 'James, I'll send my man to Mullion. We'll need your help to move Elise indoors.'

As they all crowded round her, Ellie, mortified beyond belief, began to retch again, spewing salt water everywhere. 'Oh god, I'm sorry!' she sobbed apologetically.

Despite her fine gown, Sarah crouched and ran her cool hand over Ellie's forehead.

'Shush now, Elise. Let's just get you somewhere comfortable and out of these wet clothes.' She glanced up at James. 'Can someone lift her?'

'Stand aside.' Philip said, practically wrestling James to one side in order to pick Ellie up.

*

At the water's edge, Guy gulped a few deep breaths before pulling himself to his feet. His shirt and towel had blown into the line of the surf and were thoroughly soaked, though his breeches were still on dry sand. He reached for them to dry his face, and then turning seawards for decency he peeled off his sodden undergarments and tugged his trousers up his wet legs. The adrenalin pumping through his body abated slightly as he set off wearily up the beach. He shuddered to think what could have happened to Ellie, had he not seen her. He knew without doubt, he could not comfortably live life, if lovely Ellie was not in it.

*

James had swilled the veranda clean with a pail of water before settling at a table. People were arriving in droves to bathe and set up their places under parasols. He glanced over his spectacles at Guy Blackthorn walking up the beach, and frowned. *Was Guy shirtless*? James knew Guy well having watched him thatch many a house in the village of Gunwalloe, where James owned the cliff house he used to write his best selling novels.

'Guy, my friend, come, join me.'

Guy shook his head. His dark hair hung in wet clots about his neck and the trousers he wore, though dry, stuck to his legs, revealing large damp patches. 'I can't James,' he said, his voice hoarse from the sea water he'd swallowed. 'I've no shirt to wear and Mrs Trerise will scat me, if I so much as step onto her veranda.'

'Here.' James shed his jacket and handed it down. 'Take this and come and sit. You look shattered.'

'But the sea water will ruin it I fear.'

'It's no matter, it'll launder. Put it on. I take it you were involved with Ellie's rescue?'

He nodded as he pulled the fine linen jacket on and flipped his damp hair onto the collar. 'Is Ellie alright? She looked done for when I got her onto dry land.'

'She's fine, I think. Sarah Dunstan is with her now and we've sent for the doctor. Come, tell me what happened.'

'I don't really know. I just happened to see her fall and disappear into the waves. Where's Philip?'

'He's just carried Ellie inside.'

Guy nodded resignedly and sat down.

*

Because of his swimming attire, Philip's arms were bare, and Ellie's face was in close proximity to the tufts of fair hair protruding from the top of his costume. As she glanced up at Philip, he gave a raffish wink, which despite her obvious embarrassment sent a pleasant frisson through her body - though his strong cologne threatened to turn her fragile stomach again.

As they entered her small, but spotlessly clean, box bedroom, Ellie saw Philip's eyes sweep the room, taking in the intimacy of her personal possessions. She squeezed her eyes shut, blushing through her sickly pallor.

'Don't put her on the bed, Philip.' Sarah stopped him from lowering her down. 'It will soil her lovely eiderdown.' She pulled a chair out from the desk by the window. 'Sit her here and then you can leave us.'

Reluctantly relinquishing Ellie, Philip hovered for a moment.

'Please close the door as you leave, Philip,' Sarah said firmly.

*

Betty bustled in with a pail of water to find Sarah knelt at Ellie's feet. 'Is the maid alright, my lady?'

Sarah lifted Ellie's chin. 'Are you?' she asked gently.

Ellie nodded shakily.

'She'll be fine, Mrs Trerise. Thank you for the water. I'll see to Elise. It sounds as though you're busy out there.'

'Aye, tis, and I'm on my own to deal with it.'

'I'll come and help as soon as I can,' Sarah offered.

'Oh no, my lady, I can't let you do that. I'll… I'll manage.' Betty backed out the door, bobbing a curtsy, followed by a rub of her knee and an audible 'Ouch!'

Turning her attention back to Ellie, Sarah smiled. 'Now let's get you out of these wet clothes and rinse the sand from your hair before the doctor gets here.'

*

Before they had a chance to ask after Ellie, Philip had rushed past Guy and James to retrieve his clothes from the beach, arriving back five minutes later to sit down with an exhausted sigh.

'How's Ellie?' Guy asked anxiously.

'She'll live,' he answered flippantly. 'She has quite a nasty cut to her forehead though. I do hope it doesn't permanently mar her lovely face.'

They all nodded - that would be a terrible shame.

'It was damn lucky we were here,' Philip said, leaning back to stretch his arms out. 'She'd have surely drowned if not for us.'

Although used to Philip taking all the glory, Guy forced his eyebrows not to rise.

'Good to see you back, James. I believe Sarah is hosting a dinner tonight at the manor, in honour of your newly published book!'

'Yes, Philip, she very kindly is.'

Philip yawned noisily. 'I can't be bothered to read. I've far too many more interesting things to do with my time!'

'Well thankfully Philip you're in the minority or I should be a very unhappy author. Guy, I have a copy for you, if you wish?'

'Thank you James, I'm really looking forward to reading it.'

Philip bristled unhappily. He didn't like to think that Guy was getting something he wasn't. 'Well, if you're giving them away…'

'Only to those who appreciate them,' James said dryly.

Though admonished, Philip shook the comment away. 'Where the hell is Mrs Trerise? I'm parched!'

'I should think Mrs Trerise is rather busy at the moment without Ellie. If you'll excuse me gentlemen, I'll see if I can help her. ' James stood up.

Philip folded his arms and muttered, 'Well I'm not serving tea to *anyone*.'

'I'd help but I need to get off home, James. Thank you for the loan,' Guy said slipping off the jacket.

*

When Dr Wade arrived he swept into the Tea Room and raised his eyebrows. 'Patient?' he enquired.

'Through there,' Betty gestured.

The tables were filling up and Betty was getting evermore flustered, even with James's help. The tea urn had spat scalding water at her more times than she cared to mention over the years, but today, she was at the end of her tether with it. She wondered quite unreasonably, if Ellie would be well enough to work after the doctor had seen her.

*

Having been rinsed of sand and dressed in a clean nightgown, Ellie's hair was still wrapped in a towel when the doctor knocked and walked in. After a thorough examination, the doctor cleaned and dressed the wound to her head, ordered bed rest and left.

'I can't stay in bed,' Ellie said weakly as she tried to get up.

'But Elise, you must.'

'Betty can't manage without me, my lady, and it sounds really busy out there.'

'Elise, you will do as the doctor tells you. Betty will manage. When I stepped out of the room a moment ago, James was helping.'

'Oh, that's kind of him.'

'Now, don't worry, I shall go and help as well in a moment – if Mrs Trerise allows me.' She grinned. 'You get some rest. All will be fine out there.'

'Thank you, my lady.'

As Sarah turned to leave, she noticed the lace bobbins on a velvet cushion by the window. 'You *make* lace?'

Despite the horrendous headache, Ellie rallied to speak about her passion. 'I do. Mother taught me when I was a little girl.' She paused for a moment - it was a rare occurrence nowadays to be able to show what she was capable of. 'My collection is in the top drawer, if you care to take a look.'

Sarah selected an exquisite lace collar and held it to the light. 'This is beautiful Elise, I had no idea you had such talent. Do you sell?'

Ellie shook her head, immediately regretting the movement.

'Why?'

'No one wants handmade lace anymore!'

'Elise.' Sarah placed her hand to her heart. 'I know plenty of ladies who would love to be able to purchase such quality lace.' Sarah paused for a moment, struck by a thought, 'In fact my sister-in-law, Carole, would be very interested in this for her wedding gown.'

Ellie grinned excitedly, wincing from the pain which ensued.

As Sarah pushed the drawer closed she noticed the one below had opened slightly. 'My goodness, Elise, this one is also full of lace!'

'Oh no, that isn't for sale,' Ellie said shyly. 'That is my wedding gown.'

Sarah's eyes sparkled. 'Oh, pray tell, who is the lucky man?'

'I've yet to meet him.' Ellie laughed and lowered her eyes. 'I've been making the dress since I was thirteen. It takes hours of work you see. I'd like to look special when my day comes.'

'Elise, with your looks and this dress you will look divine. I shall speak to Carole about the lace. Rest assured, you'll be hearing from us shortly.'

'Thank you so much. You're very kind.'

'I suggest you try and sleep a while now, Elise.' She pressed her fingers to her lips, blew a friendly kiss and left.

When the door closed, Ellie reclined with a sigh. Her head pounded, but her heart hammered for a different reason. Philip had been her hero today.

2

No two days were alike in Cornwall. After the glorious weekend sunshine, the rain came in squalls on Monday, drenching Poldhu Cove. The low dank clouds rendered it difficult for Ellie to work her lace by the light of the small window in her little box bedroom. The Tea Room closed every Monday, so Ellie was able to move to the window table overlooking the cove. As soon as she settled, she leant back and closed her eyes momentarily. Her head throbbed from the injury received two days ago. Every now and then a bout of nausea would sweep over her, but it was a small price to pay - things could have been far worse. She was eternally grateful to Philip Goldsworthy for rescuing her.

*

Guy Blackthorn plunged the spar down into the water reeds to staple the thatch into place, hesitating before reaching for the next bundle. It was not the best of weather to be working a thatch. The squally rain had intermittently halted the progress of his work all morning, forcing him to drag tarpaulin over the roof and retire to his wagon. As inconvenient as it was, the weather wasn't the only thing which troubled him. Having left before the doctor had seen Ellie on Saturday, he was desperate to know how she fared after her accident. As he chewed on his crust of bread, he made the decision to go and see her.

Donning his coat and hat, he harnessed his horse Mazie to the wagon and set off towards Poldhu. It was a good twenty minute drive from Gunwalloe village to Church Cove. There he re-hobbled Mazie and set off briskly on foot over the cliff path.

His heart quickened as he neared the Tea Room. Guy loved Ellie. He loved her with every single bone in his body, though she was unaware of this fact. Too bashful to tell her, instead he watched her from afar - his shyness preventing him from declaring his affection for her, for chance his love was unreciprocated.

Guy had been firm friends with Philip Goldsworthy since boyhood, and whenever possible - come rain or shine - they met at Poldhu for their weekly Saturday swim, taking refreshments at the Tea Room afterwards. Occasionally, if Ellie found time, she'd sit and chat with them, though in truth, Philip did most of the talking.

Philip's ardent attentions towards Ellie pained Guy. Philip was rich and confident and always got what he wanted. Guy was convinced that Philip would win Ellie's heart one day and then that would be the end of it. Today though, he was in an optimistic frame of mind. For sure someone would have told Ellie that it had been *he* who had rescued her from the sea, so perhaps she'd be pleased to see him. Perhaps they'd have tea together, and then he might, just might, find the confidence to tell her how much he adored her.

Knowing Ellie's love for sea glass, Guy walked down to the sea to see if he could find a piece to gift to her. Whenever he'd acquired any in the past, he'd leave it for her to find, placed on one of the rocks which surrounded the little sea garden she made by the Tea Room cottage. Today he'd place it in her hand - *if* he could find some! With his boots slung over his shoulder by their laces, he scanned the surf intently. He was in luck! His heart soared on spotting a large piece of turquoise glass glinting from the wet sand. Quickly wiping it down the front of his waistcoat, he headed to the dunes, brushed the sand from his feet and put his boots back on.

*

Ellie glanced at the figure walking along the blustery beach. She narrowed her eyes, curious as to who was braving the elements on such a day. When the figure became obscured by a clump of marram grass she lost interest, and with adept fingers began to work her bobbins quickly on her bolster cushion. As she wove her intricate patterns, Ellie felt her mother's spirit beside her, god rest her soul. She'd taught her to make lace almost as soon as Ellie could sit at the trestle table. This, along with collecting sea glass and working in her unruly sea garden, were Ellie's favourite pastimes. She truly hoped Lady Sarah would be true to her word and tempt her sister-in-law to buy some lace for her wedding gown. With the thought of weddings, she put down her bobbins, walked into her bedroom and pulled out the drawer which housed her beautiful lace wedding dress. Barely a day went by that she didn't hold it up to her to admire. Today, as she looked at her reflection, she felt a tingle in her veins at the thought of Philip. At eighteen-years-old she had yet to receive an offer of marriage from anyone - maybe, just maybe, Philip would be the one.

Lost in her reverie, the unexpected knock at the door startled her. Ellie drew her brows together - Betty was visiting her sister in Mullion and Ellie was not expecting visitors today. Quickly folding her dress back into the drawer, she walked from the bedroom to find Philip Goldsworthy peering through the window. Her heart gave an involuntary leap. Before she had a moment to straighten her skirt and pat her hair tidy, the bell tinkled and Philip stepped through the door with his arms full of flowers.

*

Guy had just finished tying the laces of his boots and straightening his red neckerchief when he heard someone knocking on Ellie's door. As he tentatively raised his head from the dune, his heart sank as he watched Philip step confidently over the threshold. *Oh damn you Philip, why are you not working at the Mill today?* From Guy's vantage point, he watched Philip hand Ellie an enormous bouquet of flowers before closing the door behind him.

A small lump formed in his throat, realising he'd not be welcome today. Guy skirted the back of the dunes, and, out of sight of the Tea Rooms, placed his gift for Ellie by her little garden before setting off back to Church Cove with a heavy heart. He'd have to wait to declare his love -

though he had an awful feeling he'd left it far too late.

*

Stepping over the threshold without invitation, Philip pressed the bouquet of flowers into her arms.

'Good morning to you, Ellie,' he said formally.

Ellie was struck by how fine he looked today in his suit and combed hair. She was used to seeing him with salt-water tousled hair and couldn't quite decide which she liked best.

'My goodness Philip, these are beautiful, thank you.' She buried her nose in their fragrance. 'I was just thinking about you.' She immediately regretted the sentence, and dared not say why.

He grinned. 'Likewise - hence my visit to you today.'

'I'm afraid I'm alone,' she said shyly.

'No-one will know,' he whispered rakishly, as he took off his jacket and shook the rain drops from it before hanging it behind the door. 'I simply couldn't wait a moment longer to come and enquire after your health.'

'I'm fine, thanks to you.'

'It was my pleasure. I must say, I thought I'd lost you, and that would never do. Whatever would I do without my lovely Ellie to serve me tea?'

Ellie lowered her eyes shyly.

'Despite your ordeal, you're looking as lovely as ever.'

Ellie unconsciously pulled her hair over the nasty wound on her forehead, but he reached over and pulled her hand from her face. She marvelled at the softness of his hands, uncalloused by lack of manual work. She shivered with anticipation as he lifted her hand to his lips to kiss it. Unaccustomed to such ardent affection, Ellie gently pulled her hand from his and stepped back.

'W ...Would you like some refreshments?'

Philip nodded thankfully. 'If you feel up to making some.'

'Oh yes, I was back at work yesterday. We're only open for a couple of hours on Sunday and I felt awful letting

Betty struggle on Saturday.'

'You should have rested though. I think perhaps Mrs Trerise works you too hard.'

'I can assure you, she doesn't,' Ellie said, warming the tea pot.

Philip settled by the window seat and leant back confidently, crossing his arms and legs. 'At least you can rest today. I feel awful now for disturbing you.'

'You're not. I was just working on my lace.' She nodded to her bolster cushion by the window.

Philip got up and inspected her work. 'God's life, Ellie, this *is* lovely. We were discussing your lace on Saturday evening at the manor.'

Ellie eyes widened. 'I'm surprised such a topic would interest the men in the party.'

He grinned. 'Any topic relating to you *always* has my interest.'

Ellie was thankful she was facing away from him as she felt her cheeks redden.

'In fact, you were the talk of the evening, what with your lucky escape, and all that. It's a wonder your ears were not burning.'

Being careful not to disturb the bobbins, Philip took a closer look at her work. 'Sarah was telling us how exquisite it was, and I must say, I agree.'

Ellie smiled broadly as she walked towards him with her tray. 'Thank you.'

'Sarah says you have trouble selling locally – I can't believe that!'

Ellie smiled. 'It's because handmade lace has fallen out of favour since manufactured lace became popular a few years ago. My mother and I had a good regular income from Lady Katherine Mason, of Barton House, Nr. Germoe - do you know the Mason family?'

'Vaguely, yes,' Philip answered dismissively.

'Well, I remember walking the twelve miles to Germoe with my mother to deliver lace, which I might add, Lady

Katherine had specifically ordered, only to be informed by her servant that our lace was no longer required! Apparently Lady Katherine had found machine made lace was much cheaper and just as good!' Ellie gave a wry smile. 'I can tell you now, it is not!' Ellie paused for a second and glanced at her lace. 'The loss in income was a terrible blow to my mother. What with that and having lost my father the previous year, I truly believed the upset caused my mother's ill health. She died of scarlet fever a few months later.'

Philip smiled sympathetically. 'But you still make your lace?'

'Yes, I enjoy making it.'

'Well if it's any consolation, I know Lady Carole was very interested in it for her wedding trousseau.'

'Well I have a drawer full enough to adorn the best trousseau,' Ellie said as she poured two cups of tea.

'I do believe she'll request you to wait on her at Bochym Manor very soon,' he said, tapping his nose.

'Well, it would be nice to have some extra money in my pocket. When is she to be married?'

'September!'

'Oh, then I hope she sends for me soon. Oh dear, I hope she realises that the only day I can go is on a Monday. I'm afraid I'm too busy here the other days....even for Lady Carole from Bochym Manor.' She grinned.

'I did explain that was the case. Carole is a very wealthy woman. She'll pay you well for your work.'

'Thank you Philip. I really appreciate that. I appreciate all you've done for me.'

'It's my pleasure,' he said, taking a sip of tea, as he swept his eyes appreciatively over her.

*

After tea, Ellie said her goodbyes to Philip. Betty would be home soon and it would not be fitting for her to be found in the company of a young man. She waved him off, took a deep breath of fresh air and walked towards her little garden.

The day was still dull, but the rain had thankfully ceased. She frowned at her flattened, waterlogged garden, but her eyes brightened when they rested on the piece of sea glass. She reached for it and held it up - it was beautiful. She remembered seeing a figure on the beach earlier - that must have been Philip, for every time he and Guy visited the cove she always found a small piece of sea treasure left here. It was as though he was too embarrassed to give her something so simple, perhaps because he was so wealthy. She smiled and kissed the glass.

'Thank you Philip for your secret gift. I shall treasure it,' she whispered.

*

The note requesting her attendance at Bochym arrived the following day. She was expected at ten a.m. Monday week. When the day arrived, Ellie felt quite nervous. She set off with mixed emotions. It had been eight years since she had been to Bochym. Her father John had been the estate steward there, but had died tragically when Ellie was ten. Not only did they lose him but also his annual wage of £120, and because they'd lived in the steward's tied cottage, she and her mother found themselves without a roof over their head. If not for the kindness of Betty Trerise taking them both in at the Tea Room, they would have floundered. Ellie had been too young at the time to question why, after their father had given the estate fifteen years unblemished service, they'd not been offered alternative employment and accommodation on the estate. It had been a constant concern to Ellie as she grew older. Betty had told her that Ellie's mother, Rose, remained tight lipped on the subject and it was her belief that Rose was too afraid to speak out about the reason. This sowed the seed in Ellie's mind that perhaps something untoward had happened before they left.

Ellie dressed carefully that day. Smart, but in sturdy

boots and clothes that would withstand the two mile walk to the manor. It had crossed her mind that Lady Carole might have sent a pony trap for her, but it was not to be. She wrapped her good shoes in brown paper and placed them in her wicker basket, along with an assortment of her finest pieces of lace. She took along a small mirror and comb so as to tidy herself when she got there.

The day was warm and dry, though the cool sea-breeze was a welcome relief as Ellie set off up the hill to Cury. Bochym Manor was situated in an enchanting, tranquil, wooded valley. She drank in the beauty and serenity of the estate as the manor came in sight. She'd taken the delightful woodland walk that ran for nearly a third of a mile up Poldhu valley to the manor. It was a walk she'd taken many times, but her favourite time was spring when the ground was carpeted with bluebells, wild garlic, orchids and campion. There was nowhere like Cornwall in the spring time, nature seemed to blanket the county with flowers - to welcome the spring and say goodbye to the winter. Today, being mid July, the blue haze of the bluebells had all but diminished, but the sweet birdsong made the walk equally enjoyable.

Ellie approached the house from the tradesman's gate. At the top of the long dusty drive, she'd changed her boots for shoes and hidden them in the hedge. Pulling a comb through her hair, she rolled it up at the back and secured it with a tortoise shell clasp. A quick glance in her hand mirror and she was ready.

Ellie only had a vague memory of living on the estate, the trauma of her father dying and having to leave the estate soon afterwards had blanked her mind to her time here. She remembered Bochym had a beautiful garden though, which she longed to be able to walk through. Ellie especially wanted to see the large mulberry tree, which she remembered her mother telling her was mentioned in the Doomsday Book. It was understood to be the oldest mulberry tree in the country. Her mother often tearfully reminisced about the many mysterious and enchanting tracks and pathways in the grounds. She told her stories of 17th century walled parterres, and how the Poldhu River had been diverted and made into a series of ornamental ponds, connected by rapids, ravines and waterfalls. There was also an early Victorian arboretum, which Ellie would give anything to walk through. She had a great love of nature and gardens, but the sea garden she'd made at Poldhu was a constant battle between wind, salt air and the occasional flood. The only flowers that would bloom were the ones that naturally clung to the cliffs in the cove, even then, her favourite wild flower, the sea pink, refused to grow where it did not want to be!

She paused for a moment at the corner of the front garden. It struck her that her last memory of this house was the day of her father's funeral. They never returned here after the service.

The manor house was truly breathtaking, with elegant mullion windows, some of which had beautiful stained glass. A large orangery sat impressively to the left of the house. When Ellie saw someone at the upstairs window looking down at her, she quickly moved on up the path to the magnificent oak front door.

'Hey, you there!' a gruff voice called out to her as she reached for the bell. Ellie turned nervously.

'Yes, you!' A portly man dressed in a black suit, the jacket straining over his barrel stomach, stood at the end of the path.

'Get yourself around the back to the tradesman's entrance. You've no right to be trespassing at the front door.'

Ellie walked back towards the man. His fat lips pursed as he drew his thick eyebrows into a scowl. Ellie thought he resembled a very cross Toby jug. There was a frisson of recognition, but she could not recall his name. Confident she had every right to be there, Ellie lifted her chin defiantly.

'I have an appointment with Lady Carole Dunstan,' she said, refusing to be bullied by this man.

She watched him sweep his eyes over her homespun clothes.

'The devil you have.' He laughed derisively. 'Present yourself to the tradesman's entrance round the back and don't loiter. This part of the house is private.'

Ellie had to almost squeeze past the man, for he refused to move to let her pass comfortably. He stank of tobacco and possessed the ugliest face she'd ever seen on a man. She cast her eyes downward, so as not to look at him and noted that his shoes were so shiny she could almost see her face in them - the sight evoked another uncomfortable recollection.

She walked purposely, but without haste, towards the clock tower. Ellie had heard talk that this was the tallest building on the Lizard Peninsula. She remembered Guy Blackthorn speaking of it once. He'd told her that once he had occasion to replace some lead on the roof of the tower for the Dunstan family and was taken in by the magnificent view from it. She smiled at the thought of Guy. He was very sweet, but she suspected painfully shy, for it was rare that he joined in the conversation whenever she'd managed a few stolen moments to sit with him and Philip. Occasionally though, he would open up and talk about his work and all the wonderful places he had thatched. She often wished he would speak more, but Philip, being Philip, often dominated their conversation. She didn't mind of course - she liked Philip, a lot, and from his last visit she suspected that he was very interested in her too.

Ellie could hear horses as she approached the stables near the clock tower, and saw several magnificent animals being brushed and pampered by a host of grooms. One groom looked up as she approached but Ellie thought it best not to make eye contact with anyone else, so she lowered her head and made for the small enclosed courtyard that led to the kitchen.

Walking past the Steward's Cottage, her childhood home, Ellie felt a mixture of sadness and affection for the old place. The sight of the honeysuckle covered porch and diamond paned windows, caught like a thorn in her heart. She remembered playing on the front lawn while her dear mother sat at the front window, lace making. Without doubt her formative years had been happy there.

As she stepped through to the cobbled courtyard, past the rear of the Steward's Cottage, an overwhelming sense of loneliness engulfed her. A cool breeze lifted her hair and a female voice whispered her name softly. She turned, but found no one in the vicinity. Feeling the fine hairs on the back of her neck stand on end, every one of her senses heightened. Something happened right here, but it was buried deep in a memory she could not recall. Conscious again of being watched, Ellie glanced at the windows facing down on the courtyard, and caught a glimpse of a figure retreating from the attic window.

Pressing her hand to her body to calm the effervescence in her stomach, she approached the kitchen door, brushed the dust from her skirt, quickly tidied her hair and cleared her throat before knocking hard.

A woman shouted an order from inside: 'Taylor, where *are* you girl? Go and answer the door. Good grief, do I have to do everything?'

'Sorry, Mrs Blair.' A fresh faced, pretty young woman opened the door to Ellie.

Wearing her best smile, Ellie said, 'Good morning. My name is Elise Rosevear.'

A woman of sizeable girth, stood by the kitchen table, sporting a crisp white apron, dropped the bowl she was holding, breaking it into four pieces. 'Oh Lord have mercy upon me,' she said, disbelief shrouding her face. 'Whatever brings *you* back to this door?'

3

Five miles away, in Gweek, on the Helford River, Philip Goldsworthy perused his newly purchased dwelling, Primrose Cottage. Set in a peaceful wooded valley, by the stream which fed the Gweek Corn Mill wheel, the cottage was ideally situated now Philip's father was in the process of handing the running of the mill over to him.

He congratulated himself that he'd bought a cottage that was in good order – just a lick of whitewash in a couple of the rooms was all it needed. The carpenter, Jeremiah Chegwin, had lived there for all of his seventy years, so the rooms were also expertly furnished. As Philip surveyed the outside of the property, his grey eyes narrowed. 'Damn it,' he muttered, spotting his immediate neighbour and friend Guy Blackthorn harnessing his pony to his thatching wagon. It was mid morning - Philip hoped Guy would have left for work by now.

Although Guy was his oldest friend, he'd hoped to keep this purchase under wraps for a little while longer. He twisted his lips as Guy approached him.

'Hello, Philip, I thought it was you,' Guy said jovially. 'So you're the mystery purchaser are you? There's been a rumour in The Black Swan that Primrose Cottage had been bought by someone!'

'I see there are no secrets in this village?' Philip said dryly.

Ignoring Philip's tone, Guy thumped his arm playfully. 'You've lived in this village long enough to know that. So you're leaving the parental palace on the river bank then. Eh? When are you moving in?'

'Soon,' Philip answered guardedly. 'You're late setting off to work aren't you?' he said changing the subject.

'I've been doing a quick job on Bramble Cottage for Ma. I'm heading back to Gunwalloe now. I'll probably see you at Poldhu on Saturday, but from Monday week I'll be working further afield.'

'Always busy. Eh? When will Silas joins you?'

'January – the lads itching to start, but I've kept him at school so he could look after Ma after Pa died. I'll have to find someone else to make my spars then. My little brother can make up to a thousand a day when he's not at school you know! He has a real knack with the billhook - I'll not find anyone as good!'

Philip snorted. 'Nonsense, I'm sure anyone can fashion a bit of hazel!'

'I bet you can't, with your soft hands. They'd be in shreds after a couple of spars.' Guy winked, before making his way back to his wagon.

Philip grimaced at Guys' ridicule. *I may have soft hands, Guy Blackthorn, but these are the hands which will very soon explore every inch of Ellie's lovely body.*

*

With his horse harnessed, Guy bid goodbye to his ma. As head of the household since the death of his father two years ago, more often than not Guy returned home on Saturdays to spend part of the weekend with his family. It felt good to come home. Being on the road all week proved a little lonely sometimes, though Guy was not averse to sharing a drink in the local hostelry should there be one nearby his work.

For all his shyness towards women, Guy was a sociable chap amongst his own gender. He wished he could converse with women, especially Ellie, but his tongue tied itself in knots whenever he tried. Flicking the reins, he set off down the leafy lane, the very thought of lovely Ellie giving him a warm feeling in his heart. How he wanted to share his love of the land and sea with her, for he knew she was at one with nature, as was he. He too had tried without success to grow sea pinks in a pot to present to her, but as with Ellie's sea garden, these prolific flowers would grow only where they chose to. She would have to settle for his gifts of sea glass - he hoped she liked these presents he left her.

*

At Bochym Manor, Ellie was completely taken aback by the shocked reaction her arrival at the kitchen door evoked. She turned expecting to find someone behind her who would warrant such an alarming response, but she found she was quite alone.

Clearing her throat again, Ellie said, 'I'm here at the request of Lady Carole Dunstan. I'm a lace maker.'

Visibly shocked by Ellie's appearance, the large woman brushed the flour from her hands and replied, 'A lace maker you say? Yes, I suppose you would be, wouldn't you? Taylor, go fetch Mr Carrington to see if Miss Rosevear is expected? Be quick about it.'

The maid bobbed her head, lifted her skirt slightly, and ran off down the parlour.

'And don't run!'

The girl faltered before setting off again.

Though uninvited, Ellie stepped into the warm kitchen. Shelves of shiny copper pots, pans and kettles hung from hooks above the scrubbed pine table. A large range was set back in the opposite wall, from where a delicious rich gravy aroma emitted. Ellie's stomach rumbled as she stood under the uncomfortable gaze of the cook, whom she vaguely remembered. Ellie smiled weakly, but the cook turned her attention to the pieces of broken bowl on the table, tutting loudly at the mess it had made.

'Betsy! Come here. Clean this mess up and scrub down the table. I can't be having any bits of crockery in my venison pie.'

'Yes, Mrs Blair, I'm coming,' a small voice called out. A young girl, aged no more than ten, emerged from the scullery, took one look in Ellie's direction, screamed at the top of her voice and shot back into the scullery.

Ellie stood open-mouthed as the commotion brought several people scurrying into the kitchen. One of which was a stony-faced woman dressed in black. Ellie felt a shiver of recognition, knowing she'd had dealings with this unyielding woman before.

'Mrs Blair. Whatever is going on in this kitchen?'

'It's Betsy, Mrs Bligh. The silly girl must be having some sort of funny turn. She's sat in the corner of the scullery, shaking like a kicked dog.'

'Well, tell her to pull herself together or find alternative employment. I will not have hysterics in my household. Now, as if you haven't enough to do, we've had a request from the Lodge. The Dowager Countess would like strawberry fool for dessert....Oh!' she said on seeing Ellie, 'and who have we got here?'

The cook raised her eyebrows. 'Elise Rosevear, would you believe!'

The housekeeper took a sharp, horrified intake of breath. 'What the devil do *you* want?'

Ellie's throat tightened, shocked by the hostility. *Come on, Ellie, you have every right to be here.* She summoned her most authoritative voice and replied tersely, 'I'm here at Lady Carole's request.' She watched the housekeeper's nostrils flare indignantly, but Ellie stood her ground until the maid arrived back with the butler.

'Mr Carrington,' the housekeeper said crossly. 'Miss Rosevear claims she has an appointment with Lady Carole?'

He looked insolently at Ellie. 'It appears so, Mrs Bligh.'

Bligh gave a derisive snort.

'Follow me,' Carrington said curtly. 'Lady Carole will see you in the Jacobean drawing room.'

Confounded at their attitude, Ellie stood up tall, lifted her chin and followed Carrington. As she left the kitchen, she was sure the cook crossed herself protectively.

The moment she stepped into the corridor towards the main house, the memories flooded back of the high ceilings and polished floors. She glanced affectionately at the servant's stairs, where she'd played when the family was away from home. As she neared the great oak staircase she felt an odd sensation of being watched again.

Carrington stopped at a beautifully carved oak door and knocked. As a lady's voice beckoned them to proceed, the hairs on Ellie's forearm stood on end, as a vaporous figure appeared before her and smiled, before melting away into the oak panelling of the staircase.

The butler cleared his throat impatiently. 'Lady Carole hasn't got all day.' As he gestured for her to step through Ellie chanced another glance at the staircase, but the figure had gone.

Ellie confidently entered the sumptuous drawing room, marvelling at the ornate, oval, roll-moulded plaster work on the ceiling. The rich walnut wall panelling gave the room warmth, and a grand piano sat by the large mullion window.

Lady Carole watched Ellie absorb the splendour of the room. She had more than a vested interest in Elise Rosevear.

'It's rather impressive, don't you think, Miss Rosevear? I live here and it never fails to make me smile as I walk into this room.'

Ellie peeled her eyes from the splendour of the room and smiled warmly at Lady Carole, who sat on one of three large sofas which flanked the great fireplace.

Unlike Lady Sarah, Lady Carole did not frequent the Tea Room, so this was the first time they had met. Ellie thought Carole was a handsome looking woman, perhaps slightly taller than herself, at five-foot-three in her stockinged feet. Carole's curly white-blonde hair was piled high and she wore a beautiful rose coloured silk dress. The garnet drop earrings and choker necklace complemented her attire perfectly. Ellie swallowed nervously, her recent bravado evading her now.

'Do take a seat, Miss Rosevear. Carrington will arrange some refreshments. Would tea suit you?'

'Tea would be lovely, my lady. Thank you.'

*

The kitchen buzzed with nervous anticipation when

Carrington arrived back. Betsy was still crying in the scullery, and Mrs Blair was mixing her new cake mixture with vigour.

'Taylor, get a tea tray ready, though I am loathed to serve Rosevear tea, but serve it I must,' Carrington said resignedly. 'Joan. Can you spare a moment?' He beckoned Mrs Bligh into the housekeeper's room.

'I cannot believe that a Rosevear has the audacity to come back to this house, John. Especially after it was made quite clear to her mother that their family was not welcome here,' Mrs Bligh muttered crossly.

'Be calm Joan.'

'Calm you say, calm! How can I be calm? Have you forgotten the disruption she and her mother caused to this household?'

'Of course not, but I think we've all made it plain to her that her kind is not welcome here. I doubt after today she'll ever venture back.'

'I hope you're right, but I have an awful feeling that her coming here today could open a whole can of worms.'

*

Ellie was conscious that Lady Carole was scrutinising her. She shifted uncomfortably and smoothed down her homespun skirt.

Studiously aware of her discomfort, Carole smiled. 'So, Miss Rosevear, how do you like your little waitressing job at the Poldhu Tea Room?'

Ellie regarded her for a moment before speaking. 'My position at the Tea Room involves waitressing, yes, but I'm also the principle baker. I see to all the accounts and I'm in charge of the general running of the place.'

'I see.' Carole gave a wry smile. 'A regular little business woman, aren't you?'

'Yes, my lady, I am!'

Carole raised her eyebrows at Ellie's assertion. 'I understand that you make the most exquisite lace too.'

'I do, my lady.'

'As you are no doubt aware, I am soon to be married. My dress, though beautiful in itself, needs some lace adornment. I'm looking forward to seeing what you've brought me.'

Ellie nodded and reached into her basket. 'May I?' Ellie gestured to the polished table to lay her lace on.

'Please do.'

Spreading the delicate lace collars, cuffs, trims and ribbons, across the table, Ellie stood back for Carole to peruse.

'Well, I declare, I can safely say this is the very best lace I've ever seen!' She fingered the work appreciably. 'And it is *all* hand-made?'

'Yes, my lady.'

'You're extremely talented, I applaud you. Philip Goldsworthy was correct when he called you 'one in a million'.'

'Did he?' Ellie felt her cheeks pink at the mention of Philip's name.

'I see from your reaction that you like Philip as much as he admires you.'

Ellie lowered her eyes, unsure how to respond to this line of questioning. Fortunately, Carole's attention on Ellie's relationship with Philip was diverted when an ear piercing scream preceded the clattering of a tea tray from behind the drawing room door.

Carole rang the bell to bring the butler scurrying into the drawing room. 'For goodness sake, Carrington, whatever is happening today? That's the second scream I have heard in the last half hour!'

'I beg your pardon, my lady. It's Taylor, one of the housemaids. The silly girl thought she saw something as she brought the tea tray to me,' Carrington glared angrily at Ellie.

'For goodness sake, what on earth did she see to make her scream like that?' Carole snapped.

'Probably her own shadow, my lady. I'll arrange

another tea tray now.'

'Very well, and be quick about it.'

As one door closed another opened and Lady Sarah entered, preceded by the faint perfume of roses. 'Did I hear a scream, Carole? Oh hello, Elise, how lovely of you to have come.'

Ellie smiled and bobbed a curtsy.

Unlike her sister-in-law's rich attire, Sarah wore a simple cream day gown and no jewellery. She moved forward and took Ellie by the hand. 'I do hope you've recovered sufficiently from your accident?'

Sarah's hand felt so soft and delicate in her own. 'Thank you, my lady, I have.'

'Oh yes,' Carole chipped in, 'I'd completely forgotten that Philip dragged you from your watery grave.'

Ellie nodded. 'And I'm eternally grateful to him. I wish there was some way I could thank him.'

'I'm sure you'll find a way to show your gratitude?' Carole said with a knowing smile.

Ellie gave a smile, though slightly perplexed at the innuendo.

'Now Carole, have you sent for refreshments?' Sarah asked as she sat and smoothed her dress down.

'I did, but apparently Taylor had a turn whilst delivering it!' Carole said dismissively.

'Oh dear, is she alright? Where is she?'

'In the hall I suspect, picking up the broken crockery and getting an ear bashing from Carrington.'

'Oh, the poor girl!' Sarah stood. 'I must go to her.'

'She'll be fine, Sarah. Come here. I need your help choosing some of this exquisite lace.'

Sarah smiled sweetly. 'Do forgive me, Elise, Carole, but I'll take a look in a moment. I really need to see if Jessie is alright.'

'Jessie?' Carole gave a puzzled look.

'The housemaid, Jessie Taylor!'

'Oh!' Carole raised her eyebrows. 'Is that her name?'

Ellie felt her heart sing at Lady Sarah's kindness.

Moments later, Sarah swept back into the room. 'Everything's fine now,' she declared. 'The poor girl believes she saw something in the shadows. I've instructed Mrs Blair to make her a cup of sweet tea. Now, let me see what you've brought.' Sarah pored over the lace with a wondrous eye. 'Did I not say how truly beautiful Elise's work was, Carole?'

As they inspected her work, Ellie became aware of a slight movement near the grand piano. She blinked furiously - her eyes seemed to be playing tricks on her today.

'I must agree I'm astonished at the workmanship.' Carole held the lace up to the light.

Sarah turned to Ellie. 'You really are a talented young woman.'

Ellie felt her heart swell with pride now. 'Thank you, my lady.'

'You must hurry and choose something, Carole. You haven't long now before the big day!'

Carole pointed her perfectly manicured fingers. 'I shall take this, and these, and…' She held up a collar and two cuffs. 'I shall also take this, to go around the empire line of my dress.' She pulled a long piece of lace from the pile and held it just under her breast. It's all so beautiful. My dress will look splendid when my seamstress adds these luxuries to it. You'll send me the bill of course?'

Ellie nodded. She would rather have been paid immediately.

Seeing Ellie's consternation, Sarah said, 'If you submit your invoice this week, you'll be paid by the end of the month.'

Ellie smiled with relief. 'Thank you, my lady.'

When Carrington arrived with a new tea tray, the lace was left on the table, as all three women sat down amiably.

'Leave the tray, Mr Carrington, we'll manage ourselves. How is Jessie now?' Sarah asked, 'I do hope she's recovered from her shock.'

'Yes, my lady. Mrs Bligh sends her profound apologies and assures you that there will be no more hysterics from the girl.'

Sarah's eyes fluttered slightly at his brashness.

'What did she see anyway?' Carole asked, taking the cup and saucer from Sarah. 'Was it a rat or something? Because I swear I heard something in the wainscot last night.'

'No, she thought she'd seen a ghost!' Sarah answered nonchalantly.

'What?' Carole fluttered her hand to her heart. 'I sincerely hope she did not. You don't believe the silly girl do you, Sarah?'

'I don't disbelieve her. Old houses such as these have a history going back centuries. Lives have been lived and lost within these walls. The house is bound to retain some of the essence and energy of its inhabitants.'

Ellie listened without comment, still diverted by the movement near the piano. She was certain it was a figure – the same she'd seen on the staircase.

Carole shuddered. 'Mama said this house used to have ghostly goings on, but I swear I've never seen a thing - thank goodness. I'm telling you though, Sarah, the moment one appears at my bedside, I am gone from this house for good.'

Sarah placed her fingers to her lips thoughtfully. *Oh, if only.*

'Anyway,' Carole flapped her hands. 'Stop all this talk of ghostly goings on. Miss Rosevear will think this household has gone quite mad.'

Sarah could also see the figure which held Ellie's gaze by the piano. *Perhaps not!*

'Miss Rosevear?'

Carole's voice drew Ellie's attention away from the vaporous figure.

'Goodness, you were in a day-dream then,' Carole

laughed.

'I'm dreadfully sorry. I was lost in the beauty of this room,' Ellie answered a little shakily. 'I should think you'll miss living here after your marriage, Lady Carole?' she added.

'Goodness gracious, I'm not leaving. Why would I? This is my family home. There is plenty of room for us all. Isn't there, Sarah?'

Sarah smiled and nodded, but Ellie noted Sarah's smile did not reach her eyes.

*

With tea finished, Carole stood up.

'Thank you for your time, Miss Rosevear.'

Realising she was being dismissed, Ellie too stood, thanked them both for tea and returned the spare lace to her bag.

Carole reached for the bell to call the butler.

'No Carole, don't bother Mr Carrington,' Sarah said. 'I will see Elise out. I'm about to go back into the garden to dead head the roses anyway.'

'Do we not employ a gardener for that, Sarah?' Carole said dryly.

'We do indeed, but I also love my garden and find great peace in being amongst the flowers. Come Elise.' Sarah beckoned her to follow.

They walked through the library towards the front hall and out of the great oak door. Once outside, Sarah took a deep breath. 'I just love the smell of the earth. Do you like gardening, Elise?'

As Ellie began to tell her about her sea garden and all its difficulties, Sarah stooped to pull a dead head from an agapanthus.

'Hey, you!'

Ellie froze as the angry voice came from beyond the garden wall. She spun round to find the unpleasant man she'd encountered earlier, striding towards them.

'I'll not tell you again. You're to stay away from this

garden. It's private!' he snarled.

Sarah stood up from where she was crouched. 'Mr Lanfear!' she shot him a sharp look. 'What is the meaning of this outburst?'

Lanfear! Ellie's heart stilled. That name evoked a deeply unpleasant memory of a terrible argument between this man and her mother, just days before they were banished. Although he stood a few yards away, Ellie scrutinised his face as he stood wringing his hands apologetically to his mistress.

'Oh! Begging your pardon, my lady,' he blustered, 'I didn't see you there.' He bowed his head. 'I called out because I thought this woman was trespassing.'

Sarah tightened her lips. 'As my husband's valet, pray tell, what business is it of yours to be loitering in my front garden, shouting at my guest?'

His mouth twitched involuntarily as he formed a response. 'I'm waiting for Lord de Bochym, my lady. His carriage is due to arrive within the hour,' he said authoritatively.

'Well I suggest you wait somewhere, *out* of the way.'

'Yes, my lady.' Resentment at being chastised clouded his face as he turned to walk away.

'One moment, Mr Lanfear,' Sarah stopped him.

Lanfear paused and took a good few seconds before turning.

It was not in Sarah's nature to dislike anyone, but Lanfear was the exception. 'I believe you owe Miss Rosevear an apology for your rude behaviour.'

If Ellie had been shocked at the mention of his name, his reaction to hers was ten fold. His fat lips twitched indignantly as he mumbled an apology.

With a nod of satisfaction, Sarah linked arms with Ellie. 'Come, Elise, we'll take a turn around the garden. Did you know that we have the oldest mulberry tree in England! Apparently it's over a thousand years old!'

Lanfear scowled darkly as he watched them walk down

into the formal gardens. *Now then, what the devil is she doing back at Bochym? And what mischief is she about to unleash?* He checked his fob watch and glanced quickly down the drive for any sign of Lord de Bochym's carriage, before going in search of Mr Carrington.

4

As Sarah watched Ellie drive away in the pony trap she'd provided, her husband's carriage came up the drive.

Lanfear had also seen his master arrive, and stepped out from where he was lurking, to open the carriage door.

Peter Dunstan, the fifth Earl de Bochym, handed his cane and hat to Lanfear and smiled broadly at his wife whose arms were full of flowers from the garden.

'Hello darling. You look more like a flower girl than the lady of the manor.' He kissed her tenderly on the cheek and glanced at the retreating pony trap. 'Visitors?' He raised his eyebrows.

'Yes, Miss Rosevear came to see us. She's made some beautiful lace for Carole's wedding gown, and we've just spent a rather lovely hour together in the garden.' She glanced at Lanfear, who lowered his eyes.

'Tell me all about it in a moment, darling,' Peter said, stepping through the great oak front door. 'It's been a long journey from Truro and I need to freshen up. Ask Carrington to arrange some lunch, I'm famished.'

Peter set off in haste through the library to the stairs, taking them two at a time. Sarah smiled - the manor came alive when Peter was home.

*

As always, the arrival of the earl brought with it a sudden hive of activity in the household.

'Hurry, Mrs Blair, his lordship requests his lunch,' Carrington said, as cook and Betsy hastily put together an assortment of cold meats and pickles.

As Carrington walked through the hall with the tray towards the drawing room, he paused momentarily. He could hear a conversation between Lady Sarah and the earl.

'Darling,' Sarah said, intent on arranging her flowers in a vase, 'I appreciate that you've a million things to do on the estate, but you need to speak to Lanfear!'

'Is there a problem?' Peter tapped a cigarette from his case and reached for the flint to light it.

'He was extremely rude to our guest, Miss Rosevear earlier. He didn't realise I was there, but his manner towards her was akin to how he would speak to a common pedlar.'

Peter sat and stretched out his weary legs. 'What the devil was he doing addressing your guest?'

Sarah stepped back to admire her floral display. 'He was wasting time, lurking by the front wall, awaiting your arrival.'

'I hope you berated him for both misdemeanours?'

'I did, but it must not happen again. I'm aware that Carole still holds the strings to the workings of this house, but *I* will not have visitors spoken to like that – no matter *who* they are.'

'Leave it with me darling, I'll speak to him. Where the devil is Carrington with lunch? I could eat a horse.'

On cue, Carrington walked through and put the tray on the table. 'Would my lord like me to serve?'

'No, thank you.' Peter waved him away. 'Darling will you do the honours?'

*

Carrington stepped back into the kitchen, deep in thought. *It seems they would all have to watch their step around the new countess.*

'Be on your guard, Albert. The mistress has complained about you berating Rosevear.'

Lanfear paused from polishing his shoes and gave Carrington an unhurried look. 'Then I'll tell him who Rosevear is, and why I spoke to her that way.'

'Go careful though, the earl is a very different man to his father.'

Refusing to be perturbed, Lanfear shrugged. 'I am well aware of that fact, John, but he's just a puppy. I can deal with him.'

*

Poldhu wore its normal sunny afternoon appearance as Ellie alighted from the pony trap. She changed out of her best clothes, donned an apron and began scouring her jam pan.

The trip to Bochym had enthralled and unsettled Ellie in equal measure. She'd spent a rather pleasant hour in the garden with Lady Sarah - enjoying the flowerbeds and marvelling at the abundance of flowers all jostling for space. They'd walked along the walled garden, where espalier plums grew in abundance, but unfortunately not quite ripe for eating. Lady Sarah had filled Ellie's basket with the last of the strawberries so that she could make strawberry jam. Ellie had been overjoyed when she was taken down to the arboretum and shown all the marvellous specimen trees there. Several of which were mature myrtle trees - the bark being soft like the antlers of a young roe dear. Lady Sarah had plucked a posy of the white myrtle flowers and given them to Ellie – their delicious fragrance now filled the Tea Room with the most wonderful aroma. Sarah had told Ellie that since Queen Victoria had included a piece of myrtle in her wedding bouquet, it had become fashionable for brides to include a sprig in their bouquets. It was thought to bring the bride good luck and Bochym was happy to provide, if some were requested.

As Ellie washed the strawberries, she smiled. Maybe one day she too would ask for a sprig of myrtle, although she didn't think for one minute that the hateful Lanfear would let her through the gates again!

Stirring the fruit into the jam pan, she puzzled as to why Lady Sarah and Lady Carole had been so welcoming of her, but their staff had been so unfriendly. Her presence at the kitchen door had provoked such an adverse response Ellie presumed it had something to do with why her family had been banished. *Oh how I wish I knew what the reason was.* She stopped stirring the jam for a moment to search her mind. *If only I could recall the argument which had occurred between Lanfear and my mother, perhaps that would give a clue to what had occurred.* She shuddered at the thought of that dreadful man.

Through the duration of their walk, Ellie had had to use all of her resolve to not ask Lady Sarah if *she* knew the reason for the banishment. She started stirring the jam again, this time with more vigour. Maybe she would ask her one day, but not yet. She liked Lady Sarah and didn't want anything to tarnish their new found friendship.

As Ellie scalded her jars, her thoughts turned to the ghostly apparition she'd seen - and heard. Without doubt this was the most disconcerting aspect of her visit. The apparition seemed to follow her throughout the manor, which had unsettled her slightly. At first she wondered if the walk in the hot sun had made her slightly delirious. She'd even considered whether the head injury she'd sustained had affected her vision, but when the maid Jessie had so obviously seen something and, she suspected, the kitchen maid had too, it was clear this was not her imagination. Strangely enough the image of the girl did not frighten her – perhaps because there was something vaguely familiar about her. Shaking the thought from her head, she tested the set of the jam on a cool saucer and set about filling her jam jars.

*

There was a cool welcoming breeze blowing through the window of the earl's dressing room that evening. As Lanfear waited upon him, Peter sensed an air of arrogance in his manner and suspected that he'd been warned of an imminent reprimand. Very little was kept secret in this house.

Peter let him help him on with his dinner jacket before speaking.

'The countess tells me you were rather rude to her visitor today.'

'Yes, my lord.'

Peter glanced at him through the mirror. 'You don't deny it then?'

'No, my lord.'

This man sorely tested Peter's normally calm composure. He was an excellent valet but he certainly wasn't going to let him answer back like this. He turned swiftly to look him in the eye. 'What insolence is this?'

Lanfear lifted his chin. 'None, my lord. It was purely out of regard for your late father that I spoke so harshly to the woman.'

Peter's nostrils flared, trying to control his temper. 'What the devil do you mean?'

Lanfear cocked his head slightly. 'If I could explain, my lord?'

Peter folded his arms and lent against the back of the chair. 'Please do.'

'Your father had the Rosevears banished from the manor eight years ago. They were threatening to bring your family's name into disrepute. Those who served him believe the disquiet surrounding the allegations caused your father's premature death a few days later. He'd turn in his grave if he knew a Rosevear was tramping over his land again!'

Peter watched as he finished the sentence with a self-satisfied nod. He regarded him disdainfully for a few moments.

'Let me make myself very clear, Lanfear. I am the earl now, and I say who is welcome at this house and who is not!'

'But..'

'Hold your tongue man. I will not have the likes of you speaking rudely to any of the guests invited to this house. I'm aware of your long service and loyalty to my late father, but if I hear of your insolence again, you'll find yourself looking elsewhere for employment.'

Lanfear's mouth twitched nervously.

Congratulating himself for taking the wind from Lanfear's sails, he said, 'Don't wait up for me. I can manage without you. I have no wish to see you again today. Your presence annoys me immensely. Good night.' He gestured to him to leave.

Peter sat to settle his jangling nerves. He'd never spoken so harshly to any of the staff before, but there had always been something in Lanfear's demeanour that annoyed him. Unfortunately good valets were hard to come by.

*

Betty had a saying, "If a month came in like a lion, it would go out like a lamb", August 1901 came in like a lion. The heady days of July became lost in the torrential rain which battered Cornwall. Ellie longed for the sun to shine, but for three-quarters of the month, not a day passed without rain. The flowers Ellie had nurtured during the early summer, now lay in tatters, covered in sand blown in from the dunes.

The inclement weather did not deter Guy and Philip though from their dip in the sea, though Ellie watched with great trepidation as they ran into the angry surf. As always, they took tea after their swim. As long as they were dressed appropriately, Mrs Trerise turned a blind eye to their damp unruly hair, but would always relegate them to the terrace, so as not to drip on the Tea Room's clean floor. Today, after ordering, Philip ran off to his carriage and came back bearing a bouquet of flowers and a package of ribbons for Ellie. Thrilled, she accepted them gratefully.

Guy silently watched the interaction. In his pocket he worked another piece of turquoise sea glass with his fingers. He'd found it earlier and hoped to give it to Ellie. How insignificant his gift felt now. Perhaps he'd leave the glass in the sand in future, for it was clear now where Ellie's heart lay.

Their growing relationship concerned Guy. Philip could be a cad at times and he was damned if he was going to sit by and say nothing if Philip wasn't true to her.

'Don't dally with Ellie's heart if you don't mean it, Philip,' he warned, unable to silence his concerns any longer.

Philip looked askance at Guy, yawned and raked his fingers through his damp hair. 'I'm not dallying with her. I adore the girl.'

'What are your intentions then?' Inwardly Guy trembled at the asking.

'Wait and see.'

Philip's mischievous grin irritated Guy. 'You told me once that your father said you were to marry into money?'

Philip sighed irritably. 'That's all very well, but to marry for money doesn't necessarily mean the woman will love me. I need someone to love me.'

'Your father will not like the match,' Guy parried.

'My father can go to hell,' he answered flippantly.

'And have you asked Ellie how she feels about you?'

Philip laughed. 'Well, I don't really think I need to ask.' He sat back folding his arms at the back of his head. 'I mean, look at the way she looks at me.'

Guy could not deny that Ellie only had eyes for Philip. He inhaled deeply, released the sea glass from his fingers and laid his hands to rest upon his lap. His heart felt terribly sore.

*

As predicted by Betty, the latter end of August saw a change in the weather. Poldhu was bathed again in sunshine. The warm weather cheered everyone, except Ellie, for she'd been dealt a blow she feared she'd not recover from.

Ellie had been aware that Betty had been quiet lately. Fearing she may be ailing, when they'd sat down after a rather busy Friday afternoon, Ellie asked her, 'Is everything alright, Betty? You're very pensive at the moment.'

Betty pulled a face – realising she could stall no longer, she took Ellie's hand in hers.

'Oh Ellie, I don't know how to tell you this but…I'm so sorry, I've decided to retire. The lease is up and Mr

Collins, our landlord, wants to sell the freehold. To be truthful, I'm too old now to run this place anymore - my knees are shot.'

Ellie's heart tightened. 'But, Betty,' she pleaded, tears pricking her eyes, 'we'll be homeless and I'll have no job!'

'Ellie don't take on so.' Betty softly patted her hand. 'I'm going to live with my sister and she says there is a small box room for you too. You mustn't worry that pretty little head of yours yet. I am sure someone else will buy the place soon.'

Ellie bit down onto her lip to stop the tears flowing. 'I hope so.' She could not comprehend not working here.

'You have your lace making. Maybe Lady Carole will buy more from you.'

Ellie pulled a face. 'I've made lace for her wedding dress. Who's to say whether she'll want any more?'

'Of course she will. If not her, she'll have plenty of rich friends baying for your exquisite lace once they have seen what you've made. You'll be fine, Ellie, I'm sure of it.'

Ellie was not so sure. She wrung her hands while she glanced at the place she called home. 'When is the lease up?'

'The 21st of September. Phew, I'm glad I've told you now. I can look forward to putting my feet up.'

*

The next morning, Philip and Guy sat on the terrace watching the masses dip their feet in the sea. They were thankful they'd swam earlier when the beach had been quieter, because by the time they'd emerged from the sea, there had been hardly a patch of sand left uncovered by families picnicking.

'I think perhaps we may have to swim even earlier next week, Guy.'

'I won't be here next week. I've a thatch to do in Lamorna.'

'Lamorna! Why that's miles away!'

'I know, but it's a favour for the builder, Jack Nance

from Cadgwith. He puts an awful lot of work my way. His daughter is marrying a fisherman from Lamorna and their cottage is in dire need of a new roof.'

'How long will you be away?'

'Three, maybe four weeks, I won't know until I've seen the job.' In truth Guy felt the need to distance himself from the situation developing between Philip and Ellie.

They both looked up and smiled when Ellie brought out their tea. As she put the tray on the table, Philip caught her hand.

Ellie laughed momentarily but quickly pulled away before Betty saw.

'That's better. You've barely raised a smile this morning. What on earth could be bothering my lovely Ellie?'

Ellie sat down on the spare chair with a sigh. 'I'm sorry. My mind is in a whirl at the moment. The Tea Room is to close. Unless someone buys it, I fear I shall be unemployed within the month.'

Philip reached for her hand again, but this time held it tight so she could not pull away.

Guy glanced away, envious of their intimacy. More than anything else, he wanted to feel her slender hand in his own.

'Listen to me, Ellie. When one door closes another always opens.'

Ellie rubbed the back of her neck. 'That is what Betty keeps telling me. I hope you're both right.'

Philip squeezed her hand. 'Trust me on this, Ellie. All will be well. *I'll* make sure it is. Now, are you going to give us one of your dazzling smiles?'

Ellie smiled uneasily and managed to pull her hand free. 'I hope you have a miracle up your sleeve, Philip Goldsworthy.'

'Miracles are my speciality.' He winked.

Guy watched Ellie collect the used crockery from the next table. When she'd taken them inside, he said, 'Don't make false promises to Ellie, Philip.'

'There is nothing false about my promises.' Philip gave a flourish of his hand.

'Well are you planning to buy this place then?'

'Good god, no. I've enough on my plate with the Corn Mill. Father is ready to take a back seat now and hand me the reins.'

'So how are you proposing to help? Are you going to marry her?' The sentence caught in his throat.

'Shush.' Philip tapped his finger to his nose. 'It's to be a surprise.'

Guy felt every nerve prickle. 'Don't dally with Ellie's emotions, Philip. The poor girl is upset. Tell her your intentions, if they're honourable.'

Enjoying Guy's anguish, Philip said evasively, 'All in good time my friend. I need to speak to my father first, but rest assured, Ellie is going to be well looked after.'

A ripple of anxiety stirred in Guy's stomach. How *he* wished he was in a position to help Ellie.

5

Guy was preoccupied with Ellie's dilemma, as he worked on Willow End Cottage in the village of Lamorna. Having been away since learning of the imminent closure of the Tea Room, he was concerned whether Philip had put any proposal to Ellie yet. It was unlike Philip to be secretive, but try as he might, he'd been unable to wheedle his plans out of him that day. Knowing Philip's father had plans for his son to marry well, suggested almost certainly he would not agree to Philip marrying Ellie. So if that was the case, what the hell was Philip proposing?

He knelt back on his heels, put down his tools, and looked around the lush wooded valley of Lamorna, berating himself for not offering Ellie the use of a room in Bramble Cottage. He'd have gladly bunked up with Silas - not that Silas would've been too pleased about it, nor his ma having another woman in the house, but still, he'd have talked her round to the idea. He scrubbed his hand over his face. If only he'd given Ellie a choice between that and whatever Philip was offering. In his heart he knew that if he could have just got Ellie away from Philip for a while, he could have showed Ellie how much he liked, no, not liked, how much he loved her! He buried his head in his hands. *Come on Guy, maybe it's not too late. Write to her and offer the room. At least you would have tried to give her a choice.*

'Mr Blackthorn, the Thatcher?'

Guy looked down at the postman below. 'That's me.'

'A letter for you, from Mr Philip Goldsworthy.'

Guy scrambled down the ladder.

'Proper job.' The postman nodded appreciably at the thatch Guy was working on.

'Thank you.' Guy took the envelope. As he read the contents, his heart sank. There was no need to write to Ellie now. It seemed she was lost to him forever.

*

Philip's parents resided in a fine house, nestled on the

banks of Richards Quay on the south side of the Helford River at Gweek. At his bedroom mirror, Philip preened himself as he listened to the seagulls heralding the incoming tide. Behind his reflection, he noted the autumnal change in the great oak trees which flanked the Helford.

He splashed a little cologne onto his clean shaven face, donned his bowler hat and bid goodbye to his mother, before heading out to his waiting pony trap. The day was thankfully fine as they headed out towards the coast. Although it was Saturday, Philip had no intention of swimming that day. Guy was working in Lamorna, but that was not why he'd changed his Saturday pursuit. No, today he was on a special mission and needed to be at the Tea Room before it opened.

*

It was blowy down by the cove. Philip cursed when he almost lost his hat in the breeze. So as to protect his clean shoes, and prevent sand blowing in his eyes, he walked to the Tea Room via the back road.

There was movement inside the Tea Room but the gingham curtains were still drawn. He settled himself by a table on the terrace to wait for Ellie to inevitably appear. She was a stickler for cleanliness and he knew that her first job was always to clean the tables.

Despite his groomed appearance, Philip's fingernails looked constantly dirty, due to his skin being naturally oily. This fact irritated him, and he was busily engaged in scraping them out with his other nails when Ellie stepped out onto the terrace. He stopped the activity immediately and brushed the offending debris from his trousers.

The wind had blown her hair across her face and as she pushed it back she saw him. 'Oh!' Her hand shot to her chest. 'Gosh, Philip you're an early bird.'

Ah well, it's the early bird that catches the worm. 'I couldn't wait a moment longer to see you.'

She felt her cheeks blush.

Philip relished in the reaction he had on her. 'So, my lovely Ellie, how are you this morning?'

'I'm well, thank you, although still worried about my future. I've tried several places for alternative employment, to no avail. It's coming to the end of the summer you see. Poldhu Hotel has offered me employment next spring, but I *need* work now. I seem to be running out of options.' She gave Philip a questioning look. 'People keep assuring me that something will come up, but nothing materialises.'

'Ellie.' Philip stood up and took her hands in his. 'Did I not say to you that you'll be fine? So you're to stop worrying, right this minute. Now, this is between me and you at the moment, so not a word to anyone - not even Betty.'

Ellie held a breath.

He pulled her into an embrace. 'I love you Ellie. I'm going to look after you from now on.'

Ellie crumpled with relief into his arms.

'Lovely Ellie, I've wanted you for so long,' he said gently touching her face. 'Now I must go. I've a lot to sort out. I'll see you next Saturday and if you could keep Sunday afternoon free, I'll take you somewhere special. Remember though.' He put his finger to his mouth. 'Not a word to anyone.'

*

In the penultimate week of trading at the Tea Room, a fierce storm hit the coast of Cornwall. During the night the massive 200ft aerials, constructed by Guglielmo Marconi, came crashing down, scattering debris far and wide. Betty's customers, whilst making the most of what they believed to be the best tea, cake and scones in the area, were buzzing with tales of the catastrophe.

As Philip emerged from his swim the following Saturday, Tobias Williams nodded knowingly towards the wireless station. 'I told ee they wouldn't last.'

Philip grunted and moved past him.

Ellie felt her tummy flutter when Philip arrived on the

terrace. It had been difficult to hide her elation from Betty, but staying true to her word, whenever Betty enquired as to why she looked constantly excited, Ellie just shook her head and smiled.

Betty was no fool. Although Ellie stayed tight-lipped about her plans, she'd seen the developing relationship between Ellie and Philip. She just hoped that he'd be true to her. Betty knew his type - all charm, good looks and false promises. She hoped with all her heart that she was wrong about him.

Ellie tidied her hair, straightened her apron and practically skipped to him to take his order. 'What can I get you today, Philip?'

His hand caught her. 'Today, my lovely Ellie, I'll have tea and a slice of apple pie. Tomorrow however…..' he kissed the back of her hand, 'I'd like you to put on your prettiest dress.'

'Oh!' Ellie squeaked. 'Where are we going?'

'It's a secret. I'll collect you at two-thirty.'

*

On Sunday afternoon, Ellie dressed in the one good frock she possessed - the one she wore if ever she needed to go to church, which in truth was quite rare. Sundays was a busy day at the Tea Room. Betty, no church goer herself, preferred instead to provide much needed refreshment to folks who had spent an hour in a draughty church. Ellie had rinsed her hair the night before, so she wore it tied back away from her face with the ribbon Philip gifted her, leaving a mass of auburn curls tumbling down her back. There was still a slight scar on her forehead from her accident, so she pulled a few wisps of hair down to cover it. As she emerged from her bedroom, she was relieved to see that Betty had taken herself back to her cottage for her Sunday afternoon snooze.

The pony trap arrived promptly at two-thirty and Ellie waited excitedly as the driver turned it around.

'Where are we going?' Ellie asked, as Philip helped her

up onto her seat.

'Wait and see.' He grinned. 'Ready to go, Yates,' he ordered the driver to set off.

Although a little nervous, Philip put Ellie at ease, chatting amiably all the way up towards the main Helston road. When Yates turned the pony trap towards Gweek, Ellie's heart flipped slightly. *Was he taking her to meet his parents*? She hoped she looked presentable enough. She was certainly not of Philip's class, but that fact didn't seem to bother him at all. A tingle ran through her body - maybe he was going to propose properly to her today.

As they passed the Gweek sign at the bottom of the hill, Yates turned the pony towards the Corn Mill that Philip's father owned, and then continued up the rocky lane towards a couple of cottages. As they came to a halt, Philip jumped down and held his hand out to Ellie.

Ellie gasped. Surrounded by a picket fence, it was the sort of cottage she'd dreamt of living in. *If this was mine I'd grow roses around the door.*

'Come.' Philip beckoned her to the door of Primrose Cottage. The grass flanking each side of the path was perfectly manicured, but Ellie was slightly disappointed that the garden borders had not been utilised. They were quite devoid of flowers! Whoever lived here must be too busy to work in the garden. Maybe Philip's parents lived here! That thought made her tremble. She consciously patted her hair tidy, just in case they were inside.

The blue door, recently painted, opened with ease, and Philip held it ajar for her to cross the threshold.

'What do you think?' Philip asked, watching the delight in her eyes.

Ellie's eyes scanned the cosy kitchen room. 'It's lovely, Philip.'

'Take a look around then.'

'Is there no one home?'

He grinned. 'Not yet.'

Room by room, Ellie marvelled at the newly decorated

rooms. There was no linen on the beds - it looked as though the cottage was waiting for someone to move in. She moved to the bedroom window, the sunlight dappled through the lace curtains. Gently pulling them aside, she looked out over the trees towards the main Gweek road. Opening the window, she allowed a cacophony of bird song to fill the room. Ellie placed her hand on her heart. *I would love to live somewhere like this.*

As she descended the stairs, Philip was waiting. 'Well, do you like it?'

'It's lovely, Philip, truly lovely. Who does it belong to?'

'It's ours, my darling Ellie. I want to spend as much time as possible with you and here is the perfect place. You'll want for nothing, once we're together. Everything will be at your disposal. You just need to say yes.'

Ellie bubbled with delight. 'I can't believe this is happening.'

He squeezed her hand. 'Say yes and you'll be mine forever, and I'll be the happiest of men.'

'Oh yes, Philip, thank you.'

'Now, Ellie.' He invited her to sit on the sofa. 'I was going to wait a few weeks before I showed you this cottage, but the imminent closure of the Tea Room prompted me to bring my plans forward. Unfortunately, I must go away for a while.'

'Oh.' Ellie felt suddenly deflated. 'Where are you going?'

'I'm spending six weeks on the continent.' He gently caressed Ellie's face. 'I'm sorry darling, I must go. It won't all be pleasure. I'll be meeting some of father's contacts over there. If I am to take over the Mill, I have to know the business inside out. Rest assured, my darling, I shall write to you often and I'll be back before you know it.'

'So, I'm to be here alone?' She glanced around the room.

'For the time being, yes, but darling, you won't be alone. We have some fine neighbours. In fact, Guy

Blackthorn lives next door with his ma and younger brother, so you will not be without friends.'

Her face brightened. 'And your parents - are they nearby?'

'Erm....quite near, yes,'

'Then I won't be alone. I could call on them and make their acquaintance,' she trilled.

Philip cleared his throat uneasily. 'Well, the thing is......I thought perhaps we could wait until I return, and then I'll make arrangements for you to meet them.'

'But Philip, I honestly don't mind going on my own.'

'Well, the thing is ....Mother is going away for a while and Father is going to be understandably busy at the mill while I am away, so he probably won't have time to see you. I'd rather you wait until I return.'

Ellie felt a seed of doubt settle in her stomach. 'You *have* told them about me?'

Philip squeezed her hands reassuringly. 'Of course, silly, I just think it would be better all round that we wait and meet them together, properly.'

With an uneasy truce, Ellie shrugged her shoulders. 'Alright, whatever you say.'

'Good, that's sorted then. So I'll send Yates to collect you and your belongings next Sunday. If you need anything, Yates will see to it, and take you anywhere you want to go. Buy what you need to make this cottage a home we can be comfortable in. Money is no object.' He glanced at her attire. 'I suggest you have some decent clothes made. I'll leave a list of shops in Helston where I hold an account.'

Ellie's immediate response to his thoughtless comment was to be annoyed but then thought better of it. She smoothed her hands down her hand-made best dress and thanked him meekly.

'Thank *you*, Ellie. You've made me very happy.'

Ellie glanced around the cottage she was to call home, with a slight tinge of melancholia. 'It's all so beautiful,

Philip, but I must say, I shall miss my life at the Tea Room when it closes.'

He lifted her chin with his hand. 'Never mind, you can make your delicious cakes for me now. Come on Ellie, no sad faces, you're about to embark on a new life with me,' he said with an air of satisfaction.

*

Betty was relieved, albeit a little apprehensive to hear Ellie's news. She would have been welcome at her sister's house, but this offer from Philip Goldsworthy was indeed heaven sent.

'So you are to be married?' Betty said cautiously.

Ellie smiled brightly.

Betty relaxed a little. 'Well, that is good news. I told you everything would be fine. My closing this place must have prompted your young man to make his pledge to you. Have you set a date?'

'No… not yet. Philip has to go away on business for a few weeks. I think because we're closing, he decided to let me live in our cottage until he returns.'

'I see,' Betty said warily. 'That was good of him.'

'I promise you'll be the first to know as soon as we set a date. Oh, Betty, the cottage is beautiful. To think I'll have my very own home, to do in as I please. You shall have to come and see it.'

'I'll see it on your wedding day, no doubt.' Despite her misgivings about Philip, Betty smiled with motherly affection. 'I knew you'd catch the eye of someone special one day. You're so lovely. I wish you all the luck in the world. Your mother would be proud that you've done so well for yourself.'

6

It was Saturday the 22nd September. The early mist which had hung in ribbons across the formal gardens at Bochym Manor had burnt away in order for the day to warm nicely for a wedding.

Lady Carole Dunstan stood before her dressing room mirror, admiring the beautiful lace of her wedding dress, as her carriage, festooned with flowers and white ribbons awaited her. Whoops of laughter filtered up from her entourage of bridesmaids as they ran about the front lawn in their fine toile dresses.

'Darling, you look beautiful!' said Lucinda, Dowager Countess de Bochym as she swept into her daughter's dressing room, dismissing the lady's maid with a flick of her hand.

'This lace is exquisite, Carole.' She fingered the delicate material. 'Finding that lace woman was a godsend.'

Carole smiled.' I couldn't agree more, Mama.'

'Tell me darling, does this colour suit me?' Lucinda said, moving Carole aside to check her own appearance. She wore an empire line dress of blue silk, scooped at the neck to show off the de Bochym sapphires. Lucinda was sixty two years old, and fortunately, age had hardly marred her beauty.

'It's perfect, Mama.' Carole wistfully admired the family jewels which would never be hers.

'It is, isn't it?' She tore herself away from her reflection. 'Now darling, are you ready to take the next step into married life - god help you.'

'Mama,' Carole warned.

'I'm sorry but you know I never agreed with this match that your father arranged for you. You do not have to fulfil his wish you know darling.'

'Mama, don't worry, I adored Papa and it was his dearest wish that I married his oldest friend's son, to secure our future finances.'

Lucinda sighed heavily. 'Yes, but….'

'No buts, Mama, I'm happy to do it.' Wearing an unashamed look, she added, 'and of course it will be financially beneficial to me too.'

Lucinda raised her eyebrows. 'The excellent marriage settlement he provided for you, and the regular allowance you'll receive that your husband cannot touch, you mean?'

'Precisely!' She smiled as she teased a curl into place. 'I do believe I've inherited Papa's business mind.'

'Darling, it's really not your place to deal with the financial issues of this house - that fell on Peter's shoulders once your father died. Peter is more than capable of securing the financial future of Bochym and I really don't want you to compromise your happiness.'

'I'm not comprised. It's not as if I'm marrying a complete stranger. Good god, I've known him all my life!'

'I know darling, but it's hardly a love match made in heaven, is it? Do you love him?'

'God no, he's more like a brother to me.'

Lucinda grimaced. 'Will that fact not pose a problem when you lay with him?'

Carole pouted disdainfully. 'It will only be until I give him an heir,' she said flippantly. 'Anyway Mama, I thought you didn't believe in love? You said it was an overrated emotion.'

'Yes, well I'm a bitter old woman who wasted her life on *your* father.'

Carole stared accusingly at her mother through the mirror. 'Did you *never* love Papa?'

'Of course I did…. at first. I loved him very much when you and Peter were little, but….' She paused, shaking the horrible thoughts of her late husband from her head, 'things went a little sour.'

'I *wish* you'd tell me what went wrong,' Carole asked pettily. 'Was it his drinking?'

Lucinda's mouth twisted. 'Among other things, yes,' she said dryly.

'Well.' Carole sighed noisily. 'I wish Papa was here today to give me away.'

Lucinda shuddered at the thought. *He never gave anything away.*

Carole picked up her bouquet, plucked out the piece of myrtle Sarah had pushed into it, tossing it to one side.

'Luck I don't need. It's fortitude to see me through the honeymoon.' She gave herself one last admiring glance. The wedding of course would be spectacular - she'd overseen the preparations herself. Well if one was to be married, even though it was to someone she didn't love, the least her family could do was to make the day as memorable as possible for her. She turned to her mother and said, 'Come on then, Mama, let's get it over with.'

*

At Poldhu Cove, the beach was full of people, enjoying the good weather. At around fifteen degrees, the water was tempting the most faint hearted of dippers.

The sky bore only the odd fluffy cloud, and the sun shone all day until the Tea Room served its last customer. With the crockery washed and put carefully away in the cupboards for the next proprietor to use, Betty and Ellie sat wistfully on the terrace and watched the people pack their belongings and head for home.

'Will you miss this, Betty?'

'My knees and bunions won't,' she quipped, easing her feet out of her shoes. Betty smiled gently at Ellie. 'I shall miss you though, my dear.

'And I'll miss you, Betty,' Ellie said tearfully. 'If it wasn't for you...'

'Shush.' Betty stopped her mid sentence. 'We've both been good for each other. You've made the Tea Room what it is.'

'It's your cakes they come for!'

'Ah but you make a good cake and scone yourself and don't deny it.'

Ellie sighed heavily. She would miss this view. Gweek

was lovely, but at low tide, the mud gave it a less than aesthetical appearance. Never mind, her cottage was situated at the back of the village, with a brook running adjacent to it, and rolling hills to the rear.

Betty smiled. 'I see you're thinking of your new home.'

Ellie nodded. 'I still pinch myself that it's happening.

'And when will Philip join you?'

'Not for six whole weeks.' She sighed.

'And then you'll be married?'

'I will.' She grinned. 'As soon as a date is set I shall send you an invitation.'

'Are you packed and ready?'

'Yes. Philip is sending the pony trap for me in the morning.'

'A pony trap! Eh?' Betty winked. 'Aren't you the fine lady then?'

Ellie laughed and lent against Betty's shoulder. They sat for an hour and for the last time, they watched together as the sun moved slowly towards Land's End.

*

Sarah and Peter Dunstan, along with a straggle of hung-over guests, gathered together on Sunday morning at Bochym Manor to wave the newlyweds off on their honeymoon. As the carriage, festooned with ribbons and flowers, disappeared down the drive in a cloud of dust, Sarah heaved a sigh of exhausted relief.

'Do you think they'll be happy, Peter?'

'I very much doubt it. But fair play to her, she did what Papa wanted her to - though I suspect the lure of an annual private income was an incentive.'

Sarah reached for her husband's hand. 'Can the estate afford it?'

Peter lifted her hand to his lips and kissed it tenderly. 'Yes, don't worry, for all his faults, Papa made sure she would be well provided for. The marriage will bring us good financial rewards, as Papa intended it to.' As they turned back towards the front path, Peter added, 'So,

Sarah, once the last of our guests decide to leave, which will hopefully be later this morning, we'll be alone at last for the first time since our marriage.' He grinned mischievously

Sarah laughed. *Alone, except for several members of the household staff and….*she glanced at the vaporous figure of the young girl at the window of the Jacobean drawing room… *a slight problem with the deceased habitants of this house.*

*

After a sad and tearful farewell to Betty and her beloved Tea Room, Ellie climbed aboard the pony trap to start her new life in Gweek.

As Ellie and Mr Yates came to the end of Cury lane to join the main Lizard to Helston road, a carriage rode past, its white ribbons flowing in the breeze.

Yates nodded. 'That'll be the newlyweds from Bochym, en-route to their honeymoon.'

'Oh yes!' Ellie craned her neck to watch it go. 'I'd forgotten all about Lady Carole's wedding yesterday. What with closing the business and packing to leave, it went completely out of my head. I'd have dearly loved to see her wedding gown. I made the lace trims for it you know?'

'Really?' Yates raised his eyebrows, before flicking the reins to pull out onto the road.

Ellie nodded – though puzzled by the strange look Yates gave her.

Half an hour later they turned into the lane behind the Corn Mill. Ellie strained her neck to look at her new neighbour's cottages. There was a row of four mill workers houses to her left, and then as they drove over the stone bridge, the next two thatched cottages came into view. The first was hers, Primrose Cottage and the one further up, Bramble Cottage, belonged to Guy and his family. She'd venture further up the lane later that day, to familiarise herself with her other neighbours.

As Yates carried her bags into the cottage, Ellie stood at the gate smiling happily. This was her home and very beautiful it was too.

'Can I do anything else for you, Miss?'

'No thank you, Mr Yates. You've been very kind, but please stay for a cup of tea. I brought everything with me to brew a pot, I'll just need to light the range though.'

'No need for that. I lit the range earlier for you. Thank you for the offer of tea, but I best be getting back. My wife will have my dinner ready. If you need anything, knock on the first cottage door nearest to the mill.' Yates doffed his hat and left.

Placing her cloth bag on the kitchen table she walked from room to room, more slowly and inquisitively than when Philip had shown her around. In the bedroom she found fresh linen waiting on the bed, and a bouquet of flowers lay on the bedside table with a simple note attached. *I love you. P*

Ellie had never felt happier.

*

After hanging her clothes in the wardrobe, Ellie boiled a kettle. Philip promised the larders would be stocked in readiness for her arrival, and they were! On the back of the larder door was a note.

Drop a list of the things you need into Moyles shop, situated adjacent to the Corn Mill and an errand boy will drop them off at the house. We have an account with them.

Ellie laughed. *I think I can manage to go shopping, Philip.*

In her normal tea room tradition she made up a tray to take out into the garden. The day was warm and birdsong was her only company, but her heart settled peacefully as she looked over the garden. It was in dire need of some flowers and though she'd been sad to leave behind her sea garden, she'd brought with her some specimen plants. Now with this blank canvas, her fingers itched to get started. A beautiful cottage such as this, cried out for a rose to scramble up its walls. She would lay a row of lavender to each side of the path and fill the garden with lupins, delphiniums and chrysanthemums – all the flowers that would never have survived in the salty air at Poldhu.

Whilst happily sipping her tea, she turned when she heard voices, to find a couple of women chatting jovially as they walked up the lane.

'Good morning,' Ellie said, standing politely to make their acquaintance.

The women, dressed in their Sunday best, halted momentarily, their smiles diminishing. One of the ladies tsked, tugging the other's sleeve to keep walking.

Bemused at their deliberate slight, Ellie watched them walk away. After clearing the tea tray away, and unaccustomed to having time on her hands, Ellie decided to set out her bobbins and bolster cushion by the front window, but as the day was so lovely, she changed her mind, put on an old dress, and set to work in the garden.

It felt wonderful to work with good soil. The leaves from the surrounding trees had rotted down over time and mulched the ground to a fine rich loam. Time swept by and several people passed Primrose Cottage as Ellie worked in the garden, but try as she might to engage with them, no one felt inclined to stop and chat. One or two nodded their heads, though the gesture seemed reluctant, but more often than not, they pretended not to notice her. Perhaps everyone was too busy to stop - it was Sunday after all and they probably had families at home waiting to be fed. Not everyone was lucky enough to be a lady of leisure. A niggling seed of doubt began to grow - settling into Gweek may be a little more challenging than she had thought.

*

Monday morning dawned bright and sunny, but Ellie lay abed long after she'd normally have risen. Unaccustomed to a life of leisure, she keenly felt the loss of being busy. She was suddenly engulfed with a strange feeling of loneliness. Knowing she needed to make friends soon, the negative reactions she received yesterday might prove a challenge. Turning to the window the dappled sun beckoned. *Come on Ellie, get up and stop wallowing in self pity. You should have called on Guy's mother yesterday. She'd have welcomed you, especially if she's anything near as amiable as Guy.* She swung her legs out of bed and groaned - her body ached alarmingly after the hours she spent in the garden yesterday.

*

Ellie knocked on Nellie Blackthorn's door after breakfast. To her disappointment she received no answer, though she was sure she saw some movement inside. *Perhaps she's busy and doesn't want to be disturbed.* Refusing to be perturbed, she returned home, put on her sturdy boots and straw hat and decided to explore her new surroundings. Locating a bridleway at the top of the lane, she walked across the fields, high above Gweek, towards the village of Constantine. Ellie was eager to see Constantine Church, where she would be married when Philip returned. It was a long walk in what proved to be a very warm September morning, so the coolness of the church brought a welcome relief when Ellie finally sat down on the first pew she came to.

Taking a drink from her flask, she relaxed. There was always something very peaceful about sitting alone in a church. Though not a church goer herself, she did occasionally visit her parents' grave in Cury Churchyard, and more often than not would sit a while inside the church, appreciating the splendour of its interior. Today she tipped her head to gaze at the ceiling and then looked towards the carved wooden eagle lectern sat upon the octagonal pulpit. A happy thought ran through her mind, imagining Philip standing there waiting for her on her wedding day. She felt such joy in her heart at the prospect of becoming his wife. These next six weeks were going to be the longest in her life.

On her walk home, she watched the men in the fields bringing in the harvest. It had been an inclement summer but the fields looked lush and abundant with crops. As she skirted the field nearest to her lane, she saw a woman and child sitting in the middle of a meadow, sketching. Dressed in white, both were blonde-headed and hatless and the sun seemed to radiate from them. Gay laughter filtered up from where they sat. Ellie smiled. *One day, I'll sit in this field with my own children.* She hesitated between wanting to approach them to say hello, but not wanting another rebuff to ruin what was turning out to be a lovely day. She decided to walk on by. There would be time enough to make new friends.

Ellie found the hedgerows in the lane leading down to her cottage were edged by a thicket of brambles. She couldn't resist picking blackberries when she saw them, so she filled her basket with an abundance of warm, plump, juicy fruit. She had a few more weeks to gather more, because she knew she could only pick blackberries up to the eleventh day of October, because tradition said that the devil spits or urinates on them! Unsure as to whether she believed that old wives tale, Ellie had her own reasons for not picking them after that date and that was so the birds could feed up before the winter set in.

Making the decision not to call on Nellie Blackthorn on the way home, Ellie had a better idea. She'd turn the fruit into pots of jam, so that when she did call the next day, she wouldn't call empty handed.

As she stood washing the glistening berries, Ellie felt that today had been a good day. Tomorrow would be even better.

7

At Bochym Manor, Jessie Taylor woke at five-thirty - she needed no call. She quickly washed, dressed in her uniform and swept her long chestnut hair in to a tight bun.

Jessie had been temporarily promoted to Sarah's lady maid, while the household's lady maid, Susan Binns, accompanied Carole on her honeymoon.

Jessie loved working for Sarah. She was kind, considerate and extremely patient with Jessie as she took on a role she was unfamiliar with. It was a role she relished, despite knowing that when Carole returned, she'd be relegated back to a normal housemaid, like her roommate Jane Truscott.

Carole held the household purse strings at Bochym, and was thrifty, to say the least, except perhaps on her own expenditure. When her brother Peter married Sarah, Carole suggested that both the ladies of the house could easily share a maid, thus increasing the workload for poor Susan Binns.

Jessie laced up her boots, made her bed and flung open the window to air the room. Sarah, herself an early riser, was never one to have a tray delivered to her bed. Instead, she would breakfast in her Morning Room at six-thirty. More often than not, Peter would join her there, but today he was away from home, so Sarah would eat alone. Jessie's first job after delivering a breakfast tray to Sarah would be to mend the garment her mistress had snagged on a rose thorn in the garden. Then she would draw a bath, select and polish Sarah's shoes and set out her garments for the day ahead.

Jessie checked her appearance in the mirror and glanced at Jane snoring in the other bed. She could leave her to sleep in, but it wasn't Jessie's way to be mean, so she shook the bed. 'Jane, wake up and move yourself or you'll be late.'

As Jessie stepped out onto the landing her world

stilled. The shape of the girl, she'd seen many times these last few weeks, was standing by the disused attic door. Jessie blinked hard and the girl disappeared. Her mouth fell open. *Where did she go? The attic was always locked!* The figure appeared again in a vaporous mist, beside the attic door. As the vapour cleared, Jessie could see that she was dressed in a calico nightdress, her arms were protectively wrapped around herself and she appeared to be deeply distressed. Surprisingly unafraid of the apparition, Jessie was confused as to why the figure appeared so often before her.

'Who are you?' she asked shakily reaching out to the girl. 'Why are you here? What do you want me to do?'

The bedroom door opened suddenly, Jane stepped out, and the figure disappeared.

'Who are you talking to, Jessie?' Jane demanded.

Jessie glanced about. 'Nobody,'

'Yes you were!' Jane retorted. 'I heard you! I'm telling Mrs Bligh about this. You shouldn't be holding the position of a lady's maid if you're engaging in some ungodly activity.'

Jessie sighed and watched in dismay as Jane flounced down the stairs.

*

After the early morning chores were complete, the Bochym staff gathered around the kitchen table for breakfast.

'Jessie's been talking to the wall again, Mrs Blair,' Jane told the cook as she settled herself at the table.

Betsy the scullery maid looked up fearfully from her meal.

'I don't wish to know,' Cook said, shooting a warning glance at the girls, as she dished out the porridge.

Determined not to rise to Jane's taunts, Jessie lowered her eyes and ate her breakfast. When she'd finished, she sat back and unable to stop herself, gasped audibly.

Everyone looked at her, but Jessie's gaze was held on

the apparition standing behind Albert Lanfear, pointing at him.

Lanfear's piggy eyes locked with Jessie's. 'Why are you staring at me girl?' he snapped.

Jessie quickly looked away.

'I wish she'd stare at me like that,' joked Joe Treen, the first footman.

'Dream on, Joe,' Jane quipped. 'Jessie only has eyes for dead people.'

Jessie elbowed Jane in the ribs.

'Ouch!' Jane rubbed her side, as cook shot another warning look.

'It's rude to stare,' Lanfear said, as he clasped his hand to the back of his neck. 'Where the hell is that cold draft coming from, all of a sudden?'

Jessie bit her lip to suppress a smile - the apparition was practically leant on his shoulder.

Betsy glanced over to the window to see where the draught was coming from. It was then she too saw the figure standing behind Lanfear. She screamed, knocked her breakfast bowl flying, and fled to the scullery.

'What the…' Cook sat open-mouthed.

Jessie dabbed her mouth with her napkin. 'It's alright. I'll go see to her.'

Betsy was cowering fearfully in the corner by the sink, as great fat tears spilled down her flushed cheeks.

'Shush, Betsy, don't cry.' Jessie gathered the frightened girl into her arms. 'I know you saw her, I can see her too, but I promise she'll not harm you.'

'But Jessie I don't like it.' Betsy sobbed uncontrollably

Jessie pulled a clean handkerchief from her pocket and pressed it into Betsy's hand. 'Please Betsy, calm yourself. You know, it takes a special type of person to see her.'

'But I don't *want* to see her,' she wailed. 'Who is she?'

'I don't know, Betsy, but I think she's trying to tell us something. Now I need you to be very brave and not scream when you see her again. I'll try and find out what she wants, alright?'

Betsy turned her distraught face towards Jessie and nodded unconvincingly.

*

Mrs Bligh marched thunderously into the kitchen.

'What's the meaning of this racket?'

'It's Jessie, Mrs Bligh,' Jane trilled. 'She's convinced the house is haunted by someone, because she keeps talking to it. Every time I walk past her, she's deep in conversation with something that is clearly not there! She's giving everyone the heebie-jeebies.'

Joe Treen jumped to Jessie's defence 'You're talking nonsense, Jane. Jessie's singing, not talking to ghosts. You know very well she sings to herself all the time. You're just jealous, that's all. I've heard you sing and you're tone deaf.'

'Treen, that's enough,' Mr Carrington scolded. 'If you've finished, go about your business.'

'Yes, Mr Carrington. Sorry,' Joe said meekly.

'And Truscott, that's enough of this silly talk. If I hear any more ridiculous stories of ghosts, you'll be looking for alternate employment. I'll not have this household disrupted. Do you understand me?'

'Yes, Mr Carrington.' Jane squirmed.

'Where is Taylor anyway?' Mrs Bligh demanded.

'She's in the scullery seeing to Betsy. Something spooked the silly girl,' Cook said, raising an eyebrow.

The bell tinkled from Lady Sarah's room. 'Taylor!' Mrs Bligh shouted, 'Lady Sarah is ringing. Go to her, *now!*'

Cook gave Mrs Bligh a grave look. 'Tell me it's not happening again,' she said making the sign of the cross at her heart.

'*Not* if I have anything to do with it, Mrs Blair.'

*

Jessie heard the bell and the shout for her.

'Betsy I'll have to go. Are you going to be alright?'

Betsy nodded tearfully.

Jessie dabbed Betsy's tears and gave her a hug. 'Come

on then. We'll get to the bottom of this, don't worry. For now we'll say you screamed because a spider crawled down your neck. Mrs Blair will sympathise with you then - she hates spiders.' She winked.

Betsy shuddered. 'I don't like them myself.'

As they walked back into the kitchen, Lanfear had gone, and to the relief of both girls, so had the apparition.

Mrs Bligh scowled coldly with pursed lips. '*Taylor*, report to my room, as soon as you've finished with Lady Sarah.'

Jessie flinched at her vehemence. 'Yes, Mrs Bligh.'

*

Mr Carrington beckoned Mrs Bligh into his room, closing the door firmly behind him, and took a seat by the window.

Bligh folded her arms. 'I don't like what's happening here, John!'

'Nether do I, Joan.'

'It's like it's all happening again, and I won't stand for it!'

Carrington tapped his mouth with his fingers. 'After all these years, I thought this episode was dead and buried.'

Bligh raised her eyebrows. 'An unfortunate turn of phrase John, in the light of things, don't you think?'

'I'm sure you can sort it, by nipping it in the bud, right now.'

Bligh gritted her teeth until her jaw ached. 'It's that bloody Rosevear girl behind this, I just know it.'

'Well, now the wedding is out of the way, we'll see no more of her. Keep calm Joan, this will all blow over.'

*

As Jessie drew a bath for Sarah, she prayed that her mistress would take her out with her somewhere today - she did not relish the interview with Bligh. It was not to be though - Sarah requested her gardening attire to be laid out.

With a heavy heart, Jessie dressed her mistress after the

bath, pinned her hair up and reluctantly made her way down the stairs to face the music.

*

The housekeeper's room stood adjacent to the laundry, so the smell of starch and hot irons permeated through the door, mingling with the strong aroma of carbolic soap which penetrated every room Mrs Bligh inhabited.

Standing before her, Bligh was dressed in black from head to toe and her greying hair was dragged back into a severe bun. She'd never married, but as a senior member of the household staff she bore the title Mrs. In reality she was as dry and pinched as any bitter old maid could be.

'Now, Taylor, I expect you to answer truthfully. Is Elise Rosevear behind all this nonsense?'

Jessie looked blankly 'Who?'

'You know very well who Elise Rosevear is.'

Puzzled, Jessie wracked her brain. 'I'm sorry Mrs Bligh, but I don't know who you mean.'

Bligh's lips twitched angrily. 'Elise Rosevear, the girl who brought the lace for Lady Carole!'

'Oh, her!' Jessie suddenly remembered the day Elise came - it was the first time she'd seen the apparition.

'Yes, her!'

Jessie bit her lip. 'But I don't know her. That day was the first time I'd seen her.'

Bligh grabbed Jessie by the arms and shook her violently. 'Yes but what mischief did she pass onto you that day?'

A piece of spittle escaped Bligh's mouth, settling on Jessie's lip. She flinched in disgust, but dare not wipe it away.

'Tell me girl.'

Jessie feared her teeth might loosen, as Bligh shook her again.

'What witchcraft are you performing, and what do you expect to gain from it?'

Jessie's throat constricted, knowing she'd be in deep

trouble and could be dismissed in a heartbeat if she told Bligh what she'd seen, so remained tight-lipped.

The door opened and to Jessie's infinite relief, Sarah stepped over the threshold.

Glancing at Jessie's distraught face, Sarah frowned. 'What, may I ask, is happening here, Mrs Bligh?'

Jessie squeaked as Bligh dug her nails into her arms.

'It's nothing for you to concern yourself with, my lady.'

Seeing Jessie's discomfort, Sarah said, 'I demand you let Jessie go, this instant!'

Bligh's fingers reluctantly uncurled and Jessie stepped away, rubbing her bruised arms vigorously.

'Now Mrs Bligh, what is the meaning of this?'

Bligh's mouth twitched. 'I am not happy with the way this girl is conducting herself in my household, my lady.'

Sarah raised her eyebrows. 'Well strangely enough, I am very happy with Jessie's conduct.'

Jessie's relief was palpable.

'That girl talks to herself all the time!'

Sarah folded her arms. 'And what pray, is the problem there?'

'Well, it's unnatural of course, and it's upsetting the other staff.' She shook her head haughtily.

Sarah's eyes narrowed. 'Jessie, would you be so kind as to ask Mrs Blair if my morning coffee could be served in the gold drawing room at eleven, and then you can get on with your chores.'

'Yes, my lady.' Jessie bobbed a curtsy and moved swiftly from the glare of Bligh.

Sarah took a deep controlled breath. 'Mrs Bligh, there isn't a person alive who does not, at some time or another, speak to themselves. It's a human trait - even you must have done it.'

Bligh's eyes flickered at her inference. She hated dealing with Lady Sarah and disagreed with her modern views and resented the casual way she addressed the staff. She was used to Lady Carole leaving the running of the household to her, and had no intention of letting Lady Sarah interfere or undermine her authority.

'The girl sees things too!' she said through gritted teeth.

Sarah tipped her head. 'Again, and the problem there, is?'

Bligh's nostrils flared. 'It's not natural!'

'And neither is your treatment of Jessie. I'll not have you bullying my staff. If I hear of it again, I *will* speak to my husband about you. Do you understand?'

'*Yes*, my lady.'

Sarah watched with relish as Bligh visibly trembled with indignation. 'Good, make sure it doesn't happen again then.'

*

After helping her dress for dinner that night, Sarah took Jessie by the hands in earnest.

'Be mindful for now Jessie, about what you do and who is listening to you.'

Jessie raised her eyebrows. *For now!* 'Yes, my lady.'

Sarah smiled and smoothed down her dress. 'I'll see you after dinner.'

8

On the third day in Gweek, Ellie woke early with an idea. She wrote invitations to everyone in her lane, inviting them to tea at two that afternoon. Perhaps they were just shy of making her acquaintance - after all she was not from this area, so she would make the first move of friendship.

After knocking on each door and receiving not a single response, even though she knew people were inside, she confidently pushed the invitations under their doors. It was quite early in the day, Ellie told herself - maybe it was too early to answer the door to unexpected visitors.

Arriving back at the cottage, she picked up her basket to go shopping. She needed to buy clotted cream, and Philip had told her there was a dairy near The Black Swan Inn. Donning her hat and coat as it was cooler that day, she set off to the village centre.

Gweek was a truly pretty tidal village. It stood at the very top of the Helford River, and from the industrial noise coming from down river it looked as though it was a thriving community. The tide was out, so the mud was visible, and Ellie stood at the bridge watching an egret wade along the muddy river bed. A couple of swans walked ungainly through the shallows. Their offspring, almost fully grown, were further down river, exploring the surroundings for themselves. There were chickens clucking on the opposite side of the bridge, and Ellie smiled at a long distant memory of her mother mimicking the buck-buck-buck of the chickens at Bochym - convinced they were saying, 'I've laid an *EGG!*'

Since her visit to Bochym, one or two memories of her childhood had begun to filter into her head, though she still could not recall who the apparition on the stairs was.

The sound of swearing and whinnying coming from the Gweek Forge shattered the peace of the morning. Ellie pitied the poor horse inside, for it sounded like there was a battle going on. Suddenly the swearing got louder, and a rather ugly man led a frightened horse out of the forge to be tied up outside.

Ellie had no wish to make this man's acquaintance, so lowered her head and set off towards the dairy.

Ellie stepped inside the Williams' farm dairy, savouring the smell of fresh milk and cheese. She was served by Mrs Williams, a ruddy faced woman with an ample bosom and a friendly smile. As she doled the clotted cream into Ellie's bowl, a young boy ran into the dairy, red-faced and excitable.

'Ma, Mr Blewett is swearing again,' he said, putting his errand basket on the table.

'Is he now? Keep away from him Charlie. He's not a nice man.'

'I heard it too,' Ellie added, 'the air was rather blue, and not for the tender ears of a child.'

Mrs Williams shook her head. 'My Eric has told him over and over again, to curb his bad language. Blewett's late father was just the same. Ugh! Horrible family.'

'Do you have any more errands, Ma?' Young Charlie tugged at her apron.

'Yes, that basket over there is for Mrs Goldsworthy.'

Ellie's ears pricked up. 'Is that Mrs Goldsworthy the Mill owner's wife?'

'Aye, it is.'

'Oh, I understood she was away for a few weeks though?'

Mrs Williams shrugged her shoulders. 'Well she sent word this morning that she wanted her normal order.' She handed the clotted cream over to Ellie, bid her good day and handed another basket to Charlie.

Ellie followed the boy out of the dairy, quickening her pace to keep up with him as he bounded over the first bridge. She was keen to see where the Goldsworthy's house was situated.

By the time Ellie had reached the second bridge, the boy was running along the river bank towards a large imposing house, nestled between two great oak trees.

Go on Ellie, knock on the door and introduce yourself. Feeling a slight effervescence in her tummy, Ellie walked down the lane, meeting the boy returning from his chore. He doffed his cap to her which made her smile. At the large carved front door, Ellie hesitated for a moment and then knocked before she could change her mind.

The great door opened slightly and a maid peeped around it to see who was there.

'Good morning. My name is Elise Rosevear.' Hesitant to introduce herself as Philip's fiancé, as she wore no ring yet, she said, 'I'm a friend of Philip Goldsworthy. I've called to make Mrs Goldsworthy's acquaintance.'

The maid's mouth formed an O and then she bobbed a curtsy. 'If you could just wait there Miss, I'll see if she's home.'

Ellie watched as she scurried off into one of the doors from the great hall in which she now stood. The house smelt of lavender furniture polish and lilies, the latter fragrance coming from a large vase on a highly polished table in the centre of the floor.

When the maid returned, Ellie noted a slight pinkness to her cheeks.

'Begging your pardon Miss, but Mrs Goldsworthy is not at home. I shall tell her that you called though.'

Ellie had the distinct feeling that the maid was fibbing, as her cheeks had now flushed up to the roots of her hair.

Ellie nodded. 'Thank you, perhaps I'll call another day?'

'Mrs Goldsworthy prefers to send out invitations to her visitors!'

Ellie felt the sting of humiliation. 'Of course she does. Hopefully I'll hear from her soon then.'

The door was held open for her and Ellie stepped out with her head held high, even though she felt slightly chastised by the young maid. As she walked slowly back down the lane from the house, she turned briefly to catch sight of a rather elegantly dressed woman watching her from the window.

*

Back home, Ellie gently kneaded the scone mixture. As she ran the scenario through her head, she could not silence the alarm bells ringing there. Why did no one want to speak to her? *Now Ellie, that's not true, Mrs Williams was very chatty this morning.* She sighed, trying to listen to the voice of reason as she cut the scones into shape. Hopefully she'd have someone to talk to this afternoon. Surely people were curious to meet their new neighbour and who could resist a free cream tea?

Because the day had turned misty, Ellie laid her kitchen table with her new crockery on a chequered tablecloth, a jug of wild flowers picked from the hedgerows was in centre stage. She made a conscious effort not to wear her best dress for the occasion, knowing most of her neighbours were not well off, so instead she wore what she used to wear, when she ran the Tea Room. The kitchen smelt wonderful as the newly baked scones cooled by the window. Several pots of jam were ready for her to give out to all her guests when they arrived. Everything was ready.

*

Mable Spargo, from the cottage at the top of Mill Lane, pulled her hat over her frizzy curls and buttoned up her coat. Never one to miss a free tea, she was curious to visit Primrose Cottage to see what all the fuss was about. The way her neighbours were reacting to the young woman down the road, anyone would think she was a mass murderer. She'd go and see for herself what she was like. Grasping the invitation, she stepped out into the mizzle and picked her way carefully down the slippery rocky path.

'Where do you think you're sneaking off to, Mable Spargo?'

Mable's shoulders drooped at the sound of her neighbour, the formidable Violet Laity.

'The shop,' Mable answered.

'In your best hat?' Violet asked accusingly. 'I have no doubt you've got that tea invitation in your pocket as well!'

Mable sighed. It was no use, nothing got past Violet. She turned to make her way back home.

'You know what we all decided.'

'I know what *you* decided, Violet.'

'It's for the best.'

'What harm would it do to meet her? Your Bert wouldn't have a job if it wasn't for Philip Goldsworthy.'

'It was old Mr Goldsworthy who gave my Bert his job.' Violet said, folding her arms adamantly.

'That may be so, but I hear Philip is taking over the reins soon, and won't look too kindly on people ignoring his chosen one.'

'Well he's asking too much if he wants us to welcome *her*!'

There was no arguing with Violet, so Mable gave up and went home, disgruntled that a cream tea was waiting for her and she couldn't partake.

*

Nellie Blackthorn, a strong, sturdy, no-nonsense woman, stood at her scrubbed kitchen table and kneaded the bread for a second time. She glanced at the grandfather clock in the corner when it chimed two-fifteen and then to the invitation on her table from the Rosevear woman next door. With one last smack of the dough, she tumbled it into her floured bread tin and pushed it into the side oven to prove again, shutting the door with her foot. With a quick smack of her hands to rid herself of excess flour, she wiped the remainder down her apron. Dabbing the perspiration from her forehead, she picked up the invitation, screwed it into a ball and threw it onto the fire before putting the kettle on to make a brew.

*

Ellie sat quietly at her table as the clock chimed three. The tea in the pot had cooled and the plates of fluffy scones lay uneaten. No one had come. A great sadness engulfed her. As much as she loved this house and all it would represent in the future, she longed to be back at Poldhu. Everyone there had been happy to see and speak to her. Every day had brought new visitors to her Tea Room. She'd been so happy there. Consciously swallowing the lump forming in her throat, she had a notion it would be a long time before she would feel happy again.

After clearing the tea table, Ellie went to stand at the front door to take the air. The mist hung heavy in the valley leaving the avenue of trees dank and dripping with moisture. The day matched her mood now. She looked up when she heard footsteps to find a young boy walking past the gate.

He stopped abruptly on seeing Ellie. 'Hello,' he said, grinning from ear to ear. All his friends at school had questioned him about his new neighbour, and were curious as to what she looked like.

Thankful at last that someone was willing to speak to her, she wiped her hands down her apron and walked over to the boy. He looked around the age of fourteen or fifteen. 'Hello,' she said, 'and you are?'

Silas's grin turned into the widest smile, revealing a good strong set of teeth, not yet rotting with lack of cleaning. 'Silas Blackthorn,' he said, reaching his hand out to her.

'Well, I'm very pleased to make your acquaintance Silas. I'm Ellie Rosevear. I take it you're Guy's brother - you have the same eyes.'

'Aye, that I am.'

'Is Guy expected home any time soon? I'd love to see him.'

'Ah well, he was going to come home last week, but sent word to Ma that he wasn't coming. Ma was furious because she'd made him a dinner. I think he'll be here this week though. He'll not risk Ma's wrath and be absent another week.' Silas shifted his feet uneasily. 'He'll not be happy when he does come home, and finds you living next door!'

Ellie laughed gently. 'Oh! I'm sure you're mistaken. I've known Guy a long time.'

'I know. He's spoken of you often. That's why he'll not be happy to find you here.' He tipped his head. 'Perhaps that's why he didn't come home!'

Ellie furrowed her brow 'Oh, I sincerely hope I was not the cause.'

Silas raised his eyebrows and it struck Ellie that maybe Guy had held a candle for her affections. She'd often wondered, but he'd never been forthcoming in telling her.

*

Ellie lay restlessly awake that night. Never a good time to mull over problems - the dead of the night always made them feel a lot worse than they were. She was dismayed as to why people were treating her so unpleasantly. It was as though they knew something about her that she did not. She recalled the shocked reactions of the Bochym staff at her reappearance there several weeks ago. Did they also know something that she did not? Her heartbeat accelerated as a very disagreeable thought jumped into her head. Was it something to do with why she and her mother were banished? Did everyone, even as far as Gweek, know what misdemeanour had occurred that led to their banishment from the manor?

*

The next day dawned bright and sunny, but the weather failed to lift Ellie's mood. She was tired and irritable from lack of sleep. The tray of scones taunted her as she poured herself a cup of tea. They'd been coated in jam, awaiting cream, so still relatively soft. Ellie would eat some of them, but the rest would go out to the birds - what a waste. She took her cup of tea to the front door and leant against the frame. *Come on girl. Don't let them get you down. It's their loss if they don't want to make friends. All will be well when Philip returns.* She sighed at the thought of five and a half long weeks before she saw him again.

She looked up as Silas came into view and had an idea.

'Silas?'

He turned and grinned at her.

'Come here a moment, please.'

Silas dropped his grin and looked back towards his cottage for chance his ma had heard.

'I'll only keep you a moment.' Ellie beckoned.

Silas stepped gingerly into the kitchen.

'I've lots of scones going begging, would you take some for you and your school friends.'

'Oh!' He licked his lips at the prospect. 'Ma won't like it.'

'Your ma doesn't have to know,' Ellie said impatiently. 'Now do you want to take them, or shall I crumble them up for the bird table.'

'Yes, I'll take them,' he said excitedly.

'Do you want one now with some clotted cream on?'

Silas nodded eagerly.

He ate the scone with relish, spitting crumbs as he thanked her.

'You're very welcome. I hope your school friends like them too. I hate waste.' She wrapped the rest in a linen cloth. 'Bring the cloth back to me, won't you?'

'Yes Miss.' He set off towards the kitchen door with his armful of scones then turned and said, 'Our Guy was right, you do make good cakes and I don't care what they say about you, I like you. I think you're nice.'

Ellie was taken aback. 'Oh, what are they saying Silas?'

'Sorry, got to go, I'll be late for school,' he said, running down the path, his head darting this way and that to make sure no one saw him leave.

She was just about to close the door when she saw Mr Yates walking his dog.

He looked up and waved and Ellie felt a tiny bit better.

*

Ellie woke with a start, and for a moment could not recall

where she was. Seconds before in her dreams she'd been walking through the corridors of Bochym Manor holding one of the maid's hands.

Ellie sat up, wiped the sleep from her eyes and heard the clock chime six times. The low light outside confused her, was it morning or night? She looked down at her attire, to find herself fully clothed. She must have gone back to bed and slept the day away.

Her mouth felt dry and sour and her stomach rumbled for food. If she was correct in her assumption, she'd slept solidly for over nine hours.

With her face swilled and hair tidied, she put the kettle on the range to boil. Cutting a slice of bread, she toasted it and decadently spread it with a thick layer of butter. With a cup of tea in one hand and toast oozing butter from the other, she stood at the front door to enjoy her supper. The muslin cloth she'd wrapped the scones in for Silas, was draped over the front door handle.

The sky was painted blue and pink as the sun set - she was cross that she'd missed a glorious day. There was music on the air - fiddle music. Ellie strained her ears to catch squeals of laughter mingled within it. Grabbing her coat and hat, she pulled the door closed behind her and set off down the lane. The fluttering scramble of rooks above her sounded eerie. At the end of the lane she turned toward the centre of the village, where the music was louder. As she neared the sound she crossed to the other side of the road and stood opposite the gate signposted Barleyfield Farm, where a harvest dance was in full swing. A band played folk tunes to one side of the house, on the other side trestle tables were set up, near where a fine looking hog was being roasted. The music lifted Ellie's spirits. It was twilight now, but the huge sycamore trees which lined the Gweek road between both bridges, threw shade upon her, so she could watch the dancing and listen to the music without being seen. The night was warm and the nocturnal creatures were rustling in the undergrowth.

The smell of roasting hog made her stomach rumble slightly, but she didn't feel confident enough to join in the merriment. As the band played, Ellie moved and swayed to the music. When they stopped playing for a quick rest and a drink, the night was filled with laughter and the crackling embers of the fire under the hog. Ellie leant back on the gate, to wait for the music to start up again. She turned her face upwards to the stars peeping through the canopy of trees, suddenly becoming conscious of someone close by.

'Well now, who have we got here, skulking in the shadows?'

Ellie turned and shuddered as the firelight lit up the man's face. It was the swearing blacksmith she'd encountered yesterday.

'Ah, tis you is it?' he said scornfully.

Ellie stepped away. She had no intention of engaging in conversation with this obnoxious character.

'No one to dance with, eh?' He grabbed her by the arm as the band started up and yanked her round in a circle.

His breath stank of beer and Ellie winced as he dug his nails into her skin. 'Let me go.' Ellie stamped on his toe and wrenched herself free from his sweaty hold. She staggered backwards, almost tripping on the grass verge.

His lips curled with resentment. 'You weren't so proud when Goldsworthy came a knocking, were you?'

Ellie's heart was in her mouth as he stepped forward to grab her again. A scream came from deep within her throat.

'Hey, what's amiss here?'

Ellie almost cried with relief when she heard Mr Yates's voice.

'Is this man bothering you Miss?' Mr Yates pulled Ellie behind him.

'Yes he is,' Ellie whispered.

Blewett snorted. 'I only wanted to dance with the maid.'

'Well she doesn't want to dance with the likes of you

Blewett, so bugger off.'

Blewett spat at the floor, turned on his heel and staggered down the road swearing angrily.

'Are you alright Miss?' Yates looked her up and down.

'Yes thank you. A little shaky though.'

'Come on, I'll walk you back to your cottage, unless you want to join the harvest party?'

'No thank you, Mr Yates, I think I'd rather like to go home.'

9

Ellie woke early with a great heaviness on her chest and feared she'd be crushed with the weight of it. Unaccustomed to low moods, she felt compelled to lift her spirits somehow. It was time to reconsider her future. Should she stay in this, her own home, or go to Betty's sister and reside there until Philip returned? The situation made her feel so confused, she knew she must get away to think.

Ellie knocked tentatively on Mr Yates's door, tidying her hair into her hat as she waited for it to open

The woman answering the door gave her a derisory look.

Ellie took a deep breath. 'Good day to you. I'm looking for Mr Yates, my name is…...'

'He's at work,' she said, closing the door on Ellie.

Ellie stepped back. *Why is everyone so rude?*

When the mill door opened, the sound of heavy machinery almost deafened her. She had to wait a few minutes. When Mr Yates was found, he stood before her in his work clothes, his mousy hair was dusty and his shirt collar was open at the neck. His smile made her want to cry.

'Begging your pardon, Miss, for keeping you waiting, what can I do for you?'

'I…I'm so sorry, Mr Yates, it's nothing. I can see you're busy.' Ellie stepped back, embarrassed for bothering him.

'Please, Miss Rosevear? Whatever you want, I'm at your disposal.'

'Well, if you really don't mind,' she said biting her lip, 'I'd like to go out in the pony trap.'

Yates's smile widened. 'That is absolutely fine. Give me thirty minutes to clean myself up, and I'll get it up to you as soon as I can.'

'Please don't rush, Mr Yates.'

Twenty minutes later, he pulled up outside Primrose Cottage, jumped down, doffed his hat, and helped her up onto the seat in the back.

'Oh, I'd rather like to sit up front with you - if you don't mind?'

'I don't mind at all, Miss.' Once she was settled and her basket was placed down by her feet, he climbed up beside her, grinned and flicked the reins to set off down the bumpy lane towards the mill.

The woman who had initially answered the door to Ellie, stood, stony-faced, arms folded, watching them pass by. Yates gave her a short nod.

'Is that your wife, Mr Yates?'

'Aye,' he said with an exaggerated sigh. He pulled up at the end of the lane and turned to Ellie.

'I'm sorry that Blewett ruined your evening. He's an unpleasant fellow at the best of times, but with a belly full of beer, we all stay clear of him.'

Ellie smiled. 'I'm just grateful you came along. Thank you once again.'

'Glad to be of service.'

'Why on earth is he so angry all the time?'

Yates shrugged. 'His father was just the same. George and his younger brother Sam were forever sporting black eyes, burst lips and bruises. It seems to be a family trait.'

'Gosh, how awful to live like that!'

Yates nodded. 'So, Miss, where would you like to go on this fine day?'

'It seems a frivolous notion of mine now to be taking you away from your work, but I would rather like to see the sea at Poldhu.'

Yates grinned. 'It's only been five days since I brought you from Poldhu. Are you homesick already?'

'A little, yes. Do you mind?'

'Not at all, Miss. Poldhu it is. I'm rather happy to be taken away from my every day work, if I might be so bold as to tell you.'

'I can imagine. It looked quite dusty. What were you doing?'

'I was bagging the flour. It's a horrible job. It catches the back of your throat and makes you as parched as a desert. I must admit, a trip to the sea will clear my lungs.' He gave a hacking cough into his handkerchief which he tried to disguise.

Ellie felt her spirits lift as they made their way out of Gweek. The sun was warm and she shed her shawl, folding it neatly onto her lap. She glanced at Mr Yates, he had a kind, clean-shaven face and though weathered was still handsome. His hair was snow-white and cut short to his collar.

He turned, knowing she was looking at him. 'What do you want to do at Poldhu when we get there? I don't suppose the Tea Room has opened again yet.'

'No, I don't suppose it has,' she answered sadly. 'I would very much like to dip my toes in the water. It's September now, so the sea will have warmed enough not to take my breath away.'

He gave a short laugh. 'Can't say I have ever tried it, whatever the month.'

'Oh! Why ever not?'

'Well, I don't often get the chance to go to the sea. This job is quite a novelty for me, and Gweek, well, though I love the village dearly, it's not the place to dip your toes into the water.' He screwed his nose and grinned. 'It's a bit muddy.'

They turned down the Lizard road, taking the first lane to the right to Cury.

'And how are you settling into Primrose Cottage, Miss?'

'Can you call me Ellie?'

Yates shifted uncomfortably. 'I don't think Mr Goldsworthy would approve.'

'Well, Mr Goldsworthy isn't here, and you're the first person who has been friendly to me. I thought I was in fear of losing my voice, if I didn't speak to someone soon.'

He gave her a pained look. He knew it was going to be difficult for her to integrate into this village, with their old fashioned ways and prejudices. He was happy that she felt she could talk to him. What harm could it do? 'Very well, as you wish, Ellie.'

'Thank you. As we are on first name terms now, what is your Christian name?'

'It's Harold, Harry to my friends.'

'And may I call you Harry?'

He gave her a broad smile. 'As my friend, you may. As long as Mr Goldsworthy doesn't hear you,' he added.

'I shall make sure he doesn't.'

The journey took well over an hour, but as they rounded the headland and Poldhu Cove came into view, it almost took Ellie's breath away.

'Isn't that the most wonderful sight, Harry?'

'Aye, it is. It's only the third time I've seen it. I'd never been here until I picked you up the other week and again last Sunday.'

'Goodness that seems like an age ago.'

'You really miss the old place then?'

'I do,' she sighed. 'I've been there since my father died eight years ago and we had to leave Bochym Manor.'

'Well, you have a new life now to look forward to.'

'You're right, I do. I can hardly wait for Philip to return, so we can begin our new life together.'

He smiled congenially. Although clearly lonely, the idea of Goldsworthy being away didn't seem to faze her too much.

'I do find it rather strange not having all my customers to speak to. I'd hoped to make some new friends, but it seems everyone is too busy with their own lives at the moment.'

Harry raised his eyebrows. If by what his wife had been saying about the gossip in the village, he very much feared that Ellie would have her work cut out making friends. He pulled the wagon up on the dunes, jumped down, but before he could offer his hand to Ellie, she had already alighted.

'I'll wait here for you,' he said, giving the pony a bag of feed.

'Oh no Harry, you must come down for a paddle!'

He tipped his head to one side. 'But I couldn't possibly do that. What would folks think?'

Ellie looked around. 'There is nobody here to think anything. Come on, Harry, you'll enjoy it.'

Harry rubbed the back of his neck. 'You must not let Mr Goldsworthy know. I'll lose this job for sure, and at the mill.'

'No one will know.' Ellie laughed. 'Come on.'

Harry watched with anticipation as Ellie kicked off her shoes. She was not wearing stockings and was quite outrageously wiggling her bare toes in the sand.

'Take off your boots, Harry, the sand feels wonderful.'

'Oh but….'

'The sand and salt water will ruin your leather boots and Mrs Yates will wonder what you've been doing. Take them off. You'll enjoy the sensation, I promise.'

Uncertain, Harry puffed his cheeks out, before exposing his feet to the elements. Stuffing his socks into his boots, he left them on the wagon. At the waterline Harry averted his eyes when Ellie tucked her skirts into her belt, exposing her legs as she stepped into the surf.

'Come on Harry, it's warm.'

Harry grimaced, convinced he'd be seen, reluctantly rolled his trousers as far up his bandy, hairy legs as they would go, and tentatively stepped into the foamy edge of the water. It was indeed surprisingly warm. Mesmerised, he watched his feet sink softly into the sand as the crystal clear water swirled around his ankles. He laughed out loud at this new and spectacular sensation. He was fifty years old and there wasn't much that excited him nowadays, but this simple pleasure brought him more joy than he'd had since he was a small boy, exploring the world for the first time.

Ellie watched in delight as he kicked the water and waded a little deeper, all the while pulling his woollen trousers further up his legs. She sighed happily as she looked out towards Land's End, remembering sunsets and days seeking shells and sea glass. It felt so good to be in the fresh sea air - to feel the elements washing over her, renewing and refreshing her mind. There was no doubt, her heart belonged here in this place.

With the beach to themselves, Ellie laid a blanket on the dunes, after they had dried their feet, and set out a picnic for them to eat.

'Nay, nay, I'll not share your luncheon, I've brought an apple and some cheese,' Harry said when Ellie gestured for him to join her on the rug.

'I've brought enough sandwiches for us both, Harry. They'll go to waste if you don't share them with me.'

Harry pondered nervously. If anyone was to see him and report to Goldsworthy, there would be hell to pay.

Seeing his dilemma, Ellie tipped her head. 'Harry, have you not been employed to do as I ask?'

Harry straightened his shoulders. 'Yes, Miss.'

'Good, then please sit down and have a sandwich.'

They passed a happy hour chatting on the dunes as Ellie told him all about her time at the Tea Room. Eventually she mustered up the confidence to ask Harry the question which had prayed on her mind for a couple of days now.

'Harry?'

He turned and smiled.

'Had you ever heard of me or my family before I came to Gweek?'

Harry furrowed his brow. 'I don't believe so, no.'

'So, you didn't hear anything about when I lived at Bochym or why we left after my father died?'

Harry shook his head. 'Why did you leave?'

'I don't know.' Ellie laughed. 'I was hoping you might know.'

'No, the first I heard of you, was when I picked you up with Mr Goldsworthy. Why do you ask?'

'No matter.' *It was clear her neighbour's reluctance to befriend her must be purely down to wariness of outsiders.*

*

Once they'd packed the picnic away, Harry made his way to the pony trap, while Ellie took a detour to her sea garden. Knowing the sand would drift to cover her flowers in a very short time, she expected to find the garden in a sorry mess. She stopped short when she saw that someone had tidied it. She glanced towards the Tea Room to see if someone *had* taken it over, but all was how she and Betty had left it. She was just about to leave, when she spotted a piece of sea glass strategically placed on the garden boundary, just where Philip used to leave them for her. Reaching to pick it up, she puzzled as to how Philip had done that? It certainly hadn't been there when she left last Sunday, and was sure that Philip had already set off on his business trip by then. Why would he do that if he knew she might not see them? Maybe he'd asked someone else to put it there and they'd done the job a day late? She popped it in her pocket to add to her collection, which now stood in a vase in her new cottage.

'All aboard Miss Ellie,' Harry said with familiarity. When he helped her up she noticed his nose was pink with the sun and his hair blown about with the sea breeze. She thought he looked so much healthier than when he'd picked her up earlier that day.

*

After a day at the sea, Ellie slept soundly that night. She woke refreshed, resolving to stick it out in Gweek. Poldhu had made her feel happy again, so she was determined to start anew in her quest to meet people, except of course the dreadful Mr Blewett.

With her basket in the crook of her arm, Ellie set out

into the bright morning sunshine. Carefully negotiating the rocky lane until she came to the stone bridge, she stopped awhile to breathe in the smell of the woodland. The stream, which meandered down from the dam, was alive with midges. Further downstream, as it met the river, grey mullet swirled in abundance in the muddy waters, but here, tiddlers swam in the shallows.

The Bridge Shop was adjacent to the Corn Mill and although she knew she could buy her groceries more cheaply in Helston, Ellie was eager to support her local supplier. With her shopping list in hand and wearing her best smile she opened the door. The shop bell tinkled to mark her arrival. The sound was welcoming unlike the looks the four women already in the shop gave her. Ellie noted that the animated voices she'd heard on entering ceased the moment she walked in. Unfazed, she said cheerily, 'Good morning, ladies.'

'This is her!' The white haired woman standing behind the counter pointed out.

Everyone ran their eyes derisively over Ellie. One sniffed dismissively, another folded her arms and shook her head, only one gave a ghost of a smile before they all turned their backs on her.

Ellie felt a familiar chill curl in her stomach. *What was wrong with everybody? Philip had told her how lovely everyone was.*

The door bell tinkled again and a rather striking blonde-haired woman entered, swiftly followed by a small, equally striking child. Ellie recognised them immediately as the mother and daughter she'd seen drawing in the field the other day.

'Good morning, ladies,' the blonde woman said, gesturing the child to sit on a chair.

'Morning Elizabeth,' the women said in unison.

Elizabeth Trevone glanced at Ellie and smiled amiably. 'Hello, I don't believe we've met.' She held out her hand to her. 'I'm Elizabeth Trevone.'

Relieved at last to experience some form of friendship,

Ellie felt the chill thaw, cleared her throat and shook her hand. 'Elise Rosevear, but everyone calls me Ellie. I've just moved into Gweek.'

'Well I'm very pleased to meet you, Ellie,' Elizabeth said, not unaware of the hostility from the others in the shop. Elizabeth actually knew who Ellie was. Nothing went unnoticed in this small village. She also knew there was a growing opposition to this young woman, and why. Unperturbed she carried on. 'This is my daughter, Jenna. Jenna sweetheart, say hello to Miss Rosevear.'

'Hello,' Jenna answered shyly.

Ellie smiled at the little girl, so obviously her mother's daughter, with her long blonde hair and eyes of emerald green. 'Hello Jenna.' Ellie turned back to Elizabeth. 'What a beautiful daughter you have there.'

Elizabeth gave a tinkle of laughter. 'Yes, I think she'll break a few hearts when she grows up.'

The three other customers, who were obviously only in the shop for a gossip, edged their way past Ellie and Elizabeth to leave, though not without a last contemptuous glance at Ellie.

'Good day to you, Mabel,' Elizabeth nodded and smiled.

Mabel Spargo nodded back to both Elizabeth and Ellie and looked sheepishly to see if Violet had seen her do it.

'Good day to you too, Violet, Joyce,' Elizabeth said brightly.

They both muttered goodbye and left swiftly.

Minnie Drago behind the counter ignored Ellie but pasted on a false smile for Elizabeth, revealing her set of rotting teeth. She disliked Elizabeth, for no other reason than she was beautiful. 'And what can I do for you today?'

'You can serve Ellie, as she was first.'

Minnie bristled. '*She* can wait,' she said tartly.

'No, Minnie, Ellie was first!'

'I'm sure we have nothing that *she* has on her list. Maybe it's best she goes up to Helston in her *pony trap*.'

Elizabeth regarded her for a moment. 'Is Mr Moyles in, Minnie?'

Minnie lifted her chin defiantly. 'He's in the back…busy.'

Elizabeth could hear the shop owner, moving boxes around. 'Mr Moyles,' Elizabeth called out, 'Mr Moyles, have you a moment?'

'What is it?' Moyles, a man of sizable girth, emerged, dusting his overall down. 'Oh,' he said happily, on seeing Elizabeth. 'Good day to you, Mrs Trevone. What can I do for you?' He swept his hand over the few hairs on his head.

Elizabeth cleared her throat. 'Good day, Mr Moyles. Apparently Minnie is reluctant to serve my friend.'

'What!' He shot Minnie a withering look. 'Why?

Minnie blanched and took on a defiant stance. 'I was only saving the reputation of your shop!'

Moyles curled his lip. 'What the devil are you talking about woman?'

'This is Miss Rosevear, from Primrose Cottage,' Minnie emphasised the latter.

Ellie's eyes widened, realising everyone in the village knew her name.

'Mr Moyles,' Elizabeth chipped in. 'If Minnie refuses to serve my friend, I will take my custom elsewhere, and I suspect the Goldsworthys would not be too happy with that.'

'No need for that, Mrs Trevone, I assure you' Moyles blustered. The Goldsworthys owned his shop, and he could not risk displeasing them - even though he did not approve of Ellie.

'Minnie, serve Miss Rosevear at once.'

Minnie folded her arms 'I will not!'

Moyles stood a moment then moved to the back room, retrieved Minnie's coat and handed it to her. 'Then you are no longer my employee.'

'What? You'd choose me, over *her*,' she practically spat

the last word. 'I'm the best shop assistant you've ever had! You'll get no better,' she answered proudly.

'You're only here for the gossip,' Moyles parried. 'Goodbye.'

Minnie snatched her coat, lifted the counter and glared at Ellie, uttering something derogatory under her breath, making Ellie shiver at her hostility.

'Ignore her,' Moyles said apologetically. 'I've wanted an excuse to dismiss her for a while. Now, Miss Rosevear, what can I get you?'

'I think I need a sit down and a cup of tea, after that!' she whispered to Elizabeth.

Elizabeth raised her eyebrows. 'Minnie has that effect on people. I don't like to speak ill of anyone, but she's not well liked. So, let's get your shopping and we'll go and have that nice cup of tea you are so in need of.'

10

Elizabeth Trevone's cottage was situated at the bottom of Chapel Hill, overlooking the centre of the village of Gweek. It had a wonderfully cosy feel as Ellie stepped into the kitchen. Feeling slightly dazed from the altercation in the shop, Ellie felt relieved to sit down at Elizabeth's table and relax. She watched Elizabeth brew the tea, as little Jenna brought plates and cutlery to the table. The day was warm and the back door was open, allowing Ellie to observe the comings and goings of this busy community.

'Will you take a slice of cake with your tea, Ellie?' Elizabeth asked while she poured. 'It's freshly made and I've sandwiched it together with some home made strawberry jam!'

'It sounds delightful, thank you.'

'Have you been into the village centre before? I've never seen you.'

'Briefly, a couple of days ago, but there didn't seem to be anyone around for me to speak to. In fact you're the first person who seems to have a kind word for me. Is it always this difficult for new people to integrate? I was told everyone in Gweek was friendly.'

'We are a friendly lot really. I'm sorry you've found things difficult. I'm sure everything will be fine from now on.' Elizabeth felt confident that she was well enough respected in Gweek for others to follow her lead and welcome Ellie into their lives. Except of course for Minnie, but she was of no consequence.

'I'll introduce you to a few people after tea, and show you where you can buy fish when the local fishermen come in. Oh, here's my husband, Jory,' she said, as a man dressed in fisherman's overalls popped his head around the door.

Elizabeth greeted her husband with a kiss on the cheek. 'Jory, this is Ellie Rosevear. We're just about to have tea. Will you join us?'

'No my lover, just popped in to say cheerio. We're about to set off with the tide.' Jory looked over towards Ellie and nodded. 'Pleased to meet you, Miss, but I'll have to go. Jenna, come and give your pa a hug.'

Ellie smiled at this happy family unit.

With another kiss and hug, Elizabeth bade farewell to Jory and then sat down with Ellie.

'I do so worry about him going out fishing, but it's in his blood and his father's before him. At least the weather is fine.' As she lifted the tea pot to pour the tea, a neighbour popped her head around the kitchen door.

'Do I hear the sound of tea on china?'

Elizabeth grinned. 'I own nothing as grand as china, Amelia, but yes, do sit down and meet my new friend, Ellie Rosevear. Ellie, this is my good friend, Amelia Pascoe.'

'I'm happy to make your acquaintance, my dear.' Amelia shook her hand. 'I've been meaning to visit, but what with one thing and another, I haven't quite found the time.'

Enjoying the first proper conversation with anyone for days, Ellie began to relax believing she could settle happily with these lovely ladies as friends.

'Among other things, Ellie, Amelia is our local midwife. She helps Dr Eddy deliver the babies in the village. She delivered me and my Jenna,' Elizabeth said proudly.

Ellie took a sip of tea and placed it carefully on the saucer. 'How lovely, maybe you'll deliver mine, when the time comes,' she said excitedly.

'I'll be happy to assist, Ellie.'

Feeling confident to speak boldly, Ellie added, 'I can't wait to be married and start a family. I've made my own wedding dress. It's so beautiful. I make my own lace you see, and I've been working on it for many years.'

Ellie noted that Elizabeth shot a furtive glance in Amelia's direction.

'I understand that because I reside in Gweek, I'll be

married at Constantine Church, so I took a walk up there a few days ago, just to look around. It's a lovely old church, I shall be happy to be married there, though we haven't set a date yet.'

Though Ellie bubbled with excitement, she couldn't help but notice Amelia and Elizabeth exchange another glance.

'Have I said something strange?'

Amelia took a deep breath. 'Forgive me, my dear,' she said cautiously. 'but who are you planning to marry? Do we know the gentleman?'

'Why, Philip Goldsworthy of course!' she laughed. 'Sorry, I thought you both knew?'

Elizabeth choked spluttering her tea everywhere.

A strange feeling engulfed Ellie. 'What, what's amiss?' Her eyes darted frantically between the women.

'Oh Ellie,' Elizabeth said, brushing the droplets of tea from her dress. 'Philip Goldsworthy married Lady Carole Dunstan last Saturday. They're on their honeymoon in Europe!'

'What?' A short nervous laugh escaped, before Ellie's lips trembled uncontrollably.

'Amelia, put some sugar in Ellie's tea quick,' Elizabeth said curling her fingers around Ellie's hand. 'I'm so sorry, Ellie. Did you really not know?'

Dazed and confused, Ellie shook her head. 'You're....You're mistaken, surely.' Her hand touched the base of her neck as she mouthed the words, 'Lady Carole Dunstan?' Her eyes darted, as she dredged the remnants of the last conversation she'd had with Philip. *"I want to spend as much time as possible with you and here is the perfect place"*. Her hand flew to her mouth. 'I thought he was on a business trip!' *"It won't all be pleasure."* His words mocked her. She hung her head, focusing on a loose thread on her skirt. 'I truly believed that he was going to marry *me* on his return,' she mumbled.

Elizabeth shifted her chair nearer Ellie. Gently

squeezing her hand, she said, 'It was very wrong of Philip to lead you on like this.'

Ellie could hardly speak for the ache in her throat. A river of tears ran down her cheeks. 'I've been such a fool. He clearly expected me to be his mistress, didn't he?'

'It seems so, my dear.' Amelia sighed as she pushed the sweetened tea towards her.

'And everyone knew, except me!' she said bitterly. 'That's why they've been so unpleasant with me, isn't it? Oh god...' She threw back her head in despair, '....the shame of it. Everyone thinks I'm his floozy! My good name will be tarnished forever.' Her shoulders began to quake.

Elizabeth pushed a handkerchief into Ellie's hand. 'No it won't, Ellie, as long as you haven't...,' she cleared her throat, '....have you?'

Ellie's eyes widened at the inference. 'Lay with him! No!' Her voice cracked. 'I'd never do such a thing before marriage!'

'Well, then your reputation will be untarnished.'

Ellie shuddered visibly. 'The very thought of his plan makes me feel unclean.' Leaving her tea untouched she stood up. 'I must go. I must think what to do. I must leave before Phil...' her face crumpled. '....before *he* returns.'

Elizabeth was quick to her side. 'Ellie sit down for a moment. He'll be gone another five weeks by my reckoning. Don't rush into anything, give yourself time to think. If we can help in any way, just let us know.'

'But I can't stay in that cottage another day, I just can't. The very thought of it makes me feel grubby.'

'Ellie, it's only a cottage - a roof over your head,' Amelia said. 'It's somewhere to stay until you can find alternative accommodation. We'll make sure everyone knows that you've not been party to Philip's plan. But if you really feel you can't stay, I have a spare room here if you feel you need it, just say the word. Now sit down and drink your tea, and I suggest you eat something too,' she said, pushing a slice of cake in her direction.

*

Guy was en-route to Gweek. He'd had a dreadful week. His mind would not settle and his heart was sore. As Philip Goldsworthy's oldest friend, he'd stood beside him as his best man, seven days ago. He'd watched him marry a woman he clearly did not love - for business reasons, he'd told him. Money attracts money - it always did and always will. Money though would not bring happiness. To the gentle clip clop of his horse's hooves, Guy's mind went over the run up to the wedding he'd attended last Saturday, and the aftermath which had broken his heart.

*

Initially, when Guy received that fateful letter - not an invitation - a request from Philip, asking him to be his best man, he truly believed that Philip was marrying Ellie. The only other information he'd received, was to collect a morning suit from Williams' outfitters in Helston, before meeting Philip at Cury Church at twelve-thirty on the 22nd September. This he'd done with a heavy heart. He stood beside Philip observing the guests arriving, noting the wedding was going to be a rather grand affair, a little too grand perhaps for Ellie's tastes - not that she didn't deserve such a day.

As the organist played Mendelssohn's 'Wedding March', Guy's heart had ached, but when he turned expecting to see Ellie approaching, he was astonished to see Lady Carole Dunstan walking up the aisle on the arm of her brother, the Earl de Bochym.

His relief was palpable. With Philip married to Lady Carole, this would surely pathe the way for him to pursue Ellie's heart. So his heart sang throughout the ceremony, willing it to be over so as to go and see Ellie as soon as he could. He just hoped that she was still at the Tea Room.

The wedding breakfast was held in the splendour of the beautiful grounds of Bochym Manor. Guy stepped into the side-lines to watch the rich people at play, feeling a little out of his depth amongst these aristocratic guests. He knew the earl and countess of course, but only in a professional manner, and wished that James Blackwell and his London entourage had been there – he felt more relaxed with them. He was keen to leave, but knew he must stay a while to be polite. It was then he spotted Jack Goldsworthy, Philip's father, making his way over, with a sandwich in one hand and a meat pie in the other.

'Guy my boy. Good to see you standing as Philip's best man.' He'd guffawed, as he reached his hand out that held the pie then laughed again when he realised he couldn't shake Guy's hand. 'It's good to see a plan come to fruition, eh?'

Guy raised a questioning eyebrow.

'This day was arranged years ago, don't you know.' Jack tapped his nose. 'Always a good business man was the old earl!'

He stood next to Guy and watched the bride and groom make their social exchanges with the guests.

'I'm not sure how good a business man Philip will be, mind. He has a tendency to spend money like water, instead of ploughing it back into the Mill. I reckon Carole will curb his spending now. If she's anything like her father, she'll be careful with her money.' He took a mouthful of pie and reminisced. 'Ah, the old earl, he was a scoundrel, you know?' He grinned. 'He liked his drink and of course his women, or should I say girls,' he dropped his voice to a whisper. 'I reckon there are a few little bastards running about the surrounding countryside, all of them sired by him.' He gave a great belly laugh. 'God, but he had an insatiable appetite for the flesh. Good friend though, salt of the earth - miss him terribly. Fair do's to him though, he kept his promise that his daughter Carole would marry Philip. He knew a good business deal when he saw one.'

Astonished at the revelation, Guy asked cautiously, 'Has the marriage always been on the cards?'

'Oh yes.' Jack belched loudly and thumped his chest, crumbling the pie down his waistcoat. 'I can't do with all this rich food, can you?'

Guy grimaced. 'So did Philip know about this match?'

'He did and relished the prospect. I told him when he was fourteen who he was going to marry – he didn't bat an eyelid, well who wouldn't be overjoyed to be part of the de Bochym family?'

'But, but I've known Philip for years, and he never spoke about it, the first I heard was today!'

'It was quite inconsequential to him, I can assure you.' He leant nearer and grinned, showing the food stuck between the few teeth he had left. 'He didn't want it to get out, for chance it frightened away some floozy he was interested in on the coast.'

Guy shuddered with indignation. Jack was clearly referring to Ellie.

Jack nodded confidently. 'Always could keep a secret, my lad.' He stuffed the remainder of the pie into his mouth. 'Right,' he said, 'I'm off to sample some of the old earl's wine cellar. Now don't you be telling Lady Sarah what I said about her late father-in-law?' He winked. 'He liked to keep his whoring quiet…the old rogue.' He laughed heartily and walked away.

Before Guy could gather his thoughts, Philip approached him, thrusting a glass of expensive champagne into his hand.

Taking the glass with a curt nod, Guy took a sip, grimacing at the unfamiliar taste - he'd tip it on the flower bed as soon as Philip turned away. With anger raging, Guy had no real wish to engage in conversation with Philip – it was clear that Philip had been tagging Ellie along! *If Philip thinks he can have his cake and eat it, he is going to be very disappointed. The first thing he would do was to tell Ellie what a false friend Philip had been to her.*

'God, but I'm looking forward to setting off on our honeymoon tomorrow,' Philip said rubbing his hands excitedly. 'What are you doing? Going back to Lamorna?'

'No, I've finished there.' Guy answered curtly. 'I may stay close by tonight, so that I can call on Ellie tomorrow at Poldhu. I'm hoping she is still there. I think I know how to help her.'

Philip laughed heartily. 'Ellie doesn't need *your* help. You'll be better off going home to Gweek. You'll have more chance of seeing her there!'

'What do you mean?'

Philip grinned broadly. 'She's to be your neighbour. I'm having her moved into Primrose Cottage.'

'So.... you've given her employment at the Mill?'

Philip snorted. 'Good god, no, I've set her up in the cottage.' He winked. 'She'll be housed, fed and clothed in the finest I can afford and I'll visit her as often as possible.' He gave Guy a nudge with his elbow. 'If you know what I mean.'

Shocked beyond belief, Guy felt bile rise in his throat. He could hardly form the next sentence. 'Ellie...Ellie's to be your mistress?'

'Correct.' Philip wore a self-satisfied smile. 'Haven't I got the best of both worlds?'

Outraged, Guy hissed. 'You've barely been married two hours. What do you think your new wife would say about that?'

Philip regarded Guy with curiosity. 'She's quite happy about it actually. She even vetted Ellie herself.'

Guy gawped in astonishment. 'She did what?'

'Oh yes, when Ellie brought the lace up here for Carole's dress. She vetted her and deemed her clean and fit to be my mistress.'

It took all of Guy's resolve not to thump Philip.

'Don't look so shocked. I saw you talking to father, he'll have no doubt told you this marriage is just for money. Carole knows it too, that's why she's happy about the arrangement.' Philip took a sip of champagne and turned to look over the vast Bochym estate with a sense of achievement. *He was going to rather like flitting between both of his abodes. After all, they both had something wonderful to offer.*

Seeing Guy's displeasure Philip said, 'It's a good prospect for a girl like Ellie.'

Guy swallowed his disdain. 'If you say so,' he answered tartly.

'I mean, what's the alternative for a girl *like her?*' He pulled a face. 'To waitress for the rest of her life? You didn't expect me to leave her to that fate, did you? This way she'll want for nothing.'

'Ellie is far more than an ordinary waitress. She has a good business brain in her head.'

Philip grinned as he waved at a passing guest. 'And she has obviously used that brain to see what's good for her!'

Guy shook his head incredulously.

'I thought you'd be happy that Ellie is settled, Guy?' he mocked.

'I'm sorry Philip, but this strange marital agreement you have, does not sit easy with me, and in truth, I'm surprised it sits easy with Ellie as well.'

'Oh she's perfectly happy. I can assure you. She was overjoyed when I showed her the cottage.'

Guy shook his head. 'I simply can't believe that is what she wants.'

'Well that proves how little you know Ellie. I'm happy, Carole is happy, and I can assure you that Ellie is very happy.' Bored now with Guy's negative response, Philip drained his glass. 'Well, I can't stand here chatting all day, I need to go and speak to my other guests. Do call on Ellie when you're home and see for yourself.'

Guy saw the smirk on Philip's face as he walked away. He may have been friends with Philip a long time, but that friendship was well and truly over now. He'd heard enough, and needed to leave. His heart felt as though it would implode. As he turned to walk away, Lady Sarah approached, halting his retreat.

'It's lovely to see you Guy, I'm so glad you could

come. You and Philip have been great friends for many years, haven't you? Philip was adamant that you were to be his best man.'

'It was an honour, Lady Sarah,' he said, the words leaving a sour taste in his mouth.

'Have you had enough to eat and drink?'

Guy smiled despite his heartache. 'I have, thank you for your hospitality. I think I might be heading off though.'

'Are you going home to Gweek this afternoon?'

Guy pondered for a moment and then shook his head. 'I don't think so.' The thought of seeing Ellie ensconced in the cottage next door, would break his heart. He knew that eventually he'd have to see her, but for the moment, he wasn't sure his fragile heart could take it.

'I fear we shall see little of you now the Tea Room has closed. I do hope someone takes it over soon. It's a shame it had to close.'

'It is, as you say, a great shame,' he answered sadly.

'Tell me Guy, do you know if Elise has found alternative employment?'

Guy swallowed hard. Lady Sarah was obviously not party to her new brother and sister-in-law's plans. 'I believe something has been put in place, yes, but not the details,' he lied.

'Oh that is a relief,' Sarah said holding her hand to her chest. 'If she hadn't found employment, I would have offered her something on the estate.'

Guy nodded, wishing with all his heart she'd done that.

*

Guy hadn't gone home to Gweek that day, in fact he hadn't been home since, but he knew he must this weekend, and the prospect made him ill. He'd spent the last few days down at Church Cove, wasting time, picking up pieces of sea glass, out of habit, that he knew now he could not give to Ellie. Twice he'd walked over to Poldhu to tidy Ellie's little sea garden and placed the sea glass on the rocks which circled it. He noted that the glass had gone on his second visit – probably taken by some child. As he replaced the glass, it felt as though Ellie had died, for his heart grieved terribly for her loss. There at Poldhu, she was still the beautiful innocent girl he coveted. He knew when he saw her again, that image would be tainted.

Now as he entered the village of Gweek and turned up the lane, he braced himself at the thought of seeing Ellie again.

11

With a heavy heart, Ellie walked back to her cottage. All her hopes and dreams for a future with Philip were now in tatters. Turning into the beautiful leafy lane, the stream babbled softly and the shade of the great oak trees shielded her sore eyes from the sun. Everything looked the same, but everything was so different from when she walked down this lane earlier that morning. Tears clouded her vision as two unfamiliar emotions bubbled inside her - anger and hatred. *How could I have been so stupid as to let him do this to me?* She hated Philip for what he'd done and how he believed that she would have agreed to such a thing. She kicked out at a stone on the path. Woe betide the next person she encountered on this lane to denounce her as a loose woman!

Shuddering with indignation she quickened her stride. She did not want to go back to the cottage, but she knew she must. Amelia had offered her a spare room, and of course Betty's sister was another option, she just needed time to think how she was going to get herself out of this sorry mess. As she neared Primrose Cottage she noticed that the lane was strewn with stray lengths of thatch. Guy Blackthorn was home! Her anger escalated. *Damn Guy, he must have known of Philip's plan.*

*

Guy was unloading his wagon when he saw the familiar figure of Ellie walk into view. Heart sore, he had no real wish to engage with her but, on watching her he noted her posture resembled that of an old woman carrying the weight of the world on her shoulders.

*

At the gate of Primrose Cottage, Ellie stopped. To her utter dismay, she saw Guy staring at her a few yards up the lane.

'Don't you dare look down on me, Guy Blackthorn. You're an utter scoundrel as is your friend, Philip!' The vehemence of her words took her completely by surprise. She turned and slammed her hands on top of the gate, pushing it open violently. Blinded by tears, she stumbled towards her front door, tripped over the hem of her skirt, and cursed as she fell flat on her face.

Winded, she felt the air expel from her lungs. Her distress intensified when she heard Guy's footsteps running towards her. 'Get off me.' She smacked his helping hands away from her.

Ignoring her protest, Guy slipped his arms around her and lifted her to her feet. A searing pain from her knee made her legs buckle and her head spin alarmingly. Although Guy's hands steadied her, she pulled away from him. 'Leave me alone.' She limped to the front door, fumbled with her key, dropped it, and then collapsed in despair into the pool of her skirt. Laying the flat of her palm on her door, she leant her hot forehead against it, sobbing brokenheartedly.

'Ellie, please let me help you up,' Guy knelt beside her, his distress matching hers, tentatively touching her arm.

'I said, leave me *alone*.'

'Ellie, please tell me what's happened?'

Ellie lifted her head. 'Oh, I think you know very well what has happened, Guy.' Her contempt for him must have clearly shone through her eyes, because she saw him flinch.

'Honestly Ellie, I really can't think what I've done to cause your distress. You must tell me.'

Ellie took a deep measured breath. 'I learnt something very shocking today. Can you imagine what it is?' She laughed caustically. 'Oh yes, I'm sure you can! For it seems I'm the last to know!'

Guy regarded her cautiously.

She gave a short pained laugh. 'I've just learnt that Philip got married on Saturday!'

Guy's world stilled.

'You may well keep your counsel, Guy Blackthorn.' She thumped him hard on his chest. 'He's your friend, of course you knew what he was planning.' Her breath came in great gulps. '*Why* didn't you tell me, Guy? I thought you were my friend too.'

Guy reeled back aghast. 'I truly didn't know until last week, Ellie.' He moistened his lips. 'You see I was summoned to attend his wedding as his best man two weeks before the date. It wasn't a formal invitation, it was a letter, and in all honesty, after the play he made for you, I truly believed he was marrying you! It wasn't until I got to the church that I realised his bride was Lady Carole. I swear to you, Ellie, he may have been my friend, but he kept his wedding plans a total secret from me. It grieved me deeply that he'd made false promises to you, and I told him so in no uncertain terms. It was then he told me the shocking news that he had extra marital plans for you.'

Ellie gasped audibly.

'He said he had set you up in this cottage and you were very happy with the situation.'

Ellie felt herself shake with indignity. 'Do you really think I am that sort of girl? If you do, you're as debauched as your friend.'

'Of course I don't.' He held her by the arms to still her trembling body. 'I questioned him about it. I couldn't believe you'd agreed to it, and I admit I was shocked when he said you were happy and excited at the prospect of moving in.'

Ellie shook her head in disbelief as she dragged herself up from where she sat. 'I *was* happy and excited at the prospect!' She stamped her foot in annoyance. 'But I thought he was going to *marry me* when he came back from his "business trip" . I had no idea that he had other plans.'

'Oh Ellie, I'm so sorry for you, truly I am.'

As his strong hands held her, Ellie felt her anger give way to sadness. She lifted her eyes to his. 'Oh Guy, everyone has been so awful to me this week. Only

Elizabeth Trevone and Amelia Pascoe befriended me. They invited me for tea and…,' the words caught in her throat, '…that's when I found out. Oh god Guy, I'll never live this shame down, and none of it was my fault.' She crumpled, sobbing into his arms.

*

Nellie Blackthorn put down the spoon she was stirring the dinner with and called out to Guy to come inside. When he didn't respond she wiped her hands down her apron and walked out into the lane. Hearing voices at Primrose Cottage she walked a little further, and was shocked to find her son embracing that floozy! A red mist descended. Storming to Ellie's front gate she punched her fists into her sides. 'Guy Blackthorn, you come away from that woman at once.'

They both spun around.

'Ma!' Guy gave her a warning look.

'I mean it Guy, if you don't come inside, *alone*, this very minute, you can find somewhere else to lay your head tonight. If you are going to associate with her type, you are no longer my son.'

'See what I mean.' Ellie buried her head into his shoulder.

'*Ma*! Go away, *now*,' he snapped.

Nellie felt herself bristle with indignation. Guy had never raised his voice to her before, but she was determined to get the last word in. 'You heed my warning. Come away from her,' she said, flouncing back up the lane.

'Don't cry, Ellie.' Guy cupped Ellie's face. 'I'll put Ma right on a few things and if Amelia and Elizabeth know of this misunderstanding, then most of the village will know soon enough too, and you'll not be judged anymore. Believe me, they're not a bad lot, they just like things done properly, if you know what I mean.'

'As do I!' She sobbed into his chest. His coat smelt of sweet thatch as she let his strong arms wrap around her, protecting her from this horrible situation.

The day had begun to cool, and dark clouds threatened rain. 'Come on Ellie, let's get you inside.' He took the key from her hand and opened the door. It was the first time he'd been in the cottage, marvelling at what money could buy. It was no wonder Ellie's head had been turned by him.

He sat her down at the kitchen table. 'Can I get you anything?'

'You can find some way for me to turn back time perhaps.' She quipped, as his dark eyes twinkled as he smiled back at her.

He smiled and looked around the room. 'You can't stay here.'

'I've no intention of doing so. Amelia has offered me a room, for a while.'

He knelt at her feet and took her hands in his, they were large and calloused but his touch was as gentle as a lamb's. 'Amelia's a good woman, and it's a good offer, but we perhaps need to get you away from Gweek. Leave it with me, I'll think of something, I promise.'

Ellie nodded and looked at Guy with fresh eyes. His hair, the colour of oak, was tousled and dusty with thatch, and his face and personality shone with kindness, it made her want to cry again. 'I'm such a fool,' she said with an exhausted sigh.

'No, you're not, Ellie. It's Goldsworthy who is the fool. Now, I must go and speak to Ma. I'll come and see you in the morning, be it here or Amelia's I'll find you, and then we'll make a plan.'

*

Guy laid abed thinking long and hard well into the night about Ellie's predicament. One thing for sure, she must leave Gweek, so his original idea of offering a room in his ma's house was not now an option.

He shook his head as he thought of his ma. He'd argued with her until he was blue in the face, that Ellie was an innocent victim of Philip's plan. Nothing he'd said though had swayed his ma's disapproval of Ellie. She could be a very stubborn woman at times!

As the clock struck four, he'd finally hit on an idea. If anyone could help her, James Blackwell could. Guy knew him well, and if there was a good deed to be done, James would be the man to do it. Fortunately James was home from his travels. He'd seen him on the coach bound for Gunwalloe yesterday just as Guy was driving the wagon out of the village. Guy was confident that, if asked, James would gladly help Ellie out of her predicament and give her a room until she could sort things out. With that settled, he closed his weary eyes and slept.

*

By the time Ellie reached Poldhu Cove that evening it was full dark. Her feet ached alarmingly and the pain in her knee from falling had hampered her journey considerably.

After Guy had left her in Primrose Cottage, she'd found a letter waiting for her from Betty:

Dear Ellie,

I have just heard some alarming news. Philip Goldsworthy married Lady Carole Dunstan on Saturday - everyone in Mullion is talking about it. I do not understand. What is going on? I am deeply concerned for you.

Betty

Never had Ellie endured such humiliation. After pacing Primrose Cottage like a caged lion for several hours, she'd made the decision to leave Gweek as soon as possible. She knew Guy would have helped her, but she just could not wait for him to come up with a solution. This was *her* problem, *she* must sort it. The naivety of how she'd got in this situation angered and embarrassed her, prompting her to pack her belongings and leave as soon as dusk fell. She had meant to leave Guy a note, but in her haste to leave she had clean forgotten to do so. Five miles and almost as many hours later, she was back at the Tea Room, exhausted and relieved in equal measure.

The smell of the sea, the sound of the waves and the

cold invigorating breeze enveloped her like a protective coat. She had planned to go to Betty's, but the hour was very late and the heel of her boot had become loose. She could go no further.

Reaching her fingers into a hidey hole under the terrace, Ellie sent up a tiny prayer that the spare key to the Tea Room was still tucked safely there. It was! With trembling fingers she fitted the key in the lock, knowing it was wrong of her to enter the building, but then if she used a key she would not strictly be breaking in.

The room smelt musty as she pushed the door open, any building near the sea could not be closed for any length of time without damp seeping through. Ellie dare not light a candle, in case anyone from the Poldhu Hotel saw, but she knew the room like the back of her hand and negotiated the stacked table and chairs to get towards her old bedroom. Bone tired with emotion, she desperately needed to lie down. Her old bed, which was stripped of linen, felt damp, but she was too tired to care. Wearily she crawled, fully dressed, onto the ticking mattress, curled herself into a foetal position and was sound asleep in seconds.

*

Nellie's lips formed a disapproving purse, as Guy informed her of his plan to help Ellie.

'She's thrown you over once for that cad, why the devil are you helping her now. You'll be tarred with the same brush if you have her in your wagon.' Nellie warned as she packed his bag with a loaf of bread, cheese and apples.

'Ma, I've explained the situation to you - Ellie was the innocent victim in Philip's plan.'

Nellie dismissed his argument with a wave of her hand. 'A likely story. It seems to me she didn't like the way us decent folk condemned her, so made up the story that she didn't know what was happening.'

Guy sighed angrily, grabbing the bag from his ma. 'I've known Ellie for quite a while now and she is definitely not that sort of girl, and for your information, she didn't throw me over, I never let her know that I was interested in her, more fool me.'

Nellie narrowed her eyes. 'More fool you for helping her now, I say,' she muttered under her breath as he set off to Primrose Cottage. She hated arguing with her son, but she also hated being wrong.

*

Guy knocked tentatively on the door of Primrose Cottage. It was early, six a.m., but he suspected that Ellie would be up and about. He peered through the window looking for movement but could see nothing. Pondering by the front door again, his hand hovered over the handle, should he try the door, but would that be too much of an intrusion? He turned the handle to open the door slightly and shouted through the gap.

The cottage was silent. Guy stepped into the hall, aware he was trespassing. He first checked the downstairs rooms and then took the stairs two at a time. The bed was made and it crossed his mind that it hadn't been slept in! He walked to the wardrobe and tentatively opened the doors, it was empty. There was no sign of her, except for her vase of sea glass that she'd obviously brought from Poldhu. Why would she leave that? He closed all the doors behind him and walked into the village. Amelia Pascoe's would be his first port of call.

*

When Amelia could shed no light on where Ellie was, Guy had no option but to set off to work. He'd been on a flying visit home to see his ma, as a job was waiting on a cottage in Berepper, near Gunwalloe. Feeling a change in the weather coming soon, he needed to finish a thatch before the autumn rain set in. Stopping only to retrieve the vase of sea glass from Primrose Cottage, he set off out of Gweek, his heart heavy knowing that he'd failed to help Ellie in her hour of need.

12

It was full daylight when the rattle on the Tea Room door alerted Ellie to someone outside. Terrified at the thought of being caught trespassing, she shot off the bed and crawled to the bedroom door. Very cautiously she peeped around it to find James Blackwell peering through the window. She pulled back, but it was too late, James had seen the movement.

'Ellie, open the door.'

Reluctantly she let him in.

'Why are you closed?' James asked, stepping over the threshold. He glanced at the stacked chairs and then at Ellie, noting her hair and clothes in disarray.

'Goodness, Ellie! Are you alright? Forgive me, but you look as though you've slept in your clothes!'

Ellie lowered her eyes when she felt tears brimming. 'I *have* slept in my clothes.'

Ignoring the impropriety, James pulled her gently into an embrace. 'Come now, tell me what has happened?'

Struggling to regain her composure, Ellie sniffed back her tears. 'I'm sorry, James, but we need to go outside to talk. The Tea Room is up for sale so I'm trespassing on private property at the moment. I'll just get my things and we'll sit on the veranda.' She retrieved her bag, locked the door and made an urgent visit to the privy. She'd tried in vain to tidy her hair, but it continued to stick out at an alarming angle.

The day was calm and the water was shimmering in the sunlight when she joined James on the veranda steps.

'Come.' He gestured for her to sit beside him. 'Tell me what's happened.'

Taking a deep breath, Ellie whetted her dry lips and began her sorry tale.

James listened without comment. When she'd finished, he cupped her hand in his and nodded. *He could gladly hit Philip for what he'd done to Ellie. In truth he'd never warmed to the man and after this never would.*

'Well, you can't stay here, that's for sure. If the constable finds you, even though you have a key, you may be in hot water. You're very welcome to stay with me at Loe House until something can be sorted.'

'I have very little money to pay you rent, James!'

'Then you can make me a cake every now and then as payment.' His eyes twinkled mischievously.

Grateful tears welled. 'That's so kind of you, thank you.'

'That is what friends are for.' He winked. 'It seems to me that you need time to take stock of everything. So dry your tears. All will be well. There is always a way out of every predicament.' He stood up and picked up her bag. 'Come on.'

Rejuvenated, Ellie stood. 'Well my immediate predicament is the loose heel on my boot. I fear I'll not reach Church Cove before it falls off completely.'

He grinned. 'Ah well you see, even that isn't a problem - I came by boat.' He gestured to the small open skiff lying lazily on its side on the damp sand.

'Oh!' Ellie's stomach churned. 'I warn you, I'm a poor sailor.'

'Don't worry, it's not far.'

She reluctantly followed him to the boat, fortunate that she'd eaten nothing since the slice of cake at Elizabeth Trevone's cottage yesterday afternoon. At the water's edge, her stomach gave a cavernous groan and then churned again at the prospect of the boat ride.

James laughed heartily. 'Come on, let's get you home and fed.'

Home. Ellie smiled. *That was a nice thought.*

Throwing her bag aboard, they pushed the boat into the surf and clambered in. The sea was relatively calm, but true to form, Ellie felt queasy before they'd even rounded the corner of Church Cove. By Dollar Cove she was heaving over the side. After what felt like an age, they grounded on the shingle beach at Gunwalloe Fishing Cove, by which time Ellie was incoherent.

James carried her limp, wreck of a body out of the boat and sat her on the beach to recover while he returned to drag the boat up the beach.

'Oh god let me die here,' she groaned, burying her head in her hands to stop it swimming so alarmingly.

James touched her shoulder gently. 'Take some deep breaths Ellie. I'll take your bag and the rowlocks and oars up to the house while you recover a little. I'll be back in a tick.'

'Fine, fine.' She dismissed him with a wave of her hand. 'Just leave me here forever.'

He returned a few minutes later, pulled her to her feet and negotiated the coast path, whilst trying to keep Ellie in a straight line.

'This is a rather alarming reaction to a short boat ride. God help you if you ever need to cross to America.'

She shuddered at the thought. 'I don't ever want to leave solid ground again,' Ellie said, trying to grasp an invisible support.

James led her to a spare room, helped her onto the bed, and once again, Ellie slept fully clothed.

*

While Ellie slept, James took her boot to the local cobblers, before calling at the Halzephron Inn to hire a horse. He had an idea to help Ellie, but he needed to go back to Mullion. As he was about to mount the horse, Guy Blackthorn rounded the corner.

'James,' Guy jumped down from his wagon. 'You are just the man I need to see. You're staying for a few days?' he asked hopefully.

James shook Guy's hand. 'I'm only here for a couple of weeks then I must return to the smoke.' He grimaced at the thought. 'I see you are doing a repair on Toy Cottage.'

Guy nodded. 'I'm rushing before this weather breaks. May I ask - do you have guests staying with you from

London?'

He grinned 'Not from London no. I actually have Ellie staying with me at the moment!'

'Oh, thank goodness for that.' Guy's relief was palpable. 'I can't tell you how pleased I am to hear that. It was Ellie I wanted to speak with you about. She had a terrible shock yesterday and then disappeared this morning before I could help her.' He raked his fingers through his hair. 'Is she alright?'

'Yes. She's resting at the moment.'

'Did she come to you?'

'No, I found her hiding in the Tea Room.'

Guy berated himself. 'Damn, I never thought of looking there.'

'Well I only found her by accident, when I went for a cup of tea. I'd no idea it had closed down.'

'Has she told you what has happened?' he asked cautiously.

'She has. I take it you know the full story too?'

'Unfortunately, yes.' Guy gave a heavy sigh. 'I could punch Philip for what he's done.'

'My sentiments exactly! I take it you didn't know what he'd planned for Ellie?'

'I truly thought, as Ellie did, that he was planning on marrying her.'

James frowned. 'You were his friend! Did you not know he was engaged to Carole?'

Guy shook his head adamantly. 'He never mentioned it. If I'd have known, I'd have stopped him from making a play for Ellie. The first I knew was when he summoned me by letter to stand as his best man - even then I believed that I was attending his marriage to Ellie! I was shocked and relieved in equal measure to find that his bride was Carole….' He paused for a moment. 'Then Philip casually told me his extra marital plans for Ellie. I blame myself for her humiliation. Even though Philip said Ellie was happy with the arrangement, I should have known that was not the case, and followed my gut instinct and gone to see her. I could have saved her all this heartache.

James patted him on the shoulder. 'Never mind, she escaped before any real damage was done.'

'I think her heart is broken though. Damn Goldsworthy. He did not deserve her love.'

James tipped his head. 'You like Ellie, don't you?'

'I do, I like her a lot and I hate to see her hurt.'

'Don't worry my friend, all will be well. Give her time to lick her wounds. She's a strong determined woman and she'll overcome this. Now I must bid you farewell, I have some business to attend to. Ellie is sleeping off a bout of sea sickness at the moment. I brought her back here by boat!' He pulled a face. 'If she's feeling better later I'm hoping to bring her to the Halzephron for dinner this evening, if you want to join us?'

Guy pondered a moment. 'I think, as you say, I'll give her time to recover from this. She was so terribly upset when I saw her last night, it might embarrass her. Tell her I was asking after her though.'

James nodded. 'I'll take good care of her for you.'

The two men gave each other a knowing look.

As James set off towards Mullion he smiled to himself. As a writer he was well versed in bringing about a happy ending to a story. Perhaps he should turn his skills to getting these two young people together.

*

When Ellie woke, it took a few seconds to remember where she was. The room faced west and light was flooding through the window, which overlooked the sea and Porthleven beyond. She brushed her teeth to rid her mouth of the metallic taste, combed her unruly hair and straightened her skirts, before going in search of James. She found him sat on the terrace writing, wrapped in a blanket, his hair in more disarray than hers.

He turned and grinned as she walked down the terrace steps. 'You're back in the land of the living, I see?' He gestured to the seat at his table. 'Do you want to join me, or is it too breezy out here for you?'

'I'd love to join you and fresh air is just what I need.' Ellie sat down sheepishly. 'I'm sorry about earlier.'

James laughed heartily. 'Don't be. I'm sorry I put you through the ordeal. Not everyone has sea legs. Are you well now?'

'A slight dizzy headache, but that's normal. Mama took me on the merry-go-round one Flora Day – the motion sickness put me in bed for two days afterwards.'

James put down his writing paper. 'I have a headache draught that should sort that out.'

'Ordeal aside, James, I'm eternally grateful to you for giving me somewhere to stay. I could have gone to Betty's sister but…' She lowered her eyes. 'I feel so foolish.'

'Ellie, you weren't to know. It's not your fault. Now, let me go and get you that headache draught, you'll feel so much better then.'

Ellie looked out towards Land's End. The sun was setting, though obscured by clouds this evening. The tension of the last few hours began at last to lift from her shoulders. James was indeed her saviour. She felt extremely lucky to have been brought here to his lovely house. She hardly knew him really, but he'd always been kind to her at the Tea Room, often tipping her generously. She was so grateful for his help and that she'd found sanctuary for the time being.

James returned with a glass of cloudy water. 'Drink this, it's bitter but it will do the trick.'

She took the glass gratefully, drained it and the liquid made her stomach rumble.

James listened with alarm. 'I think we need to feed you soon.'

Ellie smiled and shivered slightly.

'Here, pop this around you for a moment.' James put his blanket over her shoulders. 'I never like to miss the sunset. It's such a small pleasure. I do miss this view when

I'm in London.' They sat and watched until the sky split scarlet and orange. When they both shivered, James gathered up his writing material and they made their way inside.

As James stoked the fire he gestured Ellie to take a seat on one of the comfy chairs flanking it. Once it was roaring, he sat back on his haunches.

'I know you've a lot to take in at the moment, Ellie, and probably haven't given much thought to your future, but in an ideal world, do you know what you want to do next?'

Ellie smiled thinly. 'In an ideal world, I'd have enough money to buy the Tea Room and run it myself. Everyone tells me that I have a good business head on my shoulders, and I believe I have! Betty left all the finances to me.' She pulled her mouth into a tight smile. 'Unfortunately it would take years for a woman like me to earn and accumulate enough money to do that, but you know James, that's exactly what I'm going to do. I'll scrub floors and empty chamber pots, but I *will* be my own person one day, and I *will* own my own business. It's in me.' Ellie laid her hand to her heart. 'I know it.'

James nodded at her fervour. *That's what he wanted to hear.* 'I have every confidence that you'll do that.'

Elise's stomach rumbled hungrily.

'Now, how about a spot of dinner?' He pushed his hands against his knees to stand up. 'I fear if I don't feed you soon, your rumbling stomach will unsettle the foundations of my house. ' He held his arm out for her to take. 'The Halzhephron Inn does a rather tasty ale pie on a Saturday.'

13

Ellie had been James's guest at Loe House for a week now. He was a highly entertaining, gregarious person, and over that week they had gone from being casual acquaintances to firm friends. The shame of being duped by Philip still burdened her, but James's company certainly helped to diminish her unhappy thoughts.

The weather had cleared after a spell of heavy rain during the week, but the warmth of the summer had been replaced with the chill of autumn and the nights were lengthening.

Ellie spent her time searching for suitable jobs in the local newspaper. She'd written to Betty to explain what had happened and where she was. She also enjoyed the rare opportunity of having time to sit and read one of James's vast collections of books. She had been rather engrossed in a Thomas Hardy novel when a bicycle bell heralded the arrival of a telegram.

Ellie watched as James's face broke into an excited smile.

'Good news?'

His eyes sparkled. 'Yes, and I now have a rather interesting proposition to put to you.'

'You do?' Ellie blanched. *Not sure that she cared for propositions, certainly not after the last one!*

James frowned. 'Whatever's the matter? I haven't told you what it is yet.'

'W…What sort of proposition?' she whispered.

James looked crestfallen and took her hands in his. 'Oh Ellie, what are you thinking? Please don't tar all men with the same brush as Goldsworthy.'

'I'm sorry…I'

'Ellie?' He gave her hands a sharp tug. 'You have to learn to trust again, otherwise Goldsworthy will have won. Now, hear me out.' His mouth curved into a smile. 'I've bought the Poldhu Tea Room!'

'You have?' Ellie gasped in astonishment as her heartbeat accelerated.

'I have.' He squeezed her hands. 'I've been looking for a business investment for some time. I'd like *you* to run the business for me.'

An excited squeak escaped her throat. 'I.. I don't know what to say to you.'

James cleared his throat. 'Well I'd appreciate a yes, otherwise I'm going to have to learn how to bake and tame that vicious tea urn you have there.' He grinned.

Brimming with tears of joy, Ellie kissed him on his cheek. 'Oh yes, thank you James. I'd love to run the business for you'

'Phew! Thank goodness for that.' He swiped his brow. 'As you know, I am often away, so I'll need regular updates on how the business is going. You'll take a wage, buy the goods in and deposit the profits in the bank each week. If you need any repairs doing, you must send a telegram to me and I'll arrange for someone to come and help.'

Overjoyed, Ellie danced around the room. 'I can't thank you enough for giving me this opportunity.'

James grinned at her excitement. 'It's always a pleasure to help someone who is willing to help themselves. I've every confidence that you will make this a profitable business. You have a free hand to do as you wish with the Tea Room to improve profitability. So now that is settled, let's go out and celebrate. I'll hire a pony trap and take you over there in the morning to make a start - unless of course you'd like to go by boat.'

'Ugh!' Ellie felt ill at the thought.

*

It was the 11th October. The Tea Room was scrubbed clean and ready. The tables were set and cakes baked, ready to open in the morning. That evening, Ellie sat on the veranda watching the setting sun throw golden shadows across the dunes. Today had been a good day. It was down to her now to make a success of this business -

she would not let James or herself down. Because of the new moon, the tide was as far out as could be. With the weather settled, there was little or no noise from the ocean - instead the evening was filled with the trickling noise of the stream, which ran down Poldhu valley towards the sea.

Watching the night slowly begin to drift across the cliff tops, Ellie sat until the stars began to twinkle.

Later that night Ellie settled down, not in the bed she used to occupy in the back of the Tea Room, but in the cottage attached, where Betty used to live. Before retiring, Ellie had penned a letter to Amelia Pascoe and Elizabeth Trevone. They'd both been so kind and supportive to her in her hour of need, and now she was settled, and for courtesy sake, she wanted to assure them she was safe and well. And then of course there was Guy. James had told her of Guy's initial concern and his ultimate relief that she had found a safe haven. She pondered whether to write to him, but felt a little embarrassed that she'd fled Gweek, rejecting his offer of help. It also pained her to remember the accusations she'd thrown at him. It was a dilemma she would ponder on for a while longer.

The gentle sound of the stream as it meandered and bubbled over the river stones, lulled her to sleep. Tomorrow her new life would start.

*

Guy was working in Cadgwith when he received a letter from James Blackwell.

12th October 1901
My dear friend Guy

I hope this letter reaches you. Mrs Menhenick at Toy Cottage told me you are thatching a roof in Cadgwith.

I am writing to inform you that I am to return to London tomorrow, but I thought to tell you before I go, that I have purchased The Poldhu Tea Room and placed Ellie in there as manager.

She is still smarting from Goldsworthy's misdemeanours but I should think being back in the busy Tea Room, where she was always happy, will help to heal her mind. You need not worry yourself over her anymore. She is perfectly settled back where she belongs.

I shall return in a month's time and then again at Christmas with the usual crowd, and hope to make your acquaintance on one or both of those occasions.

I trust you will stay busy and that the weather is not too inclement. Mrs Menhenick sends her regards and says the roof repair is fairing well and will probably see her out.

Regards

James Blackwell

Guy clasped the letter to his chest. He'd fretted constantly over Ellie's predicament, asking here and there if anyone had any employment for an intelligent young lady, but his enquiries had drawn a blank. He longed to visit Ellie, but he felt that he needed to give her time for her heart to heal, before he would very tentatively make her acquaintance again.

*

The Tea Room had been trading for a week when Archie the postman brought two letters from Gweek.

Dear Ellie,

Thank you for your kind letter to inform me of your wellbeing. Both Elizabeth and I were anxious about you, as too was Guy Blackthorn -he is the kindest of men and was sorry that he didn't get the chance to help you. How wonderful though for you to be back in your Tea Room. Hopefully you'll keep busy and soon the past will fade into the distance and your life will feel so much better.

Kind Regards,

Amelia

*

Dearest Ellie,

Our acquaintance was so brief but I hope you will always think of me as a friend you can call on anytime. I'm so happy you're settled again. Put the past behind you now and be assured that your neighbours in Gweek now understand you were not party to Philip Goldsworthy's unscrupulous plan.

Perhaps I'll bring Jenna to Poldhu next summer, as she has

never been to the seaside.
With affection,
Elizabeth and Jenna.

*

It was the beginning of November. Custom was as brisk as ever, though no one ventured into the sea at this time of year. Ellie was turning a good profit and every Monday she took the wagon up to Helston to bank her takings. She felt proud that she was solely in charge of a business, and eternally grateful to James for making this happen. Only one cloud lingered on the horizon. It was six weeks since Philip's wedding and she knew he'd be returning from his honeymoon. Oh to be a fly on the wall to see his self-satisfied smile drop from his face when he found her gone from his cottage. She relished the moment he'd realise how wrong he'd been to surmise that she would have been party to his debauchery, but at the same time fretted about what would happen when he found out where she was. James had told her to call the constable should she encounter any unpleasantness from him, but that didn't ease her anxiety.

*

At Bochym Manor, Jessie finished dressing Lady Sarah's hair. She stood back to admire her handy work. Six weeks ago, she'd never dressed anyone's hair, except her own, and that was only to twist it into a bun.

Lady Sarah admired her reflection in the mirror and sighed. 'Well Jessie, this is where we part company, I'm afraid. Lady Carole will be home this evening with Susan Binns.' She tipped her head. 'You always knew this was a temporary position?'

'Yes, my lady,' Jessie answered.

'I just want to say thank you for all your help in looking after me.'

'It has been a real pleasure and honour, my lady. I shall miss helping you.'

Sarah looked at Jessie's crestfallen face. *Curse Carole for keeping a tight rein on the house finances. As countess, she should have her own maid! Sarah was determined to make a stand over this, but for now, she didn't want to get Jessie's hopes up.*

'May I ask you something, my lady, before I go?'

'Of course Jessie, what is it?'

'I just wondered why the west facing attic bedroom is locked…. the one next to mine and Jane's?'

'I wasn't aware it was. Why do you ask?'

Jessie nipped nervously on her lip. 'I just wondered if maybe the attic could be utilised to give us more room. When Susan comes home tonight, there will be three of us in our room and it's rather cramped at the moment. I'm not complaining, my lady, I just wondered.'

'You're absolutely right, Jessie. If the attic could be utilised then yes, I shall take a look.'

Jessie tingled with excitement. The cramped sleeping arrangements were not the only reason for asking, though more room would be a joy. It was because of the apparition of the girl she saw almost every day now, standing outside the attic door. Jessie knew that if she could get inside that room she might find a clue to the girl's distress.

*

Mrs Bligh's thin hard lips whitened as she fingered the bunch of keys she carried around on her belt.

'The key to the west facing attic, my lady?' she asked stiffly.

Sarah held out her hand. 'If you please, Mrs Bligh.'

Feeling the panic rising, she spluttered. 'But the earl had it locked many years ago. He said it wasn't to be opened again.'

'My husband?'

Bligh swallowed hard. 'No, my lady, it was the old earl - god rest his soul.'

Sarah presented her hand again.

'I really… I…don't….I don't think I have it.'

'You hold the keys to every door in the house, do you

not?'

Bligh nodded slowly.

'Well let's go through them.'

Bligh lifted the bunch of keys, surreptitiously hiding the attic key between her middle and ring finger.

Sarah smiled without humour. 'So, which one is which.'

Mrs Bligh rattled off each door key. With an air of satisfaction she said, 'No, I don't seem to have it.'

Sarah reached forward and grasped the key clamped between her fingers, dragging the bunch with it. 'I'll try this one then.'

Relishing the anxious look on Bligh's face, Sarah allowed herself a triumphant smile as she walked out of the room with them.

'I'll…I'll come with you. The lock may be stiff. I'll get Mr Carrington.'

Sarah turned and faced her off. 'Thank you, but I need no help from either of you.'

*

Mrs Bligh rushed into Mr Carrington's room, swiftly closing the door behind her. 'Lady Sarah's got the key to the west attic.'

Carrington stiffened. 'What?'

'I tried to hide it from her but she found it. What are we going to do?'

He scraped his chair backwards. 'I'm going up there.'

'No, she was adamant that she goes alone.'

'What the devil is she up to? What is she looking for?' He paced the floor.

'Nothing, she'll find nothing. Everything was cleared away before it was locked. It'll just be a dusty old room.' Bligh slumped down on the chair. 'Everything seems to be up in the air since that bloody Rosevear girl came a visiting. There was never all this upset before then. If this comes to the surface again with Lady Sarah's meddling, I fear for us all.'

'It might not come to anything. As I say, Lady Sarah will find only a dusty room up there. I'll speak to the earl and say that the floors are unsafe and then it will be locked up again. All will be well Joan, stop worrying.'

*

After a few attempts, Sarah finally unlocked the door. A chill made her pull her shawl tighter around her arms. The room housed nothing but two iron beds and years of dust. Sarah walked gingerly across the floorboards, in case of rot, but found that they were sound. The window to the left, cloudy with grime, looked out into the small courtyard, which led from the kitchen.

As she stood at the window, she had the distinct feeling that something had happened here, why else would it be locked? She also felt the hairs on the back of her neck stand up. She was clearly not alone.

'My lady!'

Sarah jumped at the sound of Jessie's voice behind her.

Jessie's hand shot up to her mouth. 'Oh, I'm so sorry to have startled you.'

Sarah stilled her thumping heart with her hand and smiled. 'Don't worry. Come in and tell me what you think of the room.'

'Gosh, it's certainly bigger than the one I share with Jane and Susan.'

'Do you…. feel comfortable in here?' Sarah raised her eyebrows.

'Yes, my lady. I do.' Jessie answered trying not to look at the vaporous figure stood by the window.

Sarah smiled. 'Then it's yours to share with whoever wants to - though I suspect you might not have any takers.'

*

In the kitchen Albert Lanfear was polishing the earl's buttons and buckles, when he heard the floor boards creak above him. His mouth dropped open. *Who the hell was in that room?* He looked up at the ceiling as a cold shiver ran down his spine.

14

Philip jumped from his carriage with gusto. 'I'll walk from here,' he told the driver. He wanted to surprise Ellie. He'd sent no word of his arrival, so that she'd be taken unawares. He'd just spent the last six weeks with Carole, and was heartily sick of looking at her powdered, sour face. If he'd sent word of his return, he knew Ellie would have tried her best to get dressed up for him. He smiled to himself. He hoped to find her in the garden or busy making cakes. He hoped her hair would be hanging loose, and her face relaxed and naturally beautiful. That's what he loved about her most of all - her naturalness.

He pulled off his tie and opened the collar at his neck as he approached Primrose Cottage. When he couldn't find Ellie in the garden, his high spirits lowered momentarily. He strode up the front path, closed his hand around the door handle, and was shocked to find it did not yield. He stepped back and looked towards the windows. Unwilling to knock at his own door, he reluctantly searched for the key under the plant pot.

'Damn you Ellie for being out when I come home,' he muttered angrily. He'd just have to surprise her when she came back.

There was a strange quietness in the cottage which knocked him off guard. A light film of dust covered the furniture, and he could see no visible signs of anyone actually living there. He tentatively opened the larder door, to a stench of rotting food and sour milk. He reeled back in disgust. *Where are you, damn it?* His mouth set hard as he ran up the stairs. He wrenched open the wardrobe door, releasing a moth which had feasted on the few hanging clothes of his which hung there.

'What is this? What joke you are playing on me, Elise Rosevear?' he yelled.

He marched to the Corn Mill, in search of Harry Yates.

'Miss Rosevear?' Philip said condescendingly.

'Sir?'

'Where is she, Yates?'

Harry cleared his throat. 'I don't rightly know, Sir.'

'Has she *gone*, gone?' he said sarcastically.

'I reckon so, sir.'

'When did you last see her?'

Harry scratched his chin. 'It'll be five weeks back.'

Philip mouth tightened. 'What made her leave?'

'I don't know, sir.' He did but decided to keep his counsel.

With a curt nod of the head, he said, 'Get back to work.'

'Yes, sir.'

Harry smiled secretly. He may be his employee, and he would miss Ellie, but he was so glad she'd upped sticks and left after learning that Goldsworthy was not the man she thought he was.

Philip was seething as he returned to Primrose Cottage. He'd fantasised about coming home and taking Ellie to bed for the first time, and now this! *Where the hell could she be? She had no home, no job, and no money. If she'd been gone for five weeks she could be anywhere!* He drummed his fingers angrily on the kitchen table. *Perhaps Nellie, next door, would know her whereabouts - she knew everyone's business.*

*

Nellie eyed her visitor with mild amusement. He looked both flustered and angry in equal measure.

'Good day to you, Nellie. I trust you're in good health.'

'Well, I'm still living,' she answered dryly. There had never been much love lost between the two of them. Philip had led her son into all sorts of misbehaviour during their youth, knowing full well that it was Guy, not he, who would get walloped whenever they were found out. Being the pampered and cherished only son of the mill owner, John Goldsworthy, Philip practically got away with murder.

'And what can I do for you?' *As if I didn't know.*

'I rather hoped you could enlighten me as to where Miss Rosevear from next door has gone.'

Nellie gave a crooked smile. 'Gone looking for a decent man to marry, I reckon.'

Philips curled his lip slightly. 'I beg your pardon?'

'I don't think I need to spell it out, Philip, do you?' Nellie didn't particularly like Ellie for throwing her son over for this cad, but it gave her great satisfaction to see Philip's face, flushed with annoyance.

With anger building, Philip flared his nostrils and without bidding Nellie good day, he stormed away. The sight of Guy's wagon trundling up the lane brought him to a halt. *Now if anyone knew where she was, Guy would.*

Guy eyed Philip cautiously as he pulled his horse to a halt.

Philip moved over and grabbed the horse's harness. 'Guy, Ellie's gone!'

Jumping down from the wagon, Guy began to untie the tarpaulin at the rear of the wagon to unload his tools.

Philip folded his arms. 'Did you hear me? Do you know why she left?

Guy expelled a weary sigh as he hauled his bag from the back. 'Need you really ask that question?'

'So you do know then?'

He threw his tool bag on the floor and rounded on Philip. 'She left as soon as she found out what a scoundrel you were.'

'What have you been saying to her? She was very happy with the arrangements when I left her.'

Guy laughed incredulously. 'That poor girl thought you were coming back to marry her!'

Philip bristled. 'I never mentioned marriage to her. I don't know where she got that idea from.'

'You never mentioned your marriage to her either, or that you were away on your honeymoon! She thought you were on a business trip abroad.'

Philip shifted uncomfortably. 'I didn't want to upset

her.'

Fuelled by anger Guy snapped. 'Have you any idea how hard it has been for Ellie in the village? Everyone knew your intention towards her, but poor Ellie was completely in the dark over her residence in Primrose Cottage. You know what people are like in this village when things are not as they should be. They all turned their back on her, thinking she was some loose woman. Damn you man, her reputation was sullied by you.'

Philip snorted derisively. 'So the silly girl has thrown everything over because of a few gossiping women? God damn it, I offered her everything any reasonable girl in her position could expect. What more did she want?'

'She assumed that you were going to marry her!'

'Only a fool assumes anything.'

Guy felt his resolve snap. 'Ellie is no fool! You duped her and you should be ashamed of yourself.'

'So where have you hidden her? Because I suspect this is all down to you giving the game away. You were jealous that I had won her affections, I could see it in your face when I told you my plans.'

'This isn't a game, Philip! This is a young girl's reputation we're talking about.'

Philip gritted his teeth. 'Rubbish. You've turned her silly head that's all. Now where the devil is she? I need to smooth this out with her and make her see sense.'

Guy threw his hands in the air. 'You really haven't heard a word I've said, have you, you arrogant bastard. For your information, Ellie is fending quite happily for herself. I can also assure you that you are the very last person she ever wants to speak to again.'

*

It took Philip only a few hours to locate Ellie's whereabouts. Lady Sarah had casually informed him over dinner that night at Bochym, that the Tea Room had been bought by James Blackwell, and re-opened with Ellie as manager.

'I'm so happy for Elise, and so thankful to James,' Sarah proclaimed. 'He knows a good business when he sees one. I must find the time to go down to see her soon.'

Philip glanced at Carole, who gave him a 'don't come running to me if your plan has backfired,' look. He pushed his dinner plate away, suddenly losing his appetite. *Damn James and his meddling. What the devil was he playing at? He hardly knew Ellie! Why would he help her?* He must think of something to get his plan back on track. He knew his new wife would not welcome his advances for much longer.

*

It was the second week in November, when Ellie received an invitation from Lady Sarah at Bochym. She had invited Ellie to take tea with her and asked her to bring another selection of her fine lace to buy. A carriage would come to collect her. Ellie pondered this dilemma. She enjoyed Lady Sarah's friendship, but was unsure how to face the new Mrs Dunstan-Goldsworthy, if she was there, knowing that her husband had planned to cuckold her with Ellie. Ellie so wanted to share her exciting news about the Tea Room with Sarah and it would be an advantage to sell more lace. After debating for twenty-four hours over the invitation, she pushed her concerns aside and attended on the day stated.

*

Ellie sat in the carriage dressed in her finest day dress and shoes. Though the latter pinched a little she knew she would be sitting for most of the time.

Passing the Lodge at Bochym Manor, Ellie felt a flutter in her stomach. Maybe she should not have come. She was confident that Philip would not be there, it being a Monday. For all his faults he took his work responsibilities seriously. After all, he'd told her he was taking over the running of the Corn Mill on his return from Europe. The thought of his trip - his honeymoon - made her shudder. *Oh the lies that man had told her.* Ellie shifted uneasily in her seat, but it was too late, the carriage had arrived at the front gates. In her heart she hoped that she would only meet Lady Sarah today, but if Lady Carole was there she would hold her head up – she had done nothing wrong.

The groomsman opened the door and helped her down. Ellie's eyes swept across the grey serpentine fascia of the manor house, until they came to rest at one of the upstairs windows, where stood the same young girl she'd seen on her previous visit. Ellie felt an odd sensation in the pit of her stomach, as though she knew the girl and knew her well. She blinked but the girl had vanished. What was it about this place that unnerved her?

The stone arched door beckoned Ellie towards it. At least she didn't have to go through the indignation of arriving at the kitchen door this time.

She glanced around to make sure Albert Lanfear wasn't around, then she rang the bell. After a couple of minutes waiting, no one came, so she rang again and turned to look down the gardens, remembering Lady Sarah's kindness at showing her around them the last time she came. The door had opened when she turned back, to see the maid she only knew as Taylor, standing embarrassed before her.

'I'm dreadfully sorry Miss, to keep you waiting, cook's cakes were burning and I had to get them out of the oven just as you rang the bell.'

'Don't worry, it doesn't matter. I am here to see Lady Sarah.' Before she could step over the threshold an angry male voice hollered from the back of the hall.

'Taylor, what are you doing answering the door?'

The maid looked stricken. 'Sorry, Mr Carrington, I thought you were still in a meeting with Mrs Bligh.'

'Meeting or not, you do not answer the door, under any circumstances.' The butler pulled the girl roughly to one side. 'Get back into the kitchen at once.' He opened the door fully to Ellie and his eyes swept over her with displeasure. 'Oh, it's you again.'

Having been summonsed to the house by Lady Sarah,

Ellie was determined not to be intimidated by him. She stood up tall, removed her gloves and announced that she was expected by Lady Sarah.

Carrington snorted derisively. 'Lady Sarah is not in. I'll see if Lady Carole is expecting you.' He left her standing where she stood, as he knocked on the large ornate door to the left of the hall.

Lady Sarah is out! Ellie's stomach tightened in trepidation. Why would she be out if she'd sent an invitation to tea? Ellie glanced through the library door which stood ajar, and stilled when she saw a movement by the window. She blinked twice and a figure appeared - it was the same young girl she'd seen before. She was dressed in a nightgown at this late hour of the morning and seemed to beckon Ellie forward. Unsure of what she was seeing, Ellie was just about to step into the library when the drawing room door opened. The girl vanished.

Carrington cleared his throat impatiently. 'Lady Carole *is* expecting you.'

Though not normally in her nature, Ellie couldn't help but smile inwardly.

'Miss Rosevear, I am so glad you could come. I fear Lady Sarah is otherwise engaged.'

Ellie took in the splendour of the room she'd entered. Ornate wall panels, pilasters, door architrave and ceiling cornices, all shimmered with gold leaf. Underfoot, a large, thick, richly ornate Turkish rug covered the wooden floor.

'I thought we'd take tea here, in the French drawing room. The light is so much better than that in the other dark oak panelled rooms. I do hope you have brought me some more of your delightful lace? My wedding gown was a sensation. I had so many people admiring your handiwork. I hope to send more work your way, if we can come to some arrangement?'

'Thank you. You're very kind.' Ellie opened the box of lace for Carole to inspect. Piece by piece Carole held the lace up to the light. The stained glass window sifted soft, colourful, watery patterns onto the chaise-longue by the window, and for a moment she was mesmerised by the display.

'Miss Rosevear?'

Carole had obviously spoken but Ellie had not heard.

'I'm sorry. I was just admiring the room.'

'It is rather nice, isn't it? Queen Victoria and Prince Albert stayed here you know, now when was it? Oh yes, 1846 I believe. It was all very hush hush of course. Even the newspapers weren't informed.'

There appeared to be a sharp altercation going on outside the door, a moment before Mr Carrington emerged with a tea tray.

'Is there a problem Carrington? I heard high words.'

'No, my lady, it's nothing.' The tea tray was placed on the table which stood in the middle of the sumptuous rug.

When tea was served and Carrington had left, Carole turned and smiled at Ellie.

'Now then Elise, my husband tells me you have rejected his proposal.'

Ellie felt every nerve in her body jangle. She glanced up from her teacup to meet Lady Carole, eye to eye.

'Philip said he offered everything to you, but you rejected it all.' Carole sipped her tea and watched Ellie with interest.

Placing her cup and saucer back on the table, Ellie poised herself to leave forthwith. The day was not warm but a trickle of perspiration began to run down her back. This was a trap. She should have known and listened to her instincts not to come. She stood suddenly. 'I think I should leave now,' she said, trying to steady her voice.

Carole placed her tea cup down and smiled. 'Please, do not feel uncomfortable, my dear. I beg you, sit down and take your tea. Do not be offended by what I have said. I knew of the arrangement Philip was preparing for you, I just thought I would invite you here to ask why it is not to your liking? After all, I thought you loved him?'

Caught off guard Ellie felt a flash of anger. 'I did!'

'Then what has changed?'

Ellie rounded on Carole. If she wanted an argument, she could have one! 'Well, if you must know, him marrying you, for a start!'

'Why on earth should that make any difference?' Carole laughed softly. 'Oh my dear, you didn't think he was going to marry you, did you?'

Ellie turned away to hide her embarrassment.

'Oh dear, you did, didn't you? Don't you realise, he could never have married you. The class difference would have been insurmountable for a start, and you have no money!'

Insulted beyond reason, Ellie snapped back. 'But he told me he loved me,' she said defiantly.

'And rest assured he still does, my dear. Please, sit down and finish your tea.'

Totally confused with the situation unfolding before her, Ellie sat back down. 'I'm sorry. I don't understand. Do you not love Philip, and if not, why did you marry him?'

'Love him, oh goodness no! Ours was a marriage of convenience, a sort of blending of money, if you know what I mean? I knew about you, of course I did, that is why I asked you to come and see me in the first instance - although I was intrigued when I heard about your talent for lace making. I could see you were clean and tidy, and though of the lower class you had a degree of intelligence. I had no qualms about him taking you as his mistress. That is what men do!'

Ellie could not believe what she was hearing. It took all her resolve to suppress the anger building inside her. 'Not in the *lower* classes they don't!' she answered through gritted teeth. 'People marry because they want to be together.'

Lady Carole dismissed this statement with a flick of her hand. 'Well, I wouldn't know about that, but what I do know is that Philip had to marry someone with money and I was quite happy with the arrangement. Unfortunately you have now left me with a dilemma.'

'Oh?' Ellie tipped her head in disbelief.

'Well, how can I put this?' She paused for a moment. 'As his wife, I need to provide an heir, and I will undertake my duties in that department until the deed is done.' She twisted her mouth disagreeably. 'What I don't want is *him* bothering me at other times. That, my dear, is where *you* should have come in.'

Ellie blanched.

'Oh come now, don't be so coy, we're all adults. So, will you reconsider? What else can we offer as an inducement? You will want for nothing.'

Ellie shook her head in disbelief. 'I'll want my unsullied reputation that is what I want! I want a husband of my own - someone who will come home to *me* every night. He never once told me about you. I had no idea he'd married you! Have you any idea how I felt when I found out? How foolish and grubby he made me feel. Well you can tell him from me, I'll never forgive him for his dishonesty. *We* the *lower* classes as you call us expect to be treated with respect, and Philip Goldsworthy and you, his wife, obviously do not know the meaning of that word!' She stood abruptly. 'Please send for my coat and hat, I should like to leave now.'

Carole yanked the bell with annoyance.

Carrington appeared at the door. 'Yes, my lady?'

'Please bring Miss Rosevear her coat and hat. Apparently she's leaving,' she said flatly.

Carrington bowed to her command, his lip curling slightly.

The two women stood in icy silence while Ellie's garments were brought.

Ellie took the coat and without another word, picked up her box of lace and made to leave.

'Go then, you silly girl.' Carole called after her.

Ellie held her head high and stormed out of the front door and into the fresh air. The carriage she'd arrived in was nowhere to be seen, so she set off up the long drive in her best shoes, which were not made for walking in.

*

By the time Ellie reached Poldhu, her shoes were destroyed and her feet harboured more blisters than skin. She had never felt embarrassment like this before. She threw her box of lace down, ripped off her torn and blooded stockings, tucked her skirts into her waistband and ran down the beach towards the sea. The icy salt water eased her blistered feet, but nothing could ease the pain of her humiliation.

15

Lady Sarah arrived home from her walk to the sound of raised voices coming from the housekeeper's room. Never wanting to make an entrance or a fuss, Sarah often came back indoors via the laundry room, which was only a stone's throw away from the housekeeper's room.

Izzy the laundry maid bobbed a curtsy, but Sarah pressed a finger to her lips to stop Izzy speaking as she moved quietly out into the corridor to listen.

'Taylor has to go,' Bligh snapped. 'I will not put up with her behaviour any longer.'

'I blame that Rosevear woman,' Carrington said. 'Every time she steps foot over that threshold, all hell breaks loose.'

'What did Rosevear want anyway, John? Does she not realise, she's not welcome here!' Bligh asked.

'She claimed she was invited by Lady Sarah, but it was Lady Carole who sent the carriage for her. I don't know what happened during the meeting, but Lady Carole was so cross with her, the return carriage was not requested to take her home!'

'Good. Rosevear is acting far above her station, expecting a carriage home. I don't know who she thinks she is.'

'I agree,' Carrington said adamantly. 'It is my opinion that since her stint as Lady Sarah's maid, Taylor has been acting above her station too. Do you know she blatantly answered the door when that Rosevear girl rang the bell? I bet she knew she was coming. Those two are in cahoots, I tell you. And then I found Taylor clearing up an upturned aspidistra in the library and berating some unseen person for the misdemeanour! She's mad I tell you, and a liability. The sooner you dismiss her Joan, the better.'

As Sarah listened in the shadows, she became aware of a presence beside her. She felt a hand grasp her arm though she could not see who it was – the grasp felt like someone in great distress. Sarah had heard enough. She entered the housekeeper's room, shocking both Carrington and Bligh with her appearance.

'Is there a problem?' Sarah glanced between them both.

Bligh lifted her chin. 'There appears to be, yes, my lady. It's the housemaid Taylor. She's being very disruptive again.'

Sarah tipped her head. 'Please explain how?'

Bligh pursed her lips. 'You will recall we've had this conversation before, my lady. The girl….' she hesitated. 'The girl sees….' Bligh glanced at Carrington for help.

Carrington jutted his chin authoritatively. 'The girl has sick fancies that she can see and speak to…… spirits… ghosts, or whatever you want to call them.'

Sarah tipped her head. 'And why is that a problem?'

'Well she's obviously insane,' Bligh said haughtily.

'Or susceptible to the spirit world - many people are!' Sarah parried.

Carrington and Bligh exchanged uncomfortable glances.

'The other members of the staff are worried that Taylor will encourage more of these ungodly beings out of the woodwork. Several have reported unusual happenings since Taylor started this nonsense,' Bligh said.

'This is an old house, Mrs Bligh. I'd be surprised if there wasn't more than one spirit.'

'But she's frightening the other staff, my lady, and she is getting above her station,' Bligh retorted fiercely.

'I for one applaud anyone who aspires to rise above their station. As for the spirits, if any of the staff are bothered by them, I suggest you tell them to find alternative employment. Jessie, and any spirits that choose to inhabit this old house, have my permission to stay!'

Lady Sarah swept out of the room in search of Carole. There was no doubt about it, the house did feel a little strange - something *had* disturbed the spirits. She found

Carole in the Jacobean drawing room.

'Oh, hello Sarah! Did you enjoy your walk?' She reached for the servant's bell. 'Excuse me, I'm just about to summon Bligh to go over the accounts.'

'Actually Carole, don't you think it's time I familiarised myself with the house accounts?'

Carole dismissed her suggestion with a wave of her hand. 'You don't need to bother yourself with that. I've done it for years, and…to be fair Sarah, I know what I am doing. It would be far too difficult for you to pick up. You just look after the flower arrangements - you're good at that.'

Sarah had to bite her tongue to refrain from retaliation. Carole could be very condescending at times. Suddenly a vaporous movement caught Sarah's attention in the corner of the room.

Carole shivered as though someone had walked over her grave. 'Goodness me, it's gone chilly all of a sudden in this room. Do you feel it, Sarah?'

She had, but shook her head.

Carole walked over to the fireplace to inspect the fire, which had been burning fiercely in the grate but was now down to an ember. 'Is it windy out there? The fire is going out!'

Sarah rang the bell for Carrington to see to the fire and watched with amusement as the disturbance in the room settled beside Carole.

'I understand Elise Rosevear visited today.'

Carole huffed. 'Little good it did though. I'm really quite put out about it.'

'Why?'

Carole waved her hand in annoyance. 'Some arrangement Philip had made to set her up, so that he didn't have to bother me in my bed chamber, but the stupid girl doesn't know a good thing when it's pushed under her nose.'

Sarah gasped in disbelief. 'I beg your pardon? Are you

suggesting what I think?'

'That she was to be his mistress, yes!' Carole replied tersely. 'I brought her here to try and make her see sense, but she took a rather haughty stance with me over it would you believe. I made the silly girl walk home though. Perhaps the walk will have brought her to her senses.'

'Carole, how could you?' Sarah said contemptuously, but before she could berate her further, the fire suddenly extinguished, puffing a great cloud of smoke into the room, covering Carole's pale green silk dress with soot.

Despite her disgust at Carole's behaviour, Sarah suppressed a smile as Carole rushed from the room, shouting for her maid and bemoaning the demise of her best day dress. By the time Carrington arrived to answer the bell, the fire had burst back into life and was blazing away in the grate.

'You rang, my lady?'

'Ask Jessie to come and see me, and I'd like a tea tray for two people please.'

'Yes, my lady.'

Five minutes later, Jessie preceded Carrington as he carried in the tea tray. Her eyes were red rimmed from crying as she bobbed a curtsy.

'Is Lady Carole joining you, my lady? Shall I wait to pour?' Carrington said holding the tea pot aloft.

'No, Lady Carole will not be joining me. Jessie, please come and sit down,' she gestured for her to sit on the sofa. 'Do you take milk and sugar, Jessie?'

Jessie edged her way towards the sofa. 'Just milk, my lady, thank you.'

'Carrington, you can pour the tea now.' Sarah watched with delight as Carrington's face turned puce.

*

At Poldhu, the day was lowering. Clouds pulled in from the sea, but the chill breeze off the ocean failed to cool Ellie's anger. She wiggled her sore feet in the surf, hoping the salt would help to heal her blisters, for they were as sore as her heart.

'Is it not a little chilly for a paddle?'

Ellie turned to find James Blackwell behind her. She smiled thinly. 'Hello, James.'

'You look lost in your thoughts.'

'Yes, you catch me in a very contemplative state of mind I fear.'

'Anything I can help you with? Is all well with the Tea Room?'

'The Tea Room is fine, James, there are no problems there.' She sighed and looked back out towards the sea. 'I've just had the whole sorry mess of Philip's debauched plan dragged up and thrown in my face again.'

James's face darkened. 'Why, has Philip been here bothering you?'

'No, I haven't seen him, thank goodness, but I've just returned from Bochym Manor and a rather unpleasant interview with Lady Carole.'

James raised his eyebrows. 'I'm surprised you went to see her!'

'I didn't! She got me there under false pretences.' Ellie raked her fingers through her hair and began to relay the whole sorry episode to him.

'Oh Ellie, I'm sorry for you. I've known Carole for a while. I'm afraid she is used to getting her own way, and does not care whose feelings she tramples on to get it.'

'Evidently!' Ellie stamped her foot angrily regretting it instantly when the action burst another blister. She reached down to cradle her sore heel. 'I was so angry James. I got up and walked out without waiting for a carriage - hence the sore feet.'

James grimaced at the sight of her blisters. 'Oh Ellie, you never walked all the way back from Bochym?'

'I did and ruined my best shoes in the process!' As she spoke, angry tears welled. 'I hate them both for this.'

James took her gently into his arms. 'Oh, don't cry, Ellie. People like that are not worth shedding tears over.'

'I can't help it James. It hurts so much. It grieves my heart to feel so sullied by their debauched plan.' She dabbed her eyes. 'I thought Philip really loved me and his love was pure. Our feelings grew and grew after he saved my life. It was like, we were meant to be.'

'Wait a minute,' he stopped her. 'Let me put you straight on that score. Philip did *not* save your life.'

Ellie pulled away from him. 'He did! He saved me from drowning a few months ago, you must remember.'

'I remember it well, Ellie, but it wasn't Philip who saved you. It was Guy Blackthorn!'

Shocked, Ellie put her hand to her chest. 'What?'

'It's true. Guy was the one that stood to the sidelines dripping wet and exhausted. Philip just took all the glory.'

Ellie's mouth formed an O in disbelief. 'Philip made out that it was him!'

'So you see, Ellie, Philip is false through and through. I suggest you put him and his schemes out of your mind. You're a lovely young woman. Don't waste your energy on him anymore. There are plenty more fish in the sea and I can guarantee there *is* someone special out there for you. You just have to open your heart to find him.'

Ellie's eyes lowered, unsure she'd ever give her heart to someone again.

'Come on now.' He handed her his handkerchief. 'Make these the last tears you shed for Philip Goldsworthy. Could this weary walker beg a nice cup of tea from you?'

'There will always be a cup of tea, thanks to you,' she said as she limped painfully back up the beach with him.

Later that day Ellie penned a letter to Guy Blackthorn, inviting him to tea Monday week.

*

No one was more surprised than Jessie when Lady Sarah invited her to sit and have tea. She'd overheard that she was going to be dismissed and thought this a very strange way to tell her to pack her bags.

Sarah handed her tea with a smile.

The cup shook violently in her hand. 'Please, my lady, don't dismiss me. I've nowhere to go.'

'Please do not distress yourself, Jessie. You are not to be dismissed, but I do need to speak with you.'

Jessie sniffed back tears and nodded.

Handing a handkerchief to her, Sarah said, 'Tell me Jessie what you can see? Because I see something too, but I can't make out what it is.'

Jessie lifted her watery eyes to meet Sarah's. 'It's a young girl– about my age. She's dressed in a nightgown and very distressed about something.'

'And you're not afraid of her?'

'No, my lady, there is nothing to be afraid of.'

Wondering if it was the same person who had grasped her arm earlier, Sarah asked, 'Do you know why she's distressed? Mrs Bligh tells me you speak to her.'

Jessie shook her head. 'She doesn't speak back to me, but it's the way she presents herself that worries me.'

Sarah raised her eyebrows. 'Enlighten me.'

'I think something must have happened in the attic, where I sleep now, because she constantly stands by the window which overlooks the back courtyard. She also presents herself behind Mr……..' Jessie looked downwards.

'Behind who, Jessie?'

Fearful of saying the words, Jessie's lips moved but she dare not speak.

Sarah moved to sit beside her. 'Tell me?'

'She appears behind Mr Lanfear,' she whispered. 'The girl points at him and her distress is ten fold.'

'I see, and are these the only places you see her?'

'Normally yes, except…….I know it sounds strange, but whenever Miss Rosevear has been a guest in the house, the girl seems happier and appears everywhere. It's as though she follows her about. The girl was deeply distressed after Miss Rosevear left following the argument this morning with Lady Carole. All sorts of strange things began to happen then. Plant pots were knocked over, ashes from the fireplaces were scattered over the rugs and the library curtains had been pulled from their fastenings. That was when Mr Carrington found me talking to her. I was trying to make her stop.' She lifted her gaze to Sarah. 'She was making a lot of work for me, you see.'

Sarah tapped her fingers to her lips. *Maybe Elise could shed some light on what was going on here.*

Jessie lowered her voice to a whisper again. 'Mrs Bligh thinks that I'm in cahoots with Miss Rosevear, but I don't know her, my lady, I promise.'

'It's alright Jessie, you're not to worry about what Mrs Bligh thinks. I have made it quite plain that I will not tolerate her bullying tactics towards you. Now would you like a slice of cake with your tea?'

*

That evening, as Sarah prepared for bed she turned to face her husband Peter as he entered her bedchamber. He looked tired after his journey and was unsure as to whether to bother him with her questions, but she knew she wouldn't sleep if she didn't.

'Have you eaten, darling?'

'Yes, I had dinner with Leonard Cunliffe at Trelissick.'

'Is he well?'

'He is and sends his regards along with an invitation to spend New Year with him, if we choose. I think he rather likes renting Trelissick House. I wouldn't be surprised if he buys it one day.'

'Have you told him how much money a house like that costs to run?'

Peter laughed. 'As a banker and director of Harrods, I don't believe money is an issue.'

'Shall we go on New Year's Eve?'

'Perhaps, though it is a long way, and the roads are terribly muddy at the moment,' he said draping his housecoat over the chair. He clambered into bed and lay down with a sigh.

Sarah stopped brushing her hair and joined him in bed, kissing him softly on his furrowed brow.

'Darling, can I ask you something?'

'Yes my love,' he answered sleepily.

'Do you recall if there has ever been any accidents in the attic?'

'Gosh, what a question. Why do you ask?' He gave a cavernous yawn.

'I just wondered if anyone had died following an accident there.'

'No, not that I'm aware of.' He yawned again and his breathing deepened.

Sarah watched him slip into a deep slumber, but sleep was not an option for her. Her interest had been piqued. Something had happened there and she was determined to get to the bottom of it.

*

As Ellie lay in her bed that night, she ran through the events of the day. Her anger had abated and her thoughts were dominated by the figure she'd seen in the library. Ellie racked her brain. She knew it was the same girl she'd seen during her first visit to Bochym, but who was she? She could feel her eyelids droop - the emotion of the day was taking its toll. Eventually Ellie relaxed and slept, but in the early hours a name jumped into her head and woke her with a start. Sitting up in bed, she rubbed the sleep from her eyes. Pearl Martin, the young housemaid who used to look after her when Ellie's mother went out selling lace - that's who she'd seen in the manor, well her spirit anyway. Where on earth had that come from? Ellie felt a strange sense of melancholia. Of course, something happened to Pearl just before Ellie and her mother left Bochym, but what? And hadn't Pearl been mentioned during the argument between her mother and the horrible Mr Lanfear? Ellie sat in the dark, searching her mind for more information. *Come on Ellie, think.* But try as she might, no more information came to mind.

*

Ellie was not the only one to have a disturbed night. At Bochym, Lady Carole woke to a curious sensation - someone was in the room. She sat bolt upright and pulled the sleep mask from her eyes.

'Who is it, who's there? I hope that's not you Philip, because I'm not interested.'

The room, lit only by the moon, revealed a vaporous movement which stirred the heavy velvet curtains. Carole's skin began to creep. She pulled the bedcovers up to her face for protection. Knowing she had closed all the windows before bed, her senses heightened as an icy breeze moved the curls of her hair. Unnerved, she fumbled in the dark to locate the candle, meeting instead with an ice cold hand. Emitting a piercing shriek, Carole leapt from the bed and made for the bedroom door. She tried the handle, but it would not open. In her panic her scream intensified, as a strange, clawing sensation of depression and hopelessness settled over her like a shroud.

Alerted by her screams, Peter burst into Carole's bedroom, knocking her flying across the floor. 'What the devil is going on Carole? You'll wake the whole household with your hysterics.'

Carole scrambled to her feet and fled the room with a speed unbecoming of a lady.

After a quick search of the house, Peter finally located Carole in the corner of the kitchen. She was pale, tearful and shaking like a gibbering wreck. Carrington and Bligh had been roused from their slumber and were stood over her in their nightgowns.

'I'm not staying here a moment longer, Peter,' Carole declared as he lifted her to her feet. 'Something is amiss with this house. Things are happening that should not be happening.'

'What on earth are you talking about?'

'There are ghosts, spirit energies, or something, evil in this house.'

'Don't be absurd, Carole. You've lived in the house for the last twenty years. I've lived in it twenty-five years and never have I seen a ghost! It was a dream…a nightmare. You'd do better to curb your drinking, and then you would not have these ridiculous fancies.'

'I was *not* dreaming!' she yelled.

The conversation had developed into a full blown row by the time Sarah joined them. 'Is everything alright here?'

Carole turned her wild eyes on her sister-in-law. 'Do I look alright?' she snapped.

'If I'm honest, no you don't. Pray tell.'

'My lady claims she is being spooked by a ghost,' Bligh stated haughtily.

'I'm not claiming anything…I *was* spooked!'

Though highly amused, Sarah desperately tried to keep her face straight.

'I see *you* don't believe me either,' she directed the accusation at Sarah, but before Sarah could answer, Carole's eyes widened. 'Look, look, it's behind you, look!' she shrieked pointing her trembling fingers.

'Oh for Christ's sake, Carole, pull yourself together,' Peter said turning to look behind him.

Everyone else had turned to look, but only Sarah could see the apparition Carole was pointing at.

'Peter stood with his hand on his hips. 'I see nothing, do you Sarah?'

The apparition vanished and Sarah shook her head.

'There, see, you are completely deranged, Carole. If you don't stop this nonsense I shall send for the doctor to give you a sleeping draught. Where is Philip?'

'I'm here,' Philip said tying the belt of his housecoat. 'What's going on?'

'Carole's had a funny turn.' Peter turned back to Carole. 'Now do I send for the doctor or not?'

Carole stood up shakily. 'You will not. You will send for Binns to bring my clothes down from the bedroom and then you will send for the carriage. Once I'm dressed,

I'm going to stay with Mama in the lodge. I'm not spending another moment in this house, *ever*.'

Sarah's heart sang hearing this statement. She glanced at Bligh's stony face. At last she would be in soul charge of the household accounts, whether Bligh liked it or not.

16

Although it was November, Ellie was surprised at how busy she was. Relieved at last to be clearing the last of the tables ready to close, her shoulders drooped when she saw Lady Sarah riding over the dunes. *Oh no, please say she hasn't come to plead Lady Carole's cause.* Putting aside the pain of her tired, blistered feet, she put down her tray with trepidation and ran to grab the reins while Lady Sarah dismounted.

'Thank you, Elise. I do hope I am not too late for tea.'

Ellie smiled and bobbed a curtsy. 'Will it be just you, or are others coming?' she asked, scanning Poldhu Hill for other riders.

'No, I'm alone today. Forgive me, I know you're closing, but I'd like afternoon tea for two and I'd very much like you to join me.'

Ellie nodded wearily.

Settling at the table by the window facing the sea, Sarah laid her kid gloves neatly by her table setting and admired the view. She pulled her gaze away from the sea and smiled gently as Ellie approached the table.

'I'm so happy that James bought the Tea Room for you to manage, Elise.'

Ellie nodded. 'I'll be eternally grateful to him,' she answered, placing the cake stand on the table.

When Ellie returned with the tea, she knew Sarah was about to say something about Carole, because she clearly looked uncomfortable. Ellie took a deep breath. *Now keep calm and tell Lady Sarah in no uncertain terms, that you're not to be persuaded to be her brother-in-law's mistress.*

'Elise,' she said grasping her by the hand. 'What can I say? Except that I am truly sorry for my sister-in-law's conduct towards you yesterday. I was appalled when I learnt the nature of your visit, and that Carole sent you away without ordering the carriage for you. It's all too awful and unforgivable. I do hope you will accept my apologies.'

Ellie felt her body relax. 'You have nothing to apologise for, my lady.'

Sarah squeezed Ellie's hand. 'Oh I think I do. Carole's requests and actions, along with my new brother-in-law's expectations of you, have brought our good family name into disrepute. Rest assured I *shall* bring this to my husband's attention.'

Ellie eyed her cautiously. 'Did you really not know?'

Sarah shook her head. 'Believe me, I had no idea. Pray tell me, how did this all come about?'

Very reluctantly Ellie relayed the sorry tale again.

Sarah listened in shocked disbelief. 'I'm appalled at their underhand treatment of you.' She curled her elegant fingers around Ellie's hand. 'Please tell me this will not affect our friendship? I would hate to think that you would feel uncomfortable visiting the manor again. I so enjoyed walking around the garden with you. It's lovely to have someone to speak to who has a love of flowers, as I do. Please tell me you'll come again?'

Ellie's smiled faltered. 'You've always been welcoming, Lady Sarah….'

'Please Elise, call me Sarah, we are friends after all.'

Ellie nodded. 'Then you can call me Ellie.'

'Oh but Elise is such a beautiful name. I'd much rather call you that, if you don't mind?'

Ellie laughed. 'I don't mind at all. As I was about to say, you've always welcomed me, but….' She moistened her lips. 'I'm not sure you are aware but on my visits I've met with unprecedented hostility from several members of your staff.'

Sarah grimaced. 'You mean Lanfear?'

'Among others, yes.'

Sarah sighed, recalling the overheard conversation between Carrington and Bligh about Elise.

'I'm so sorry for that. I shall certainly look into the reason why – unless, you know the reason?'

'Well!' Ellie pondered for a moment. *In for a penny in for a pound.* 'I believe it may be something to do with why my mother and I were banished from Bochym eight years ago.'

'Banished?' Sarah's hand shot to her heart. 'Why?'

'I don't really know. I was only ten at the time. But it was shortly after my father, Thomas Rosevear, who was the old earl's steward, died in an accident on the estate. All I recall of that time was a violent argument between my mother and Mr Lanfear and then later that day, being told of my father's death. Two days later we left Bochym Manor for my father's funeral, and never returned. Betty took us in here, and she told me that Mother was fearful of speaking about it.' Ellie took a deep emotional breath. 'Mother took the eviction very hard - she died a year after my father.

Sarah reeled back in shock. 'I'm so dreadfully sorry, I had no idea. Of course the new steward appointed would have needed your cottage, but… you and your mother should have been given alternative accommodation. She should have received a widow's pension if the accident happened on the estate. I believe that has always been the Dunstan policy.'

'We received nothing,' Ellie answered flatly.

Sarah sat in stunned silence. 'I am so sorry. When did all this occur?'

'Well my father died on the 16th September 1893.'

'I cannot imagine how terribly uncomfortable you must have been when you were invited to visit the manor after all that had happened.'

Ellie laughed. 'Strangely enough, despite being unwelcome to your staff, the manor itself felt friendly - as though it welcomed me back. Sorry, that sounds silly I know.'

Sarah smiled. 'No, I know exactly how you feel. I felt the same about the house when I came to live there, it seemed to embrace me.' Sarah smiled. 'I'm going to find out what happened, Elise. I'll not rest until I have some answers.'

Ellie's lip trembled. 'Thank you, Sarah.'

'Now let's have tea shall we, for there is something else I'd like to speak to you about.'

Ellie tipped her head.

'There has been, how shall I say this...a little bit of upset in the manor since you first visited.'

'Upset?' Ellie raised an eyebrow.

Sarah cleared her throat. 'Perhaps not the right word….shall we say, a disturbance, strange happenings and the like…..of a spiritual kind, if you understand me?'

'Oh, I see….'

'You seem unsurprised?'

Ellie nodded cautiously.

'Did *you* see anything at the manor?'

'Yes. For risk of sounding foolish, I saw Pearl Martin, well the spirit of her at least - she called my name when I walked through your courtyard and then she followed me through the manor.'

'Pearl Martin?'

'Yes, it only came to me last night who she was, because I saw her again yesterday in your library. Pearl was a dairymaid at the manor. She used to look after me when I was little. She was very kind and I remember she used to read to me, I liked her a lot.'

'Do you know what happened to her?'

Ellie twisted her mouth. 'My memory of that time is sketchy but I believe something happened to her that week we were banished….I just can't recall what.' Ellie paused for a moment. 'I do know that Pearl's name was mentioned in the heated argument I told you about between my mother and Lanfear. But strangely enough, I also remember Pearl watching us drive away with my father's funeral carriage - at least I thought it was her.'

'Or, her spirit?'

Ellie shrugged. 'Maybe.'

'Well if it is Pearl, she is quite distressed at the moment

and very disruptive. One of my other maids can see her and she tells me that Pearl nearly wrecked the library when you left yesterday.'

'Oh dear!'

'Jessie and I believe you might have the answer to Pearl's distress. Perhaps you might come back to the manor and see if you can help?'

Ellie must have looked dubious because Sarah added, 'If it's any consolation, Carole is no longer residing at the manor. Our mutual friend, Pearl, scared the living daylights out of her last night.' Sarah paused to smile. 'Carole is residing permanently with the dowager at the lodge, as too will Philip.'

Ellie smiled too. 'Perhaps I will venture back one day then.'

'Good.' Sarah got up from her chair and reached for Ellie's hand. 'I can't imagine the hardship we have caused you. I shall find out why that happened to you Elise, I promise you.'

*

With the bit between her teeth, Sarah summoned Bligh, Carrington and Lanfear to the library. For too long, these older members of staff seemed to be a law unto themselves, to feel free to bully younger staff members and speak disrespectfully to visitors to the manor. Not only that, but they appeared to treat her, the lady of this house, with a degree of contempt. After speaking with Elise, Sarah had had enough and was determined to cut out the rot that had set in over the years. This was going to be a happy household from now on! Sarah relished the job of bringing them down a peg, although they were clearly indignant at being severely reprimanded for their unwelcoming conduct towards visitors - Elise was not mentioned, but they all knew who Sarah meant.

As she dismissed Carrington and Lanfear back to their work, Sarah, much to the displeasure of Bligh, asked to be shown the household accounts.

Still smarting from the reprimand, Bligh was clearly affronted when Sarah then informed her that she wanted to look over the accounts on her own.

It took several volumes of accounts and very dusty work before she came across the one she was looking for. Written in faded ink she saw. *Household Accounts for 1893.*

Sarah flipped the pages of the account ledger until she came to September. The following names were scored from the page

Saturday 16th September – Pearl Martin – Chambermaid – AWOL

Saturday 16th September – Thomas Rosevear – Steward – Deceased - Accident

Saturday 16th September – Ruby Sanders – Chambermaid – Dismissed - Theft

Tuesday 19th September – Rose Rosevear – Stewards wife – Dismissed.

Under the heading, wages due, all were marked *None* and signed by Mrs Bligh.

*

It had been laborious work but Sarah put a bookmark in the account ledger and went in search of Peter.

Not normally one to bother Peter in his study, he looked quite surprised when Sarah breezed in.

'Hello darling. It must be something important, for you to venture into my stuffy study.'

'Sorry darling, I don't mean to disturb you.'

'You're not.'

She placed the account book down in front of him and kissed the top of his head.

'You look like you've been rummaging in the attic. You have dust in your hair.'

She smiled, patted her hair and sat down.

'I understand you've been asserting your authority.'

Sarah's smile faded. 'Why, who has complained?'

Peter laughed. 'No one darling, I don't think they dare. I was listening at the library door. Well done, but what prompted it?'

'I went to see my friend, Elise Rosevear this morning at Poldhu, to apologise for Carole and Philip's behaviour towards her.'

Peter raised his eyebrows.

'Apparently they tried to set Elise up as Philip's mistress!'

'What?'

'Apparently Carole and Philip tried to set Elise up as Philip's mistress!'

'What?'

Sarah took a deep breath and told Peter about Philip and Carole's unscrupulous plan.

Peter shook his head in astonishment.

'I know she's your sister, but I find the way she and Philip have treated Elise is totally unacceptable. Also for Carole to bring Elise here yesterday under false pretences, and then send her home without a carriage when refused to conform to debauched plan, is frankly despicable and not fitting as to how we want our family to be portrayed.'

Peter's nostrils flared angrily. It was times like this that Carole reminded him of their father. Thankfully he did not share their unpleasant traits. 'Rest assured Sarah, I *will* speak to her. Did your friend accept the apology?'

'She did, thank goodness, but Peter, she told me something quite alarming. Did you know her family used to work here? Her father was your father's steward.'

'I do, he met with an unfortunate accident I believe a few days before my father died!'

'Do you know why Elise and her mother were banished, without warning or financial recompense?'

Peter leaned back and steepled his fingers. 'From what I understand from Carrington, my father dismissed Mrs Rosevear for defamation of character, though in truth I always thought she was the sweetest of women - she used to feed me warm scones and homemade jam.' He smiled at the memory. 'So that's all I know. Father died a few days later and by the time I came home from university to deal with his death and appoint a new steward, the Rosevears had gone. The whole affair was over.'

'Well apparently some of our staff think otherwise. Three of them have been unforgivably cruel in their behaviour towards Elise. My goodness, she was only ten when it happened!'

'Ha! Hence the reprimand?'

'Yes.'

Peter glanced at the ledger on his desk. 'I'm curious, why have you brought this to me?'

'Well I was looking to see if anything was said about the Rosevears and I came across these names. Do you remember two maids, called Pearl and Ruby? Look, here they are listed in this ledger.'

He smiled broadly. 'I do actually. They both resided in the attic, affectionately renamed the jewellery box, because of their names. Though to be truthful, it was only Pearl who shone like a diamond. Ruby was lovely but was overshadowed by Pearl when it came to looks, but from what I recall they were great friends. What of them?'

'Well look at the entry for this particular week in September 1893. It's the same week your father died. Not only did the Rosevear's troubles start, but Pearl went missing and Ruby was dismissed. Do you know what happened?'

He leant over for a closer look. 'To tell you the truth, I don't. As I said I had a lot to deal with that week, and never gave them another thought. In those days staff came and went and were replaced. I haven't thought of Ruby and Pearl for years.'

Sarah sighed. 'I wonder why Ruby was dismissed.'

'Why do you want to know?'

'I'm just curious that's all.' Sarah knew Peter was annoyed about the previous night's escapade with Carole, and suspected that to mention Pearl was now their resident ghost probably wouldn't go down too well at the moment.

'I suggest you ask Mrs Bligh, darling. She made the entries.'

*

The air in the room was thick with anticipation as Sarah confronted Bligh.

'I don't remember. It was a long time ago.' Bligh remained stony-faced through the interview.

'Oh come, come, Mrs Bligh, we all know *you* forget nothing! I shall not leave this room until you tell me why Pearl left, and the reason you dismissed her friend Ruby,' Sarah said, settling herself in the chair behind Bligh's desk.

*

Mr Carrington set a cup of strong sweet tea down in front of Mrs Bligh.

'Damn her for her meddling. I had to tell her about Ruby, John. She wouldn't have left my room until I did.'

'Don't worry yourself, Joan. Ruby Sanders will have left the county years ago, if she knows what's good for her.'

'I hope you're right. I don't like it, John. Lady Sarah is stirring up old bones, if you'll excuse the turn of phrase.'

'What did you say about Pearl?'

'Just that she'd gone missing, of course.'

17

Guy Blackthorn dressed in his best clothes. His curly hair had been rinsed under the hand pump that morning and it now shone like jet in the morning light. Clean shaven, he stood by the cracked mirror in his bedroom to adjust his scarlet neckerchief before peeking out of the window. Light rain was falling, but nothing could dampen his spirits. Ellie had invited him to tea.

Nellie glowered as he grabbed his coat from the hook. 'I know where you're going. Silas saw your letter.'

'It's not a secret, Ma.'

'You'd do better to stay away from her. She may have played the innocent card over the Goldsworthy affair, but mud sticks and you'll be tainted by association.'

Guy sighed heavily. 'Goodbye, Ma.' He kissed her soft cheek. 'I'll be back before dark.'

'Bring us some cake back, Guy.'

'I'll try my best, Silas.'

*

The view of Poldhu Cove as Guy steered his horse and wagon down the hill, never failed to take his breath away. Even on a day like this, with fine rain drifting across the dunes, the sight of the sea would lift any heart - as if his heart could lift more! He pulled Mazie to a halt, jumped down and gave her a drink and feed before checking his fob watch - he was a little early, but he was sure Ellie would not mind. Running his fingers nervously through his hair, he undid all the good he'd done with a comb earlier that day.

Ellie was returning from the beach as he walked to the terrace.

She clutched her skirt with one hand and waved happily with the other on seeing Guy.

'I'm a little early, sorry.'

Ellie reached out and gently touched his arm. 'No its fine, I'm so glad you could come. Let's go inside. I'm afraid I'm not properly dressed for tea yet.'

With the wind in her hair and her clothes ruffled by the salty breeze, he smiled. 'You look just fine to me. Has it been a good day for collecting?'

'It has! Look!' She rummaged in her pocket and produced her treasure.

'Excellent, you can put it with the others now.' He produced the vase of sea glass she'd left at Primrose Cottage from his bag. 'I found it when I was looking for you that morning - I suspect it was too heavy to carry……' He paused when he saw the pained look on her face. 'What's the matter?'

'Oh Guy, I left it because Philip gave most of them to me.'

'Philip?'

'Yes. He'd leave them on my garden rocks for me to find.'

Guy shook his head. 'I can assure you, Philip has never left you sea glass.' He cleared his throat. 'It was me. I left them for you. I wanted to give them to you in person, but Philip always had some expensive trinket to offer you, I always felt my gift paled into insignificance.'

Ellie felt her shoulders droop and gratefully took the vase from him. 'I have been so misled by Philip, haven't I?'

Guy took a seat by the window while Ellie tidied herself up. 'Right, she said emerging from the curtain. 'I think tea is in order.'

As always Ellie had made a wonderful selection of cakes and sandwiches. 'I hope you like this. It's to say thank you, Guy.'

'For what?'

'For being my saviour, that's what. I found out last week that it was you, not Philip, who pulled me from the sea.' She shuddered at the mention of his name. 'He let me believe he'd done it.'

Guy shrugged his shoulders.

'So thank you, Guy. Thank you for saving my life and for offering to help me out of my predicament. I'm sorry I fled Gweek without letting you know where I'd gone to. James told me how worried you were.'

'Please don't apologise for leaving Gweek. You knew what you needed to do. As for the incident in the sea, well, I was just so grateful I'd seen you fall and got to you in time. I'm also glad you've settled back here now. It pained me to see Philip treat you so unworthily.'

Ellie nodded sadly as she filled the cups. It still pained her too. 'We've never really chatted before, have we?'

Guy shook his head. 'You only had eyes for Philip,' he said softly.

'Then I was a fool.'

'I've told you before. You're nobody's fool, Ellie. May I?' He reached for a sandwich.

As the afternoon wore on, Ellie urged Guy to tell her all about his work as a Thatcher. As he spoke in his soft melodic voice, his lovely kind eyes twinkled gently. Ellie felt she could listen to him all day long. When the day cleared slightly, they took a walk on the beach, and then all too soon it was time for him to leave - neither wanting the day to be over.

Ellie pressed a parcel of sandwiches and cake for him to take home.

'My brother will be thrilled with these.'

'I met your brother Silas when I was in Gweek. He was one of the few people who would pass the time of day with me……though I suspect it was the lure of scone and jam.' She grinned. 'Say hello to your ma for me too. I know she's not too fond of me, but hopefully a slice of cake may make her like me a little more.'

'Thank you, Ellie. I don't believe I've ever spent a more enjoyable day.'

'Well I hope you'll come again soon. You're always welcome.'

'Thank you, I'd like that.'

There was a moment where he was not sure if he should kiss her lightly on the cheek. He wanted to, but something stopped him. It was enough just to have her close to him.

Ellie stroked Mazie as he climbed aboard. 'Bye, Ellie. Thank you again.'

'It was my pleasure.' She waved as the wagon moved away over the bridge and then she climbed the sand dune to watch as he slowly made his way up the steep hill out of Poldhu. She smiled broadly, feeling happy for the first time in many weeks.

The Tea Room felt a little lonely as she cleared away the tea tray. As the evening slowly began to drift across the cliff tops, Ellie made to close the curtains and lock up for the day. Suddenly a furious banging came upon the door. Startled, Ellie ran to turn the key in the lock, but Philip burst through the door and into the room.

Ellie watched fearfully. His anger seemed to fill the room as he paced up and down.

'I see you've been entertaining a guest, even though you're supposed to be closed on Sunday afternoon.'

'What do you want Philip?' She was annoyed that her voice wavered slightly.

'I thought I'd come and see for myself why you changed your mind about me, and now I know. I should have known better than to purchase a cottage next door to Guy Blackthorn. I bet as soon as I'd gone to Europe, he was round baying for your attention, wasn't he?' He stepped forward menacingly. 'You belong to me and if you think I'm going to let some low born Thatcher whisk you away from under my nose, you are very much mistaken. I've invested a lot of time and money in you. Now, let's start again shall we?'

Ellie grasped the top of a chair and tried desperately to still her hammering heart. *Remember, bullies only win if they think they can control you.* 'I belong to nobody,' she said through gritted teeth. 'I'll thank you to leave my premises,

Philip Goldsworthy, otherwise I will lodge a complaint of harassment with the constable tomorrow.'

'Don't be absurd.'

Ellie stood her ground, despite her knees turning to jelly. She stared icily at the man she used to love, seeing him for what he really was. 'If you do not leave within the minute there will also be a charge of trespassing on my property.'

'It isn't your property.'

'The Tea Room was purchased for me by James Blackwell. I run this establishment in a managerial role. You *are* trespassing.'

'And what's Blackwell after, I wonder?' he chided.

'Not all people are as conniving as you,' Ellie snapped.

Philip gave a short derisive snort.

'I'm sure James will be very interested to know that you came harassing me after dark.'

Philip regarded her for a moment before his face softened. 'Ellie.' He stepped towards her, but she stepped back. 'How have we come to this? We've never had harsh words before. Come on, we can settle everything.'

Through the narrow aperture of her lips she hissed, 'Go back to your wife, Philip. You deserve each other.'

His eyes narrowed. 'You promised me you'd be mine forever.'

'That was before I knew what a scoundrel you were.' She opened the door for him to leave.

'This is not over,' he snarled as he left.

When the door shut, Ellie fumbled with the key to lock the door. Tonight she'd sleep in her old cot in the Tea Room. Her courage having left her, she dared not venture out to her cottage.

*

It was purely by chance that Sarah met with Guy the following week. She'd ridden over the hills from Bochym down to Church Cove, passed the time of day with the tenant Farmer at Winnianton Farm, Gunwalloe, and was on her way to visit the church which was tucked into the hillside. Although Cury Church was the Dunstan's place of worship, St Winwaloe's Church, also known as The Church of the Storms, due to its exposed location on this windswept coast, always felt wild and romantic to Sarah. She'd been lucky that day, the bell ringers were practising for a wedding and the cheerful tune rang out across the dunes.

'Good morning to you, Lady Sarah, what a fine morning for a ride.'

Sarah turned to see Guy walking along the beach. Noting his wet hair she held her hand to her chest. 'Goodness have you been in the sea? It's the first of December tomorrow! Is it not freezing in there?'

'A little, but I do like to swim.'

'I thought you always swam at Poldhu?'

'I do, but I don't have time to go over today.'

'That's a pity. I understand from Elise you took tea there last week.' Sarah noted the twinkle in his eyes at the mention of her name. 'You like Elise, don't you?'

'I cannot tell a lie, yes I do.'

'Have you told her?'

Guy just smiled but said nothing.

'Have you been back since?'

He shook his head. 'I don't want to impose.'

'I am sure a visit from you would not be an imposition. Elise was very animated about your last visit.' Sarah watched his reaction. *It would be nice to bring these two young people together*. 'I have three bags of rich soil which I think will help Elise with her garden. I understand she's struggling to grow things in her sandy soil. I know it's perhaps a little out of your way, but if at all possible, could you find time to come and pick them up and take them to her?'

Guy's face lit up. 'I'd be more than happy to. I remember being with my pa when he collected some good rich top soil from Bochym. He was always a keen gardener.'

'So, you've been coming to the manor for a lot of years then.'

Guy nodded. 'I helped my pa thatch some of the cottages on the estate.'

Sarah paused for a moment. 'Guy, you don't remember a young girl at the manor called Ruby Sanders do you?'

'I do yes,' he answered cagily.

'You don't happen to know where she is now, do you?'

'I'm afraid I don't,' he lied. He did know where Ruby was - she was a bar maid down at the Cadgwith Arms, but he had his reasons to keep that information private. 'Begging your pardon, my lady, but why are you enquiring?'

Realising that Guy was hiding something from her, she said, 'I found an entry in a ledger. It stated that she was dismissed a few days after her friend Pearl went missing, I'd just like to speak to her about what happened. Elise and her mother were also dismissed at the same time, shortly after Elise's father died in our employment. I believe something very untoward happened that week, and I would really like to get to the bottom of it.'

Guy pressed his lips together but remained silent.

'If you do ever hear of her whereabouts, rest assured, she has nothing to fear from me.'

'Yes, my lady,' Guy answered sheepishly.

He watched as Sarah gathered the reins. 'When you come for the soil, ask for me or Richard the gardener.'

'I'll come next Monday.'

Sarah nodded. 'Goodbye then.'

Guy felt an uneasy stir in his stomach. He'd warn Ruby when next he was in Cadgwith. He didn't know the reason why she'd been dismissed. He just knew she was fearful of speaking of it but adamant that she had done no wrong.

*

December unfolded in a whirl of mist and chilly breezes. The weather however, did not deter Guy from collecting the soil from Bochym the following Monday. He suspected Lady Sarah was matchmaking, and wasn't going to miss an opportunity to see Ellie. Knowing Ellie took the wagon to Helston on a Monday morning, he waited until the afternoon to deliver the soil.

'I know it's not the weather for gardening, but Lady Sarah sent this good topsoil for you,' he told her.

Overjoyed, Ellie clasped her hands together. 'How kind of her.'

'If you don't mind getting soaked through with this mist, we can dig it in now if you want?' he offered.

They laboured for over two hours, by which time the mist had cleared and the wintery sun was warming their backs.

Guy brought more rocks from the beach and built up the small retaining wall around the garden. 'There, I can't guarantee an abundance of flowers like those at Bochym, but it will give a little more sustenance to your sandy soil. Sarah sent these lily bulbs down for you too.'

'Oh lovely. I'll send a note of thanks to her.' Ellie had only seen Sarah briefly last week when she'd called to tell her what she'd gleaned about her mother's banishment. She was still reeling from learning that her mother had threatened to bring the earls name into disrepute.

'Sarah seems quite busy at the moment, having taken over the running of the manor from Carole. Apparently Carole and Philip have moved out and are residing in the lodge.'

'So I understand.'

'You'll never guess why, Sarah tells me Carole was spooked by a ghost!' He laughed heartily. 'Can you believe that? She refuses to return until an exorcism has been carried out. Sarah and Peter have point blank refused so they are in stalemate at the moment.' A broad smile swept across Guy's face. 'By all accounts Philip is furious. I think he liked to lord it up at the manor, but it seems all his well laid plans are falling around his ears.'

They glanced at each other sharing a secret little smile.

With the day clearing, Ellie invited Guy to eat with her on the terrace. So, wrapped in their warmest clothing, they feasted on mackerel, caught and landed that morning at Mullion, which Ellie had fried in butter and served with hunks of fresh baked bread.

'A feast for any table,' she said placing the plate down with a flurry.

There was a familiar easiness growing between them - a joint friendship that both parties enjoyed. Guy would have liked there to be more to the relationship, but until Ellie could move on from what Philip had done, he was content just to be in her company.

With the meal finished, and the day brightening by the hour, Ellie walked Guy to his wagon.

'Are you going far?'

'Only up the road to Cury.' He looked up - the sky was the clearest blue now, not a cloud in the sky meant the day would turn cold as night fell. 'There'll be no moon tonight, so the night sky will be something to behold I think.'

'I shall look out tonight, now you've told me.'

'Good bye, Ellie, thank you.'

Ellie waved him off, feeling a warm glow despite the chill of the day. 'Goodbye Guy, please come back soon,' she whispered on the breeze.

As Guy's wagon trundled up Poldhu hill, he must have known she was watching him, because he turned and raised his hand to wave.

Ellie felt a strange emptiness at his departure. Perhaps her damaged heart was mending at last. This time she would choose the right man.

*

Later that night as Ellie sat by the lamp light working on her lace, she heard the soft melodic sound of a flute. She opened the door and her eyes were drawn up to the starry night sky. Pulling her warm coat on, she stepped off the terrace and walked to the sand dunes, where the music was coming from. It was the most perfect sound on a night such as this.

The music stopped suddenly. 'Hello, Ellie,' Guy said as he saw her silhouette standing there. 'Forgive me, as it's late I didn't want to knock and frighten you, so I let my flute call you. It's such a splendid night you see - I wanted to share it with you.'

As Ellie lifted her skirts to climb the dune, Guy scrambled to his feet to help her.

His hand felt wonderful in hers, but she consciously pulled away. 'I didn't know you could play the flute. It sounded lovely.'

'I can't read music. I normally just play whatever tune comes to mind, I'm glad you liked it.'

The night was crisp and cold and Ellie could see Guy's breath as he invited her to sit on his rug. Pulling her knees to her chest she looked up into the sky. Guy settled beside her and they sat for a long time, silently watching the stars.

When Guy saw Ellie ease the stiffness out of her neck, he beckoned her to lie beside him. 'It's so much better to watch if you lay down.'

Tentatively she did, and soon they became at one with nature, listening to the gentle lapping waves embrace the beach below, and losing themselves in the great vault of stars above.

'It's so vast you cannot really comprehend what is up there, can you?' he whispered.

Ellie sighed. 'I admit, sometimes it's too much for me to take in.'

'It's fascinating - I love it, just as I love Mother Nature. There's not a day goes by when I don't see something wonderful in the world we live in.'

Ellie smiled. She loved Guy's spirited approach to life.

'Look, Ellie, a shooting star. Quick make a wish.'

Before she could think of one, another jet of light skimmed right across the sky.

'There's one for you now.'

They laughed as another flashed across the sky. In their excitement, her hand fell on Guy's hand and he curled his fingers around it. She felt her heartbeat accelerate and shivered at the intimacy.

'Are you cold?' He squeezed her hand tighter.

'No, I'm fine.' This time she did not pull away from his hand, but closed her eyes, briefly enjoying the moment. She was happy tonight - really happy. Life felt so much better when she had someone to share it with.

Eventually they both suppressed a yawn. They knew it was time to move, though neither wanted the magic to end. This was a night they would remember - a night when something had shifted in their tender relationship.

As Guy helped Ellie to her feet, she shook out her skirt as he picked up the rug. They took one more look at the sky and made their way back to Guy's wagon.

Mazie whinnied as they approached.

'Poor old girl, you thought you were finished for the night didn't you,' he said, patting her.

'Well you could sleep in the wagon here.'

'I could.' He laughed gently. 'But I won't. It wouldn't do for my wagon to be seen here all night.'

'Well its one a.m. already. I might have to demand you marry me to save my reputation,' she joked shyly.

'Well Ellie, I might just do that,' he answered in all seriousness.

Ellie felt a tingle down her spine. 'Come and play the flute for me again one night,' she said softly.

'I will, in fact the tune you heard was one I made up for you. It's called Ellie's Smile.'

'Oh how lovely.'

'Good night, sweet Ellie.' He reached for her hand and pressed a kiss into her palm.

As Ellie walked on air back to her cottage, locking the

door behind her, Philip Goldsworthy climbed back into his carriage which was hidden secretly on the hill behind the Tea Room. He'd seen enough for now. It was time to put a stop to Guy's meddling. He waited a few minutes then hit his cane on the roof to tell his driver to head home.

18

On Saturday 15th December 1901, the Tea Room buzzed with exciting news from their very own cove. Alan and Angie, morning regulars, sat huddled round the newspaper with their good friend Sally, to read the newspaper. Three days earlier, on the 12th December, Guglielmo Marconi had received the first trans-Atlantic radio signal, sent 1,700 miles from Poldhu in Cornwall, to Signal Hill, St. John's in Newfoundland in Canada. Exciting though the news was, no one realised just how significant this breakthrough would be to the world!

*

While Guy was working in Cury, he took the opportunity to breakfast with Ellie on Mondays before she took the wagon to Helston. The week before Christmas, whilst en route to Poldhu, a horse and rider passed him at speed, came to a halt at the bridge and tossed a hessian sack into the stream. Guy tutted loudly, a sack in the stream meant only one thing, puppies or kittens or god forbid, an unwanted baby! As the rider set off, again at speed, Guy jumped from his wagon and ran as fast as he could to the bridge, waded into the freezing stream and retrieved the sack from the water. Quickly undoing the string, he released two squirming puppies and three dead ones. He sighed heavily. He knew times were hard and unwanted animals could not be fed, but he wished these people would find a more humane way to dispose of them. The puppies were cross bred with a collie and by the look of their ears, a spaniel. Guy suspected they were probably only six weeks old. The mother dog must have hidden them for them to reach this age. He picked up the first one and rubbed its belly in case any residue water had got into its lungs, the second one was crawling about squeaking pitifully, so he concentrated on the one in hand. As soon as that one squeaked, he popped them both into his own bag. The dead puppies he could do nothing for.

Without a shovel he could not bury them, so he tied the bag tight and scraped the muddy bank with a sharp stone, dropped them in the hole and covered them with more stones. Knowing the puppies would need milk, he set off across the dunes to Ellie. He found her working, as always, in her sea garden.

Her smile lit her face on seeing Guy, and as always, this settled on his heart like nothing else could.

'Hello,' she said shyly. 'I'll just clear my things and then we'll have breakfast.' She heard a squeak coming from his bag and gave him a questioning look.

'Ellie, I need a favour before breakfast.'

'Oh'. She said cautiously.

'May I beg some milk from you?' He opened his bag and two squeaking puppies popped their heads out. 'I have two orphans in dire need of sustenance.'

Ellie clapped her hands in delight as she reached out for them. 'Oh bless them, wherever did you get them? They're not even weaned yet.'

'They've just been dumped in the stream. God knows, I don't want a dog, but what can I do?'

Ellie was smothering the pups in kisses and Guy watched in delight.

'How old are they?' she asked snuggling them into her neck.

'Around six or seven weeks I think.'

'You'll have to leave the poor things with me until they're weaned I suppose.'

Guy relaxed. 'Thank you, Ellie, I'd really appreciate that.'

She laughed as one tried to lick her face. 'You must come back for them though Guy,' she warned. 'I've always been a little nervous of dogs. I definitely never wanted one.'

'You'd never know to look at you.' He grinned. 'But yes, I promise I'll take them both back when the time comes.'

'Come on then little ones - let's get you settled somewhere warm.'

*

On Saturday 22nd December, Guy called early in the morning. He was en route to Cadgwith to quote for a new roof, and promised Ellie he'd return later that day to collect the puppies now that they had weaned.

The Tea Room was incredibly busy that weekend. Visitors to the Poldhu Hotel had heard about her delicious cakes and left their spectacular location for an equally spectacular tea. It was a lot for Ellie to do on her own, but she managed admirably.

James Blackwell was down from London with two friends and they all occupied the best table on the terrace.

James, seeing how busy she was, left his friends periodically to help Ellie.

'Thank you,' she mouthed every time he came back for more trays.

'You're welcome. Maybe you need to get some help in soon.'

'I can manage normally,' she said in her defence.

'I know, I know,' James said holding his hands up. 'I'm just saying. This is as busy as I've ever seen it. It's all credit to you, Ellie, for making this business a success, but don't run yourself into the ground. Think about getting some help.'

*

By four p.m. Ellie was exhausted. She put the 'closed' sign on the door and went to see to the puppies. As tired as she was the puppies were a constant source of joy and trouble in equal measure. By the time Guy returned later that day as promised, despite herself, she'd set her heart on keeping one of them. Philip had once told her that he had a fear of dogs, so it would be a perfect deterrent to keep him away, should he ever come bothering her again.

Guy looked tired when she handed him a cup of tea and piece of cake. He looked deep into her eyes and smiled and Ellie felt her heart miss a beat.

'Ellie, what are you doing for Christmas?'

'Sleeping,' she joked.

He grinned. 'That's a very good idea. What about Christmas Day though.'

'I've nothing planned. What about you?'

'I've to go home naturally to Ma, but I was thinking you could come too. I could pick you up on Christmas Eve and you can stay with us.'

Ellie raised her eyebrows. 'And what would your ma say about that?'

'She's fine, now that all that misunderstanding has been cleared up.'

Ellie was unsure. 'Do you have room for me to stay?'

'I'll bunk down with Silas. He won't like it of course.' He grinned. 'But when I tell him you're coming, I think the promise of cake may sway him.' He reached for her hand. 'Say yes, Ellie. I don't want to spend Christmas without you.'

The thought of spending Christmas alone didn't actually appeal to Ellie either, though she knew Betty would probably invite her to join her at her sister's. Christmas with Guy did rather appeal. With a dazzling smile she said, 'Well, yes then Guy, I'd love to, as long as your ma doesn't mind.'

Guy's joy was palpable. 'That's wonderful, Ellie.' He reached out and cupped her hand softly. 'We're going to have the best Christmas ever.'

Yes Guy, I think we are.

Guy finished his cake and drained his teacup. 'I'll have to go now,' he said very reluctantly. 'Come on little fellas.' He called the puppies to him.

'Guy, would you mind awfully if I kept this one?' Ellie asked hopefully. 'I've rather fallen in love with him. I've called him Brandy.'

'Thank you. It would be a weight off my mind if you would keep him!' Guy tickled the other's ears. 'Well, I'm going to call this one Blue because of his bluish tinge to his coat.' He looped a choker rope around his neck. 'Say goodbye to your brother. Thanks again for looking after them, Ellie.'

'It's been a pleasure,' Ellie said, feeling a small pang of sadness at seeing Blue go as well.

'I'll come back for you and Brandy on Christmas Eve around about midday.'

'I shall bake a very special cake for you all.'

Guy leaned forward and kissed her lightly on the cheek. 'Until then.' His eyes twinkled with joy.

*

Lady Sarah dismounted her horse at Poldhu and pulled the bag from her saddle. That morning she'd collected a bundle of laurel, ivy and holly together and weaved and teased the leaves into a beautiful Christmas wreath for the front door of the manor. Having found that she had plenty over, she decided to make one for Ellie, to adorn the Tea Room door.

She swept through the door, a waft of expensive perfume preceding her. 'I'm here for a moment of sanctuary before I host a dinner tonight. We've invited James Blackwell and his friends, who are always great company. Unfortunately, Philip and Carole will be joining us. I had hoped Carole's unease at the manor would keep them away, but alas, no. Though I'm not too sure what the atmosphere will be like when James sits down with Philip.' Sarah raised her eyebrows. 'They've never been the best of friends and this matter between you and Philip seems to have stirred up animosity between them. Hopefully Peter will keep the peace between them.' She took off her riding coat and hung it on the peg behind the door.

'Here you are, Elise, I've made you something.' Sarah handed the bag over to Ellie.

Ellie pulled the wreath from its hessian bag with delight. 'Ouch!' She sucked the pin prick of blood from her finger.

'My apologies, Elise, it's an occupational hazard handling Christmas wreaths I'm afraid. My own fingers and forearms are like pin cushions at the moment.' She smiled gently.

'No matter, it's lovely, thank you.' Ellie grabbed some twine from the drawer and tied it to her front door knocker.

Sarah watched with amusement. There was something very different about Elise today- she radiated happiness. 'You look like the cat that got the cream,' Sarah said as she settled herself at the table by the window.

Ellie admired the wreath on the door and then came to sit beside Sarah, excited to share her Christmas plans with her.

This was music to Sarah's ears. It seemed these two young people were beginning to find each other at last. 'Guy is a lovely man, is he not?'

'He is and very kind.' Ellie's eyes shone at the thought of him.

Sharing her joy, she said, 'I do believe you'll have a wonderful time.'

'Now, they are my plans, let me bring some tea and you can tell me your plans for Christmas at the manor.'

*

Nellie stilled from her kneading and put her floury hands on her hips. 'You've done what?'

'I've invited Ellie for Christmas and don't look like that,' he said in response to Nellie pursed lips. 'Ellie and I are friends, more than friends really, but I want to take things slowly. I'd like her to be my wife one day, so I want to invite her here, to meet all my family.'

Nellie didn't respond, she just looked down at Silas on all fours playing noisily with Blue. 'Where has that dog come from? Get it out of my kitchen.'

Guy look puzzled. 'I've just brought him home with me, you saw me bring him in! I found him and another almost drowned in the stream at Poldhu! Ellie's been weaning them for me. Don't you remember me telling you?'

Nellie looked flustered. 'Of course I remember. I still don't want it in my kitchen.'

'So it's alright about Ellie coming?'

'Coming where?'

'Here, for Christmas!' Guy shook his head in despair.

'Don't raise your voice to me. You're not too old to feel the back of my hand.'

Guy lifted his hands in bewilderment. He looked to Silas who just shrugged his shoulders.

'Come on, Blue, let's get you settled outside.'

'Aww can't he sleep with me,' Silas moaned. 'It's cold outside.'

'He's a dog - he'll not feel the cold!'

Silas followed Guy into the back shed.

'Is Ma alright?' Guy asked as he settled the dog on a bed of old thatch.

Silas shrugged again. 'Where is Ellie going to sleep?' he said with a cheeky grin.

'In my room, of course.'

Silas's mouth dropped open. 'Ma won't like that.'

'She'll be alone. I'm sleeping with you.'

'Oh no.' His face dropped.

'Hey, you're not my ideal bedroom companion either.'

Silas thumped his brother playfully.

'There is one consolation, Silas, she'll bring cake.'

'It'll have to be bloody good cake,' he said flatly.

'Come on let's get back inside.'

As they rounded the front of the house, Guy bid goodnight to Harry Yates who was out walking his terrier.

*

There were eight for dinner that night at Bochym. Sarah, Peter, Lucinda - the dowager countess - Philip, Carole, James Blackwell and his two friends Glen and Gerald. There had been a noticeable coolness between James and Philip whilst partaking of pre-dinner drinks, this being the first time the men had met since James had bought the Tea Room for Ellie. Unfriendly looks had been exchanged but thankfully nothing yet had materialised.

Although Sarah had not known James as long as her husband had, she was confident that he would not willingly cause any upset around the dinner table. However Philip, she noted, seemed to be spoiling for a fight.

At seven p.m. they all made their way into the French drawing room, which was laid out with Bochym's finest new table wear. Since Carole's departure from the manor, Sarah had purchased a brand new dinner service, much more in keeping with the style of the manor. Carole of course, did not approve. This was just one of many changes Sarah had decided she'd make to the manor. Another was reinstating Jessie as her lady's maid in the New Year. It was ridiculous that Susan Binns was expected to run between the manor and the lodge to see to both ladies.

As they took their seats, Sarah watched Carole nervously looking about her. Sarah smiled inwardly. Having been spooked once Carole would have died of fright if she could see the figure standing in the corner of the room.

The meal consisted of a beef consommé, roast duck and partridge pie with root vegetables followed by syllabub, custards and mince tarts. The conversation was light, and most of the party wanted to know about the new novel James was writing, having just returned from France to research it.

Eventually the ladies retired to the Jacobean drawing room, while the port and cigars were handed around the dinner table. On leaving, Sarah shot Peter a 'don't let Philip start anything' look.

Philip's eyes held a malicious glean, as he leant back on his chair and yawned noisily. 'With all your time taken up novel writing, James, I'm surprised you found the time to acquire a business!' he said tartly.

James took a long measured breath. 'There is always time to go into business when the right one comes along.'

Philip regarded him reproachfully. 'I wouldn't have thought a *Tea Room* was your kind of thing.' He drained his second glass of port in addition to the six glasses of claret previously consumed.

'That's because you know nothing of me.' James raised his glass to sip his fine ruby port.

'I know you saw a pretty woman in Ellie,' he said under his breath.

James's eyes narrowed. 'I beg your pardon?'

The table silenced, waiting to see if this conversation would turn unpleasant. The circumstances of his acquisition of the Tea Room were known to James's friends. It was unsurprising to them. James had a good heart. He had wealth and liked to use his money to help others in need. Only last year he chose to help his local postman, who'd had the misfortune to trip and fall under the wheels of a horse drawn carriage, crushing his left leg. The injuries which ensued ended the poor man's ability to do his postal job. James decided to put the money up to buy a small premises in Gunwalloe to set him up as a cobbler. It was not the hardest of trades to master, and with the next nearest cobbler being in Helston, the man had never looked back.

'Hold your tongue Philip.' Peter gave him a warning look.

Philip shrugged his shoulders indignantly. 'I'm only saying, that it's obvious what his game is, Peter. I mean, why else would he pay out all that money, unless….' He left the question unfinished.

'I saw her potential as someone competent to make a business a success, yes.' James said with a note of exasperation.

'Humph, a likely story.'

Refusing to be perturbed, he answered in a low, calm voice. 'You really are a disagreeable character, Philip. You seem to judge everyone by your own standards.'

'Disagreeable?' Philip thumped his fist on the table. 'You come into our house and dare to call me disagreeable?'

Peter sat back to observe the situation. He knew he should stop this, but it was time Philip was brought down a peg or two and he suspected that James was the man to do it.

James shot a quick glance at Peter, who gave him a slight nod of approval. He sat back and folded his arms, confident now that what he was about to say would not constitute as speaking out of line in his host's house.

'I do indeed call you disagreeable. I came here as a dinner guest of Peter and Sarah, and I don't expect to be charged with some misdemeanour that you seem to have got into your head. I might also tell you that I, and everyone around this table, know of your indiscretions towards that poor woman. I suggest you stop acting like a petulant child who hasn't got his own way with her and be thankful that Ellie has found her footing again, after you so casually tripped her up.'

Philip flushed. 'Are you going to allow him to speak to your brother-in-law like this, Peter?'

'I am, yes,' Peter replied tersely.

Philip flared his nostrils and reached for the decanter, but Peter took it from his grasp.

'I think you've had enough, Philip.'

Philip sat back in astonishment. 'Not only do you refuse to defend me, but also your hospitality?'

'That's about the measure of it, yes.' Peter nodded.

The corner of his lip twisted. 'Well that's damned unfriendly of you.' He sat back in a sulk, tapping his fingers with agitation. Eventually his head cooled as he watched as the rest of the table enjoyed a drink and a laugh. He was not insensible as to where his bread was buttered, and causing bad feeling between himself and Peter was probably not the thing to do. He leant forward towards Peter. 'I apologise, you're right, I've had too much to drink.'

'It isn't me you need to apologise to,' Peter answered pouring himself another port and turning away.

*

The three ladies of the group sat around a roaring fire, their skirts spread out across the settees and hands settled gently on their laps while the maid served tea and coffee.

'Tell me Sarah, why are your arms scratched and raw? I was looking at them earlier and thought them quite frightful,' Carole said in amusement. 'I do believe she looks like a ruffian who's been hiding in the bushes, Mama, don't you agree?'

Lucinda, the Dowager Countess let her eyes rest on Sarah's exposed forearms and raised her eyebrows enquiringly.

Folding them closer to her chest to hide her injuries, Sarah answered in her defence, 'I was making three holly wreaths. I've made one for the manor, one for you, which I will bring down to the lodge tomorrow, and the other I took down to Elise at the Tea Room earlier today.'

Carole snorted in a very unladylike way. 'Well I suppose it's the only Christmas cheer the silly woman will get this year. If she'd have stayed in Gweek where Philip put her, she'd have enjoyed a bountiful Christmas like the rest of us.'

Sarah gave a ghost of a smile. 'Rest assured, Elise is going to Gweek.'

'Really?' Carole's attention was peaked. 'Oh please tell me she's seen sense at last?'

'Yes, she's made a very sensible decision to spend Christmas with Guy Blackthorn - Philip's best man!'

'I beg your pardon?'

'I'm so pleased that Elise has found a real friend in Guy – someone she can rely on and *trust*.'

Carole scowled. 'Well there is no accounting for taste there then.'

'Oh I think Elise has got the measure of men now and I for one, hope that the relationship develops over the Christmas festivities.'

Carole's nostrils flared as she turned her head towards the flames of the fire.

Lucinda placed her tea cup in her saucer and demanded, 'Who are we talking about?'

'Elise Rosevear.'

'Do I know her?'

'Elise and her parents used to live on the estate!' Sarah offered.

Lucinda and Carole turned to Sarah and said in unison. 'Did they?'

'Yes, Lucinda, you must remember them,' Sarah pressed. 'Thomas Rosevear was your late husband's steward!'

Lucinda tipped her head and searched the depths of her mind. 'Mmm, now you mention it, I do recall Rosevear. The poor man slipped on something in the rear courtyard. Hit his head and died almost instantly, am I right?'

'Yes and his widow and child were dismissed shortly afterwards by your husband,' Sarah said flatly.

'Were they, why?'

Sarah felt her heart race. 'Do you really not know?'

'No, my dear, I'm sure I don't.'

Sarah's eyes narrowed. *Someone was not telling the truth, and she was fairly certain it wasn't Lucinda.* 'Apparently it was defamation of your husband's character.'

Lucinda shook her head. 'That's news to me. Anyway tell me, why are we discussing the Rosevears? I seem to have lost the thread of this conversation.'

Carole bristled with irritation. 'Sarah has befriended the woman!'

Lucinda shot Sarah a sharp look. 'What has possessed you to befriend an *ex* employee?'

'I'm friends with Elise. Unfortunately her poor

mother died shortly after being dismissed,' Sarah answered firmly.

Lucinda shook her head. 'But what on earth do you speak about. Surely the class divide would be a barrier to any decent conversation!' Lucinda pulled the shawl closer to her body. 'You modern ladies don't seem to understand the class system as my generation did. The friendship will go nowhere, you mark my words. It doesn't do to mix classes.'

'Elise Rosevear is a very intelligent business woman actually.'

'Rubbish! From my dealings with her, she hasn't the sense she was born with!' Carole said dismissively.

Lucinda looked to her daughter. 'Why, do you know her too?'

'She made the lace for my wedding dress, mama,' Carole said nonchalantly as she inspected her nails.

'If she is as good a business woman as Sarah says, and she is able to make exquisite lace, I fail to see why you think she has no sense, Carole,' Lucinda parried.

'The silly woman refused to let Philip set her up as his mistress, Mama. I mean, apparently she was in love with him, so I simply can't see what the problem is! As you know, I don't want him in my bed, and she would have been the perfect solution, but she threw it all back into his face. If that doesn't make her silly I don't know what does,' she answered with a toss of her head.

'Oh, I see,' Lucinda replied.

Sarah listened in astonishment. 'Don't tell me you condone what Carole and Philip did, Lucinda?'

Lucinda shrugged her shoulders. 'Frankly I see nothing wrong with it. All men take mistresses. It stops them from bothering us.'

Sarah blanched. 'My Peter would not do such a thing.'

Lucinda and Carole exchanged glances.

'He wouldn't, I know he wouldn't.'

'Well maybe you're right, Sarah,' Carole said. 'But the

fact is Philip is pining for Elise.'

'Well he'll have to pine, Elise has found someone else!'

Carole smirked. 'Philip is confident that everyone has a price.'

It took all Sarah's resolve to keep her anger in check. 'I do not believe I am hearing this, Carole. You're speaking about Elise as though she's some sort of commodity you can buy. Elise has been through a terribly emotional time because of you and Philip. You are both to leave her alone, do you hear me?'

A sudden movement in the room caught Sarah's eye.

As Carole stood up to take a visit to the water closet, she shuddered violently. 'Has it gone cold in here?'

'No,' the other two women said in unison.

'Well there is a distinctive chill in this room!'

A knock on the door heralded Carrington, informing the ladies that the gentlemen were about to join them.

'Oh, Carrington, build up the fire,' Carole ordered as she swept out of the room.

Carrington looked first at the roaring fire and then at Lucinda for guidance.

'The fire is fine, Carrington, leave it.' Lucinda dismissed him with a wave of her hand.

As Carole gathered up her skirts and petticoats to sit on the pot, she became acutely aware of another presence in the room. The hairs on her forearm stood on end, something moved and then a face flashed before her. Without waiting to finish her ablutions she ran screaming from the WC, wrenched open the great oak front door and flew down the path.

The gentlemen of the party, alerted to her screams, found her utterly distraught by the front gates, demanding that a carriage be brought to take her home.

'Goodness me, what on earth ails the girl?' Lucinda said, sweeping past Sarah to aid her daughter.

Sarah glanced at the apparition of Pearl and knew exactly the cause!

19

It was the 22nd December. As Harry Yates passed Primrose Cottage with his dog, a strange noise brought him to a halt. The cottage was illuminated, so Harry surmised that Philip Goldsworthy must be home, and whatever he was doing he was making a hell of a racket. The moon was waxing, so there was a glimmer of light in the night sky. Harry pulled his dog to heel and watched a while longer. Much to his surprise a long pole emerged through the thatch of Primrose Cottage. Once the pole had found air space, it was agitated violently until a large hole formed.

'Now why the devil would he do that to his roof?' he said to his dog. He shook his head, shivered with the cold and set off home, giving Philip no more thought.

*

Guy was both surprised and annoyed to find Philip knocking on his door the next morning. There had been a marked coolness in their relationship since Guy had told him in no uncertain terms what a cad and blaggard he was.

'Philip!' Guy's tone was as cold as the look he gave him. 'What can I do for you?'

'I've a hole in the roof. As you're the best Thatcher I know, well….' He laughed, '… in truth you're the only Thatcher I know. I wondered if you could do something about it.'

Guy scratched his head thoughtfully. 'I'll get my ladder,' he said reluctantly.

Philip followed Guy down the lane not bothering to help him carry the ladder.

'Is there any chance of fixing it today?' Philip said hopefully.

'Why? Are you staying here for Christmas?' With Ellie coming, Guy hoped very much that he was not.

'No, I'm leaving today to spend Christmas at Bochym, but I can't risk the rain getting in. It's quite a big hole.'

Guy felt the tension in his shoulders relax - he didn't want anything to upset Ellie during her stay.

'Well,' Philip continued. 'I'm saying I'm spending it at Bochym, but if my silly wife has anything to do with it she'll want to have Christmas lunch at the lodge with her mother the dowager countess. I don't think the dowager likes me. In fact I don't think she likes men at all.'

Guy ignored Philip's prattling as he negotiated the front gate.

'Carole is refusing to set foot in the manor, stupid woman. Apparently something spooked her last night when we dined there. Well, I can tell you, she can sit in the lodge with her mother if she wishes, I intend to dine in the luxury of the manor – and partake in the earl's fine claret.'

Guy's ladder was a thirty foot long pole ladder. It had been made in the wood yard at Gweek, especially for the craft of Thatching. It had been made simply, from a tree reduced to the right diameter and split straight down the middle, creating two identical sides that gave it great strength. It was splayed at the bottom, for extra stability and Guy dug it deep into the soil. At the top of the ladder Guy puzzled as he surveyed the hole. 'What the hell happened?' he shouted down to Philip.

'It's those damn rooks, taking the reed to build their nests.'

'It's a bit early for them to be nest building, and this is one hell of a hole,' Guy grumbled. He eased himself off the top rung of the ladder to take a closer look.

Philip watched as Guy practically jumped back onto the ladder to descend it. 'I'll have it fixed in an hour.'

'I'll leave you to it then. I'll settle up with you later,' Philip said.

Assuming Philip had left his cottage, Guy retrieved his tools to start the job. He tied his sacking knee protectors around his legs and pulled on his leather mitten to protect his palm. Many a Thatcher didn't care to wear such things, but a skilful pair of hands, that were well looked after, combined with a good eye, were the most important tools any Thatcher could possess, and Guy was determined to look after himself. With a shock of thatch over his shoulder he scrambled back up the ladder and set about his work. From his vantage point, he could see Silas walking Blue over the hills. He'd have to watch Silas, for he knew he'd smuggle the pup into his bed if he could and that would just make the dog soft.

As Guy was busily repairing the hole, Philip stepped out of the cottage, and after making sure there was no-one around, he very quietly pulled Guy's ladder away, carefully swapping it for his own rotting one. He stepped back inside and waited.

With the last spar in place, Guy wove the tar coated twine to secure it, gathered his tools and jumped onto the ladder. The feeling of slimy mould as he grasped the edge of the ladder alerted his senses that something was very wrong. He released his grip, glanced at the state of the wood then felt the rung under his feet snap and give. His stomach lurched, he grasped hold of the thatch, but his feet dropped through to another rung and then another before he lost his grip completely and his feet broke through the next four rungs. Every nerve in his body jarred as he plunged helplessly to the ground and oblivion.

When Guy landed with a heavy thud, Philip rushed out of his cottage, and quickly swapped the ladder back, before running to where Guy lay.

Guy was unconscious, his right leg lay at an alarming angle and his arms were splayed across the path. A small pool of blood was forming from the back of his head.

Seeing the extent of Guy's injuries, Philip felt a pang of guilt. He'd only really meant for him to break a leg - just something enough to hinder Guy's Christmas plans.

'Christ, is he dead?' Harry Yates shouted frantically as he raced up the lane dragging his dog behind him.

Philip, shocked from his reverie, felt a frisson of fear. *Had Harry seen it all?* He quickly fell to his knees feigning distress, as Harry ran up the front path. 'Oh god, Harry, Guy has fallen from the roof!'

'I know, I saw him fall from way down the lane,' Harry said, kneeling beside Philip.

Alarm bells rang in Philip's head. *Christ, the one thing he didn't bank on was a witness.* 'I think the ladder must have been at an odd angle, which made him slip.'

Harry nodded as he looked up at the offending article. 'It doesn't look cockeyed though!'

'That's because I've just had to straighten it up, otherwise it would have fallen on us. Anyway don't just sit there man,' Philip snapped, 'go tell Silas to run and get Dr Eddy.'

Philip watched as Harry rushed up the lane dragging his terrier behind him. He sighed angrily. 'Damn his eyes.' He then looked back at Guy. 'At least you'll not be bothering my Ellie for a while. I found out you see, I found out that you were going to steal her away for Christmas.'

*

When Dr Eddy arrived with Silas, they were carrying a stretcher between them. After a quick observation, it was clear to Dr Eddy that Guy's injuries were serious.

'Right,' Dr Eddy warned everyone. 'We must lift him carefully in case he's broken his back.'

Guy was carried to Bramble Cottage and placed by the fireside, while his ma fussed about him and Dr Eddy began to deal with his many broken bones. Guy remained unconscious throughout.

'We just need to wait until he regains consciousness, Nellie,' Dr Eddy said gently. 'Until then, I've no idea if his back is broken or not.'

'How long will he be unconscious?'

'I don't know, Nellie. We just have to keep a watch over him. I'll go now but I'll send Amelia up to help. She'll know what to do when he comes round.'

Nellie nodded miserably as she pulled a chair nearer

her son and sat down.

'Look after your ma, son.' Dr Eddy ruffled Silas's hair and left the cottage.

Philip too made his excuses and left.

Harry waited a few minutes more and then also took his leave when his dog threatened to pee up Nellie's kitchen table leg. Harry pulled the dog outside and waited as it relieved itself by a tree. As he stood waiting, he heard Philip cursing and grunting. He walked down the lane towards Primrose Cottage to find Philip struggling to drag several pieces of old timber to the back of his cottage. Disinclined to go and help, as it looked like a rather heavy job, Harry held back. He glanced at Guy's ladder still leant against the cottage and thought it was best if he made himself scarce. He had no doubt, that if Guy hadn't finished the roof job, Philip would send him up the ladder instead to cover the hole with some tarpaulin if he saw him.

'Come on boy, let's get home' he said, as he pulled the dog down the lane as fast as its little legs would carry it.

*

On Christmas Eve, Ellie dusted her hands together. Everything was ready. Her bag was packed and waiting by the door. She had a box full of Christmas goodies - a Victoria sandwich cake, a tin of ginger biscuits, and a jar of plum jam and one of chutney. It was five past midday, Guy would be here soon. She hadn't lit the range in the cottage that morning, so she sat with her warm coat and scarf on to keep out the chill. Brandy was sat near her feet and she enjoyed the warmth from his body next to her ankles.

Ellie watched as the clock ticked by. At two o clock, her tummy rumbled and her hands were getting colder even with her gloves on. She roused herself to light a fire to make some tea. It was strange how different a room could look when it was cold - a good fire made the room look homely and cosy, but at the moment the room looked almost blue with cold. She shivered violently.

The beverage warmed her, and after taking Brandy out for a walk on the beach she realised, that for some reason Guy wasn't going to come today.

With a heavy heart she returned to the cottage, brushed the sand from Brandy's paws, lit the range and threw another log on the fire. Once the flames were crackling in the grate, she stood up and wrung her hands not knowing what to do next. Her stomach rumbled again and Brandy lifted one eyelid at the noise. The evening was slowly beginning to drift across the cliff tops. It was time to make something for them to eat. By the time a pot of vegetable soup had cooked, the night sky had fallen.

All that evening the same thing hung heavy on her mind. Had something happened to Guy? Was he ill? She tossed every single scenario over and over. She knew it was not in him to let her down, unless it was for a very good reason. She tried very hard to not panic.

At eight-thirty the fire had collapsed into a pile of grey ash. She stood and stretched her stiff limbs, opened the door and let the night air in. She knew Guy would not be there outside, but was impelled to look anyway. She took Brandy out onto the dunes for a few minutes, before closing the cottage up for the night.

In the gloom of dawn, Ellie woke to a lonelier Christmas Day than she could ever have imagined.

*

Nellie, Silas and Amelia took it in turn to sit in vigil. As always, Amelia Pascoe gave her enduring, moral support and this kept the family's spirits up. Though never having any real medical training, Amelia assisted Dr Eddy on many occasions, not only in her role as midwife, but as a nurse too. Just having Amelia around seemed to make any situation bearable. Dr Eddy had left strict instructions not to move Guy for chance his back was broken. Over the last forty-eight hours, Guy had regained partial consciousness several times, but had been incoherent and agitated, so a sleeping draft had to be administered to keep him still.

When he finally woke on Christmas morning, he was lucid enough to understand the enormity of his situation. He could hardly swallow, his mouth was so dry. He glanced at the three worried faces looking down on him.

'Oh my god, what's happened?' he moaned, trying to lift his arms. A searing pain shot through his body. His stomach heaved making him choke as vomit rose into his throat.

Unsure of the damage he may cause, Amelia had no option but to cup her hands firmly around his face and turn his head allowing him to vomit over the floor.

Nellie's hands flew to her face, the tears running through her fingers. Silas dropped to his knees to comfort his brother, while Amelia wiped Guy's face with her apron.

'You've fallen from next door's roof, Guy,' Silas said, unable to keep his own tears in check.

Guy tried to move but sweat glistened as his face contorted with unimaginable pain.

'Don't move,' Amelia said, 'You've broken all your limbs and Dr Eddy thinks you have a back injury too.'

'Oh, god, no.' A hot thumping feeling of dread swamped him. 'Am I paralysed?'

'We don't know. Please keep still, Guy,' Amelia reiterated. 'Silas, can you fetch Dr Eddy please.'

Guy's head hurt alarmingly, but he could not lift his hand to investigate. 'My head?' He shot a frightened look to Amelia.

'You've a gash just above your left ear. Dr Eddy has stitched it and I've put a soothing balm on it, but it will hurt for a while. When Dr Eddy returns he'll give you a draft to make you sleep.'

Guy gave a harsh half stifled cry as another pain ripped through his body. He panted, waiting for the hot white pain to subside, consciously counting the seconds until his body calmed and he was able to breathe more comfortably again. A tear escaped and ran down his cheek, which Amelia wiped away before anyone saw. He glanced around the kitchen.

'How long have I been here on the floor?' he asked breathlessly.

'Two days, it's Christmas Day now.'

'Christmas Day!' Guy tried to lift his head and his whole body screamed in agony. 'Ellie!' he gasped.

'Ellie?' Amelia looked at Nellie who just shrugged her shoulders.

'He means Ellie Rosevear from Poldhu,' Silas said, as he shrugged his coat on. 'With all this going on I forgot that Guy invited her here for Christmas. She was going to bring cake!' he added.

'Ellie Rosevear?' Amelia looked down at Guy curiously.

'Argh! Yes, I should have picked her up yesterday,' Guy said between gasps of pain. His face contorted and more tears fell. 'She'll be wondering what has happened.'

'Guy, don't get upset. I promise I shall send word to her as soon as I can. Now stay calm, until Dr Eddy gets here. He'll give you a draft for the pain.'

*

Rain fell like a veil of tears across the countryside on Christmas Day. Ellie stood at the water's edge with Brandy on a rope by her side. The tide was as far out as it could be, so she was almost under the shadow of the vast Poldhu Hotel. The beach was deserted, as empty as her heart felt. Whoops of laughter could be heard on the breeze from around the headland at Church Cove, no doubt coming from James Blackwell's house guests who were taking their annual Christmas Day dip in the icy waters. There had been no word from Guy, though with it being Christmas she didn't really expect it. In her heart, she knew that something major must have happened for her to be excluded from the Christmas festivities Guy had been so looking forward to sharing with her.

'Come on boy, it's just you and me for Christmas, Brandy.'

Ellie would have to make the best of what was in her larder today. There was some cold pressed ham which she'd have with the chutney she'd gift wrapped for Nellie Blackthorn. When it was apparent that there was to be no trip to Gweek, she had made some bread first thing that morning and it should be just about ready when she got back to her cottage. The only thing she would be starved of today was company.

20

There had been no post on Christmas Day, so Ellie waited anxiously for the postman next day. She always had a pot of tea and a scone waiting for him in case he did deliver. For some reason Brandy had taken a great dislike to Archie and seemed to sense him coming even before he had turned the corner of the hill, so as soon as Brandy started grizzling, Ellie pushed him into the back room and tried to settle her drumming heart. She knew a message would come today, she just dreaded to think what it would say.

'Seasons greetings to you, Ellie, I hope you had a good Christmas?' Archie said, laying his bicycle against the cottage wall. He grinned when he heard Brandy whining in the back room.

'Sorry,' Ellie mouthed. 'Brandy has no issues with anyone else. I don't know what is wrong with him.'

Archie laughed again. 'It's an occupational hazard, it's the uniform.'

He followed Ellie into her cottage and pulled his bag from over his head. 'This is a deal lighter now Christmas is over!'

Taking the tea gratefully from Ellie he handed a letter to her.

Ellie's tummy churned, but when she studied the handwriting, she found it wasn't Guy's. Apprehension turned to disappointment as she pushed it deep into her apron pocket to read later.

As soon as Archie left, she ripped open the envelope.

Dear Ellie,

Guy Blackthorn has asked me to write to you, first to apologise profusely for letting you down at Christmas, but more importantly, the reason. He has met with an unfortunate accident. He fell from a ladder and landed on his back. I have to inform you that his injuries are catastrophic and Dr Eddy fears he may never walk again. It is Guy's wish that you do not see him in his predicament - he just

wanted you to know. Having said that, I strongly urge you to defy his wishes and come to him as soon as possible. We all fear for Guy's well being.
Yours truly
Amelia Pascoe

Ellie could hardly breathe for the crushing feeling in her chest. She glanced at the clock - if she hurried she could catch the first wagon out of Mullion and by luck she'd be at Guy's side by midday.

There was no connecting wagon to Gweek so Ellie jumped off at the crossroads of the Lizard, Helston, St Keverne road, from there she would have to walk the two miles to Gweek.

*

Philip stood pondering at his office window in the Corn Mill. Although he'd successfully managed to ruin Christmas for Ellie and Guy, his own festivities had not been at all agreeable. Carole had point blank refused to return to the manor for Christmas lunch, insisting Philip stayed with her and his mother-in-law to eat at the Lodge. The incessant chattering over dinner about the latest fashion in London had driven him to distraction. He had hoped to be invited to the manor for drinks on Christmas evening, but no invite had materialised. He suspected Peter was still smarting over his row with James. Damn them all, damn James for his interference, Peter and Sarah for their churlishness and Carole for this ridiculous notion about ghosts. His privileged life on a country estate was not going to plan. He was just about to turn away from the window when he noticed Ellie walking into Gweek. His mouth curled into a smile. *Go on, go to him. Because he'll not be coming to see you for a while and that's a fact!* He hadn't meant to, but he'd done a proper job on Guy. He'd seen for himself the state Guy was in when he'd visited that morning. Once Ellie had seen him, she'd realise there was now no future for her with Guy.

*

It was with great trepidation that she turned into the lane which would pass Primrose Cottage. The very thought of the place made her shudder. The trees were bare now, and the lane was rutted and slippery with great pools of muddy water. She lifted her skirts, quickened her step and averted her eyes. At the door of Bramble Cottage, she hesitated to gather courage to knock.

Nellie opened the door but began to close it again before Ellie could speak.

Ellie put her foot in the door and grimaced as Nellie pushed against it.

'Please, Mrs Blackthorn, I need to see Guy.'

Nellie stood her ground. 'He doesn't want to see you. He doesn't want to be bothered by anybody. He's had a terrible accident.'

Hearing the commotion outside, Guy shouted, 'What's happening, Ma?'

Nellie stared Ellie down. 'It's nothing. It's no one.'

Silas knelt beside Guy. 'It's Ellie,' he whispered.

Guy groaned inwardly. He couldn't let her see him in this state.

'Let her in Guy. She'll not go away until you do,' Silas said, knowing that if anyone could lift his mood, Ellie could.

'Please, Mrs Blackthorn, I beg you. It's because of Guy's accident I've come.'

'There is nothing anyone can do, so you might as well go back where you came from.' She tried to kick Ellie's foot from the gap in the door.

'Please, Guy, let her in,' Silas pleaded.

'Oh, god,' Guy's voice cracked with emotion.

Silas got up and ran to the door. 'Ma, Guy says to let her in.'

Ellie tipped her head hopefully and Nellie huffed and stepped aside.

Ellie rushed inside, saw Guy on the kitchen floor by the fire and fell to her knees beside him.

Her dark eyebrows came together as she ran her eyes over his broken splinted body. His skin glistened with perspiration and a sour smell of sweat and dried blood caught in her nostrils.

'Guy,' she whispered as her cool fingers touched the dark beard which shadowed his jowls. She glanced at the bandage covering the wound to his head, noting the hair protruding was caked in dried blood. 'Why has no one washed you?'

'The doctor says he's not to be moved,' Nellie snapped back.

Ellie bit her lip. 'Can you not move at all,' she whispered.

Guy looked deep into Ellie's beautiful, concerned eyes. 'I can move my head, but I dare not move anything else. The pain is excruciating. I fear I'm destined to die on this draughty kitchen floor.'

She gently laid her fingers to his lips. 'No you're not, Guy. Don't ever give up hope. How often does the doctor come?'

'Dr Eddy comes most days. We can't pay him, but still he comes.'

'Did he say what could be done for you?'

Guy's mouth twitched. 'Nothing we can afford. Apparently there is a doctor in Truro who specialises in back injuries, but I don't have the money to get there or pay for his services.'

'How much is it?'

His lip curled. 'More than any of us can afford, I'm afraid.'

Ellie could not bear the devastated look on his face, she had to do something. Seeing he was bare-chested, she asked, 'Are you wearing clothes under this blanket?' She ignored Nellie tutting disapprovingly behind her.

'Dr Eddy removed most of them to splint my limbs.'

'Have you any movement in your limbs?'

'They're all both broken, but I can move my fingers

and toes, though I have terrible pins and needles.'

'Well, that's a good sign, is it not?' Ellie paused a moment then asked, 'Forgive me for asking, but are you in control of your bodily functions?'

'Oh for goodness sake,' Nellie protested. 'What a thing to ask a man you hardly know.'

Guy nodded. 'I am.'

'I know nothing about back injuries, Guy, except that if you have movement and control, there is real hope that you'll recover.'

'Stop this at once.' Nellie grabbed Ellie and pulled her away from Guy. 'Stop putting fanciful notions into his head. Look at him - he'll never be fit for anything again.'

Ellie shrugged Nellie off. 'Guy, could you endure the pain while I try to clean you up a little? You'll feel so much better.'

'Oh, god, Ellie, I know I smell awful, but you can't do that, it wouldn't be proper.'

She gave a crooked smile. 'Guy, I've seen you swimming in your underclothes. Let me help you,' she whispered tenderly.

Guy nodded thankfully.

Nellie stood with her hands on her hips. 'I told you she was a hussy. Send her away, Guy.'

Ignoring Nellie's protests, Ellie turned to Silas. 'Would you be kind enough to bring me a cloth, a bowl and a jug of hot water please.'

'I'll get it,' Nellie snapped as she scuttled to the kitchen sink. 'Silas, watch her,' she warned.

Very gently, Ellie unwound the bandage from Guy's head to inspect the wound, apologising when he flinched as the dressing caught on his stitches.

After sponging the blood from his hair, she looked up at Nellie who was watching with pursed lips. 'Could I have some more hot water please?'

Dipping the cloth in the fresh water, she pulled the blanket down to his waist and began to sponge his chest and armpits.

Nellie was beside herself. 'Whatever are you thinking? Have you no shame woman?'

'The shame is, that not only is Guy in terrible pain, he needs to be washed. If there is nothing else we can do for him at the moment, we can make him clean and comfortable. Can you not see how wretched he is?'

Nellie stood with her hands on her hips. 'The doctor says he shouldn't be moved, that's why I've done nothing!'

'Please, Mrs Blackthorn,' Ellie said more gently. 'He'll feel so much better.'

'I can't watch, I just can't watch.' Nellie flounced out of the kitchen.

Ellie pulled a face at Guy, making him smile for the first time.

After towelling dry Guy's chest, she re-covered him with the blanket when he started to shiver.

'Now, I've never shaved a man before, so I don't know how to do it. Do *you* shave yet, Silas?'

'He'd like to think so,' Guy quipped.

Silas poked his tongue out at his brother.

'Well then I shall have to leave you with a beard for now.' Her eyes twinkled.

Guy lay in silence for a good few minutes after the ordeal - his pain and embarrassment slowly subsiding.

Leaving him to recover, Ellie helped Nellie clean the bowls. There was no conversation between them, but Ellie guessed that Nellie felt relieved something had been done to make Guy feel a little better today.

Very reluctantly Nellie brewed a pot of tea for them all. Ellie had brought with her a cake and Silas salivated as it was cut into pieces. Nellie refused a piece on principle.

Ellie settled back down beside Guy. She fed him small pieces of cake, and spoon fed him tea from her mug.

'Mmm,' he said with heartfelt gratitude. 'Thank you.'

She took his hand gently. 'What happened?'

'I was repairing a leak on Primrose Cottage for Philip.

When I stepped on the ladder, it just gave way under me and I fell. I can't understand it, Ellie. I always make sure my ladders are as sound as a bell. I would never use one that was rotting. I asked Silas to go and inspect the ladder, but he says it's intact! It just doesn't make sense. I definitely felt the rungs break under my feet.' He tried to move as he spoke, but his face contorted in pain and a film of perspiration formed again on his body.

'Try to relax, Guy.' She gently dabbed his damp forehead with her handkerchief.

'Ellie.' His eyes looked up at her in earnest. 'I had hoped….you and I,' his face crumpled as he spoke. 'But now…..'

Ellie put her fingers to his lips. 'Let's just get you better.'

'But, Ellie, I may never walk or work again!'

'Shush.' She smiled, but her heart broke for him. 'Tell me, how is Blue getting along? Brandy is pining for him.'

'The poor thing is locked in the shed. I can't do with him in here - the little bugger licks my face.'

Ellie grimaced. 'Ugh! I can imagine that would be a problem.'

Guy sighed heavily. 'God knows how I am going to afford to keep him now this has happened. I can't feed Ma and Silas if I don't work - the dog is just another problem.'

'Do you want me to take him back to Poldhu with me?'

'No.' Silas heard and stood in protest. 'I'll find work to pay for his keep. Please Guy, don't send him away.'

Guy raised his brows.

'Well the offer is there, Silas, should you need me to help. He'll be well looked after until Guy is up and about again. Just let me know.'

Silas gave a grateful nod.

Ellie looked up as the clock chimed two. 'Guy, I am so sorry but I must go now or I shall miss the three p.m. Mullion coach. I promise I'll come again soon though.'

'Thank you for today, Ellie. You have made this wretched man very happy.' Guy felt a searing pain as he tried to stretch his fingers out to touch her.

She kissed him lightly on the mouth, much to Nellie's disapproval.

Guy closed his eyes, savouring her kiss. The touch of her soft, clean hair as it brushed across his face filled his senses with a painful longing.

'I'll show you out,' Nellie said scathingly as Ellie pulled on her coat.

Ellie gave Guy a dazzling smile and a wave, but as she stepped out of the door, she stopped suddenly - Philip was waiting outside.

Nellie slammed the door shut behind her.

'Bloody hussy, she comes here pretending to be bothered about your welfare and then has the audacity to meet her lover out there.'

'What?' Nellie's words jarred every nerve in Guy's body.

'It's true. She's there now, talking to Philip Goldsworthy. I've told you, she's no good.'

'Silas,' Guy yelled at the top of his voice, cringing at the pain that ensued.

'What?' His brother stuck his head around the door.

'Go out the back door, keep out of sight, but tell me what you hear said between Ellie and Goldsworthy.'

With great stealth, Silas rounded the side of the house, where high words were being spoken.

'He needs help, Philip. He fell from your roof for goodness sake!' Ellie pleaded.

Philip was clearly enjoying Ellie's distress. 'What do you expect *me* to do?'

'Apparently there is a doctor in Truro who specialises in back injuries, but Guy can't afford his services. You can. I know you have the means to help him. He's your friend, Philip. It's the least you can do for him.'

Philip looked towards Guy's cottage and his face

softened. 'You're right, Ellie. I can afford to pay for his treatment.'

'So will you?'

Again he enjoyed the desperation in her voice.

'Yes, of course I will.'

Ellie felt tears of relief brimming.

'On the proviso you return to me,' Philip added.

Ellie clenched her fists, unable to comprehend what he'd said. 'I beg your pardon?'

'That's the deal, Ellie - the quid quo pro. I'll leave it with you to think about. If you want to help him, the ball is in your court.'

Ellie staggered backwards, trying to distance herself from his indecent proposal. Too angry to speak, she picked up her skirts and stomped off down the lane.

Philip jutted his chin out and gave a crisp satisfied nod.

When Silas returned to Guy, he knew not what to say to him for fear of his reaction.

'Well?' Guy asked anxiously.

Silas fidgeted uncomfortably.

'Silas!'

Silas swallowed hard. 'I think Mr. Goldsworthy is going to pay for your hospital treatment.'

Nellie gasped in disbelief.

Guy groaned, trying in vain to calm his breathing. 'What else did you hear?'

'I don't know for sure, but I think Ellie has promised to return to him.'

Guy felt his world implode. 'God, no!' he cried, 'Please don't tell me that.' He tried to quell the dreadful ache in his heart that far outweighed any pain from his broken body.

'See, Guy!'

His ma's voice jarred him back to the present.

'I told you she was no good. She comes here pretending to care for you, crooning over you, touching you intimately and telling you everything is going to be alright, when all the time she is planning to go back to him! She's nothing but a hussy!'

'Stop calling her that! Argh!' His body shuddered in pain. 'Ellie cares for me, I know she does!'

Silas watched in horror as the argument between them escalated. He dropped to his knees to comfort his brother. 'Guy, if it's any consolation, I don't think Ellie looked too happy about going back to him.'

'See, Ma, I believe Goldsworthy is forcing her hand. I will not go with his money, if it means Ellie has to go back to him!'

Nellie punched her fists into her hips. 'Stop being such a bloody fool. Do you want to lay there for the rest of your life? For god's sake, have some sense. She wouldn't throw herself at him if she didn't want him!'

'I won't go, I tell you,' he cried pitifully.

'Oh yes you bloody will!' Nellie retorted.

*

Ellie could not believe Philip's audacity. If there had been a shred of feeling left for him, it had well and truly gone now. Her anger at Philip's disgusting proposition propelled her up the hill out of Gweek. He clearly did not possess one ounce of decency.

*

Her anger surpassed any attempt at sleeping that night. Hour by hour she lay awake fretting until she decided what to do. At six a.m. she rose and dressed warmly for it was chilly, and was tramping over the coast road towards Gunwalloe Fishing Cove before the sun had started to push through the dawn mist. It was a good three-quarter of an hours walk, but the heavy rain during the night had made the cliff path slippery with wet mud. As she rounded Halzhephron Cliff, James Blackwell's house came into view. James was Guy's only chance, she just hoped he was still at home. He would know what to do. She picked her way gingerly down the slippery path and when she reached the door, she patted her damp hair and brushed down her skirts before knocking loudly on the kitchen door.

'Yes? Hello, Miss,' Jane the cleaner said.

'Hello Jane, I'm looking for James.'

'Oh my luver, you've just missed him. He's been gone these last ten minutes.'

'Is he coming back?'

'I should think so, yes.'

'When?'

Jane shrugged. 'When he finished what he's doing in London I suppose.'

'So he's catching the wagon?'

'Aye, that's what I said. He's been gone these past ten minutes.'

Without taking her leave from Jane, Ellie lifted her skirts and ran like the wind up the lane towards Berepper Farm, where the wagon picked up its passengers. James was just about to board when he heard Ellie's frantic shouts.

'Can you wait one moment?' James asked the driver.

'Not really, I've people waiting up the line for me.

'Just one moment, I beg you.' James stepped back down from the wagon and watched Ellie approach, red faced and breathing hard with exertion.

'Whatever is the matter? Is there something wrong at the Tea Room?'

Ellie stopped, bent double to catch her breath and shook her head. 'It's Guy,' she gasped.

James frowned and grasped Ellie by the arms. 'What about him?'

'Oh James, he fell from a roof three days ago and damaged his back. He's been laid on his kitchen floor since, unable to move.'

James was horrified. 'Is it broken? Has the doctor seen him?'

'He's injured it badly. Dr Eddy in Gweek says there is a doctor in The Royal Cornwall Infirmary, who might be able to help him, but Guy cannot afford to get there or pay for his services. I just wondered if there was anything you could do? I don't know who else to ask.'

'Mr Blackwell, we need to go. If you don't board now I shall go without you,' the driver of the wagon shouted.

'I'm coming,' he shouted back. 'Leave it with me, Ellie. I'll send a wire to Dr Eddy. We'll sort something out.'

Ellie burst into tears at his kindness.

'Ah.' He gathered her into his arms. 'Don't worry Ellie. We'll get him sorted, I promise. Now I must go.' He patted her warmly on the arm and climbed aboard the wagon.

Drained with emotion, Ellie sat down heavily on the damp grass until she regained her composure. 'Thank god for men like James.'

As the wagon trundled through the village, James pondered on Guy's predicament. He'd known him for a while now, and knew he was a proud man. Helping him financially might not sit too well on Guy's shoulders, but help him he must.

21

Guy too had experienced a sleepless night. Not usually a praying man, he made an exception and prayed all night that Ellie would not take up Philip's offer. It seemed his prayers were in vain, because a wagon turned up for Guy at two p.m., swiftly followed by Dr Eddy.

'I'm *not* going,' Guy protested, when Dr Eddy told him everything had been arranged.

'Doctor, make him see sense!' Nellie pleaded.

'Who is paying for this doctor?' Guy demanded.

'Don't you fret about that, it's all being taken care of.'

'I demand to know!

'Your benefactor said you would do so, but he was adamant that if you asked I was to tell you that it is a friend, and you must thank god for friends like this, Guy.'

Guy's heart sank. 'I can't go. What will Ma do?'

'Your ma will struggle for a lot longer if you don't go. You need specialist treatment if you're to make a proper recovery. We'll all make sure your ma is looked after. I'll ask around to see if I can find work for Silas. You mustn't worry.'

'How could she do this, Ma,' Guy bemoaned as Dr Eddy went out to make the wagon ready for its patient.

'Well, she's done it and if it gets you better, then all well and good!'

'But to beggar herself with that man, I just can't bear it, Ma.'

Nellie pursed her lips. 'I don't know why you're so surprised. We all know what sort of woman she is. After all, she had no qualms about stripping you bare yesterday. What decent woman would do that? I thank the lord she is what she is though, otherwise you, my poor son, would lie festering by my kitchen fireside for the rest of your life. Now, lie quiet while the good doctor makes you ready for the journey.'

Once securely strapped to a pallet, he was loaded onto

the flat bed wagon.

'Oh Christ,' Guy said to no one in particular.

Silas climbed aboard. 'I'll look after everything, Guy.'

Guy fought the tears in front of his brother. 'Silas, the wagon is full of reed. Ask Farmer Ferris if he'll store it in his barn, but god knows when I'll be back.'

'I will, Guy.'

'Look after Ma,' he said resignedly.

Silas nodded. 'I'll write to you. I'll tell you all the news.'

'I'll not be able to write back though, think on.' He flexed his fingers causing a severe pain to shoot up his arm.

Dr Eddy climbed up beside Guy and waved to Silas and Nellie. As they passed Primrose Cottage, Guy turned his head away. His heart was heavy with melancholia at the thought of what Ellie had done. He would not have wished her to do that for him. He'd have rather rotted on the kitchen floor than see his beloved Ellie with that hateful man.

*

Ellie received a telegram that same day which made her weep again, but this time tears of joy.

EVERYTHING SORTED STOP JAMES STOP.

*

After a long and arduous journey to Truro, first via wagon, then train, then wagon again. Guy and Dr Eddy arrived at The Royal Cornwall Infirmary.

On his new doctor's orders, Guy was laid on a waterbed - a contraption which took a lot of getting used to. It was a box lined with and covered by a rubber sheet and was used, the doctor informed them, for patients whose injuries will not allow them to be on a less yielding surface. The rubber stank, and the constant movement of water gave Guy terrible motion sickness.

Guy reluctantly bid farewell to Dr Eddy, thanking him for his kindness, before submitting himself to the first day of his long journey of rehabilitation.

*

As 1901 came to a close the weather in Cornwall was almost spring-like. Ellie had taken to walking Brandy over the cliffs most mornings, and the fields of daffodils, which Cornwall was so famous for, were already bursting into colour. This earlier than normal show of blooms meant that the local pickers would make a little money sooner than planned. At least there would be full bellies during the coldest of months.

Walking back home, the euphoria of knowing that Guy was to be treated began to wane, replaced by a great sadness that Guy was going into this New Year with such uncertainty. One thing she was confident of was that she had left Guy in no doubt that whatever the outcome was to his rehabilitation she would always be with him to help. She just wished she'd told him that she loved him - because she did, of that she was certain.

*

On the 29th December, Ellie received a letter from Gweek.

My dear Ellie,

Further to my last letter informing you of Guy Blackthorn's accident, I thought you'd like to know that he was taken, very reluctantly I might add, to hospital in Truro yesterday, to start his treatment. Guy is a proud man and was quite concerned as to who had paid for his treatment. Dr Eddy tells me he is sworn to secrecy as to who his benefactor is, so I too am completely in the dark. Whoever it is, I'm so grateful to them. Dr Eddy tells me the treatment will take many months, but the doctor in charge of his specialist treatment has every confidence that Guy will fully recover, so that is good news. Guy is residing in the orthopaedic ward, should you wish to send him news of home, which I'm sure you will. Let's hope his recovery is quick. We both know that Guy is a man at one with nature and will not be the most patient of patients being forced to lie abed. The address is - Royal Cornwall Infirmary, Infirmary Hill, Truro. I'm sure Guy would be more than happy to get a letter from you and know that others are thinking of him at this difficult time.

Dr Eddy said that Guy's greatest concern was for the welfare of his ma and brother. Rest assured this tight knit village will look after them. In fact Dr Eddy has secured a job for Silas at the Forge. Not ideal I know, George Blewett can be a difficult man, but I'll keep an eye out for him.

I'll close this letter now, wishing you every success in the coming year with your new venture at the tea room. Let's hope and pray for Guy together.

Kind Regards

Amelia Pascoe

Ellie shuddered at the thought of Silas working for Blewett. She'd only encountered Blewett once and that was enough. Ellie knew that would not be enough to keep starvation at bay. Yes, she was sure the other villagers would help, but times were hard and people were poor.

Reaching for her ledger, Ellie flipped through the Tea Room's accounts. As Guy had been instrumental in saving her life, Ellie felt it was the least she could do to help his family, now they were in need. If she budgeted carefully she could put a percentage of her takings in an envelope and send them to Nellie each week. She would make sure she kept enough back to run the business efficiently. She had few needs other than food for her own table, so she would not miss giving some of it back to Nellie.

The clock struck nine-forty-five - it was almost time to open. Only a few regular customers ventured down in the winter time. Alan and Angela never failed to drop in, en route from walking their dog Tan, to meet up with their friend Sally and her dog George to chat over tea and toast. Gillian too and her dog Poppy were never far behind them. Since Betty had left, and on acquiring a dog of her own, Ellie relaxed the 'no dogs allowed on the premises' rule in the winter time, as long as the dogs stayed tied up outside.

Ellie put Amelia's letter to one side. She'd write to Guy early in the New Year, hopefully he would have settled into his treatment by then. Knowing of his disabilities, she knew she wouldn't receive any correspondence back, but it would be important that he knew how much he was missed during his stay in hospital.

*

There was an influx of visitors at The Poldhu Hotel over the New Year, which in turn made Ellie busier than normal. At midnight on New Year's Eve, Ellie wrapped up warm and sat on the terrace. Her only companions were Brandy and the moon. As the clock chimed midnight, a cheer went up from the vicinity of the Hotel. Ellie had never felt lonelier.

'Darling Guy,' she whispered into the night sky, 'I hope with all my heart that you mend soon, so that we can be together. Happy New Year, my love.'

Brandy lifted her head from Ellie's lap and gave a comforting sigh.

*

Guy stared at the stark white ceiling. He kept as still as possible to prevent the waterbed from moving underneath. He hated the contraption.

'Happy New Year, Mr Blackthorn,' the nurse removing his bed pan said cheerily.

Guy responded with a grunt. The embarrassment of a nurse helping him when nature called plunged him deeper into a depression.

The nurse took away the bed pan and returned to straighten his bedclothes, the action making his water bed move.

The nurse looked down as he grimaced. 'Sorry, Mr Blackthorn, you'll get used to it, I promise. Can I get you anything?'

'No…thank you,' he added.

'If you're not sleepy, be mindful to spend several minutes, deep breathing, to keep your lungs clear.'

Again Guy grunted.

The nurse gave a crooked smile. 'I'll say goodnight

then.' She put the tiny hand bell near his fingers. 'Ring if you need anything.'

'I need to die,' he whispered despondently.

*

For the early part of January 1902 the coast of Cornwall was drenched in a fine mist. Ellie shivered, pulling her shawl over her shoulders. On days like these, even a good fire could not diminish the damp chill air in her little cottage. Custom had been minimal that day, only seeing her regulars, so once they left, Ellie locked the door and retired to her cottage to do her paperwork. First though, she would write her letter to Guy.

She sat for a long while tapping the pen on her teeth as she thought about all the things she wanted to say without being too forward.

Dear Guy,

I hope this letter finds you more comfortable than last I saw you. I received a letter from Amelia Pascoe shortly after you went to hospital. She told me that Dr Eddy assured her your treatment will work, though it will be a long process.

I think about you daily and pray for your swift recovery so that you can return to your family.

Rest assured that your ma will be financially taken care of, so please don't fret about that.

Life goes on as usual at Poldhu, though I miss you terribly. I miss your visits, your humour and zest for life. I hope that when you return, we'll pick up where we left off. I admit I'm lonely without you. Those last few weeks before you befell that terrible accident were full of joy. My life was so much happier when you were by my side. Get well soon Guy. I'll be waiting for you.

Your dearest friend, Ellie.

Ellie sealed the letter with a kiss and gazed out of the window at the waves gently rolling onto the beach. She'd shared happy times with Guy down at the water's edge. She hoped with all her heart, he would walk again and they could let the surf lap against their ankles.

'Come back to me soon, Guy,' she whispered.

'You look lost in your reverie.'

Ellie spun around to find Lady Sarah at her doorway. Automatically she stood up and bobbed a small curtsy.

'Elise, please don't stand on ceremony for me. We're friends remember.'

'Sorry it's just habit.' Ellie laughed as she beckoned her into the cottage, whilst casting her eyes round the room to make sure all was tidy.

'I'm sorry I haven't been down to see you before now, we spent the New Year at Trelissick House. I do hope I'm not disturbing you, I thought I heard you talking to someone,' Sarah said as she took off her riding jacket.

Ellie smiled. 'It's just me talking to myself. It's probably a first sign of madness. That's what you get for living alone.'

'Well I might just have the solution to that, but first I want to know all about your Christmas with Guy.'

Ellie pushed the letter aside to post later. 'Goodness, you don't know, do you? I didn't get to share Christmas with Guy after all.'

'Oh Elise!' Sarah reached out and cupped her hand. 'Why ever not?'

'Let me put the kettle on the stove. I have such a tale to tell you.'

Sarah listened in amazement. 'Oh my goodness, I can't believe it, poor Guy. But it beggars belief why Philip has not mentioned this, if it was his roof Guy fell from! Granted, we didn't share Christmas lunch with him or Carole, but I do recall we saw him on Christmas Eve morning. You would have thought he'd have said something then, would you not?'

'Nothing surprises me with that man,' Ellie said sternly. 'Do you know that Philip offered to pay for Guy's treatment, on the proviso I became his mistress.'

Sarah shuddered. 'Goodness me! The scruples of that

man! So who *is* paying for Guy's treatment?'

'James Blackwell, but I think he's keeping that fact secret from Guy. He's a proud man - Guy would never ask anyone for anything.'

Sarah smiled. 'Good old James, he never fails to come to the rescue.'

'I agree. I've a lot to thank that man for.'

'Well, Guy's treatment sounds positive, let us hope for a speedy recovery.'

Ellie lifted her cup in agreement.

'Forgive me for asking, Elise, but do you need any help in the Tea Room?'

Ellie's lip curled. 'I can scarcely believe you need a job!' she joked.

Sarah laughed. 'I think I have enough on my plate running…or trying to run the manor.' She rolled her eyes. 'No matter, I'm not here to grumble to you. It's just that one of our housemaids is finding working at the manor a little strained at the moment, and I am looking to relocate her.'

'Why, what'd happened?'

'Do you recall I told you that Jessie, our housemaid, could also see the ghost you call Pearl.'

'I do.'

'Well!' Sarah crossed her arms. 'It seems some of the household's staff have been making things very uncomfortable for her. One or two have threatened to leave because they think Jessie is encouraging spirits from the dark side.'

'I'm sorry to hear that. Unfortunately people are afraid of what they don't understand.'

'Personally I am of the mind that if people don't want to stay in our employment they can go, but I can see this is all a strain on the poor girl. I want to help her. I had hoped to promote her to the position of my lady's maid, but I think it will cause more problems for her.'

'How long has Jessie worked for you?'

'For about four years now. Her mother worked in the laundry but she died when Jessie was twelve, so Jessie was kept on, first as a scullery maid and then a housemaid.'

'So you want to settle her here at the Tea Room?'

'I would be so grateful if you could, but Elise, can you afford to employ someone? I can help with the finances if need be.'

Ellie tapped her finger on her mouth for a moment. James did say she could employ some help and take the money out of the profits. 'Thank you, Sarah, I can. I was actually looking for someone to help me. So you have offered me a gift. I'll be happy to have Jessie here with me.'

'You won't be disappointed in her. Jessie's a fine worker and I for one will be sorry to let her go.'

'If you like her, Sarah, I know I will too. Bring her down tomorrow. I'll get a room ready for her in the cottage.'

*

Jessie arrived with Sarah promptly at ten the next morning and though the Tea Room was closed on Mondays, Ellie had set a table by the window for tea and cake.

After introductions, Jessie gave a nervous curtsy to Ellie and looked around for somewhere to place her bag. Jessie was sixteen, but had already taken on a womanly body. She stood five-foot-two in her stocking feet, with an abundance of unruly curls which she'd clearly tried to tame with several pins. She wore a confident smile, and to Ellie's delight, possessed a pleasant disposition. Ellie took to her immediately.

'Pop your bag on the table, Jessie.'

'Yes mum, and then what would you like me to do.'

Ellie smiled warmly. 'Well you can start by calling me Ellie, and you can come and join us for tea and cakes.'

Jessie looked apprehensively at Lady Sarah. 'Me, mum, sit with you and Lady Sarah?'

Ellie grinned and nodded. 'We're all just friends having

tea now.'

Jessie bit her lip nervously, patted her hair and straightened her skirt while Ellie held out a chair for her.

'I'll just pop and get the tray. The tea is brewing.'

Jessie jumped back up. 'Let me, mum…Ellie.'

Ellie held out her hand. 'Sit, please.'

Jessie looked sheepishly at Sarah, who patted her hand. 'I know you're going to be very happy here, Jessie. I am so sorry for the trouble you've encountered at the manor, but I think this will be the making of you.'

'Thank you my lady, you've been so very kind.'

*

After a very pleasant hour, Sarah took her leave.

Ellie smiled at Jessie. 'I'll show you to your bedroom. The cottage is small but I'm sure it will be to your liking.'

Jessie stopped dead at the bedroom doorway. 'Is this all mine?'

Ellie grinned and nodded. 'I'm just next door.'

'Oh, Ellie, it's lovely.' Jessie dropped her bag and ran her hands across the neat bedspread. Turning to the table by the window she glanced at the array of gifts from the sea - shells, unusual pebbles and sea glass.

'Move them if you don't want them there.'

'Oh no,' Jessie answered, fingering the sea glass as though it was a precious stone. 'They're lovely too.'

'I like to collect them. It's a lovely day, so why don't you slip on your coat and take off your stockings and we'll take a walk down the beach to find some more?'

*

With his pain, coupled with boredom, loneliness and heartache, Guy's mind was in a terrible state. A black mood engulfed him, making him quite unwilling to communicate with anyone.

'There's a letter come for you, Mr Blackthorn,' the nurse said. She held the envelope up for him to see.

The handwriting was clearly Ellie's - the last person he wanted to receive a letter from.

'Shall I open it so you can read it?'

He shook his head, so the nurse left it on the bedside table.

The letter sat where the nurse had left it mocking him. His head told him to read it, but his broken heart urged him not to. The day seemed endless. He ached beyond belief and though he lay on a waterbed, his back and buttocks pained him terribly. Never in his life had he felt so miserable.

As the sun set on another day, Guy watched from his tiny hospital window as the sky turned pink. How he longed to sit at Poldhu and watch the sun set over Land's End and witness the blue black night sky creep up from the east, each moment revealing another star twinkling in the darkness. Only a few weeks ago, he'd sat on a blanket on the Poldhu dunes and watched the shooting stars with Ellie. Life had been good. A future had been in the making. His plan to propose marriage to Ellie had been on his lips so many times, but because she'd been hurt by Philip, he wanted to give her more time to adjust to someone else's feelings. So he'd waited. He gave a short snort. Look where waiting had got him. He'd lost her forever now.

Darkness had descended, not only in his room but in his heart. Soon the nurse would light the gas lamp and bring him a meal he had no desire to eat. He glanced at the letter - her letter. What could she possibly say that he wished to know?

As the nurse came to light the gas lamps, she saw the letter on his table and frowned. 'I'm sorry, Mr Blackthorn. I should have left the letter on your bed. You can't possibly reach it from there.

When Guy had arrived at the hospital he had both arms re-splinted as soon as the doctor had seen him. His left shoulder was shattered, so his arm was now strapped to his chest, and his right arm was broken just above the wrist, so he was just about able to use his hand to hold a book or a letter. It was this hand she pushed the letter into. When the nurse left he looked again at Ellie's handwriting and his eyes watered. Leaning the letter on his thigh he slowly ripped the envelope open, took a deep breath and began to read.

Dear Guy,

I hope this letter finds you more comfortable than last I saw you.

Guy squeezed his eyes shut to steady his feelings.

I received a letter from Amelia Pascoe shortly after you went to hospital. She told me that Dr Eddy assured her your treatment will work, though it will be a long process.

I think about you daily and pray for your swift recovery so that you can return to your family.

'But not to you!' he whispered.

Rest assured that you ma will be financially taken care of, so please don't fret about that.

'Oh no, Ellie, not with *his* money!' He could read no more, he screwed the letter into a tight ball in frustration, throwing it as far as his arm would permit. 'Aargh! The action produced a pain so severe it almost made him vomit. 'Damn you Goldsworthy.'

'Mr Blackthorn, whatever is the matter?' The nurse stood at the doorway with a tray of food, her eyes glancing at the screwed up letter.

Guy turned his head away from her. Angry tears pricked his eyes. He felt so helpless. Goldsworthy was helping his family financially, while he lay prostrate on this damn moving bed. He thumped the mattress hard making the bed undulate under him. He was glad of the seared pain in his wrist which ensued - it took away the ache in his heart.

The nurse placed the tray heavily on the bedside table and thumped her fists into her hips.

'Mr Blackthorn, please do not do that to the bed, it may burst, then I shall have a terrible mess to clean up,' she scolded. 'Now, you need to eat some of this lovely dinner we've prepared for you.' She pulled a chair alongside the bed, placed the tray on his chest and handed him the fork. Cupping his head she lifted him slightly, waiting for him to start to eat. 'Mr Blackthorn, I do have other patients to see to.'

Guy closed his eyes and willed the nurse to leave him to his misery.

'I can't leave you to your own devices otherwise you will choke. Now please.' She manoeuvred his hand holding the fork and scooped some potato onto it. 'I will not leave until you have eaten at least two mouthfuls.'

Guy's mouth remained tightly shut.

'Mr Blackthorn.' The nurse looked back toward the door and whispered, 'Guy, please, eat something, otherwise I shall feel Dr Sandringham's wrath if I allow you to wither and die of starvation. Please, take a little nourishment, for my sake if not your own.'

Guy noted the blue of her eyes intensified as they began to water, and reluctantly took the fork and ate a mouthful of food.

The nurse smiled weakly as he took three more mouthfuls and then he was done.

'Thank you,' she mouthed as she stood, gave him a drink of water and straightened the bed. Picking up the discarded letter, she placed it in the cupboard with his belongings.

Guy watched her go. He swallowed down the food which threatened to make another appearance, wondering whether it was the food or the thought of Goldsworthy's filthy money taking care of his ma that made him sick. He tried to rationalise it in his head. Of course he was thankful that someone was helping his family, he just didn't want it to be him!

22

After a relatively quiet winter, it was the first week of February 1902, when a storm hit the South West coast of Cornwall. Jessie, having lived most of her life inland at Bochym Manor, quaked at the ferocity of the wind and rain, which battered the windows and whipped the sea to an angry torrent.

Brandy too was experiencing his first taste of wild weather and cowered in the corner of the cottage with his tail between his legs.

Ellie watched apprehensively as the tide pushed higher up the beach. It had breached the perimeter walls three times since she'd lived here. She didn't relish the mess if it reached the Tea Room. She glanced at the clock – it was three-fifteen, by her estimation high tide was about now, so they should be alright. She just hoped that the storm would blow itself out before nightfall. Dealing with a flood in the dead of night was no laughing matter. Just to be on the safe side, she and Jessie had banked up all the doors with hessian filled sand bags.

With nothing else to do but wait, Ellie made a brew of tea for her and Jessie and they sat amiably by the fireside.

Jessie had settled nicely into Ellie's life. She was popular and friendly with the customers, and Ellie wondered how she'd ever coped without her. She was an absolute godsend in helping fill the void left by Guy.

As Ellie took the first bite of cake, a blast of wind shook the windows and the fire blew back, sending smoke billowing into the room. Both Ellie and Jessie jumped from where they sat, coughing to clear their lungs of smoke.

'This is awful,' Jessie moaned.

'Well, hopefully the storm will move off soon. It's bad for business. No one dare venture down to the cove when the weather is this vicious.' They moved cautiously back to the fireside. 'Still, it's nice to put my feet up.'

'I'll say.' Jessie dropped into the armchair with a sigh.

'Is it harder work here than the manor/'

'No, this is wonderful. I love it here. At least I don't have Mrs Bligh, the miserable, dry, old 'spinster of this parish', scowling at me anymore.'

Ellie laughed at the apt description.

'I miss Betsy though, and I know it sounds strange but, I miss Pearl's ghost as well. Lady Sarah said you knew Pearl. What was she like?'

Ellie smiled. 'I did know her. She used to look after me when I was little. She had lovely red curly hair, vivid green eyes and a line of ginger freckles across her nose. She was really bonny and always smiling.'

'Gosh, how lovely, I can only see a grey image of her, but it's really clear. There is one thing for certain, she doesn't smile now. I feel like I've abandoned her now I've left. I'm sure she wanted to tell me something. I used to see her standing at the attic window looking out to the courtyard. She'd also stand behind horrible Albert Lanfear, pointing at him in great distress.'

'Oh!' A sudden memory jumped into Ellie's head and then just as quickly left her again, leaving her disoriented.

'Are you alright, Ellie?' Jessie reached out to her. 'You've gone deathly pale.'

'Yes, I'm fine, it's just that when you mentioned Pearl standing behind Lanfear, it struck me that I'd seen that image myself, but years ago. I just can't recall the incident.'

'There must be something significant in it then. Maybe Pearl knows that you know what happened to her. That's why she gets excitable whenever you visit the manor and terribly upset when you leave.'

Ellie sighed. 'I can't tell you how it grieves me to hear that. I really don't know what happened, except for what Lady Sarah told me, that Pearl ran away.'

Jessie shivered. 'I have a notion that she died in the manor and no one found her body, because for some reason, the girl is in torment there. It breaks my heart to think no one can help her, now I've left!'

'Oh Jessie, I'm not sure anyone can help. What has happened to Pearl is in the past, and the past can't be changed.'

'I know, but I just want her to be at peace, and she really isn't at the moment.'

*

The storm abated as the evening drew in, so Jessie risked a quick walk with Brandy. She'd already mopped up two puddles from the frightened dog, she didn't want another. They supped at seven, and then Jessie curled up to read her book while Ellie penned another letter to Guy.

Dearest Guy,

I hope my last letter made you feel a little bit better and I pray with all my heart that you are making a good recovery. It has been six weeks now since your accident and if I'm not mistaken most broken bones heal in that amount of time. I know you have a more serious problem with your back so I wish you god speed in that recovery. I do not mind admitting that I miss you terribly. Hopefully once your arms are out of their splints you will be able to pen a letter to me to put my mind at rest. Don't worry if you can't though, I will understand.

Spring came early at Poldhu. Although we are just experiencing the first storm of the season, the sun, when it shines, has real warmth in it. The daffodils have been picked already. I saw this lone sea thrift flower yesterday and picked it for you. It made me smile as they should not make their appearance for many weeks yet. It grieves me that you are not here to see it all, so I've enclosed it for you to enjoy.

I admit I have not ventured over to Gweek to see your ma and Silas, but as you have always been so kind to me, I am managing to send a little money from my takings to them, just to keep the wolf from the door, so to speak.

I would dearly love to visit you, but being so far away makes it impossible for me to be there and back in a day. As much as I want to be by your side, I cannot leave the tea room at the moment. I have

taken on a young girl, to help out, but I fear it will be some time before I could leave her in charge, so my visit to Truro must wait. Rest assured Guy, I pray for your speedy recovery every night. In fact you're all I think about. I miss you so much. Get well soon and hurry home to me.
Your dearest friend, Ellie x

Ellie retired to bed early to read for a while, safe in the knowledge that the storm had blown itself out and all risk of flooding had subsided. She read a few lines, but her mind would not be still. Jessie's heartfelt concern, over basically someone who had died long ago, also worried her. Something was gnawing at her mind. Why did the spirit of Pearl need Ellie? What did she know that might free her from her eternal torment? Ellie put her book down and pulled the covers high. She sent a silent prayer up for Guy's recovery, and then another for Pearl to rest in peace.

As Ellie fell into a deep sleep, she began to dream. The years slipped away and she was sat with her mother around the kitchen table at Bochym Manor. The entire household staff had been summonsed - something had happened. Ellie glanced around the people seated at the table. The room felt sombre and a hush had fallen as they waited for Mr Carrington the butler, to take his seat.

Ellie smiled at Pearl, who was standing just behind Albert Lanfear and Ellie wondered why she wasn't taking her seat.

Mr Carrington cleared his voice - clearly he hadn't noticed that Pearl hadn't sat down. 'It is my duty to tell you that Pearl Martin has done a wicked thing by running away after getting herself in the family way, leaving us without a dairymaid or a bye-your-leave.'

Ellie frowned and turned to her mother. 'Pearl hasn't gone, Mummy! She's standing behind Mr Lanfear right now, look, she's pointing at him!'

Ellie woke suddenly from her dream as though she had

been pulled through a vortex. She sat up in the dark emptiness of her bedroom. Unable to get her bearings, Ellie grasped for her candlestick. With a strike of the flint, the room was illuminated and she realised she was at home in her own bed and no longer ten-years-old. It worried her how real the dream was. She pulled her pillow up to prop herself up and pondered on her dream. Had she conjured that scene up because of what she and Jessie were talking about? The more she thought, the more she realised, that deep down that was no ordinary dream - that was real, she'd just pushed it to the back of her mind. Pearl hadn't run away, she must have died! She had a very strong inclination that Albert Lanfear had something to do with it.

*

It was Valentine's Day. After the storm two days ago, the weather in Cornwall was more in keeping with May now. Ellie was troubled by her dream, but as yet she could do little about it. Try as she might she was struggling to recall any other detail, but none would come. As the sun rose in the east it had real warmth. The sea however was icy cold as she paddled her way over the rocks in search of sea glass treasure. She had a mind to enclose a piece to send to Guy in her next letter. It would be something he'd appreciate. She'd sent her letter two days ago in a hope that he would receive and read it today – this day for celebrating love. Hopefully the letter would leave him in no doubt of her feelings for him.

Ellie's feet were icy cold as she padded up the beach. A soak in a bowl of warm water would be just the ticket. Brandy was in a playful puppy mood and circled her legs as she walked, almost tripping her up. As they rounded the dunes to the Tea Room, Brandy began to growl. She grabbed him by the scruff thinking the postman had arrived, only to find Philip standing on the terrace with his arms full of flowers. It took all Ellie's strength to hold Brandy - the dog seemed to sense that her visitor was unwelcome.

Ellie gleaned some comfort in the fact that Philip looked fearful of the dog. Brandy's growling and barking brought Jessie outside. She looked first at Ellie then at Philip Goldsworthy.

'Shall I take Brandy from you, Ellie?'

'No, thank you, but could you bring me her lead, please?' The dog gave her confidence to deal with Philip.

Once on the lead she quietened the dog the best she could, and then looked questionably at Philip. 'Why are you here?'

'I should think that was obvious. It's Valentine's Day. I've brought you flowers.'

'I don't want your flowers, Philip. I suggest you take them back to your wife.' Ellie began to walk towards her cottage.

'But Valentine's Day is for people in love, and I love you Ellie.' He stepped forwards but Brandy lurched at him stopping him in his tracks.

Ellie pulled him to heel. 'Go to hell, Philip and take your flowers with you. I cannot bear to look at you after what you said to me when I asked you to help Guy.'

He glanced warily down at the dog. 'But Ellie, Guy is being helped, did you not know?'

'Of course I know,' she snapped.

'Well then.' He held his free arm out.

'Well then, what?' she rounded on him.

'Come on Ellie. Did you really think I wouldn't help my friend?' he said in a deep authoritative voice.

Ellie blanched with indignation. 'What exactly are you inferring?'

'Do I have to spell it out, Ellie? I paid for his treatment. Of course, I've kept it secret from everyone in the village. Guy probably wouldn't have accepted it from me if he'd known. Now I understand that you're still angry with me over the marriage misunderstanding, but Ellie, I love you. Can we not be friends now?' He held out the flowers.

Ellie looked at him incredulously. 'I honestly didn't think you could sink any lower than you already have done. You have the audacity to stand there lying to me, pretending you've been a good friend to Guy. I know exactly who has paid for Guy's treatment, Philip and it certainly wasn't you!'

Caught out, Philip gave an embarrassed shake of his head.

Enjoying his humiliation, she said, 'I'd very much like you to leave now and take your flowers with you. You're not welcome here, ever again.'

As Philip narrowed his eyes, Ellie could see cold anger in them. If it hadn't been for the fact that Jessie and the dog were by her side she would have been much more afraid than she was. Thank god Guy had brought Brandy to her before he was injured.

Philip's voice hardened. 'You belonged to me once. You will again one day.' He threw the flowers to the ground and heeled them into the sand until they were destroyed. 'This is what you are doing to my heart, Ellie.' He turned on his heel and left.

Jessie stood agog. 'Bloody hell, Ellie! What was all that about? He's married to Lady Carole! What's he doing coming here with flowers for you?'

Ellie sighed. 'It's a long story Jessie. Philip wants to have his cake and eat it, if you'll excuse the pun. Come on, let's go indoors and I'll tell you all about it.'

*

Guy had endured his prostrate state now for six weeks and was thoroughly miserable. First with boredom from the tedious monotony of the days and more so, the embarrassment of having a nurse see to his every call of nature.

He could not sleep at night, for no matter how he tried to still and empty his mind, Ellie always came into his head. The sight of her suntanned bare legs exposed as she tucked her skirt into her belt, and the wind blowing her long curly hair into her face. That smile on her rosy lips, the one she'd only just started to wear for him, and those lovely eyes that looked upon him with love. All these things tortured him. Once she was his, now she was another's.

And so this was his lot, strapped to a contraption which kept his spine immobile and still on this hated water bed to avoid blood poisoning from pressure wounds. He was unsure how much more he could take.

'Two letters for you, Mr Blackthorn,' the nurse trilled as she slipped the envelopes into his hand. 'It's Valentine's Day, maybe there is something from someone special for you.'

When she'd gone he glanced at the first one - his lips curled into an unaccustomed smile. It was from Silas, he'd know that scrawl anywhere. The other however was clearly from Ellie - 'someone special.' He screwed his eyes shut to blot out the pain stabbing his heart. *Please stop writing to me, Ellie, you're breaking my heart.* He crumpled the unopened letter into a tight ball and threw it into the corner of the room.

For a good few minutes, uncontrollable demons flew around in his head. The more agitated he got, the more his bed moved, which made his situation worse. He took several deep breaths to calm himself before he could pick up Silas's letter to read.

Dear Guy,

When are you coming home? I miss you. I've made all the willow I had into spurs ready for you. Farmer Ferris has taken your wagon of reed and put it in his barn. He sends his best wishes for a speedy recovery and says you're not to worry about anything. He's taken Mazie too and she is grazing in the top meadow. I promise I will ride her every week so that she doesn't get fat and lazy. Ma misses you and sends her love. I think she is going a bit soft in the head though. She thought she had made a stew the other day and all she had done was boil her petticoat and drawers in the pot over the fire and put the potatoes and carrots in the dolly tub.

Guy rested the letter for a moment. He hoped all was well with his ma, that sort of behaviour was very uncharacteristic of her.

I bet it's great laying in bed all day. I wish I could.

'No you bloody well wouldn't, Silas.'

Please get better soon, so that I can work with you. I have to work at the forge with horrible Blewett. I want you to come home and thump him for me because he keeps thumping me if I don't pump the bellows fast enough.

Guy felt his fists curl into a ball at the mention of Blewett. God damn it, he would brain the man when he saw him next….if he ever got out of here!

Blue is growing daily, he follows me everywhere. He can even climb the ladder up to the roof. Come home, Guy, we need you back.
Silas

He laid the letter on his bed and sighed in frustration. He heard the nurse come, but ignored her. He didn't see her pick up the balled letter from the corner of the room, straighten it out and put it with the other letter in his bedside cupboard.

'Mr Blackthorn,' she said, 'Dr Sandringham is coming to see you in a few minutes. Let me just tidy your covers.'

As he saw Dr Sandringham approach with a young woman in tow, Guy turned his face away. How many more times could he listen to him saying "Not long now before we can start your rehabilitation." Damn the man, he was sure he was just trying to appease him.

'How is my patient today?' Sandringham asked, as he checked the notes at the foot of his bed.

Guy said nothing.

Ignoring Guy's silence, he said, 'Today the splints will be removed from your arms and legs, so I think it's time we tried to move you.'

Guy turned and saw the young woman smile down at him - she had very blue eyes.

'This is Nurse Young. She specialises in getting patients moving again.'

Nurse Young gave Guy a dazzling smile. 'Good day to you, Mr Blackthorn.'

Not having spoken for many weeks, Guy answered hoarsely, 'Good day nurse.'

'You can call me Clara,' she said with a twinkle in her eye, 'Right then. Let's get this poor body of yours moving again.'

23

Gweek valley, being low lying, was often covered in a fine layer of fragile white crystals of frost from late autumn through to the early spring, whereas further down the Helford River no frost gathered at all.

Knowing the icy wonderland would soon warm and dissipate, Amelia Pascoe began to do her weekly washing. She was up to her elbows in suds at the kitchen sink when she spotted Nellie Blackthorn standing by the bridge, without her coat! It was early March, not the time of year to be without warm clothing. Amelia dried her arms, pulled on her own coat and stepped out into the chill of the morning.

Elizabeth Trevone too had spotted Nellie, and was making her way towards her, swiftly followed by her daughter Jenna.

'Great minds think alike.' Amelia grinned at Elizabeth. 'What on earth is she doing?'

'Are you alright, Nellie?' Elizabeth and Amelia called in unison.

Nellie heard the voices, but momentarily didn't register them calling her name. She furrowed her brow. *Come on woman, stop day-dreaming.* She heard a voice again and jumped when Amelia touched her on the shoulder.

'You were miles away then!' Amelia laughed.

Nellie smiled shakily. 'I was, wasn't I?'

'Why are you not wearing a coat?'

Nellie looked down at her apron and shivered. 'Erm?'

Amelia took her by the arm. 'Come on. You're chilled to the bone. Let me brew you a cuppa. Would you like to join us Elizabeth?'

They all settled in Amelia's comfortable kitchen, while Amelia brewed a strong cup of tea, helped by little Jenna.

'Where were you going without your coat? There is still a chill in the air.' Elizabeth laid her hand on Nellie's arm.

'It must have been warm when I left home. I've just

been to the dairy.' Nellie looked around her for the can of milk she'd purchased. 'What the devil have I done with it?'

'You had nothing in your hand when we found you,' Amelia assured her as she put the tea pot on the table.

Nellie tutted loudly. 'I'm in such a day-dream today.'

Amelia had given Jenna a plate of biscuits to take to the table and as she offered them up, Nellie took one gratefully. 'Thank you, Emma.'

Little Jenna smiled. 'It's Jenna, Mrs Blackthorn.'

Nellie frowned. 'That's what I said.'

Jenna glanced at her mother, who put her finger to her lips not to say anything else.

'Do you feel alright otherwise?' Amelia moved in to take a closer look at her eyes. She didn't know what she was looking for, but she'd seen Dr Eddy do much the same thing.

Nellie moved back slightly. 'I'm fine, thank you. You keep your doctoring to yourself.'

Amelia laughed. 'I can't help myself. Here.' She handed a cup to Nellie. 'How are your boys?'

'Dr Eddy says Guy is doing well, thank goodness. All his splints have been removed and he's moving about now, though lord knows when he'll be home again.'

'Gosh, that is such good news. Are you still okay for money?'

'Yes thank you.' Nellie had received another envelope with money in this morning, though she had no idea where it was coming from. 'Silas is working at the forge, of course.'

Elizabeth pulled a face. 'Oh yes, poor Silas. How's he getting on with George Blewett?'

Nellie tsked. 'He keeps belting Silas for not working fast enough. I'm afraid of the man 'else I would give him a piece of my mind, but we need all the money we can get.'

'He really is an unpleasant individual. I'll keep an eye out for him. If I hear raised voices, I'll intervene. I'm not afraid of him,' Amelia said.

Nellie nodded appreciatively and sipped her tea. 'I pray to god that Guy will recover enough to go back to thatching - at least Silas can work with him then.'

'Will he return to full fitness then - I mean enough to thatch again?' Amelia asked cautiously.

Nellie shrugged her shoulders. 'The doctor seems to think so, though it'll take time. Silas worked with Guy during the school holidays so he knows the ropes and it's in the blood. My Rory, god rest his soul, said Guy picked the skill up in an instant, there is no reason why Silas won't do the same.'

'Have you heard anything of Ellie since Guy went into hospital?'

Nellie puzzled. 'Who?'

'Ellie Rosevear from the Poldhu Tea Rooms.'

Nellie's face blanked.

'You must remember her. There was all that misunderstanding over Philip Goldsworthy last year. I understand she came to see Guy before he went into hospital.'

Nellie tsked, 'Oh that hussy.'

'Ellie is *not* a hussy. In fact I always thought she would make a good wife for Guy.'

Nellie pursed her lips. 'Over my dead body - she'll always be tainted by association with Goldsworthy.'

Amelia bristled. 'No she won't, and you know it.'

'I think we'll agree to disagree there,' Nellie said getting up. 'Thank you for the tea and chat, but I shall have to get back.'

'Don't forget to go back to the dairy.'

'What for?'

Amelia shook her head. 'The milk you said you'd bought!'

'Oh yes, I forgot all about that. Where's my coat?'

'You didn't have one on!'

'Of course I did. What fool would go out in the cold without one?'

'Here, I'll lend you one of mine.'

'No wait a moment, when I come to think about it, I took it off in the dairy. I was having a warm moment, you know?' She fanned her face.

'Oh, god, yes, you don't have to tell me about them!' Amelia agreed.

'Tell you about what?' Nellie asked.

'Nothing.' Amelia shook her head and laughed. 'Now can you remember where you live?'

'Don't be cheeky - you'll be old and forgetful one day.'

Amelia and Elizabeth watched as Nellie set off down the lane and turn right. 'Nellie, you're going the wrong way to the dairy.'

'I know, I know,' Nellie answered impatiently as she turned back and walked over the bridge.

Elizabeth and Amelia glanced at each other.

'Is she losing her mind, Amelia? You heard her call Jenna, Emma, and she's known her eight years.'

'I don't know. She may have a water infection. I've seen many a person go doolally because they haven't drunk enough water! I'll get Dr Eddy to go and see her.'

Elizabeth laughed. 'On your head be it, she won't like that!'

*

Over the last two weeks, Clara had coaxed and cajoled Guy to begin to move his weak body. As well as his broken limbs, his spine had sustained a fracture, which with the help of bed rest and immobility, had thankfully mended. He was still in considerable pain, but it was nothing he could not cope with. Thankfully he no longer resided on his water-bed hell. He now had the luxury of a nice firm straw mattress which did not move when he breathed.

Guy was unsure of Clara at first and proved quite unwilling, if not a little bit stubborn, when she tried to touch his fragile limbs.

After several attempts to massage his body without

success, Clara folded her arms and gave him an ultimatum. 'Do you want to rot away on this bed for the rest of your life, Guy Blackthorn?'

Guy swallowed hard.

'Do you?'

'No!' he snapped. 'Of course I don't.'

'Then let me help you!'

'I'm frightened you'll set me back months if you move me!' As soon as he said it he felt guilty for questioning her ability.

'You're not a special case, Guy, believe me. I've managed to help many people walk again after worse back injuries than yours. Now, are you going to let me help you or not?'

Guy lowered his eyes but lay silent.

'Trust me.'

He gave a slight nod of the head and resigned himself to another kind of hell.

First Clara gave him gentle stretching exercises whilst he was lying in bed. She massaged his limbs every day and made him flex his feet, knees and elbows. After a week of stretching and flexing, he was fitted with a bone corset to keep his trunk stable in order to bring him to a standing position. This was the very worst part of his rehabilitation. Clara and another nurse swung his legs off the side of his bed and very slowly they lifted him to a sitting position. Every nerve in his body protested. His head swam alarmingly and he promptly vomited into a chamber pot which Clara swiftly pressed against his chest.

He glanced up at her apologetically.

She smiled. 'Don't worry, that always happens.'

They gave him a few minutes to regain his balance, before pulling him to a standing position.

Guy felt as though his legs were made of jelly. There was no strength in them and his feet felt huge, as though they were three inches bigger than they should be. Suddenly horrendous pins and needles set into his legs.

'Christ, what is this hell?' he moaned as they sat him down again, and lifted his legs back onto the bed to rest. 'I'm not going to be able to do it, am I?' he cried as the pins and needles subsided. 'I'll never be able to walk again.'

Clara raised her eyebrows. 'Don't be so defeatist, Guy. You've just done it!'

'But you don't understand, my legs, they feel odd, like they don't belong to me.'

'They're lazy that's all. We just have to get them going again. Trust me the next time will be easier.'

'Tomorrow?'

'I'll be back in two hours and we'll do it all again. I promise you'll not need a nurse to bring you a bed pan by the end of the day.'

Sure enough before he settled down to sleep at the end of that day, he'd stood up supported by two nurses and relieved himself into the chamber pot strategically placed on a chair. As he gave a long satisfied sigh, Clara and the other nurse exchanged a smile.

Clara returned to his bedside before lights out to check on him.

'Are you alright?' She smiled.

He nodded contentedly.

'I'll see you tomorrow.'

Guy reached out and grasped Clara's hand as she turned to leave. 'Thank you.'

As she smiled her eyes twinkled. 'It was my pleasure. Goodnight, Guy.'

Although exhausted from the day's activities, Guy felt an overwhelming feeling of achievement today. He closed his eyes and thought of nothing except his own well being and slept peacefully for the first time in a long, long time.

*

Twice a month since Guy had been admitted to hospital, Ellie had penned a letter to him. She told him news of Brandy growing daily and the mischief he got into. She wrote about the extraordinary people who visited the Tea

Room, mostly guests staying at the Poldhu Hotel - many of them here from Europe, enjoying the delights of the Cornish coastline. She wrote about the moon and the stars, reminding him of the night they watched the shooting stars together. She also wrote about her flourishing garden, now in the throes of spring. They were just little things, but she hoped that it would help to pass his lonely days. Ellie had hoped that now almost eight weeks had passed, Guy would have been able to pen a short letter back to her by now. The fact that he hadn't, lay heavy on her mind.

*

Clara Young had worked at the Royal Cornwall Infirmary for five years. Having escaped the clutches of her licentious step-father, she first worked as a skivvy, before lying about her age in order to train as a nurse. She was twenty-two-years-old, time was ticking by and there seemed to be no sign of a husband on the horizon for her. Unfortunately the long shifts at the hospital seemed to hinder her meeting any eligible young men.

Taller than the other nurses, standing at five-foot-six in her stocking feet, Clara had long straight brown hair which would not hold a curl no matter what she did. This didn't matter as she wore it scraped back into a bun at the back of her head. Her eyes were blue and her lips thin. People had commented that she was more handsome than pretty.

Her work in rehabilitation seemed mostly to be with the older, well-to-do-patients, who had fallen and were learning to walk with the aid of a stick. Guy Blackthorn however, was very different from her normal patients. She gloried in the time she spent with him, though it grieved her that he suffered greatly from melancholia.

After observing him for a couple of weeks it was clear there was no sweetheart on the horizon, otherwise he would have had visitors or letters from someone. When mentioning this to the nurse who'd looked after Guy from the start, she'd told her, 'Oh yes, he's had letters from someone! He read the first one and then screwed it up, and when the others came he did the same without even opening them!'

'Did you see who the first one was from?'

'I didn't read it of course, but couldn't help seeing that the letter was signed by someone called Ellie.'

'Did you throw them away?'

'No, I've put them with his belongings.'

'Why? He obviously doesn't want to have anything to do with this girl.'

'Not at the moment he doesn't, no. But you know he is prone to very dark moods. I thought perhaps when he's feeling a little better he'll reconsider and want to read them at a later date.'

There was no way Clara could go through Guy's things without him knowing but she was determined that if the letters were from a sweetheart, she was certainly going to find out one way or another.

Guy was into the third week of his rehabilitation and as soon as he could be helped to a standing position without his head spinning, Clara had begun the next phase to help him take his first tentative steps. It was a slow and laborious session and the effort drenched Guy in sweat, but with Clara's help and his own dogged determination, Guy slowly began to feel the ground under his feet.

By the end of the week, he'd managed to walk four steps almost unaided towards his chair where Clara let him sit and rest.

She pulled up the other chair and sat beside him while he took a long drink of water. Clara noted that his face showed relief at being able to rest, but apart from that it was devoid of all other emotion.

'Are you not happy with your progress?' she asked tentatively.

'I am yes, thank you.'

'It's just that.....well, you never seem happy with your achievements. In fact you always look so sad!'

Guy lowered his eyes and shrugged his shoulders, immediately regretting the action when a pain shot through his newly mended collar bone.

'Whatever can be bothering you? You're making excellent progress now, you should be happy.'

Guy did not know how to answer her.

'Talk to me Guy. A problem shared and all that. Have you no sweetheart who could visit and lift your spirits.'

'No!' The ferocity of his answer shocked him.

Clara rested her hands on her lap and waited for him to say more.

Guy glanced at Clara. She was always so kind to him. He'd trusted her to help him walk, could he trust her with his painful story? She clearly wanted to help. Would it help? He saw her hand move over to his hand, she cupped it gently and squeezed. The action thawed a tiny part of his heart. 'I had a sweetheart, but…..' He hung his head.

'But?'

'She….Ellie.' He closed his eyes to the pain of speaking her name.

'Ellie?'

He took a deep breath. 'Ellie gave herself to another man…..to get the money for my treatment.

'Oh, I see. Did she know this other man, or…'

Guy's eyes widened at the inference. 'Oh yes...yes she knew him.' He pulled a tight smile. 'She knew him well.'

'Are you sure she did this…thing.'

'I'm certain. The conversation between them was overheard and the next I knew I was on my way here.'

'Well I'm sorry for you, Guy. But perhaps… she was more his sweetheart than yours.' She cupped her other hand on his and added, 'Anyone who really loved you would not do that. If it had been me, I'd have moved heaven and earth to find another way to help you.'

Guy pulled his hand from hers and looked away.

Immediately berating herself at saying the wrong thing, she added, 'I'm sorry, I spoke out of turn.'

Guy shook his head. 'Don't apologise. What you say has already gone through my head a million times. In truth I'd rather have died on that kitchen floor than suffer the consequences and heartbreak of her doing what she did. I can only surmise that she did not love me as I loved her.'

Loved, he said loved, not love. Clara reached again for his hand. 'The pain will ease in time, Guy. Someone will come along and mend that broken heart of yours, I promise that. But you'll have to let go of the past. You're beginning a new phase of your life now, learning to walk again, and living life to the full when you get back home to your work. Make sure you open your heart to everything on offer now. You deserve to be happy. This is your second chance.'

This time Guy didn't pull his hand from Clara's.

*

With the weather being so inclement during February and March, and life at the manor busy with household affairs and social events, Sarah hadn't found a moment to visit the Tea Room. This she needed to rectify. So on the 30th March – Easter Sunday - Sarah brought with her a group of ladies to take tea after church.

As she watched Ellie at work, Sarah noted that although she had a smile for everyone, something was worrying her. Concerned at first that all was not well between her and Jessie, though to watch them, she very much doubted that, she decided there was something deep rooted that perhaps needed her help to sort out.

*

On Easter Monday, the weather was rather blustery but the sun tried in vain to warm the day. As Ellie turned to make her way back up the beach, she lifted her hand to shield her eyes from the sun. Sarah was standing on the terrace.

With her skirt hem damp, sand on her feet and her hair blown loose, Ellie felt she was hardly in a fit state to receive visitors, but she smiled happily.

'Sarah! What an unexpected but lovely surprise. Please forgive my appearance.'

'No matter, I've brought some primroses from Bochym for your tables.' She handed a huge bunch of fragrant yellow flowers.

'These are lovely.' Ellie buried her nose into the posy. 'Come on in, I'll brew us some tea.'

Sarah sat down as Ellie took the kettle from the fire, brewed the tea and then poured the remaining water into a bowl and quickly washed her sandy feet. A few minutes later, Ellie sat down stockinged and booted.

'I'm sorry to have called so early, but I wanted to speak to you.' Sarah leant forward and took Ellie's hands in hers. 'I need to know what is worrying you.'

Ellie felt her throat constrict. 'It's Guy! My heart aches for news of him. I've written a few letters, obviously not expecting a reply at first, because of his injuries, but it's been over three months now. I'm desperate for word of him. He was in such a black mood when I saw him in December before he was admitted. It will not sit lightly on Guy should he be crippled.'

'Well, that's easy enough to rectify. You need to make a trip to Truro to put your mind at rest.'

Ellie grimaced. 'There's the thing you see. I can't make the trip to Truro and back in a day. I would stay over somewhere but I don't want to leave Jessie in sole charge just yet.'

Sarah stood and smoothed down her fine dress. 'Well, I am planning a trip to Truro at the end of April to shop for my upcoming European trip. If you can wait a few more weeks, I'll take you in the carriage. We can be there and back before nightfall.'

Ellie's eyes watered. 'Thank you, Sarah, you're so kind.'

Sarah sighed. 'I wish I'd thought to take you earlier, but I've been so busy at the manor. So shall we say the 28th April? I can go shopping and you can visit your young man.' She smiled knowingly. 'I suggest you send him word to say you are coming. It will give him something to look forward to. Now Elise, I must rush. I'm going to Helston to see about having new drapes made. I'm trying to get everything spic and span in the manor before we go away.'

Ellie was in two minds whether to tell Sarah about the disturbing dream she'd had about Lanfear, but as she was in such a rush to leave, she thought to save the information for the long journey to Truro.

24

The trip to Truro could not come soon enough. The thrill of seeing Guy again filled Ellie's heart with joy. She was not indifferent to Guy's plight and did wonder if his lack of correspondence was his way of releasing her from their budding relationship. Perhaps he did not want to be a burden on her with his disabilities and was giving her a chance for her to be free of him. This she swept aside. From their past relationship, she knew she could break down any barriers the injuries would throw up.

Ellie packed her basket on Sunday evening with a small pot of jam - she would bake scones first thing in the morning to go with it. She took a cake for the nurses and a bunch of very early blooming sea pinks. As she rummaged in her wardrobe to find her prettiest dress to wear the next day, she heard Jessie answer a knock on the door.

'Who is it?' she called through.

'A message from Bochym - Lady Sarah has a dreadful cold and cannot go to Truro tomorrow.'

Ellie felt her world implode, until Jessie popped her smiling face around her bedroom door. 'But she's sent word that the carriage will come for you at ten a.m. as promised, for you to go on your own. Why are you crying?'

'Tears of joy Jessie, that's all. They're tears of joy.'

*

Clara had the letter Ellie sent in her pocket. She'd intercepted it from the ward nurse and toyed with the idea of giving it to Guy several times, but something deep inside told her not to. So instead she'd read it. It was clear from the letter that this woman cared nothing for how much she'd hurt him with her actions. Why else would she come and taunt him so. Clara knew how Guy felt about Ellie and the last thing he needed was to plummet back into his melancholia over her visit. Besides, Clara had set her hat at Guy. She wasn't going to let anyone get in the way of her attempts to mend his broken heart.

Clara watched from the hospital door as a beautiful carriage drew up and a lone woman in a very pretty dress emerged with a basket on her arm. She knew this must be Ellie. The note stated that she would be accompanying a 'Lady Sarah' in her carriage.

Clara felt every nerve prickle. It would only be a little white lie! She stepped forward as Ellie entered the hospital doors.

'Hello, can I help you?' Clara asked.

'Yes, thank you,' Ellie said brightly. 'I'm Ellie Rosevear - here to see Guy Blackthorn. I believe he's expecting me.'

'Guy Blackthorn?' Clara frowned.

'Yes, he was admitted in December with spinal injuries.'

'One moment.'

Clara pretended to check the resister as Ellie glanced at the stark white walls of the hospital. *How bleak this must be for Guy.* She was glad she'd brought him the bunch of sea pinks, though she feared they would be wilting now in her basket. She turned as Clara approached her.

'I'm afraid there is no one called Guy Blackthorn residing here.' She gave Ellie a sympathetic smile.

'Oh!' Ellie felt her heart sink. 'Are you sure?'

'I'm quite sure. He may be in Plymouth or even Exeter. Many spinal patients are sent there for specialist care.'

Ellie felt her throat restrict. 'But… I was told he was here!'

Clara smiled pleasantly. 'He might have been initially and then transferred out of the county. Have you come far?'

Ellie nodded.

'I'm sorry. You seemed to have had a wasted journey.'

Ellie looked around for a chair to sit on. Her disappointment was such she sat with her basket on her lap trying very hard to suppress her tears. No wonder he hadn't answered her letters.

Clara worried at Ellie's reluctance to leave. She knew she must return to her patients - she was already late, but she could not risk Ellie asking anyone else.

'Miss Rosevear, let me walk you to your carriage. This has obviously been a great disappointment to you.'

Ellie looked up. 'Of course, I'm sorry. I'm taking up your precious time. Here, let me give you this.' She fished into her basket and drew out a cake. 'I baked this for the nurses to share and there are scones and jam. I baked them for Guy, you may as well share them out,' she said her voice trailing.

'How very kind of you.' Clara felt a pang of guilt at her dishonesty.

'There is also a bunch of very early sea pinks. Perhaps you could give them to one of your patients.'

'Thank you, I will.'

Clara walked Ellie to the carriage and waved her off. *She and Guy would enjoy the jam and scones with their afternoon tea.*

*

It was the longest, saddest ride home for Ellie. Grieved to think Guy was out there somewhere but completely unattainable, she found it hard to comprehend how to get through another few months without seeing him. She would pen a letter to both Plymouth General Hospital and the Royal Devon and Exeter Hospital when she got home, but even if she could find where Guy was, there was no chance of her visiting him so far away.

*

A letter arrived from Bochym the very next day.

Dear Elise,

I do hope you feel better for seeing your young man, though the carriage did return sooner than I thought it would. I hope he is well and it has put your mind at ease. I am afraid I shall not see you now for some time. We are embarking on a European tour today and will

not return until July. I do hope the sunny weather revives me as I am struggling to regain my strength after my illness.
Take care, Elise and give my love to Jessie.
Your friend, Sarah.

*

Ellie waited three weeks before receiving a reply from the hospitals, only to be told that no such patient was residing there. Heartbroken, Ellie dearly needed to speak to someone about her plight, but with Lady Sarah away she wrote to the only other person who would understand - Amelia Pascoe.

The letter that came by return post shocked Ellie to the core. It was edged in black and read:

My dear Ellie,

I am so sorry you are having difficulty in locating Guy's hospital. I hope you will forgive me, but unfortunately, my heart and mind are sore with grief at the moment and I feel unable to help you. You see, our dear mutual friend, Elizabeth Trevone, passed away quite unexpectedly yesterday (Thursday). The circumstances of her death are quite frightful. She caught her leg on a lump of wood in her hen coop last Wednesday evening and to all intents and purposes it just looked like a superficial bruise. Dr Eddy and I were called out by her distraught husband, Jory, on Thursday morning and we could both see that Elizabeth was mortally ill. We lost our friend on Thursday afternoon. We were all with her when she died, Jory, little Jenna, Dr Eddy and I. Dr Eddy believes the bang caused a clot in her blood which travelled to her heart and killed her. To say I am devastated is a complete understatement. I am numb with grief, not only for myself but for her poor husband Jory and of course little Jenna. The funeral is at eleven a.m. on Monday 26h May at Constantine Church. If you wish to come, meet at my cottage at ten.
I close this letter with sadness.
Amelia

Ellie put the letter down and sat with her head in her hands. Her worries over Guy seemed so trivial after reading this. She remembered with affection Elizabeth's kindness to her when everyone else shunned her. And Jenna, that poor beautiful little girl who so adored her mother, however would she cope now without her. Ellie felt a great empty sadness engulf her. What ill luck to befall such a lovely little family unit. It was times like these she wondered where God was and why had he let this happen.

*

Dressed in her mourning clothes, Ellie pushed aside her feelings about her time in Gweek, and set off to attend Elizabeth's funeral. Amelia greeted her warmly and quickly arranged for Ellie to go to church with the Williams's from the dairy. Neighbours, who had once shunned her, reacted quite differently today as they nodded to acknowledge her presence. It seemed that Amelia and Elizabeth, bless her, had set the record straight, and Ellie had been forgiven for any misdemeanours they thought she'd committed.

The church was full to capacity that day and many mourners stood in the churchyard outside to pay their respects. Ellie knew the sorrow of losing someone close, but the saddest sight she'd ever seen was little Jenna walking hand in hand with her father, Jory, behind the shiny black coffin. In her hand she clutched a posy of wild flowers, and when the coffin came to rest at the altar, Jory picked her up for her to place her flowers on the lid.

The wake was held in Elizabeth's homely kitchen. Jory sat by the fireside quietly broken-hearted. Little Jenna, always the hostess, walked from mourner to mourner, offering slices of cake to one and all, just like her mother had shown her.

'I fear for Jory's sanity,' Amelia said as she put another kettle on to boil. 'He's a quiet man at the best of times, but he loved Elizabeth with all his heart.' She turned and watched Jenna. 'He has no idea how to look after her. He left that to Elizabeth. Having said that, she's her mother's daughter. Look at her - she's a proper little housewife. The child is devastated at the loss, but when I came to see them both this morning, Jenna had made breakfast, washed up and made the beds.'

Ellie's lip trembled. 'Poor little mite. I feel for her. I too lost both my parents by the tender age of eleven. As long as you're there for her Amelia, she'll come brave. My saviour was Betty Trerise at Poldhu. Without her I would have floundered.'

Amelia sighed heavily. 'I'm going to really miss Elizabeth, more than you can ever imagine. I've known her since she was born. Her family lived in Sunnyside, over there by the river, until her parents and brother succumbed to consumption, some eight years ago.' She shook her head. 'It wiped the whole family out. Even though I am a good twenty years her senior, we became great friends after the tragedy and have been ever since. Elizabeth was the warmest, most giving human being I have ever come across. As you know, she made friends with everyone.'

Ellie gently laid her hand on Amelia's arm when she saw her eyes fill with tears.

'I know. You were both so kind to me when I needed a friend.'

Not one to let her emotions show, Amelia quickly whipped out her handkerchief and dabbed her eyes. 'We were glad we were able to help.' She sniffed. 'So tell me Ellie, how is that Tea Room of yours?'

'It's fine, but it's Guy's whereabouts I'm fretting over, if you remember I wrote to you to say he was no longer in The Royal Cornwall Infirmary, but of course this awful thing happened with Elizabeth, so…..'

Amelia rubbed her hand on her forehead. 'I'd completely forgotten. I wasn't aware that he'd been moved, Nellie hasn't said anything. Why don't you ask Dr Eddy? He'll know for definite where Guy has been moved to.'

'I had thought Guy's ma might be here today, I could have asked her,' Ellie scanned the room. 'I might go and call on her.'

'Maybe it's best you don't, today. Nellie has come down with the most dreadful cold. I called on her this morning to make her a hot toddy. She's confined to her bed and rather irritable with it too.'

'Oh dear. How is Silas? Are they managing without Guy's wage?' She did not disclose that she sent money to them every week, for chance of embarrassing Nellie for accepting charity.

'They're managing very well. Silas is a good lad, he's working at the forge and clears pots at The Black Swan in the evening. I don't think they want for anything.'

'I'll tell her you were asking after them,' Amelia said setting off with the tea pot to refill everyone's cup.

Ellie had to wait for over an hour to speak with Dr Eddy as he'd been temporarily called away. By the time he'd returned, Ellie knew the last wagon had departed from the Lizard crossroads, which meant she would have to walk the five miles home.

It was with a heavy heart that Ellie set off on her journey. Dr Eddy had left her in no uncertain terms that Guy had not been moved, and was still in residence at Truro. He'd told her that he was improving every day and had the care of a specialist nurse who was working miracles with him. He'd told her that he'd seen Guy only last week and found him to be so much happier than when he'd last seen him at the end of January. "Perhaps the pretty nurse who is looking after him has something to do with the upturn in his mood," he said with a wink.

Of course Dr Eddy knew nothing of her feelings for Guy, or how his thoughtless words had pierced her heart. *Had Guy made way in his heart for someone else's affection? He must have. Why else would he ignore her letters and have her sent away?* As her mind swirled with mixed emotions, she did not see the pony trap pull up beside her.

'Ellie!' Harry Yates doffed his cap. 'I thought it was you.'

Ellie pulled a smile from the depths of her heart. 'Hello, Harry. It's good to see you again.'

'Are you walking home to Poldhu?'

She nodded. 'I've missed the last wagon.'

'Hop aboard then.'

'Oh, but won't you get into trouble? I'm not sure Phi....Mr Goldsworthy will like you helping me.'

'Mr Goldsworthy can go to hell - begging your pardon for swearing. Hop aboard, I'll take you home. I'll think of some excuse for being late back.'

Ellie climbed aboard and settled beside him.

'You look somewhat distressed. Goldsworthy hasn't been bothering you again, has he? I know I work for him, but I'll not see him hurt you again.'

She shook her head morosely. 'You're very kind, Harry. I've just been to Elizabeth Trevone's funeral - the day has been quite emotional.'

Harry shook his head. 'Terrible, terrible tragedy that. That poor little girl and Jory will never, ever get over losing her. That's a fact!'

'I thought I'd see you there today.'

'I had planned on attending, but Mr Goldsworthy wanted me to take him to Bochym. Apparently his wife is having the place exorcised today!'

Ellie gasped. 'You're joking.'

Harry pulled a face. 'It's as true as I sit here. His wife believes there are evil spirits floating about and she's determined to rid the manor of them. I think she's mad if you ask me. You don't believe in ghosts do you?'

'Well, for risk of sounding mad as you say, I believe that sometimes, spirits get a little bit lost, en route to the other side.'

Harry gave her sideways look and grinned. 'Do you now. Well, I've never seen one and I'll not believe until I do.'

They sat for a while in silence until Harry asked, 'Tell me, have you had news of Guy since his accident?'

Ellie, who'd been thinking about Guy, turned her head in surprise as though he'd read her mind. 'Not personally no. I think by all accounts he's getting the care and help he needs.'

'He's a good man, Guy.'

Ellie nodded.

'Were you not walking out with him before his accident?'

'Not really. We liked each other, but…..'

Harry frowned at her response. 'I thought maybe you and he would make a lovely couple.'

Ellie smiled. 'Perhaps I did once too.'

Harry cocked his head. 'But not now?'

She shrugged her shoulders.

He flicked the reins. 'That's a shame.'

Ellie nodded sadly.

As they pulled up at Poldhu, Ellie offered him tea and cake. Harry thought 'in for a penny in for a pound' and accepted graciously. 'I'd love to, but first, I'm going to dip my feet in the sea - it lifted my spirits last time I did it. Perhaps you'd like to join me to lift your spirits too Ellie?'

Ellie smiled through her heartbreak. 'Perhaps I will. It will be a pleasure to paddle with you Harry, though I warn you, it will be mighty cold at this time of year.'

*

At Bochym, a small group of people gathered in the Jacobean drawing room. Carole and Philip stood by the fireside, certain that they would be ensconced back into the family home in the next few hours. The local vicar, Andrew Ellis, was donning his black cassock, while Carrington and Bligh stood with folded arms, surveying the scene with disapproving eyes. In the corner of the room stood Betsy, shaking like a leaf, brought against her will to witness the cleansing of the room.

'Maybe the silly girl will stop dropping things every time she thinks she sees something,' Bligh said haughtily.

'This had better work,' Carole snapped at the vicar.

'I'll not tolerate being ousted from my own home for another minute by this…this...,' she shook her head, '..ungodly thing!'

The vicar gave a gracious smile. 'Lady Carole, leave everything to me. I shall make this house spectre free. I'll burn incense and sage leaves to help cleanse the house, and call upon my own spirit guides and use the power of prayer. It's quite a simple technique. I will aim to draw in all that energy and send the spirit to where it needs to go,' he said with a flourish of his hand.

Philip moved nervously from one foot to the other. He'd been spooked once before playing with a Ouija board years ago. He didn't relish the action of calling on spirits. 'I'm off to The Wheel Inn. I'll see you after all this palaver.'

'Coward,' Carole sneered.

Philip raised his eyebrows. 'That's the pot calling the kettle black. You're the one who won't sleep here anymore!'

'Oh go on.' She shook her head disapprovingly. 'Go and drink yourself stupid then.'

Philip stomped out of the room. *Better to be drunk, if I'm to share the cold comfort of your bed!*

Carrington and Bligh watched with envy as he left.

'It is understood that unpleasant spirits feed on fear, Lady Carole. The earlier you evict these unwelcome guests, the better. Rest assured, they are generally harmless and easily removed,' the vicar said as he piled rice onto a plate and placed it by the open window. 'A spiritual possession is not necessarily "evil." Most spirits are simply lost, confused, or still clinging to life, and will leave when asked.' He piled salt onto another plate and stood it on the jardinière stand by the door. He dusted his hands together and smoothed down his cassock. 'Once I start, please, I beg you to keep silent.'

Betsy emitted a frightened cry in the corner of the room.

'Be quiet child,' Bligh scolded.

The vicar stood in the middle of the room with his hands held aloft. He cleared his throat before reciting the Latin rites. 'Ecce crucis signum, fugiant phantasmata cuncta.' Translated meant - 'Behold the emblem of the Cross - let all spectres flee.' He cleared his throat again. 'This is not your place anymore. The spirit world awaits you and you will be safer there.' He lit the sage leaves and coughed as the smoke swirled upwards. He stood back and let the smoke fill the room.

Betsy covered her eyes with trembling hands – never had she felt so terrified.

The vicar sprinkled holy water around the room, droplets of it landing on the silk curtains. 'Go to the light,' he urged as he walked around the room. 'Everyone repeat after me the Lord's prayer.'

As much as Carrington and Bligh abhorred this procedure, they all joined in with the Lord's Prayer.

When they'd finished, the vicar walked around the room, sniffing the air. 'There, my lady. That should have done it!'

From the shadows, Pearl watched with interest as the vicar walked out of the door. She looked at the burning sage and the piles of white rice and salt everywhere, adamant that she was *not* leaving until she'd seen justice done. Pearl scowled with distaste at Carrington and Bligh, but her glare was wasted on them, only Betsy could see her and she was staring slack-jawed at her. Pearl gave her a friendly smile, which was not returned.

'Well, Bligh,' Carole said as she entered the room with a self satisfied smile. 'I shall be moving back into the manor this evening. Please get my room ready.'

'Yes, my lady.' Bligh bobbed a curtsy.

As Carole walked towards the window, Pearl blew the pile of rice into her face. Carole stopped dead, watching the plate of burning sage extinguish. Suddenly all the candles in the room extinguished and Pearl ran her icy fingers down the back of Carole's neck. The scream could be heard in the scullery.

Carrington and Bligh stood open- mouthed as Carole shrieked, lifted her skirts and fled the house as fast as she could. They'd not seen anything, but Betsy grinned as she witnessed Carrington and Bligh trying to vacate the room at the same time only to get stuck in the door jamb.

When they'd gone, Pearl allowed the candles to re-ignite themselves. She glanced down at Betsy cowering in the corner like a frightened mouse. She smiled sympathetically at her before returning to her usual haunt in the attic bedroom.

*

At Poldhu, Ellie would not let Harry go home until he had soaked his feet in a bowl of hot water. They'd both been caught out by a wave and Harry's trousers were soaked to the thigh. So it was a strange sight Jessie found when she returned home to the cottage. She stood open-mouthed at the stranger sat by the fireside with Ellie, enjoying a foot bath.

'Jessie, come and meet my old friend, Harry Yates.'

'Pleased to meet you, Mr Yates,' Jessie said trying to keep a straight face.

'And you, Miss Jessie. Do forgive my exposed hairy legs, but Ellie here insisted that I soak my feet after my paddle, for chance I catch a chill.' He coughed as he spoke.

'I think perhaps we're a little too late.' Ellie frowned.

Harry thumped his chest and nodded.

'Your wife won't be happy when she sees the state of your trousers, Harry.' *Ellie remembered well, the scowling face of Harry's wife. It put her in mind of someone eating pickled onions.*

Harry pulled a face. 'My wife died in November.'

'Oh Harry, I'm so sorry,' she said feeling guilty now for thinking ill of her. 'What happened?'

'Dr Eddy said it was Bronchopneumonia. A bad chill went to her chest and took her in five days.'

Ellie reached over to comfort him. 'Are you coping

alright?'

'Aye, I've got Terry, so I'm alright.'

'Is Terry your son?'

'No, we were never blessed with children. Terry is my little terrier dog.' He grinned. 'He's been a godsend and gives me more attention than my wife ever did!' He gave a wry smile. 'I know I shouldn't speak ill of the dead, but....' He laughed gently, followed by a violent coughing fit.

'Are you looking after yourself Harry? Are you eating properly? Now I look at you I can see you're thinner than you were.'

'I'm not the best cook in the world, but I manage.'

'Well, we have a pot of broth on the range for supper, I insist you join us.'

'Oh no, maid, I'll not be sharing your supper.'

'Yes you will!' She passed him a towel to dry his feet. 'Jessie, could you set another place at the table, please?'

Harry lifted his rheumy eyes to give Ellie a grateful look. 'Thank you.'

'It's my pleasure. It will be lovely to have your company.' She needed something to take her mind off the terrible realisation that Guy might no longer want her.

*

After a fitful night, tossing and turning, hearing the clock chime every hour, Ellie gave up trying to sleep and rose early. The noise of her clearing the fire grate of ashes roused Jessie.

'Sorry Jessie, I didn't mean to disturb you.'

Jessie yawned and stretched, regarding Ellie sympathetically. She knew she was hurting, but because of the nature of her sadness, she did not know how to help, other than being there for her, even if it meant getting up at this ungodly hour in the morning.

With the fire lit and the kettle boiled, they settled down to a silent cuppa and watched the dawn break red and gold over the hills. A sudden knock on the cottage door made them both jump, and were surprised to find

Betsy, the scullery maid, in great distress on their doorstep. On seeing Jessie, she sobbed uncontrollably in her arms.

'Shush now.' Jessie comforted Betsy. 'Have you run away?'

'No,' she sniffed. 'They think I'm in bed poorly. I sneaked out early this morning and ran all the way.'

'What on earth is wrong?'

'Something really frightening has happened at the manor.'

Ellie paused as she was making Betsy a strong cup of tea. She'd completely forgotten about the exorcism Harry had told her was happening. She pushed the mug of sweet tea into Betsy's hand and sat down while Betsy blurted the whole story out to them.

Jessie looked up at Ellie. 'What are we going to do?'

'There really is nothing we can do until Lady Sarah gets back and that won't be until July!' Ellie knelt at Betsy's feet. 'But you say Pearl's ghost is still in the house.'

Betsy trembled as she nodded. 'I'm frightened, Miss, I don't want to be there anymore.'

'Oh Betsy, don't take on so.' Jessie put her arm around her. 'I've told you, there is nothing to be frightened of - the girl you can see was just like us once. She's not evil - she's just lost in time. Ellie will speak to Lady Sarah on her return, nothing like this will happen again,' she said, without the confidence she spoke with. 'Now drink your tea, and I'll walk back with you.' Jessie glanced at Ellie who agreed she should go. 'I'm sure we can smuggle you up the back stairs without Bligh seeing you.' She winked. 'And next time you see Pearl, tell her, we are trying our best to help her. Will you do that?'

Betsy gave a nod as her bottom lip quivered.

25

As spring melted into early summer, the Sand Martins were busy feeding their young at Poldhu. Ellie had to rely on these small pleasures to lift her sore heart. With Sarah away until July and having just received a letter from James to tell her he wouldn't be home until August, Ellie would have floundered if not for Jessie's companionship. Ellie prayed that Guy had not really forsaken her. She hoped that he would mend enough to realise he was not going to be a burden on her. Then he would come back to her and all would be well.

*

By the third week in June, Guy was six months into his stay at The Royal Cornwall Infirmary and, as Dr Sandringham said, it was almost time for him to go home.

Clara had been his constant help and companion these last four months and she had grown into his life. Over the latter weeks, they had spent more and more time together. When she finished her shift, she would sit with Guy to keep him company. Sometimes they would walk into the hospital grounds and she would make a picnic to share. It had helped him to fill the void left by Ellie.

One evening, after enjoying the warmth of the June evening, he said his good nights to her and watched her go back to the nurse's house. He liked Clara - she made him laugh when he believed there was no joy left in the world. He'd miss her. She was brilliant at her job, though she'd disclosed to Guy that once he'd recovered enough to go home, she too would re-evaluate her position in the hospital. She loved her job, but it was time to settle down. She wanted a home and a family.

Guy exhaled heavily - everyone deserved a happy ever after, maybe *he* should marry her! He was sure they would make a good match, but she wasn't really who he wanted to spend the rest of his life with. Was it fair to marry someone else when he loved another? For he did love

Ellie, he loved her with all his heart and always would, even though she was lost to him now. He'd pondered long and hard that night, and by the morning, he'd made a decision.

As they took their tea in the morning sunshine in the hospital gardens, Guy took a deep breath. 'Clara.'

Clara smiled and waited, she'd felt a shift in their relationship - dare she hope for more?

Guy cleared his throat. 'Clara.'

'Guy?'

'You've been my rock these last few months. I've spoken to you at length about my feelings for Ellie. You've listened and understood my pain and sadness.'

Clara's heart accelerated. 'I know you still have feelings for Ellie, even after what she did to you, you still think of her don't you?'

'I do, I admit, I'm sorry, but…' The image of Ellie entered his mind, fresh faced and wind-swept. 'I realise that I have to let her go and move on. You understand me - you understand the limitations of my body at the moment. I wondered, could you, would you consider spending the rest of your life with me? Would you marry me?' He could feel his body tremble as he waited for her decision.

Clara's heart sang. This is what she'd dreamed of and could hardly comprehend that he was actually asking her.

Guy misjudged her hesitation. 'I'll understand if you say no, my world is very different to your life here in this hospital.'

Clara put her fingers gently to his lips to quieten him. 'It is my greatest wish to marry you and I shall do everything in my power to make you happy again.'

Guy stood unaided, reached up, slipped his hand under her hair resting it on the back of her neck, and very gently Clara's hand rose to his.

'Then as soon as I am fit and well, we *will* be married, Clara,' he said, kissing her tenderly on the lips.

*

On the 12th July Guy packed his belongings in readiness to return home. It had been seven long months, but he was on his feet and walking with just one stick now. His recovery to his mind, heart and body was down to Clara, of that he was truly grateful.

Clara entered his room with familiarity, sat on the bed and kissed him on the lips.

Guy smiled. Clara was dressed in a pretty floral dress and cardigan. He'd never seen her out of uniform before.

'I love you,' she said gaily.

Guy nodded, but something stopped him from declaring his love back. He berated himself. Ellie was lost to him - he knew that. He was moving on, he was going to marry Clara - she had stemmed his heart from bleeding, but oh, it was proving so hard to let Ellie go.

'I hope your ma likes me,' Clara said nervously.

'I'm sure she will. Now are you absolutely sure you want this? You have a fine career in nursing here. Life will be very, very different in Gweek. Once I return to work, I'll be away all week!'

'It'll be fine.' Clara fingered the cloth of the new shirt she'd bought him. 'I'll be your wife, what more could a girl want?'

'As I said we must wait a while. I'm not strong enough to be your husband yet. Dr Sandringham says I'll have regained my strength in a few more weeks, and then I'll marry you.'

Clara didn't really want to wait, in case he changed his mind. 'So I'm to live in sin with you, am I?' she joked.

'Certainly not! Ma will be there to chaperone us and believe me she's not one to put up with any shenanigans. I've told you I'll bunk down with Silas and you'll have my room. Everything will be above board.'

'I'm only teasing you.' She kissed him again. 'Now come on, get your things together, I can't wait to start my new life.' *Of leisure!* 'I'm just going to say my last goodbyes to everyone. I'll wait outside for you.'

As he knelt down to drag his belongings out of the cupboard, Ellie's screwed up letters tumbled out. He sat and looked at them for a few moments - he'd never read them properly and hadn't realised they was still there. *Don't read them Guy, not now you've moved on.* Very tentatively he gathered the letters together and smoothed them out into a neat pile. He looked around for a bin, but it had been taken away to be emptied, so he pushed them into a side pocket of his bag to dispose of later. It was time to start again…without her.

*

All Guy's neighbours were out to greet him back home to Gweek. As he passed them he secretly prayed Ellie was not among them.

Clara watched in awe, overwhelmed at the constant crowd of people patting him on the shoulder and wishing him well.

Silas hung on to Guy's arm as they walked the last few steps to the cottage and Nellie flew tearfully into her son's arms, before he could even get through the door.

'Oh, Rory, I thought you'd never come home.'

Guy shot Silas a confused glance, but he just pulled a face.

'Come and sit down.' She dragged him to the kitchen chair and sat opposite him. She picked up his soft hands in her work worn hands and let the tears of happiness run down her face.

'Don't cry, Ma. Everything is fine now, thanks to Clara.' He beckoned her over to meet her.

'Ma, this is Clara. Clara has been my nurse and it's down to her that I'm able to walk again.'

Nellie looked up at the woman in the pretty dress. 'Well thank you for escorting my Rory home.'

Clara glanced at Guy with raised eyebrows.

'Ma, it's me, Guy, you keep calling me Rory. That was Pa's name.'

Nellie pursed her lips. 'No I don't!'

'You've called me it twice and I've only been home a few minutes.'

'She does it all the time,' Silas chipped in.

'Hold your tongue, Silas,' Nellie scolded. 'You're making out that I'm losing my mind.'

She is, he mouthed to Guy.

'Ma, Clara didn't just escort me home, she's staying. I wrote and told you.'

Nellie glanced again at the woman then back to Guy. 'Of course I remember! She's staying until you're completely fit?'

'No Ma, Clara is staying forever.' He reached out and pulled Clara to him. 'We're to be married as soon as I'm fit enough.'

The welcoming crowd still gathered at the door began to murmur with excitement.

Nellie bristled. 'Well you could have let me know you were bringing a bride-to-be home. Where is she going to sleep?'

The murmur from the crowd intensified.

Guy sighed. 'I did, I wrote and told you. She'll sleep in my room and I'll bunk down with Silas until the wedding.'

'Oh.. I see. Well I hope she can cook!'

Before Clara could answer, Guy said, 'Ma, let's just have a cup of tea and say goodbye to everyone before you interrogate her.'

The crowd laughed and began to disperse, wishing Guy well in his new life as they left.

When Guy returned to the kitchen, Nellie had gone upstairs.

'Where is Ma, Silas?'

'She's gone to sort your room out.'

'I don't think your ma likes me,' Clara said, taking her cardigan off.

Guy stood beside her and held her by the arms. 'She'll be fine. This is her kitchen and it'll feel strange for her to share it. But once she realises you're here to help her, everything will settle down. You *can* cook, can't you?

Clara looked sheepish.

'Oh!'

Silas sniggered.

'Now don't be rude, Silas. Clara is an extremely competent nurse who has managed to get this broken man back on his feet. I'm sure Ma will teach her all she knows about cooking. Now, where is Blue? I long to see him, I bet he's grown.'

'I'll fetch him, he's in my room,' Silas said guiltily.

Guy shook his head as Clara looked around the tiny kitchen.

She didn't know what she expected, but to share this cramped space with three other people was going to take some getting used to.

Seeing Clara's consternation, Guy pulled her into an embrace. 'Everything will be fine, I promise.'

Clara very much thought the opposite.

*

As Clara lay in Guy's bed that night, between the non-too-clean sheets, the flickering candlelight illuminated a vast collection of cobwebs along the dark oak beams, many of which were supporting flies. Her eyes focused on the most enormous spider, which was busily spinning another web. Clara, used to the hospital's clean and pristine environment, screwed her nose up - this place was absolutely filthy.

Clara disliked Guy's mother immensely, and suspected the feeling was mutual. Dinner that evening had been a fraught occasion. Nellie dominated the chat around the table. She'd been excitable and loud, telling Guy all the news from the village, though Silas kept interrupting when she got a fact wrong, which was quite often. Whenever Clara tried to contribute anything, Nellie pressed her lips together, and shot a baleful glance in her direction. Clara was thankful that Guy would be around for at least another month, so he could deflect any initial problems as she tried to integrate into this tiny cottage.

*

The same day Guy and Clara made their triumphant return to Gweek, Lady Sarah arrived back from Europe. Eager to ride out, she saddled her horse the next day and rode down to Poldhu. Her arrival was preceded with a waft of *Edwardian Bouquet* perfume by Floris of London, followed by squeals of delight as the two women greeted each other.

'Ellie.' She reached out and took her by the hands. 'Oh how I've missed you and your lovely Tea Room. One just can't get a proper cup of tea anywhere in Europe! How are you? How is Jessie doing? Oh, speaking of which, here she is,' she said as Jessie came through the door and curtsied automatically.

'Come tell me all about what has been happening here.' She beckoned Ellie to sit with her while Jessie made the tea. 'How is that young man of yours?'

*

Sarah rode home an hour later, shocked and dismayed at what she'd learned that morning. Dismayed that Ellie had not seen Guy since December, something she would try to rectify as soon as possible, though she knew not how. More pressing though was what Ellie had said about Albert Lanfear, and perhaps the implication in Pearl's death. That coupled with learning that an exorcism had taken place to rid the manor of that same ghost, Sarah went in search of her husband.

*

After the excitement of arriving at Gweek, Clara was late rising the next morning, much to Nellie's disapproval. She refused to take a cup of tea up to her when Guy asked, stating that 'if she wanted tea, she could jolly well get herself out of bed and make it herself.'

Guy rolled his eyes and stepped outside into the summer sunshine. The dragonflies were out in force - their iridescent loveliness was a sight to behold. He took a deep breath of clean Cornish air, something he'd been starved of these last seven months. He slowly walked down to Barley Field Farm where Mazie was grazing lazily in her field.

Silas followed Guy down the field with Blue in tow – it was apparent who Blue's master was now.

'We need to get Mazie working again soon - she's getting fat and lazy by the look of her.'

'I've ridden her whenever I could, but I've been working all hours to keep us in food.'

'Have you managed alright? That alone worried me the most.'

'Aye, someone sends Ma two shillings every week in the post, without it we'd have struggled.'

Guy grimaced. He'd stop that money coming immediately. He was not having Goldsworthy pay another penny to this family, and he would make damn sure he would pay every single shilling back to him.

Silas watched Guy pensively. 'Are you alright?'

Guy nodded. 'So, Silas, are you ready to take on your apprenticeship?'

Silas's face brightened. 'I can hardly wait. When can we start?'

'The doctor said in about four weeks, though I fear you will have to take on all the heavy work for a while.'

'I'm ready and strong, look!' He flexed his arm muscles.

Guy laughed and squeezed the tiny bicep on Silas's arm.

'In truth, I'll be glad to get out of the house. Ma is going daft in the head.'

Guy bit down on his lip. 'She's just getting forgetful that's all. Clara will be there to look out for her now.'

'Good.'

'How do you like Clara?'

Silas shrugged. 'She's alright. She's not like Ellie though is she?'

Guy lowered his eyes. 'No, she's not. Do you see Ellie much?'

'I've not seen hide nor hair of her since that day she came here before you went to hospital.'

Guy looked down the lane. 'So she doesn't come next door.'

Silas shook his head.

'Good.' His relief was palpable

*

At Cury Church, the Reverend Andrew Ellis cowered in the corner of his vestry as the earl bore down on him.

'How dare you enter my house and perform an exorcism on it while I am out of the country.'

The reverend's lip trembled. 'I do beg your pardon, Sir, but Lady Carole is a force to be reckoned with. With the best will in the world she's not an easy person to say no too.'

'Nevertheless I am the master of Bochym Manor. No one enters my home without an invitation from me. I do not expect this outrageous behaviour from our own vicar. I have a good mind to write to the Bishop about this.'

The reverend's lip quivered again as Peter stormed out of the church.

*

At Bochym Manor Lodge, Carole was taking a leisurely breakfast with her mother when Peter stormed in and confronted Carole about the exorcism.

Carole turned to him in fury. 'How…how dare you berate me?' she was so angry she could hardly speak. 'It's my house too you know and I'll not be kept from it by some...some, ghost! The reverend obviously had no idea what he was doing, because the damn thing is still in there! We need to get someone else in, Peter. Someone who can do the job properly.'

Peter's face darkened with rage. 'You can forget that idea. I forbid anymore tom foolery in the manor again, do you understand? Have you any idea how much you have frightened the staff with your stupid actions? You will never, ever do anything like this again.'

Carole was taken aback, he had never spoken to her so harshly before. Her lip quivered slightly. 'But how will we ever rid the manor of ghosts?'

'Oh, for Christ's sake, Carole, I do not believe in ghosts, but if they are there, there they *will* stay! You, madam, will just have to put up with that fact. God damn it, you lived in that house for twenty years and saw nothing. You're going soft in the head.'

*

Sarah was in the drawing room when Peter arrived home from the Lodge. He slammed every door he went through until he came upon the room Sarah was in. She had never seen him so angry.

'I'm going to my study,' he said. 'Have some tea sent in to me will you, please?'

Sarah nodded and pulled the bell for Carrington. She'd not told him what Ellie had said about Lanfear, that would have to wait until he'd calmed down a bit, but the more she thought about it, the more the thought of Lanfear made her skin crawl.

Albert Lanfear and Susan Binns had accompanied them on their European trip. It had not gone unnoticed by either Sarah or Peter that women shied away from Lanfear. Susan Binns in particular gave him a wide berth. There was obviously something unpleasant about him, but as all she had to go by was Ellie's vivid dream about him and Jessie's theory of Pearl pointing at him, she needed more solid evidence.

26

It was Tuesday 16th July. All was ready for another busy day at Poldhu. Brandy heralded the postman's arrival long before he knocked on the door, which gave Ellie time to lock him in the bedroom. Ellie surmised that Brandy must sense her nervous apprehension whenever the post arrived, because the only other person he growled at was Philip!

'Morning.' He grinned at Ellie. 'She still doesn't like me, eh?' He nodded to the whining behind the bedroom door.

'Sorry, Archie. What have you for me?'

'Three for you, today.'

Ellie recognised Amelia Pascoe's handwriting on one of them and had ripped it open almost before the postman had left, hoping it contained the news she'd been waiting for - that Guy had returned home.

Jessie watched Ellie's animated face as she sat down, anticipating good news. After watching Ellie fade like a wilted flower over the last few months, she crossed her fingers that all would be well soon.

Leaving her to read the letter, Jessie crossed the dunes to open the Tea Room. Moments later she noticed Ellie walking slowly down the beach towards the incoming tide. *Where on earth was she going? It was almost time to open up.* Stepping out onto the terrace, she watched in astonishment as Ellie dropped to her knees at the waterline.

*

The letter, now balled up in her hand, evoked a pain in her heart unlike any other Ellie had experienced. Sat in the surf with the swirling tide dragging at her skirt, she truly believed she would never recover from this blow.

My dear Ellie, Amelia had written.

I am writing to let you know that Guy is home from hospital, and having seen him, appears to be fit and well and able to return to

his thatching in due course. I'm sorry Ellie, but my letter also bears news that will upset you. Guy has brought home a young woman who nursed him through his treatment. She's a nice girl, her name is Clara, and she seems very kind and caring, which I'm thankful for, as Nellie seems to be quite forgetful nowadays. She will no doubt be a great help to her. It is my understanding that the banns for Guy and Clara's wedding will be read in a month's time. They plan to marry in Constantine Church sometime in September. Forgive me, Ellie, for being the one to have to tell you this news. I think perhaps you would rather hear it from me than anyone else. I know you had deep feelings for Guy and these last few months have been difficult for you. I'm sorry for the way things have turned out again, but rest assured, Ellie, one day your prince will come, I promise.
Your friend, Amelia

Slowly Ellie let the waves wash the crushed letter from the palm of her hand. She watched in desolation as it sank and disappeared. Oh how she wished she too could disappear. Why had Guy saved her, to let her drown again in misery? Yet again she'd been thrown over for some other woman. The day was hot but she shivered uncontrollably. How could Guy do this to her, when he knew how much she'd suffered at Philip's hands? Was her heart to be forever toyed with? Did men think she had no feelings, that they could promise the earth then casually toss her aside when someone better came along? There were no tears - none would come, for the shock of the news bewildered her. She hardly felt the hands under her arms pulling her from the rising tide.

'Ellie.' Jessie knelt in the surf, and wrapped her arms around her. 'What are you doing? What's happened?'

Ellie circled her wet arms around Jessie, thankful for some form of human contact, but it would take more than a friendly pair of arms to help. Ellie felt damaged beyond repair.

*

Bochym held its annual garden party on the first Sunday of

August. This was the first Sarah had hosted as the new Countess de Bochym. Sarah had overseen the whole affair and relished in the opportunity to make her mark and show the beautiful, well-maintained estate to her fellow members of the local gentry. In her own cool and calm way she stepped out into the summer sun, thankful that the weather was perfect.

The huge ornate marquee sat to the right of the formal gardens, housing the vast table, laden with delicate sandwiches, fancy cakes and hot and cold drinks. Vases of fragrant pink lilies filled the space with the sweetest smell.

Outside, the carefully manicured lawns adjacent to the manor held several chairs with deep cushioned seat pads, and tables draped with crisp, white tablecloths.

The windows from the Jacobean drawing room stood open in order for the pianist to play for the guests for the duration of the afternoon. Further down the garden, a band had set up to play softly to the strolling crowds.

A flurry of servants scurried from the kitchen to the garden, making sure everything was in the right place. She smiled every time they bobbed a curtsy whenever they saw her. She would rather they didn't, wanting her relationship with the staff to be more informal, but Peter insisted that they must, as a mark of respect for their betters. Sarah's family was not without money, but her father had been frugal and only kept two servants, both of whom Sarah classed as her friends. It did not sit well to have so many staff, but she was no fool, this manor would not run itself. She just wished she could replace one or two of them, namely Carrington, Bligh and the dreadful Lanfear. She shuddered at the thought of him.

'Hello Sarah,' her mother-in-law joined her on the front lawn. She was resplendent in her navy and white striped dress and wide brimmed hat. At her throat she wore the most exquisite necklace. 'This all looks rather splendid.'

'Thank you, Lucinda.' This was high praise from

someone who was renowned for her garden parties.

'That's a beautiful necklace, Lucinda. If I remember correctly, you wore it to our wedding. Are they the de Bochym sapphires?'

'What these?' Lucinda touched the gems at her throat. 'No my dear, they're rather spectacular replicas, don't you think? The de Bochym sapphires are incredibly valuable, so we keep them in a safe box. I very rarely take them out, except for special occasions and yes, I did wear them to your wedding.'

'Well replica or not, it's beautiful.'

'The real ones will be yours one day, Sarah… when I'm gone of course. They've been passed down to each generation of countesses.'

'Well then, I hope that I am not in possession of them for a very long time.'

Lucinda raised her glass. 'I'll drink to that, my dear.'

'Forgive me for asking, but was it the de Bochym necklace the dairy maid Ruby Saunders was dismissed for allegedly stealing?'

Lucinda's grey eyes narrowed. 'I'm not sure I know what you're talking about, Sarah,' she said taking a sip of sherry.

'I've been looking through some old ledgers and came across a dismissal of one of our maids. When I questioned Mrs Bligh, she told me that Ruby Saunders had been found in possession of a priceless sapphire necklace. She was dismissed immediately on your orders!'

Lucinda shook her head. 'I don't recall that name at all, but then I always left Mrs Bligh to deal with the staff. Mark my words, my dear, should this Sanders girl have taken it, she would have been hanged, not dismissed, but that would be highly unlikely. As I just told you, the de Bochym necklace is always either around my throat or locked away.'

This information sent a frisson through Sarah's body. Again she had the impression that s*omeone was not telling the* *truth.*

*

At two p.m. everything was ready. The gates opened and a stream of visitors, both gentry and locals, walked leisurely up the long drive from the lodge, Ellie and Jessie included.

It was with great trepidation that Ellie agreed to attend. She knew the work Sarah had put into this event and she didn't want to be churlish by not accepting.

It had been three whole weeks since learning of Guy's impending marriage, and the pain still cut deep. After the initial shock, Ellie could do nothing except accept her fate. She had a business to run and this being summer, was her busiest time. The work numbed her senses. The night time was the worst. Hour after hour, Ellie lay in the darkness. Try as she might, she could not process why Guy had treated her so monstrously. Each morning, she watched the sun rise on another lonely day, drained of emotion, desperately trying to find a smile for her customers. This definitely was her lot now. No man would ever hurt her again - she would not allow it.

Jessie could hardly contain her excitement at returning to the manor as a guest. For the last few years she had been one of the servants busy running backwards and forwards. Today she stood with Ellie, in her best Sunday dress with a glass of chilled white wine in her cotton gloved hand.

Sarah was busy with her guests, so they took a turn around the garden. Ellie again stood in awe of the beautiful array of flowers in the formal borders. They watched a game of croquet, joined in one, and then made their way up to the marquee for a bite to eat. When Betsy saw them, she squealed with delight and hugged Jessie. Jane Truscott, her former roommate however, stood stock still and nearly dropped the sandwich platter she was holding.

'Well look at you, all lardy dardy, drinking the earl's wine cellar dry,' Jane said sarcastically.

'Hello Jane, it's nice to see you too,' Jessie replied

amiably. She held her glass high. 'Cheers.'

Jane pulled a face and flounced off with the platter of sandwiches.

Jessie and Ellie exchanged a smile and made for the buffet table, spread out with more food than Ellie had ever seen.

'Well now my beauty, fancy seeing you here.'

Ellie felt her skin creep at the sound of Philip's voice. She was not ignorant of the fact that the chances of running into him at this party were very high, but she was ready to ignore him the best she could. Ellie began to walk away without acknowledging him.

'Come come, Ellie. Have you no kind word for the man who loves you?'

'Come on, Jessie, let's go outside, the air in here has turned sour.' Ellie grabbed Jessie's sleeve and headed towards Sarah standing by the marquee opening.

Philip snorted angrily. He was not going to allow this little minx to dismiss him in the grounds of his own home, so he followed them.

'Talking of love or ex lovers, I see Guy is back on his feet now, no doubt accelerated by his upcoming nuptials to the pretty little nurse he brought home with him.'

Sarah turned on hearing Philip's voice, excused herself from the guest she was speaking to and went to Ellie's aid.

Ellie was trying desperately to suppress her tears when Sarah reached out to protect her from Philip.

'Philip. What is the meaning of this? What are you saying to upset Elise?' she demanded.

Philip's lip curled into a smile. 'I'm just giving her an update on our mutual friend, Guy. He is to be married next month to Clara. I believe that's her name, am I right, Ellie?'

'How can you be so insensitive, leave her be. Come Elise - Jessie, you come too. Philip, go back to your wife and stop causing trouble. This is meant to be a happy event and I'll not have you upsetting my guests.'

A middle aged lady with an ample bosom came to their aid. 'Is there anything I can do, my lady?'

'Oh, Mrs Parson, yes thank you. Please could you take Elise and Jessie to your cottage for a moment, I'll be along shortly.

*

For the first time in eight years, Ellie walked through the door of the Stewards Cottage - her old home. Everything looked familiar as Mrs Parson sat them down in the front room and went to make a cup of tea for them.

'Are you alright, Ellie?' Jessie cupped her hand over hers.

'I am. I'm just angry at myself for getting upset in front of *him*. I do hate how he gloats.'

Jessie looked around the room. 'This is where you used to live, isn't it? Does it seem strange to be back here?'

Ellie glanced through the window to the clock tower - a view she remembered so well. 'Yes. It's like I've never left.'

Mrs Parson came in with a tray. 'Did I just hear you say you used to live here, my dear?'

Ellie nodded. 'My father was the old earl's steward on the estate until he died in an accident eight years ago.'

'Oh, bless my soul. It was my husband who took over from your poor father. The old earl died that same week and the young earl had to come home from university to interview my husband for the position. It was a terrible tragedy – I believe he slipped in some blood in the courtyard and cracked open his head. Am I right?'

'Slipped in some blood?' Ellie said in astonishment. 'I didn't know that. Ma just told me that he'd slipped and died.'

'I'm sorry I thought you knew the circumstances.' Mrs Parson looked abashed as she poured the tea, and then changed the subject, 'I must say you look a little calmer than when you came in. What happened?'

Ellie shook her head dismissively. 'Someone just said

something unpleasant to me. I should not have let it bother me.'

'Humph, probably some ruffian from Cury, no doubt. As long as you're alright now, that's all that matters.'

She passed a cup to Jessie. 'And how are you, my dear, are you settling in at the Tea Room? Mrs Blair said that's where you'd gone to.'

'I have settled in nicely thank you, Mrs Parson. It's lovely working with Ellie in such a beautiful location.'

Mrs Parson watched as Ellie cast her eyes around the room. 'You'll be recognizing some of the furniture I suspect. We only replaced our own bed - everything else was in lovely condition. Tell me, where did you go to when you left here?'

'Poldhu.'

'Ah nice, the sea air would have been good for your poor mother's soul. I'm glad she decided to have a complete change when you moved.'

Ellie lowered her eyes. 'Yes.'

'You can have a look around the cottage after tea if you want, for old time's sake. It might bring back some happy memories.'

'Thank you, I'd like that.'

After tea, Mrs Parson gave Ellie and Jessie permission to go upstairs to look around. The cottage was spick and span and Ellie lovingly ran her hand on the highly polished wooden banister as she climbed the stairs. She first glanced into what was her parent's bedroom and then walked into the one she'd occupied. The wallpaper was the same - tiny pink rosebuds on a cream background. Ellie stared at the wicker chair beside the bed, her head awash with long forgotten memories of her ma reading to her from it. Lost in her reverie, she barely heard Jessie say her name.

'Ellie,' Jessie whispered again. 'Look!'

As Ellie turned she saw the figure by the window. 'Pearl?' her voice, almost inaudible.

Ellie glanced at Jessie before moving towards Pearl. Their eyes met, Ellie's full of wonder, Pearl's full of woe. Ellie gave a long faltering breath, overwhelmed at the sense of familiarity. Pearl pulled away from Ellie's gaze and looked out from the window, up towards the attic window of the main house. Following her gaze, Ellie gasped audibly, staggered backwards and sat heavily on the bed. Her hands covered her face as though to hide from something. 'Oh god, oh god, what have I seen?'

'What?' Jessie glanced out of the window, goose pimples rising on her skin. 'Ellie, I can't see anything! What have you seen?'

Footsteps alerted the girls that Mrs Parson was climbing the stairs. Ellie stood up and straightened the bed clothes.

'Ah, there you are! I suspect this was your old bedroom, yes? Gosh you look deathly pale, Miss Rosevear. Are you sure you're quite well?'

Ellie folded her arms quickly to hide her shaking hands. 'Yes, I'm fine, Mrs Parson. As you can imagine this is all very emotional for me. I had some happy times here.'

Mrs Parson nodded sympathetically. 'Come on down, Lady Sarah is in the front room.'

*

'Elise, my dear,' Sarah hugged her. 'I'm so sorry about Philip.'

'I'm alright, Sarah, really I am.'

'Come, sit. I'm sure Mrs Parson won't mind if we commandeer her front room for a few more minutes.'

'Take as long as you need, my lady,' Mrs Parson bobbed a curtsy and retired to the kitchen.

'Words cannot describe how shocked I was when you sent word about Guy. He always gave me the impression that it was you he cared for.'

Ellie's lip trembled. 'I suspect when someone has nursed you so closely, you do form a deep attachment. What is done is done, Sarah.' She sighed resignedly.

'Oh, Elise.' Sarah hugged her tightly. 'Would you like to come back to the garden party? Philip has gone. Peter had a few harsh words with him, so he took himself off to The Wheel Inn.'

'No thank you. I think I'll go home now. Jessie can stay if she wants.'

'No, I'm coming with you,' Jessie said, desperate to know what Ellie had seen in the bedroom.

After thanking Mrs Parson for her hospitality, Ellie was the first to step out of the Stewards Cottage.

'Hey, you there!'

Ellie froze at the sound of Lanfear's voice.

His face was blood red angry as he growled. 'I thought I'd made it quite clear…..'

Sarah put her hands on Ellie's arms and moved her sideways in order to pass. Ellie saw Lanfear blanch at the sight of his mistress.

'Mr Lanfear,' Sarah said authoritatively. 'Get out of my sight this instant. My husband will speak to you later, regarding this matter.'

Lanfear gave a curt bow and scuttled back from where he'd come, leaving Ellie visibly shaken.

'Elise, I simply do not know how to begin to apologise for the upset the men of this house have caused you today,' Sarah said in a fluster.

'Sarah, please do not be distressed. I perhaps should not have come.'

'Oh rest assured, Elise, I will make sure this never happens again. I want you as my guest to always feel comfortable visiting this house and I will do my upmost to see that respect will be given to you from now on.'

*

As Ellie and Jessie walked the path through the woods towards Cury, Ellie told her about the shocking memory which Pearl had helped her to remember. It was what she'd witnessed from her old bedroom window eight years ago.

Shocked to the core, Jessie could hardly breathe. 'You've got to tell Lady Sarah, Ellie.'

'I know. I just need to process it in my own mind first. This is a serious allegation I'm about to make.'

*

The last of the garden party guests left just after seven that evening. Apart from the altercations she'd dealt with, Sarah thought her first garden party was a huge success. Now there was just one more thing she needed to sort out. She went in search of her husband.

*

After dressing his lordship that evening, Lanfear returned to the kitchen, seething from his disciplinary. Peter had left him in no doubt that a dismissal would follow any further aggressive behaviour directed to a visitor to the manor. Lanfear slammed his shoes on the table and began to scrub polish into them. 'If I see that Rosevear bitch again, I'll make her pay for undermining my position in this household,' he muttered.

27

Cornwall was basking in a heat wave which had lasted for almost six weeks. Because of the good weather, Ellie had neither time nor energy to ponder on the disturbing recollection she'd had at Bochym. Without doubt, The Poldhu Hotel visitors were making August the busiest she'd ever experienced. Ellie was so grateful she had Jessie with her now – Betty's knees would not have coped!

*

It was the third week of August before Sarah found time to visit Ellie. She rode down Poldhu valley early one Monday, before the searing heat of the day. She flaked down upon a chair on the terrace and fanned herself furiously.

'My apologies, Elise, for not coming to see you before now, I have been so tied up engaging a new lady's maid, time seems to fly by.'

'Have you employed someone then, my lady?' Jessie asked arriving with a tea tray. She secretly hoped that Jane Truscott, her fellow chamber maid, had been overlooked for the job after being so horrid to her.

'I have, Jessie, she's called Lowenna Kernow and she's wonderful.' She turned to Ellie. 'I refuse to continue to work under Carole's archaic rules of sharing a lady's maid, now she no longer resides at the manor.'

'Good for you,' Ellie said. 'Jessie come, sit with us.'

'I do hope all is well after your unpleasant altercation with Philip?' Sarah placed her hand on Ellie's.

'And the unpleasant recollection she had in the Stewards Cottage!' Jessie added.

'Shush Jessie,' Ellie scolded. *She wasn't sure if she had decided to divulge what she'd seen, as it was so incriminating.*

'What unpleasant recollection, Elise?'

Ellie glared at Jessie, but the girl stood her ground. 'If you don't tell Lady Sarah, I will.'

Sarah's eyebrows arched with interest, so Ellie

reluctantly told Sarah word for word, the memory she'd experienced that day.

*

When Sarah dismounted on her return from Poldhu, her horse was lathered up and whinnying.

'Is everything well, my lady?' her groom asked anxiously.

'Yes, sorry.' Sarah stroked the sweating horse. 'I think perhaps I rode her too fast in this heat. Give her some extra feed and a good drink, will you?'

Once inside, Sarah swept past Mrs Bligh and collected the account ledger for 1893 again. She ran her finger along the entry for the week Pearl Martin had allegedly run away and the Rosevears had been dismissed. Her fingers stopped:

Saturday 16th September – Ruby Sanders – Chambermaid – Dismissed - Theft

Peter once told her that Ruby was Pearl's friend, and Sarah did not believe she was a necklace thief - therefore she needed to speak to her, but how? No one knew where she'd gone. She looked at the other people listed as employed around that time. Derek Bray – Dairyman, he'd retired and by all accounts had moved away. John Carrington – Head Butler, Joan Bligh – Housekeeper, Albert Lanfear – Valet to the Earl, Dora Sands – Lady's Maid to the Countess, gone now. Hilda Blair – Cook - maybe she would know. Isabel Breag – Junior Laundry maid. Issy! She was still in their employment! Sarah slammed the book shut and went in search of her.

The laundry smelt of hot damp linen when Sarah entered. Issy wiped her hands down her apron and bobbed a curtsy.

Sarah closed the door behind her and sat down on an old rickety chair.

'Issy, do you remember Ruby Sanders?'

Issy hesitated. 'Yes, my lady.'

'Do you know where I can find her?'

Issy's eyes clouded with concern.

'I believe Ruby was falsely accused of stealing something.'

Issy remained silent, not daring to disclose anything.

'Do you know where she is, Issy? It's really important that I find her. I want to make amends.'

Still Issy remained silent.

Sarah dropped her shoulders in resignation.

'The Cadgwith Arms, my lady. That's where she was the last I heard. Please don't tell her I told you.'

The relief was palpable on Sarah's face. 'Thank you, Issy.'

Issy nodded. 'Ruby is as honest as the day. That necklace was planted on her!'

'I know. I intend to have Ruby's name cleared.'

*

Sarah found Peter in his study and placed the ledger on his desk.

'Ah, the ledger again?' he grinned.

'Sorry Peter, are you busy? '

'No, I'm just finishing a few things before I set off to London. What is it my darling, you look troubled.'

'I need to tell you something very worrying about Lanfear.' Sarah took a seat. 'The ledger says Pearl Martin ran away, but Ellie remembers that while Carrington was informing the staff of Pearl's disappearance, she could clearly see the image of Pearl standing behind Lanfear, pointing at him!'

'That doesn't make sense Sarah.'

'It does if Pearl was already dead!'

Peter sighed wearily. 'Are you saying Elise saw her ghost?'

'Yes, but hear me out.' She then told him of the second and more chilling revelation of what Ellie had remembered about the night Pearl allegedly ran away.

Peter sat back in the creaky leather chair and listened intently. 'The latter part of the story is a grave allegation,

Sarah.'

'I agree, but Lanfear's manner towards Elise tells me he's frightened that she'll reveal something he doesn't want revealing.'

'And now she has!'

Sarah nodded.

Peter glanced out at the garden and picked at the skin around his finger nails - a bad habit while he pondered on a problem. Presently, he said, 'To be honest, Sarah, you and I both know there is a history of unpleasantness between your friend Elise, and Lanfear. She could be making it all up.'

'Why would she do that?'

'Revenge perhaps, because of his unpleasantness! After all, the ledger clearly says that Pearl Martin went 'absent without leave'.' He prodded the writing, 'See.'

'But I don't believe that, Peter. Something more than unpleasant has gone on here.' She took a deep measured breath. 'I know you don't believe in ghosts…' She waited for his reaction but with none forthcoming, she continued. 'Jessie has seen the ghost of Pearl, so has Elise, and in truth, so have I…..'

'Mmm,' Peter murmured, unconvinced.

'Jessie told me that when she lived here, she witnessed Pearl standing at the attic window, crying. She also told me that Pearl appears regularly behind Lanfear. Now with Elise's revelation, I truly believe some grave misdemeanour occurred that day, eight years ago and Lanfear is behind it. I don't like him Peter, he gives me the creeps, and if he has done what I believe he has, I do not want him in my house!'

'Have you thought that Jessie and Elise could have made this story up?'

'I am certain they have not!'

Peter leant forward and steepled his fingers. 'I cannot dismiss the man on a ghost story and the recollection of a ten-year-old, which is what your friend Elise was at the time. You have to understand that, Sarah.'

'I do. That is why I need your help.'

Peter furrowed his brow 'I'll help you of course, but I know not how?'

'Do you remember telling me about Pearl and her friend Ruby? They were dairy maids here together. You said yourself they were inseparable and shared the attic called the jewellery box.'

'Yes.'

'Well.' Sarah opened the ledger. 'According to this, Ruby was dismissed the same day that Pearl ran away. When I questioned Mrs Bligh, she said she dismissed her on your mother's orders for stealing a priceless necklace.'

'Was she? I'd have never thought Ruby would have done such a thing.'

'Well, she didn't. I spoke to your mother about the incident and she has no recollection of it. The only priceless necklace is the de Bochym sapphires and they, I am told, are locked away.'

'Gosh you have done your detective work, haven't you? So how can I help?'

'I think Ruby was dismissed because she knew what had really happened to Pearl. I spoke to Issy in the laundry, who knew Ruby and spoke to her before she left. She said Ruby was in a deeply distressed state, firstly for the disappearance of Pearl, and secondly that the necklace had been planted on her for some reason. Issy believes Ruby is innocent and I believe that too. According to your mother, a theft, such as was stated, would have been a hanging offence, instead Ruby was just dismissed. Don't you see Peter, none of it rings true. If Ruby was falsely accused, then I think we should put the situation right. Issy says Ruby has lived in fear and secrecy since leaving the manor, terrified the family would press charges for something she didn't do.'

'So Issy knows where Ruby is?'

'Yes, though she was reluctant to tell me, for chance

we were going to press false charges. I assured her that was not the case. I told her we would clear everything up. I'd like you to go and see Ruby. If I go, you will think I've put words and thoughts into her mouth. But if you go and ask her for her version of her dismissal and the events leading up to it, you might find it is similar to Elise's story and then we have some real evidence.'

Peter remained silent for a few minutes.

'Please, Peter. If Lanfear has done something wicked, I do not want him in this house a moment longer.'

He nodded. 'Lanfear will be coming with me to London. We'll be away three weeks, so you don't have to worry about him. On my return I promise I shall speak to Ruby.'

'Thank you, darling.' Overwhelmed with relief Sarah left Peter's study to find the vaporous image of Pearl standing on the stairs, smiling.

*

It was late August. Clara stepped out of the hot kitchen, away from Nellie's incessant chatter. The initial resentment Nellie had felt for Clara had diminished when Clara took it on herself to clean and sweep the cottage from head to foot. Clara had no desire to be a skivvy, but also had no desire to live in a pigsty.

Nellie knew she'd let things slip during Guy's absence but having this woman share her house, made coping with what was going on in her head a little more manageable. Nellie knew something was amiss, but she wouldn't admit it to anyone. It worried her though that she suffered great bouts of forgetfulness, only to come to and find that she had put her clean linen on the compost heap. She tried to cover her mistakes, but sometimes Clara found out before she could rectify them and would give her a look, but thankfully never scold her.

Clara leant on the front wall and sighed. She was bored, and totally discontented with her lot. Guy had been back at work these last two weeks and was seldom home during the week, sometimes only returning on Sunday for the day. Although he'd warned this would be the case, she'd not envisaged having to look after his mother when she'd agreed to marry him. Nellie was becoming a handful, forever harping on about her childhood, mistaking her constantly for her long dead sister. Clara could hardly leave Nellie for an hour before she'd done something ridiculous like burned the sheets on the fire or added coal to the dinner. Clara suspected the woman was losing her reason completely. In her line of work, she'd seen many people like this and most were confined to the mad house. Her concerns fell on deaf ears. Guy put Nellie's behaviour down to her age, so there it was, Clara's sole job in life now was to look after this old woman and she was very disgruntled about it!

Wiping the perspiration from her forehead, she set off down the lane, ignoring the calls from Nellie within Bramble Cottage.

At the bridge near the bottom of the lane, Clara lifted her skirt and petticoats, tucked them into her belt and picked her way down the bank of the stream. The water was icy cold as she stepped in, making her shiver with pleasure. She waded up to her knees and let the water run past her bare legs like silk flowing in the wind. Flinging her head back she basked in the glory of the coolness and did not see Philip Goldsworthy watching her from the bridge.

*

Philip raised his eyebrows as his heart picked up a beat at the sight of this woman's bare legs. He smiled appreciatively. She was not a local lass, for he knew them all, having lived in the village all his life. No, he knew exactly who this woman was. It was Guy Blackthorn's intended - and a rather handsome woman she was as well. He watched with delight as she scooped handfuls of water in her hands to run it through her long brown hair. His loins tingled when she gave a squeal of pleasure as she kicked the water playfully. He lifted his bowler hat and wiped the perspiration from his head then replaced it and left her to her enjoyment.

*

Refreshed and invigorated, Clara walked slowly back up the lane. As always her eyes gazed appreciatively as she neared Primrose Cottage. It was well maintained and from the window, which Clara had often looked through, it seemed roomy and comfortably furnished. She wished it belonged to Guy. His mother's cottage was a lot smaller. The furnishings were meagre and the walls were dark and foreboding. Clara longed for Guy to whitewash them, but Nellie wouldn't allow it.

As she neared the gate, she heard a moan and found a gentleman prostrate on the pebble path.

'Are you alright, sir,' she said running to his aid.

'Damn me, I slipped on the path. I think I've hurt my shoulder.'

'Come, let me help you up.' She pulled him to his feet and from the sound of his grunts surmised that he'd probably broken a bone.

'Help me inside. The key is in my pocket, see.' He turned and offered up his trouser pocket for her to retrieve it.

Without reserve, Clara fished the key out of his warm pocket and fiddled with it in the key hole until the door opened. With a swift look of appreciation through the open doorways, she walked him into the kitchen. He was pale and sweaty as she assessed him. 'I'm a trained nurse, if you'll allow me to examine you I'll be able to help.'

Philip nodded, but through the pain he observed the girl with great admiration - she had nice eyes.

'I don't believe we've met before.'

'No, I'm from St Agnes,' she answered, gently pressing his arm. 'Tell me if that hurts?'

'Ouch,' he said, as her fingers ran along his collarbone. He blew a painful breath, before feigning ignorance about her. 'You're a long way from home, what brings you to Gweek, Miss….?'

'My name is Clara. I helped rehabilitate your neighbour, Guy Blackthorn, after his accident.'

'Ah I see, and has he fully recovered from his…accident?'

'He has.'

'And still you're here?' He raised his eyebrows.

'As you see,' Clara answered flatly.

Philip's mouth twitched into a slight smile, she didn't look too happy about the prospect.

'Guy and I are to be married soon. I would have thought being his neighbour, you'd have heard.'

'I'm barely here to see my neighbours and I've not seen Guy for many months. May I offer my congratulations on your upcoming nuptials?'

Philip noted Clara could barely raise a smile at the thought of her impending marriage. 'Forgive my manners. I've not formally introduced myself. Philip Goldsworthy at your service, ma'am.'

Clara gave him her best dazzling smile. 'I'm pleased to meet you.'

Philip reached out to her hand and pressed it to his lips. 'Enchanté, Clara.' He held her gaze as she held his.

'I think you may have fractured your collarbone, Mr Goldsworthy.'

'Damn it.'

'Do you have a tablecloth?'

'A tablecloth?' he frowned.

'To make a sling.'

'Oh I see, yes, you'll find one in the drawer over there.'

Clara ran her fingers admiringly over the dresser, before pulling a white linen tablecloth from the drawer. She swiftly folded it into a triangle and tied it around Philip's neck to support his arm. Her face was very close to Philip's and she was not unaware of his reaction. 'You'll need to keep it close to your body for a few weeks. No lifting, leaning or reaching and you will be in some considerable pain for a while.'

'I'm indebted to you, Clara.'

'Think nothing of it. It's nice to be able to do some proper nursing again.' Clara sighed audibly as her eyes took in her surroundings. 'I've wanted to look inside this house since I came to live next door. It really is lovely. Do you never live here?'

'No,' he said sadly. 'Unfortunately it needs someone to look after it. The path for instance, it's slippery with moss, that's why I fell. I should really employ a housekeeper to come and air and sweep the place.'

'Well, I could do that for you. After all, I'm only next door.'

Philip smiled thoughtfully. 'I'm not sure your husband-to-be would like that.'

'He wouldn't have to know,' Clara answered seriously. 'He's away most of the week.'

'Nellie would have something to say.'

'Phish, her! The woman is going mad! She doesn't know her ar….foot from her elbow anymore. No one would know,' she whispered.

Philip's stomach flipped. 'I see. Well then, let me show you around the place.'

Clara sighed enviously at every room she was taken in to. When it came to the master bedroom, they both paused and looked at the bed.

'It looks comfy.'

'It is.'

As their eyes locked, Clara pouted her lips. 'I would gladly look after the place for you, Mr Goldsworthy. It would certainly give me something constructive to do while Guy is from home.'

Philip felt the stirring of an exciting prospect. *This one was a little minx*. He cleared his throat. 'You'll put my mind at rest then, if that is what you propose. I'll leave you the spare key. You can come and go as you please but if, and only if, you call me Philip. After all, we're friends now.'

Clara felt a tingle of exhilaration. 'Thank you....Philip. Tell me, how often do you visit? I've not seen you here before.'

'Not often, I agree, but then there was nothing to come for.' He raised an eyebrow. 'Perhaps I shall rectify that now. Unfortunately I have this to contend with at the moment.' He lifted his arm and winced in pain. 'How long did you say it would take to mend?'

'Two, three weeks before it is functional again I'm afraid. Though it will ache longer than that.'

Philip blew a reluctant sigh. 'Am I not to do anything?'

'Oh, there are certain things you will still be able to do,' she said suggestively.

Philip's mouth curled into a wide smile. 'Is it me or is it getting hot in here? I think we had better go downstairs.'

As they said their goodbyes in the kitchen, Philip said gently, 'I thank you for your nursing skills, Clara.'

'It was my pleasure.'

'Well then, I'll take my leave of you for the present. I'll leave you to lock up.'

'When might you return,' she asked, not even trying to hide her enthusiasm.

'I'll send word. Any letter through this door, you have my permission to open.'

*

Fortunately for Clara, Nellie napped in the afternoons, allowing her to slip away to Primrose Cottage. It was so much nicer and much more peaceful than Guy's. She was always careful that no one saw her enter the cottage after learning that there was a deep animosity between Guy and Philip. He'd not like her doing what she was doing, but what Guy didn't know, he couldn't grieve over. My god, but she needed something to relieve the boredom of life with Guy's mad mother. Besides, Primrose Cottage had a huge array of books to read and soft comfortable furnishings to curl up and read them on.

Clara didn't have long to wait before a note dropped on the doormat heralding a visit from Philip.

I intend to visit Primrose Cottage on Wednesday 3rd September at 4:00p.m.

Please air the bed for an overnight stay.

*

When Philip stepped through the door, Clara was waiting for him.

'Well, well, this is a nice surprise to come home to.' He sniffed the air. 'The cottage smells so fresh.'

'I've aired the bed linen…as you're staying,' Clara said without a hint of shame.

'How have you managed to get away from Nellie?'

'She's dozing in the chair. I'll have to return soon.'

'That's a pity. I was hoping you could come and share some supper with me. I admit my culinary skills are non existent, but I've brought with me some cold ham, tomatoes and bread.' He grinned boyishly. 'Do you think you could get away this evening?'

Clara pondered for a moment. Although Nellie slept a good part of the afternoon, she still took herself off to bed at eight and slept through until six the next morning. 'It'll be a late supper I'm afraid. After eight?' she asked with a raised eyebrow.

'Perfect, I'll see you then.'

*

Clara picked through the offerings Nellie had served up, knowing she was to eat with Philip later.

'Eat up girl, you'll waste away.'

'I'm not hungry.'

'In my day I was made to eat everything on my plate.'

'I'm not a child, Nellie,' Clara snapped. 'So stop treating me like one.'

Nellie pursed her lips and got up from the table and started to wash up. She knew she was bossy - it had always been in her nature. In fact it was the one trait that wasn't altering in the way she felt at the moment. *I must be more accommodating to Clara, after all, she is such a good help.*

Clara glanced at the clock - it was already seven-fifty. Desperate to get Nellie upstairs as soon as possible, Clara said, 'Here let me do that, you go on up and I'll bring you a cup of tea.'

Nellie's mouth relaxed and nodded gratefully.

Once the pots were washed, Clara added a generous amount of whisky, normally used for medicinal purposes only, into Nellie's tea.

Clara watched Nellie slurp her tea with relish. She bid her goodnight, closed her door and began to make herself presentable for Philip.

It was still light outside when she pulled the front door to, but just as she stepped into the lane she saw Guy's wagon trundling towards her. Clara felt a curl of resentment in her stomach.

*

At Primrose Cottage, Philip's fingers reached into his waistcoat pocket, retrieved his watch and tutted. She was late. The trundle of a horse and wagon making its way up the lane alerted him to the reason why.

'Damn his eyes!' Philip sighed resentfully as Guy rode past.

*

Clara could barely hide her irritation as the wagon pulled up.

'You said nothing about coming home tonight,' she said, punching her fists into her hips.

Detecting an air of accusation in her voice, Guy jumped down and kissed her on the cheek. 'We thought to surprise you. Are you alright, Clara?' he said noting the high colour on her cheeks. 'You look a little feverish.'

'I'm fine. A little hot perhaps,' she snapped.

'I'm not indifferent to your plight of being left alone all week with Ma, so as we were looking at a job in Garras, I thought it would be nice to come home and keep you company.'

Clara smiled tightly.

Guy tipped his head. 'Are you not pleased?'

'Of course I am,' she said, helping Silas to take the tools from the wagon.

Guy regarded her for a moment. 'You look nice. Were you going somewhere?'

Clara narrowed her eyes. 'Just because I'm stuck in a tiny cottage in the middle of nowhere, doesn't mean I can't pretty myself up for an evening stroll!'

Silas raised his eyebrows as he walked past.

'I wasn't criticising or questioning you, Clara,' Guy said flatly.

'I'm glad to hear it.' Resigned that her plans were in tatters, Clara returned to the cottage to put the kettle on the fire, while Guy and Silas finished unpacking.

Guy detected a distinct chill when they walked into the kitchen, despite the warm temperatures. As Silas entered, Blue trotted behind him, putting damp paw marks on Clara's scrubbed stone floor.

'Get that filthy dog out of my clean kitchen.'

Silas shot a worried look at Guy as he pulled Blue to heel.

'It's our kitchen too, Clara,' Guy said softly. 'Blue stays.'

Clara flashed her eyes angrily. 'You don't have to scrub this floor!' she snapped and turned away, but Guy knew her look was derisive.

Silas and Guy glanced uneasily at each other.

Presently Guy asked, 'Where's Ma?'

'She's in bed, fast asleep. Do you want something to eat?' she asked shortly.

'No thank you, we've eaten at The Old Court House at Mawgan. A mug of tea will suffice.'

He reached out and caught Clara's hand as she placed two mugs of tea on the table. 'We could still go for that stroll after this? Silas can feed Mazie.' His request seemed to be problematic judging by the serious furrow on Clara's brow.

'It'll be dark by then. The evenings are drawing in now. I'll go another night.'

'As you wish.' Guy let her hand go and watched as she slumped down opposite him and folded her arms.

'So, are you working at Garras now then?' Clara trilled.

'No, just arranging a job. We're down in Cury for a few more days, then in Gunwalloe next week, so there'll be no more surprise visits.' He could see the sting in his voice made Clara's demeanour change in an instant. He had never met anyone whose mood ran so hot and cold.

Her face softened. 'I'm sorry, Guy, It's been so hot today and your ma can be very tiresome. I also have quite a headache.'

*

As soon as Guy and Silas departed the next morning, and with Nellie still sleeping off her whisky induced sleep, Clara slipped out to Primrose Cottage. To her dismay, she found Philip had also gone. As she moved despondently from room to room tidying up, she found the bed in disarray and a note waiting for her on the pillow.

I saw you had a visitor. I'll be here again tonight. Will you? P

28

As Guy set off the next morning back to work, he knew all was not well at home. Clara had been in such a strange mood last night. For the first time in their relationship, he really didn't know what to say to her, nor had he any idea how to mend what was clearly going wrong between them.

Guy thought back to when he'd asked Clara to marry him – she'd been so thrilled at the prospect. But now, it seemed life in a sleepy village was not to her liking. He couldn't blame her, life here was vastly different to a busy hospital, and though he hated to admit it, his ma *was* becoming a problem too. Her sharp mind was failing it seemed. He was so thankful Clara was there to keep an eye on her, but of course there was the crux. Clara had not come to nurse his ma, she'd come to be his wife. He knew he must go up to see the vicar at Constantine with Clara this weekend to arrange a wedding. That would give her something to occupy her mind. But then what about after the wedding? Nothing was going to change dramatically. Maybe Dr Eddy could use Clara's nursing skills. He'd enquire when he was next home. He might also ask the doctor to take a look at his ma, though she would not look on this very favourably. His ma had ailed nothing in her lifetime and shied away from doctors. The only person she'd consult on certain 'woman matters' was Amelia Pascoe, though (he smiled to himself) Amelia would always consult Dr Eddy before advising Nellie on anything medical. He sighed heavily, flicked the reins and set Mazie into a trot.

Silas glanced at his brother. He knew to keep quiet when Guy was in a pensive mood. He too had seen how moody Clara was last night. She could barely hide the irritation from her face when they'd arrived home unexpectedly. He wished with all his heart that Guy wasn't going to marry her, because he knew Guy would not be as happy as he would have been with Ellie.

*

The cool breezes of September were a welcome relief for all. With the start of the month a letter from James had arrived for Ellie. He'd been away in Europe since January researching his new novel but had sent regular letters charting his many ventures. There was never an address to reply, as James was travelling through several countries, so as yet he knew nothing of Guy's impending marriage. Ellie sat on the dunes to read his letter, while Brandy snuffled in the marram grass for tasty treats the visitors to the beach had left.

August 1902
Dear Ellie,

Greetings from Paris. He'd enclosed a colour drawing of Notre Dame.

I trust all is well with you and the Tea Room. I understand from my lawyer that Guy is recovered and no longer in hospital. I should think you are quite relieved at the prospect. I hope he is fit and able to enjoy tea and scones and your company again.

I shall be making my journey back to London at the end of August and onward to Cornwall by mid September.

I look forward to seeing both you and Guy on my return.
Regards
Your good friend, James

Ellie folded the letter up. She would never share tea and scones with Guy again, that was for sure. What puzzled her was why Guy had not even had the decency to come and explain why he'd passed her over for another woman. Perhaps he was uneasy about her reaction. She gave a short laugh - and so he should be! For in truth, she was as angry as she was sad. If she lived to be a hundred she would never understand how he could have led her on and made her fall in love with him, only to toss her aside like a discarded rag when someone better had come along.

She fingered James's letter - she'd be glad to see him

again. He'd be pleased to find that his business was thriving, but equally unhappy to find its manager wasn't.

*

In Primrose Cottage, Philip relaxed back into the pillow with a deep sigh, feeling very pleased with himself.

'So, you were a virgin?'

Clara lay in the hot twisted sheets. 'Of course!'

'So you and Guy haven't….'

'No! He wants to do everything properly and wait for the wedding night.'

Philip snorted. *More fool him.* He rewarded himself with a satisfied smile - he'd bedded Guy's wife-to-be, before he had.

'What is Guy going to say when he finds you didn't wait?' he said, lighting a cigarette.

'He'll never know. I'm a good actress.'

Philip smirked. *Actress or not, Guy was no fool.* 'When is your wedding anyway?'

Clara propped herself up on her elbow. 'Soon, but that shouldn't affect my visits here.' She ran her fingers suggestively down his chest.

'Is that so,' he grinned. That was not what he envisaged. Once Guy was married and out of the picture, he intended to do everything to woo Ellie back. She'd loved him once and in his own arrogant way believed that Ellie would succumb to his charms again - after all, no woman wants to live the life of a lonely old maid! Once he had Ellie, Guy could have his trollop of a wife back. Until then though, he'd have some fun with her.

'What are you grinning at?' Clara asked.

'Oh the future looks rosy that's all.' He yawned, stubbed out the cigarette, closed his eyes and was asleep almost instantly.

Clara listened to him breathing deeply as she stretched lazily, luxuriating in the fine linen sheets covering her. She congratulated herself on finding a husband for respectability and a lover to keep her warm when Guy was away.

*

After his impromptu visit earlier that week, Guy spent the whole next weekend with Clara. During that time, they'd arranged for the banns to be read and the wedding date was set for Saturday the 27th September. The wedding breakfast was to be held at the cottage for all Guy's neighbours and friends. Clara had no one, except her depraved step-father and she had no intention of inviting him!

Because Clara couldn't administer Nellie's whisky sleeping draft when Guy was home, Nellie had taken to wandering about in the lane in her night clothes. This forced Guy to speak to Dr Eddy about her. There was very little Dr Eddy could do for Nellie, she wasn't the easiest patient to administer medication to, so all he could offer Clara and Guy, was that they be kind to her, humour her whenever possible, not to scold her for doing strange things, and if things were to get out of hand they were to fetch him and he'd give her a sleeping draft. Clara smiled inwardly - the whisky tea she would administer, when Guy was away from home, would be the only sleeping draft Nellie would need.

Before Guy left on Monday morning he left strict instructions for Clara to make sure the front and back doors were locked securely and the key hidden every night. So that evening, she left Nellie snoring in her bedroom, secured the doors of the cottage, covered her head with the hood of her cloak and skipped happily down the lane to Primrose Cottage.

Harry Yates pulled his little terrier back behind the tree and watched with interest, as Guy's intended let herself into Philip Goldsworthy's cottage.

*

Nellie woke in the dead of the night with a dizzy headache. She shivered, realising she must have fallen asleep without pulling the blankets up. It took her a while to locate her bed warming pan and then set off downstairs to refill it with embers from the fire.

Once in the kitchen, she stopped for a moment, wondering what she was doing there. The firelight flickering reminded her. Laying the warming pan on the floor she picked up the coal shovel and pushed it into the glowing embers. Sparks flew everywhere as she pushed and shoved until the shovel was full of hot coals. She turned towards the door, leaving the waiting warming pan on the floor and walked carefully up the steps to her bedroom. Pulling the covers back she laid the shovel on the bed and moved it around to warm the covers. The bed sheets ignited immediately. Nellie jumped back in shock, accidently kicked over her night soil bucket and fell heavily against her bedroom door. The flames were licking higher and higher, but Nellie couldn't move for the dreadful pain in her hip.

'Rory,' she screamed. When no one came, she screamed for her late husband again and again.

The heat in the room intensified, and her body prickled with perspiration. Burning linen had fallen on the rug beside her bed, and one by one the rags of the rug ignited, coming ever closer to where she lay. Her bed was ablaze, the flames licking up to the beams and smoke filled the room. Nellie gagged and choked as she tried desperately to move her limbs. Suddenly her nightgown was alight. She shrieked and slapped her hands on the flames.

'Rory', she screamed, but nobody came.

*

Clara woke with a sense of quiet contentment. Her eyes flickered open and then sleep pulled her back for a moment. It was the crack of timber that brought her to full wakefulness. Pushing the covers back, she padded quickly to the window.

Bright orange sparks flew up into the night sky to mingle with the stars. It took but a moment for the awful truth to sink in. Her cottage was on fire!

'Oh Christ!' She twisted back to look at Philip who was stirring in the bed.

'What is it, come back to bed,' he beckoned sleepily.

'No, Philip, come here quick.'

Thinking Guy had returned unexpectedly and found his wife-to-be not at home, he leapt naked out of bed in a panic. It was one thing cuckolding someone - it was another being found out. 'Come away from the window.'

'No, look, I think Bramble Cottage is on fire!'

'Jesus!' He pushed her out of the way. 'Get your clothes on and go out the back door. The neighbours hereabouts will most probably have seen it and started to deal with it.'

As predicted, the neighbours were out in force. From the side of her cottage Clara stood hiding under the hood of her cloak. She could see Bert Laity ramming the front door with a fallen tree trunk, and several people were running down the lane with ladders and buckets. It was clear by the flames from the thatch that the fire had started in Nellie's room.

Clara panicked. Thankfully no one had seen her yet, otherwise they would wonder why she was outside in the middle of the night, while the doors of her cottage remained securely locked. There was no question about it - she had to risk her life to get back inside the cottage.

*

Harry Yates, who due to ill health could do nothing more than help fetch ladders to the scene, knew exactly where he could find one. He'd seen Philip Goldsworthy move a ladder around to the back of Primrose Cottage, the day Guy met with his accident.

The light from the blaze lit the night sky, giving enough light for him to locate the ladder in the long grass behind Philip's Cottage. He grasped the wooden sides, grimacing as the slimy wood slipped through his hands. He dragged it away from the grass for a closer inspection and ran his fingers down the rungs – the top first five were broken and splintered. A sudden unpleasant thought popped into his head. *Had this been the ladder Guy fell from?* Everyone hereabouts had inspected and puzzled over how Guy had fallen from the ladder which was leant against Primrose Cottage which was as sound as a bell! *Had Goldsworthy swapped it?* He shook his head in disbelief. *Why would he do a thing like that? But..!* He stepped back from the ladder as though it was contaminated, and as he did so, he saw a dark figure running towards the back of Bramble Cottage.

*

Clara fumbled with trembling fingers to open the lock of the back door and entered the kitchen. She grabbed the tablecloth, pushed it against her face to stop the thick, penetrating, choking smoke and made her way through the room to unlock the front door, so as to make the neighbours think she'd been indoors. Her eyes were watering as she skirted the fireside and promptly fell over the warming pan Nellie had left on the floor. Before she could scramble to her feet, the front door burst open and Bert Laity stormed into the room, quickly followed by a stream of neighbours all carrying buckets of water.

'Hello!' Bert yelled. 'Hello! Where are you Nellie? Clara?'

'Nellie is upstairs, please help her!' Clara shouted from were she lay on the kitchen floor.

Someone came to Clara's aid, she did not know who, but he picked her up as though she was a bag of feathers.

'Come on maid. Let's get you out of here.'

Clara felt the damp grass beneath her as she was laid down. The cool night air filled her lungs and she rolled over coughing and spluttering. When she collected her breath she sat up and found Harry Yates holding a lamp over her – he had a strange expression on his face.

'Nellie's upstairs,' she sobbed.

Harry nodded. 'It's alright, Bert's gone in for her,' he

answered flatly.

*

Guy felt deeply troubled, though he knew not why, but whatever it was, his mind was not on his work. Twice Silas had to nudge him with the next shook of thatch. The third time Silas nudged him, Guy waved him away.

'I need to rest my back awhile, Silas. You carry on.'

Very cautiously he stepped down onto the top rung of the ladder. Something he'd never given a second thought to before his accident. He'd never been tentative on the roof. You couldn't be a Thatcher if you were. It troubled him deeply that he'd fallen, it just didn't make sense. His equipment was checked constantly – as were all his working tools. He could still hear his pa telling him, "A neglectful workman ends in dire consequences". How he had fallen from that ladder, he did not know. Silas had retrieved it after the fall and as far as either of them could see, there was nothing untoward about it, which made him more cautious about using it.

They were working on the thatch at Winnianton Farm, Gunwalloe. Guy sat on the grass and took a long quenching drink from his water bottle. He watched with amusement as Silas scrambled up the ladder, swiftly followed by Blue. Guy had never seen a dog climb a ladder before, but Blue seemed to have no trouble negotiating the rungs nor the thatch. He'd scramble to the ridge of the house and would sit quite contently as Silas worked.

It wasn't only the ladder mystery which bothered him - it was Clara's discontent and the fact that he was indebted to Philip Goldsworthy. Damn his eyes for stealing Ellie back. Thankfully the envelope of money, which Silas told him had come every week, had ceased as soon as Guy had returned home. As soon as he could he would return the money. He shook his head, he was thankful to be better, but oh my goodness, at what cost?

'Thirsty work, eh?'

A familiar voice broke into Guy's thoughts. He looked

up to find his old friend James Blackwell holding out his hand to him.

Guy stood and clasped hands with him.

'Guy my friend. It fills my heart with such joy to see you back on your feet again.'

Guy grinned. 'Thank you, it's good to see you too. It's been a long process.'

'Are you completely well?' James stood back to take a better look.

'I'm still in a little pain, but that should subside over the coming months. At least I can work again, albeit a lot slower than I used to. Thankfully I have Silas to help me. I couldn't do it without him.'

James looked up at Silas on the roof. 'Glad to hear he is following in the family's footsteps. Good god, is that a dog up there with him? I've never seen anything like it!'

'I swear they're inseparable.'

'I'm just this day back from my travels. I was en route for a swim in Church Cove if you'd care to join me?' James grinned and patted Guy and the shoulder.

'Thank you but I am still a little too fragile to be battered by the waves.'

James nodded. 'My goodness, but it's good to see you. I should think Ellie is pleased to see you back on your feet.'

Guy blanched at the mention of her name.

'Are you alright? You've gone very pale.'

Guy moistened his dry lips but found it difficult to speak for a moment.

'What is it? Is something other than the pain bothering you?'

Guy sighed and nodded. 'It grieves me deeply, James, that I'm indebted to Goldsworthy and Ellie.'

'Why are you indebted to Goldsworthy?'

Guy nodded sorrowfully. 'He paid for my treatment you see.'

James raised his eyebrows. 'Did *he* tell you that?'

'No, I've seen neither hide nor hair of him since the day before I was taken into hospital.'

James cleared his throat uneasily. 'Guy .... I don't know how to tell you this, forgive me, I'm not looking for any praise or such like, but...it was I who paid for your treatment.'

Guy felt his knees soften. 'You?'

James nodded. 'Ellie came to me in such a state of panic in December. She'd just come from you, frantic that you'd be crippled for life if you didn't get the care you needed. Forgive me, but I thought she would have told you once you had mended.'

'Oh god.' Guy felt his world tip on its axis. He sat back down. 'What have I done?'

'What is it, what's amiss?'

Guy thumped his head hard with his hand. 'I thought Ellie had given herself to Philip Goldsworthy in return for him paying for my hospital care.'

'What? Why the devil did you think she'd do that?'

Guy balled his hands into fists. 'Silas overheard a conversation between Ellie and Goldsworthy.'

'Surely you know Ellie would not do that! Has she not been in touch with you during these last months?'

'She has.' Guy hung his head shamefully. 'I'm ashamed to say that I ignored all her letters, believing she was with Goldsworthy. Damn my pride. Oh god, James, what have I done.'

'So you've had no contact with her since December?' he asked incredulously.

'None.' He cast his eyes downward.

'Well, you must go to her immediately. It's never too late to make amends.'

'Oh but I'm afraid it is.'

'Why? You and Ellie are made for each other. Go and explain and all will be well, I'm sure of it.'

'I can't James. I'm to be married on the 27th of this month.'

James looked at Guy's crestfallen face. 'Oh… I see!'

'I met a nurse, Clara, at hospital. She helped me through the darkest of days. We sort of grew into each other's life, so I asked her to return home with me after I'd been discharged. I thought my future with Ellie was over!'

James took a deep breath. 'I should think Ellie will be deeply saddened at your news. She really cared for you, Guy.'

Guy felt his world implode at the thought of the hurt he'd caused her.

'Guy, my friend. I still think you should go and explain to Ellie.'

'Have *you* seen her yet?'

James shook his head. 'I've been on the continent since January. As I say, I only returned from London this morning, so I haven't been over to Poldhu yet. But if I can make a suggestion, I think you should go over there right now.'

Guy nodded sadly as he watched James walk down the lane. He thought of the letters Ellie had sent him, still stuffed down the side pocket of his bag! Very slowly he flattened the screwed up letters and opened them one by one. His eyes blurred with emotion as he read the rest of the first letter she had sent him.

……I miss you terribly. I miss your visits to the Tea Room, your humour, and your zest for life. I hope that when you return, we will pick up where we left off. I admit I'm lonely without you. Those last few weeks before you befell that terrible accident were full of joy. My life is so much happier when you are by my side. Get well soon, Guy. I'll be waiting for you.

He looked at the others and shook his head –he hadn't even bothered opening them! He picked one at random, and scanned the letter.

….. I admit I have not ventured over to Gweek to see your ma and Silas but as you have always been so kind to me, I am managing to send a little money from my takings to them just to keep the wolf from the door, so to speak.

His eyes ran to the close of the letter.

Rest assured Guy, I pray for your speedy recovery every night. In fact you are all I think about. I miss you so much, Guy. Get well soon and hurry home to me.
Your dearest friend, Ellie x

'Oh Ellie!' He dropped his head into his hands. 'What have I done to you?'

29

At the Tea Room, Ellie was disconcerted with the unwelcome presence of Carole Dunstan-Goldsworthy. She watched her cautiously – their last meeting being less than friendly.

Carole was sat on the terrace in the shade with three other well-heeled ladies. They ordered tea and scones, without actually engaging Ellie in any real conversation, but Ellie had the distinct impression that Carole was watching her, because whenever Ellie glanced at her, she swiftly turned away.

When they rose to leave, Ellie came out with her tea tray but Carole held back from the others.

'Hello Elise.' She pulled on her kid gloves with an air of superiority. 'I'm so glad you've seen sense at last. This place…,' she flicked her hand casually, '...would hardly give you enough income to live on, so I'm sure the accounts Philip has set up for you will come in handy.' She cast her eyes derisively over Ellie's clothes. 'Though for some reason, it seems you are still not using the outfitter's account!'

Ellie almost dropped the tray back on the table. 'I beg your pardon?'

'Come, come Elise. Don't be so coy about it. I'm glad to see the back of Philip from my boudoir. Philip is too, by the look on his face, and it certainly won't do you any harm financially.'

Ellie felt her stomach bubble with anger. 'I can assure you, Madam, I do not know what you are inferring.'

'Please yourself, but I suggest you spend his money on a new wardrobe of garments though - Philip prefers his women to be well dressed.' She tapped the side of her nose with her gloved hand and walked off.

Speechless, Ellie punched her fists into her hips in consternation. *What the hell was all that about?*

*

With the last of the customers gone, she left Jessie to wash the crockery, for fear of breaking something, and stormed down to the sea hoping the water would cool her fury. *What the hell had Philip been saying to his wife?*

The sound of someone clearing their voice made Ellie spin around. Her hand shot to her mouth, stunned into silence at the sight of Guy before her.

Every muscle in her body tensed. Her knees weakened and a whole range of emotions bubbled up. The most immediate was to administer an angry slap to his face if he came any closer.

'Ellie,' he whispered as he advanced with his hand outstretched.

Ellie stepped back, as though his touch would burn her. She saw him falter, as his posture crumpled and he retracted his hand. She stared him down - her mind was working furiously as she tried desperately to control her emotions.

'What do you want, Guy?' Much to her annoyance her voice was tearful.

Holding her gaze with his haunted eyes, he said, 'I'm here to apologise, Ellie. I fear I have done you a great wrong.'

Suddenly finding it difficult to breathe, Ellie turned and made to walk away.

'Please, Ellie.'

Despite herself, she hesitated, turned and snapped accusingly, '*What*, Guy? What do you want to say to me? Are you going to explain why you ignored all the letters I sent to you, and apologise for sending me away from the hospital without a bye-your-leave after I'd come all the way to Truro to see you? Well you've left it *too* late!'

Ellie saw his pained expression turn to puzzlement.

'You came to see *me*?'

'*Yes I did!* I came all that way in April, only to be told by a nurse that you weren't there! But you *were* there, *weren't* you Guy? You just didn't want to see me! You couldn't face me because I'd already been replaced in your affections by someone else, hadn't I?'

Guy raked his hands through his hair. 'No, Ellie, I…I had no idea that you had come, I swear. I can't understand why you were told that I wasn't there.'

'But you have replaced me with someone else, haven't you?' She stopped for a moment to swallow down a sob. *Stay strong Ellie, stay strong.* 'I hear you're getting married! Tell me Guy. Is it something all men feel impelled to do to me? Because it seems to me that I'm to be used and then discarded like some old rag!' This time she could not control her emotions.

'Oh, Ellie, let me explain.' He held both hands out towards her.

A flare of adrenalin fired her brain to respond. 'Explain! How are you going to explain to my broken heart?' Unable to control the hot tears running down her face, she shook her head. 'I'm glad you're back on your feet, Guy, now please, leave me be. I've nothing more to say to you.' She picked up her skirts and ran up the beach.

Already exhausted from the long walk over Poldhu cliff, Guy did not have the strength in his legs to follow her quickly, so by the time he reached the cottage he found the door securely locked.

Guy peered through the window and could see Ellie in the arms of a girl who was clearly comforting her.

He tapped on the glass. 'Ellie, please, let me in, so I can try to explain properly. I'll not leave until I've done so.' He collected a chair from the terrace and sat behind the closed door of the cottage.

*

When her distress dissipated a good ten minutes later, Ellie sat and stared down at her hands. She was spent and emotionally drained. Her throat and lungs were sore, as though she'd been burned inside.

'Is he still outside, Jessie?'

She glanced outside. 'Yes.'

Ellie sighed with hopeless despair.

Jessie poured Ellie a drink of water and knelt at her feet.

As she drank thirstily, Jessie pleaded with her, 'Ellie let him in. Let him explain. You need to know why he's done what he's done. He's not going to go away until you hear him out.'

Did she want to know? Did she really want to know why it was so easy for him to discard her? Was there some real flaw in her persona that impelled men to do this to her? She would never know if she didn't hear him out. Ellie squeezed her eyes tightly shut and nodded.

Jessie quickly unlocked the door and Guy stood up stiffly and walked inside.

Ellie stood as he entered, rubbed the back of her neck, but could not make eye contact with him.

'Shall I leave or shall I stay?' Jessie asked uncertain.

'If you could just leave us for a few minutes, Jessie, thank you,' Ellie said hoarsely.

Jessie nodded, turned to leave and on the way out gave Guy a look that told him he was in big trouble.

Feeling calmer now, Ellie glanced at the man she loved with all her heart, but it was too much to bear, and quickly looked away.

'Ellie.' There was a sad plead in his voice. 'I've just seen James Blackwell. He explained what you did for me…..how you asked him to help me. I'd no idea it was James who paid for my treatment and that you had instigated it. I thought…..' He lowered his head shamefully. 'I thought you…..'

Ellie lifted her gaze to his. 'What, Guy, what did you think?'

His throat thickened with emotion. 'It was something Silas overheard you and Goldsworthy speak of …' He felt unable to meet her gaze. '…about him paying for my treatment if….'

Ellie felt the colour rise in her cheeks. 'Oh I see! You really thought I'd take up that disgusting offer of helping you, if I went back to him?' Her mouth tightened as though she tasted something bad. 'Do you really think my morals are so loose that I would have done such a thing?'

'But, Ellie!' Guy clamped his hands together. 'What was I to think? Silas heard the conversation, then the next I knew a wagon arrived to take me to hospital.'

'My god, Guy, I'd have moved heaven and earth to help you, but do you honestly think I'd have done that?'

He nodded, shook his head and then shrugged his shoulders helplessly.

Ellie threw her hands up in the air in frustration. 'I thought you knew me!'

'I thought I did too, that's why I couldn't comprehend why you'd agree to his offer. I couldn't bear it, Ellie, the thought of it made me ill.'

'But I wrote to you, Guy!' Her voice trembled. 'I filled my letters with my love for you!'

His shoulders slouched. 'I didn't read them, Ellie. Just seeing your handwriting on the envelope was too painful. I just tried to put you out of my mind.'

'Which you clearly managed to do, hence your upcoming marriage,' she reposted bitterly.

She watched him bite his lip guiltily - unable to comprehend that he would think she would have gone back to Philip. Suddenly the conversation she'd had with Carole that morning popped into her head. She felt her face drain of colour. 'Who else believes that I have gone back to Goldsworthy, Guy? Who've you told?'

Guy's eyes widened. 'Silas and Ma knew of my concerns of course, but apart from that, no one - it hurt too much to speak of them.'

'Well someone is spreading malicious rumours about me! I've just had the humiliation of Philip Goldsworthy's snooty wife, practically thanking me for taking Philip off her hands again! Are you sure you've not inferred to *anyone* else that I have prostituted myself with that man? Because if you have, I swear I'll *never* speak to you again, Guy Blackthorn.'

'And I swear I don't know why she said that to you. It hasn't come from me!' He ran his hand through his hair, making it stand on end. 'Ellie, I'm so sorry for all the hurt and misunderstandings, truly I am.'

Ellie shook her head. 'You should have trusted me, Guy,' she whispered.

'I should have, yes.' His voice matched her sadness. He reached out to touch her but pulled back as though unworthy.

As her resentment abated, Ellie felt calmness settle between them. 'The treatment worked I see?' she said softly.

He smiled weakly. 'It was a terrible struggle. It still is, but yes, thank you for doing what you did. Without you and James I would still be laid on my kitchen floor.'

And you would have still been mine, Ellie thought selfishly.

As though he'd read her mind, he added, 'I'd gladly turn the clocks back to that time if I could. As good as it is to be mobile again, I feel that I have ruined something quite wonderful between us, and I shall be forever saddened by that.'

Ellie twisted her mouth grimly.

'I hope we can still be friends, Ellie?' he said as he made for the door.

'I hoped we'd be so much more,' she whispered.

He turned to face her and the room was loaded with unspoken sorrow.

'I'd better go now.'

As Ellie nodded sadly, Jessie appeared at the door.

'Mr Blackthorn, someone is shouting for you from the cliff path.'

Guy's eyes narrowed. They both stepped outside to look.

'Guy, Guy,' Silas shouted from the top of his voice.

'It's Silas! What the devil…?' Guy ran out onto the dunes with Ellie hot on his heels.

Silas ran into Guy's arms almost collapsing on contact.

Guy held him tight to his chest. 'Silas, what is it?'

Tears and mucus ran down his blotchy face. 'It's Ma,' he cried as he pushed the crumpled telegram into Guy's hand. 'There's been a fire and Ma's dead!'

Guy felt his head swim. 'Oh, god! Clara?' He scanned the telegram for more information. .

Ellie stepped forward and touched him gently on his sleeve. 'Guy, I'm so sorry for your loss.'

He rubbed his weary eyes. 'We must go, now.'

Ellie nodded sympathetically. 'I hope Clara escaped unharmed.'

Guy's lip quivered, the shock rendering him speechless now.

Ellie watched as Guy led Silas back up the cliff path. He'd aged almost ten years in the last few minutes.

*

When Guy and Silas returned to Gweek, they found their cottage in a terrible state, but not uninhabitable, and to Guy's infinite relief, found Clara well, though very shaken.

Clara greeted him at the door, with nervous anticipation. *Would he question why she'd survived, when his ma had not?* To all intents and purposes everyone hereabouts believed her to be inside the house when it caught fire. She just had to convince Guy to that fact.

'Oh Guy!' She flaked into his arms sobbing. 'I'm so very, very sorry. I couldn't save your ma! I tried, but the flames beat me back.'

Feeling his strong arms embrace her, caused relief to sear through her veins.

'Shush, Clara. Don't blame yourself. It's not your fault,' he said, his voice breaking with grief.

Clara sent up a prayer of thanks.

'Where is Ma's body?'

'At Mr Trewin's the undertaker. Dr Eddy thought the

cottage was in too much of a mess to have her laid out here.'

Guy nodded sadly. 'I'll go and see her in a few minutes.'

'I think Amelia is sitting in vigil at the moment and has made arrangements for someone to be with her until the funeral.'

Guy felt his eyes burning with unshed tears. *Thank god for good friends like Amelia.*

Slowly they walked around the cottage together. Everywhere stank of smoke, but only Nellie's room was burned charcoal black.

'Dr Eddy says that your ma must have fallen when the bed went up in flames, because her hip was broken. By the time I realised the cottage was on fire, it was too late. I feel awful, because I didn't hear anything.' She feigned a sob.

Guy reached for her hand and squeezed it tightly. 'Please don't upset yourself. I'm sure you did everything possible to help, Clara, you're such a caring person.' He looked at the burned shell of the bedroom and shuddered. *What a dreadful way for his ma to die.* He cast his eyes skywards to the gaping hole in the roof. Fortunately, the quick thinking of his neighbours, climbing ladders to drag the smouldering thatch off, had saved the whole roof from setting alight. Guy sighed. 'At least we can still live here, while we repair it.'

'Oh well you see, Philip Goldsworthy has offered to help us. He says I can live in his cottage until ours is habitable again,' Clara said happily

'No! You keep away from that house and Goldsworthy!' Guy could hardly keep the venom from his voice. 'We don't need *his* help.'

'But, everything is in a terrible mess,' she argued.

'I said no, Clara. We'll make your room habitable and Silas and I will sleep in the wagon.'

Clara pouted her lips sulkily and wriggled her hand free

from Guy's. She did not relish sleeping in this stinking cottage.

As Guy and Silas set to work immediately repairing the roof, Clara reluctantly cleaned and aired her bedroom the best she could. As she lay in the acrid room that night, her dissatisfaction with life and Guy escalated.

Two days prior to the funeral, Clara had the unenviable task of scrubbing the greasy soot from the walls in the cottage to make it habitable for the wake. It was a disgustingly obnoxious job, which made Clara's mood as filthy as the soot under her fingernails. Each night she lay abed, thoroughly disgruntled at being denied the hot clean water and fresh bed linen next door.

Eventually the cottage was presentable, but having no time to organise the wake, Guy's immediate neighbours had rallied to make a splendid funeral tea and laid it out on Nellie's scrubbed pine table. The cottage still smelt of smoke, but Guy promised Clara that the walls would be white-washed once the funeral was over. Clara's mood lifted slightly, she rather looked forward to putting her mark on the cottage. She had ideas in her head taken from Philip's cottage and now she was mistress of the house, she was going to make a home she was proud of.

*

It was a sad and sombre procession which made its way through Gweek up to Constantine Church. Many villagers attended Nellie's funeral. She'd been a well respected, no-nonsense member of the community since her husband Rory brought her home from Constantine as his new bride. She'd be sadly missed. Everyone was shocked at her frightful demise. Many had witnessed her memory decline over the last few months, so on hearing how she'd mistaken her coal shovel for a warming pan, they crossed themselves and muttered, 'There but for the grace of god go I.'

As the procession returned to Bramble Cottage, several of Guy's neighbours expressed their relief that his Clara had escaped the inferno. Only Harry Yates knew exactly how she'd escaped. He stood in the corner of the kitchen barely eating anything. The very sight of Clara Young turned his stomach.

*

It was mid September. Ellie was lovingly tending her little sea garden late one afternoon. It was the one occupation that took her mind off Guy for a couple of hours.

The soil Sarah had sent down to her from Bochym had encouraged some different varieties of flowers to bloom that summer, but she knew they would be short lived. The wild Atlantic Ocean would do its best to blow in damp, salt-laden air which would soon turn the rich soil to sand, no matter how much she tried to protect it.

Without doubt May had been the best time for flowers in Cornwall. The coast paths and hedgerows, especially, were an array of colour and so too her little garden had come to life. Ellie had worked hard in her garden that year. She'd salvaged stones from rock falls in the cove and made herself a rock garden to mimic the cliffs. In early summer, despite the salt-laden air, it bloomed with white star-like sedum angelica. yellow kidney vetch had settled neatly into the crevices of the rocks, and bunches of wild garlic and bluebells found their own place in the garden, punctuated with mounds of hedgerow cranesbill - it was these small geranium flowers that always made Ellie smile. At last she'd managed to tame a few clumps of her favourite sea pinks, but no matter how many clumps of common storksbill she planted, this sticky little plant, with hairy stalks and a purple, white or pink bloom, managed to relocate itself back into the sand dunes.

Ellie stretched the stiffness out of her back. Business had been quiet today. The locals had stayed at home knowing a storm was brewing - the first of many that would batter the Cornish coast from now until spring time.

Jessie had caught the wagon up to Mullion to get some shopping, if she didn't come back soon, she'd surely be caught in the storm.

The wind had risen while she'd been working, and rain began to fall almost horizontally. Ellie quickly put her garden implements away in the outhouse. The wind began to build and was pushing in from the sea - the tide was already higher than normal. Ellie watched apprehensively, hoping the sea would not breach the wall which circled the dunes directly outside the Tea Room. She shivered in her thin dress and ran for shelter. Once inside she turned the door sign to 'Closed'- no one would come now. She made herself a cup of tea, and covered the uneaten cakes. The scones of course would not last another day, so she'd toast them this evening and enjoy them with a pat of butter. After sitting the chairs on the tables and sweeping the floor, Ellie noted that the waves had whipped up alarmingly and watched in trepidation as the tide encroached further up the beach than she'd ever seen before. She shivered as the cold draught normally associated with the winter months crept under the door. Ellie knew the sea and its tides like the back of her hand. She also knew that a spring tide, along with this south-westerly storm, would cause great damage, unless she did something to protect her property.

Tying a headscarf around her hair she ran onto the terrace and began stacking the outside tables and chairs around the back of the building, away from the prevailing winds. The tide had reached the dunes by the time she'd finished. This was going to be a big one! First she moved the sand bags into position at the doors. All her windows had shutters, so she battled against the wind to secure them all.

Ellie had never moved her lace collection from her old box bedroom into the cottage she now lived in, because she still preferred to work near the Tea Room's sea- facing window. It was this particular window shutter that had stuck fast to the wall, corroded with salt. It took all her strength to free the catch and by the time she did, the tide was swirling around her ankles. With all shutters secured, Ellie battled with the elements as she edged her way back to the main door to retrieve Brandy who was inside whining pitifully.

She was thoroughly drenched when she forced the door shut behind her. After securing a leash to Brandy, Ellie scanned the room to make sure all was secure, before trying to make her way to the safety of her cottage. As she opened the Tea Room door, she watched a huge wave burst over the wall and swamp her lower lying cottage! Another larger wave swiftly followed smacking against its walls making the wooden building shudder. As the Tea Room stood on higher ground, Ellie decided it was best to sit the storm out there. Heavy dark clouds shrouded the cliffs bringing in the night where there should have been at least two hours of daylight left. Ellie lit the candles and waited apprehensively for high tide. Lightning struck and Brandy shivered with fear. 'It's alright boy.' She stroked his silky ears. 'We're safe in here.'

*

Guy was partaking in a welcome glass of ale in The Black Swan when the storm blew up the Helford. He was bone tired from white-washing walls, but his cottage was almost back to its original state, except his ma's room - that would have to wait. He'd been repairing the front door all day, replacing the lock after it had been battered down by Bert Laity. He'd been away from his work for over a week now and was itching to return to it, to make some much needed money.

He nodded at Constable Treen as he entered the Inn, preceded by a strong gust of wind.

'Good god, what a day!' Treen said, shaking the rain from his helmet. 'I've just come back from Helston and my colleague from Mullion tells me Poldhu, Church Cove and Polurrian Cove are getting a real beating. This is a bad one, there is going to be some real damage on that coast tonight, that's for sure.'

In less then a moment, Guy drained his glass and bid everyone goodbye. All he could think of was Ellie. He ran the length of the village, called for Silas from Bramble Cottage and began to harness Mazie.

'Where are you going?' Clara asked. 'Dinner is ready!'

'Sorry Clara, I'll be back as soon as I can. Silas come on, are you ready?'

Clara folded her arms and watched the wagon set off down the lane. *Where on earth could they be going in this weather?* Lightning lit the southern sky and Clara surmised that perhaps a thatch had caught fire.

30

Never normally afraid of anything, this storm unnerved Ellie. Shedding her wet clothes, she dressed warmly and pulled a shawl around her shoulders and hoped that Jessie had found shelter for the night in Mullion. Though the building was secured against the weather, the candle guttered as the wind whistled down the chimney. She glanced around the room and prayed that the business she had grown successfully would survive this night. She shuddered as a howling scream of wind wrapped around the building and made the roof tiles chatter. The sea sounded very close, but unable to see out of the shuttered windows, she could only imagine just how close it was. Having being used to the sound of distant waves, this was deeply alarming. It was going to be a long night.

Ellie doubted her prayers were being answered when the boom of water, as it hit the side of the building, shook the structure to the very core. Sea water began to seep under the door and Ellie scrambled to push a rug into the gap to stop the seepage. Another wave hit, and water gushed down the chimney, splattering the room with soot and ash. Ellie flinched and cowered as debris tumbled down the roof and crashed just outside the door, surmising that the chimney pot had been knocked off. With her heart in her throat, she dragged a table to the back of the room and crouched on it with Brandy.

The sea boomed and battered the building incessantly, each wave sounding larger than the other. Brandy whimpered pitifully on the table beside her, nuzzling closer for comfort. The Tea Room had suffered many storms and minor damage in the past, but this…this was something else. She knew she should leave, but she was fearful of going outside.

Lightning lit the room through the slight gaps in the shutters. The thunder which followed preceded a powerful wave, which from the sound of it, rearranged the outside furniture Ellie had stacked around the back. Unable to look outside, she could only imagine the destruction of her garden. If she'd been afraid before, the next wave that hit terrified her, as it ripped part of the roof off and blasted the seaward window and shutters from their fastenings. Glass and rubble flew everywhere when the next wave hit, and though Ellie tried to cover and protect Brandy, he leapt from the table and made for the door, dragging Ellie with him. The swirling seawater was knee deep and Ellie watched in infinite horror as the splintered remains of her old bed and chest of drawers, was swept out of the great gaping hole where the windows had been.

'My lace! My dress!' she screamed, as the next wave took her feet from under her. She knew then she must get out of this building for fear of being washed away with the next wave.

*

As Guy and Silas rounded Poldhu hill, the sheer force of the storm hit them. Though it was fully dark, flashes of lightning illuminated the destruction of the cove. They pulled into a small derelict homestead at the top of the hill and tied and hobbled Mazie under a lean-to building.

They set off down the hill, battling against the wind. The sea foam, waist deep, hindered their advancement. The sea had breached the bridge and the current running underneath threatened to take them off their feet, forcing them to feel their way across the granite coping stones. As they rounded the entrance to the beach, a massive wave confronted them, making them backtrack up the road towards the Poldhu Hotel.

'Stay here, Silas. I'm going to see if Ellie is still here. I'll shout if I need you.' He picked his way through waist deep water and the debris of broken furniture towards the cottage door.

'Ellie, Ellie are you in there?' He hammered on the door.

Holding Brandy by his leash Ellie had just opened the

door of the Tea Room to make her escape when she heard Guy shouting.

'Guy?' she screamed. 'I'm over here!'

Guy swung around to face a huge advancing wave. He waded towards the safety of the road, waited a moment for the water to retreat, before climbing up onto the terrace. Most of the wooden terrace boards were destroyed, and what was left creaked alarmingly underfoot. Another wave threatened to take his feet from under him, but he held onto the shutters as the water rushed past.

Ellie had stepped back inside, though she was no safer in than out.

As soon as he was able, Guy made for the door and Ellie fell into his arms with relief.

'Guy, thank god you're here.'

After a very soggy embrace he held her at arm's length. 'Are you alright?'

'Yes.' She shivered uncontrollably. 'But I think I've lost everything, except the takings for the week.' She patted the bag across her shoulder.

He glanced at the destruction and the huge gaping hole. 'Come on, we need to get out of here. It's not safe. Where's Jessie?'

'She's not here.'

Another wave hit the building, ripped the rest of the roof off and a torrent of water engulfed the room from every direction. Grasping Ellie around the waist and scooping Brandy under his arm, they were involuntarily pushed outside by a great wave into the swirling vat of foam and sandy seawater. The dog panicked and struggled moving its legs as though to swim, but Guy held tight as he helped Ellie coughing and choking to her feet.

'Silas,' he yelled. 'Come and help.'

Silas waded through with his arms aloft.

'Here.' Guy thrust Brandy into his arms then took a firm hold on Ellie. 'Right Ellie move as fast as your feet will carry you.' They waded through the undulating sea of foam. Once out on the main Mullion road, they gathered their breath, ready to take on the now shoulder deep foam by the bridge.

'Go careful. Feel your way with your feet. There'll be boulders underneath this lot,' Guy warned.

Brandy whimpered and struggled, but Silas held fast. Almost as soon as they cleared the foam at the other side of the bridge, another great wave took their feet from under them.

'Oof!' Ellie fell forwards and banged her knee.

Completely submerged, Guy flayed about in the foam until he found her. 'Get up, Ellie.' He pulled her to the surface. 'Are you alright?'

'Yes,' she lied, '…apart from looking like a snowman!' She spat the foam from her mouth.

He pulled her along but realised she had a noticeable limp. 'You're not alright, are you?'

'I'm fine. Let's just get out of this hell.'

*

Though thoroughly exhausted by the time they'd struggled up the hill, Ellie turned. The night sky flashed with sheet lightning and a pitiful cry escaped her throat at the destruction of her world.

'Come on Ellie, don't look back yet. Let's get out of this storm.' Guy led her to the wagon and fetched a blanket for her. He wrapped it around her shoulders and pulled her into a tight embrace.

The chill wind clawed at her skin and she shivered uncontrollably in his arms.

'Climb into the wagon and shed those wet clothes, Ellie, or you'll catch pneumonia.'

Reluctantly she left his embrace and did as he bid.

'May I come in?' he said, popping his head in a few minutes later, to find her curled up in the blanket at the far corner of the wagon. 'I need to find you something to wear.'

'Of course,' she said through chattering teeth.

He pulled his bag from the back of the wagon and handed her a shirt, jacket and trousers to wear. After selecting some clothes for himself, he grasped Silas's bag and backed out of the wagon.

Silas had settled Brandy and Blue in the corner of the barn, and had started to shed his own clothes.

'Once I find a sheltered spot, I'll get a fire going,' he said to Silas, who was hopping around naked as he tried to drag a pair of dry trousers up his legs.

Guy located a wood-store around the back of the barn, and rummaged in the back to find some dry logs. Within half an hour he'd found a sheltered spot and had a good fire blazing and water on to boil. There was little to eat in the wagon, but there was tea and some dry biscuits. It would suffice - it would have to.

Although the shirt was coarse and the wool trousers tickled, Ellie found Guy's clothes to be wonderfully intimate next to her skin.

As they sat around the camp fire listening to the storm raging, Ellie reached out to Guy and laid her hand on his. 'Thank you for coming to my rescue again.'

Silas raised his eyebrows as Guy cupped his own hand over Ellie's.

'It's always a pleasure to rescue you, Ellie.' He grinned broadly.

His smile made her heart sing. 'Even though I must look like a drowned rat whenever you do?'

'You'll always look beautiful to me, wet or dry.' He winked.

'Ugh! If you two are going to get all soppy, I'm going over to the barn to sleep with the dogs,' Silas said, shrugging the rug around his shoulders.

They both smiled bashfully across the firelight.

'Was it very bad when you got home to Gweek, Guy?'

'Bad enough, but we're on top of things now.'

'And… Clara?'

'She escaped unscathed, thank goodness.'

After hearing Guy tell her what had happened, Ellie sighed. *'It has been a week of catastrophes.'*

'Where is Jessie, Ellie?' Silas asked tentatively.

'She went to Mullion. Hopefully she had the good sense to stay there. I'm sure someone will have put her up for the night.'

Guy stretched his legs out towards the fire. 'Maybe we should all settle down and get some sleep. I fear tomorrow will be another trying day for you, Ellie.'

Ellie nodded sadly. 'I suspect I've lost everything now.' She looked straight at Guy and he knew immediately what she was inferring.

*

It was a wild, noisy and uncomfortable night for the trio, though Ellie had the warmest bed. When Guy woke her the next morning and helped her down out of the wagon, his hair smelt of wood smoke and his face had that early morning crinkled look. Her heart warmed at the sight of him, wishing she could see him first thing every morning, but that was not to be now.

*

The storm had gone and after a meagre breakfast, the trio returned to Poldhu, astonished to find a group of local men already working on the Tea Room. There was also staff from the Poldhu Hotel there, to give a helping hand bearing beverages and food.

The devastation was astronomical. Ellie's garden, now buried beneath stone, sand and driftwood, looked as though a tropical cyclone had ripped through it. This was the least of her worries. The terrace balustrade was hanging off and her chairs and tables were strewn across the sand dunes.

The once golden beach had changed beyond recognition. It was now strewn with stones - the tide having washed the sand right up to the Tea Room and cottage door. Her cottage, though flooded, had thankfully not suffered any structural damage, but the whole roof and seaward side of the Tea Room was completely destroyed.

When Jessie arrived back from Mullion, she shed an ocean of tears at the devastation before her - tears that shock prevented Ellie from shedding.

Silas took it on himself to comfort Jessie, as Ellie and Guy walked down the beach hoping to salvage some of her lace - especially her precious wedding dress.

They stood at the water's edge and looked out at the jagged edges of the coastline. It looked as though large bites had been taken out of the cliff.

She scooped the odd piece of lace out of the foam, explaining to Guy why the lace was in the Tea Room and not in her cottage.

Guy bent down and picked up another scrap of lace and handed it to her. 'Was there a lot of lace?'

Ellie nodded sadly. 'Everything I've ever worked on, including my wedding dress.' She felt her lip quiver. 'Still, I've no need for it now.' She turned her gaze to the sea.

Guy gently touched her arm. 'I'm so sorry.'

Ellie smiled tightly and began to walk back up the beach.

James Blackwell was waiting for them when they returned. He took Ellie into his arms and hugged her. As he did, he gave Guy a thankful smile.

'James, I am so sorry. Your business, it's in ruins.'

'Shush now. Do not bother yourself, Ellie, it will be rebuilt.' He released her from his hold and held his hand out to Guy. 'I'm glad you're here with Ellie.'

Guy nodded in acknowledgment. 'Did you arrange for all this help, James?'

'No, I've just this moment arrived. From what I can gather, they've taken it on themselves to come and help.' He smiled at Ellie. 'It seems that you and your Tea Room are very popular, and you're held in much regard.'

Ellie gave a heartfelt sigh. 'I'm so grateful to them.'

'Come Ellie. Let's see what can be done to get you back up and running once the structure of the building is safe.'

'I'm going to see if we can help with mending the roof, James.' Guy glanced at Silas and Jessie. 'That's if I can prise my brother away from his new friend.'

*

James worked with Ellie and Jessie for the rest of the day. They managed to salvage the cutlery and scalded it clean, but the napkins and tablecloths had long gone and most of the crockery was smashed to smithereens. They scrubbed clean the tables and chairs which had been swept onto the beach, but some were beyond repair and were burning on the bonfire.

Fortunately the day was warm, dry and breezy. The Cornish weather would throw hell and fury at you one day, and caress you with warmth the next. As the day progressed, it was hard to imagine the anger of the sea yesterday, as the gentle waves lapped the beach.

After digging the sand away from the cottage door, Jessie had thrown open the windows, so it had dried sufficiently for them to sleep there that night. James took his leave late afternoon, telling Ellie he would arrange for a new tea urn and crockery to be delivered to her. Anything else she needed, she was to go to Helston and purchase and have the bills sent to him. He'd be residing at Loe House for the next two months, and promised to come daily to help. Guy and Silas stayed for supper before retreating back to their wagon, with a promise that they too would stay until the Tea Room was habitable again.

*

The next morning, Ellie made an inventory of everything she needed. The curtains would wash, but along with the table linen, she needed to purchase fresh food and ingredients to bake with. She needed to feed the many helpers who had arrived again that morning to repair the damage, shift debris and move great piles of sand back down onto the beach. Ellie was overwhelmed at the goodwill of all these people. With their help she would be open for business in a few days time.

As Ellie packed her bag ready to catch the early morning wagon to Helston, Brandy began to snarl and bark. She glanced at the clock – it was early for Archie the postman.

Ellie gave Brandy a sharp tap on his nose and shut him in the cottage. She stepped out to greet Archie, only to be confronted by Philip, dressed to the nines, complete with bowler hat and cane.

Ellie gave him a contemptuous look. 'What do *you* want, Philip?'

He tutted audibly. 'Now, Ellie, what sort of greeting is that? You know, you look so much better when you smile - you should try it more often. Tell me, why such hostility towards one who comes offering help?'

'I'm not interested in your help,' she said acidly. 'I recall when I last required your help, you refused.'

He raised an eyebrow. 'I did not refuse you, Ellie. I merely told you my terms.'

'A real friend helps and asks for nothing in return. Now I'll thank you to *leave*.'

'Ellie,' his voice softened. 'I love you. That's why I want to help you. Look at the state of this place!' He waved his arm about. 'Face it, Ellie, this silly venture of yours is over, it's finished. Come back to me and all your troubles will be over.' He stepped towards her.

'Go away. I do not want *or* need your help.' Ellie halted his advancement with the palm of her hand.

'For god's sake woman, be reasonable. Now that this…this….' he racked his brain for the right word, '…ridiculous idea of trying to run a business has failed - as I knew it would!' he added derisively. 'You must cut your losses and do what you're good at – looking pretty.'

Ellie gasped incredulously. 'You really are the most deplorable, obnoxious person I have ever come across, Philip Goldsworthy.'

Philip's lip curled angrily. 'It wasn't so long ago you

were fawning all over me.'

Her eyes narrowed. 'I was blinded for a while with your lies and false promises.'

'Well, you're blinded by stupidity now. Have you lost your reason? You cannot live on fresh air, you silly woman.'

What with the devastation of her business and now Philip's insults, Ellie could suppress her anger no longer. 'If I was destitute and living in the gutter, I would never ask you for help. The thought and sight of you makes my skin crawl.'

'How dare you?' He raised his arm and moved to strike her. 'No woman speaks to me like that.'

Guy, who had quietly observed the altercation from the Tea Room, stepped out from the shadows.

'Raise your hand to Ellie ever again and I will floor you once and for all, Goldsworthy.'

Philip faltered, and then laughed sardonically. 'I didn't think you'd be far away. Ellie wouldn't have the nerve to say what she just said to me, without knowing you were covering her back.'

'Then you don't know Ellie at all, do you? She's more nerve and courage than you could *ever* possess. It's only money that makes you strong, and you had to marry that.'

Philip rounded on Guy. 'Talking of marriage - is it not time you were getting home to your bride-to-be. I believe you've a wedding next weekend.' He glanced at Ellie, enjoyed watching her flinch at the mention of it. 'What are you going to do, Guy? Marry Clara and keep Ellie on the side?' He turned back to Ellie. 'It seems you are always to be second choice, eh?'

Before Philip had finished his sentence Guy lurched and grabbed Philip by his freshly starched collar.

Philip, unready for this attack moved back a step, but Guy tightened his grip, forcing his clenched knuckles under his chin, making him gasp for breath.

Knowing Guy's strength, Philip made to knee him in

his groin, but Guy was ready with his fist. The punch was swift and the power of it lifted Philip off his feet, so that he landed in a pile of Brandy's excrement in the sand dunes.

All the workers had stopped what they were doing to watch the unfolding scene before them.

Stunned for a moment, stars burst around Philip's head as he spluttered blood from his split gum and nostrils. 'You'll be thorry you dit that,' he wailed through cupped hands.

'I think not.' Guy smiled, rubbing his sore knuckles. The pain in his hand was excruciating, but strangely satisfying. 'I think perhaps a thump was long overdue.'

Philip scrambled to his feet and fumbled for a handkerchief. 'The conthable will hear of thif.'

Guy nodded. 'I'll look forward to hearing from him.'

Picking his hat up, Philip brushed the sand from it and shot Ellie a withering look, before stomping off across the dunes.

With the fight over without the need to intervene, everyone returned to their work.

Ellie lifted Guy's hand to inspect it. It was red and bruised and slightly swollen. 'You're hurt!'

The gentle touch of her hand caught his breath. 'It's nothing. I'll go and wash it in the sea. The salt water will help. I'm just sorry you had to witness that, Ellie. I'm not a violent man, it's just…..'

'He has a tendency to bring out the worst in people,' she said finishing his sentence.

He smiled and made to pull his hand away but Ellie held on and gently kissed his swollen knuckles. 'Thank you, for once again being there when I need you. You may soon be someone else's husband, but you'll always be my knight in shining armour.'

Guy looked deep into her eyes and the sorrow in them for what could have been. The sorrow transferred to his eyes at his coming nuptials and did not go unnoticed by

Ellie.

*

As Guy washed his hand in the surf, a froth of lace washed up by his feet. Picking the material out from within a clump of kelp, he held up the dripping, ruined mess of a dress. Squeezing the water from the garment, he rolled it up and stuffed it into his leather bag, knowing Ellie would be devastated to see her fine work ruined like that. He knew exactly who could help restore the dress to its former glory.

While Ellie was in Helston, Guy made a trip to Bochym. He knew several of the staff at the manor, having worked on the estate cottages. He also knew that Issy the laundry maid would be able to launder the dress for him. He couldn't give Ellie a wedding ring, but he could give her precious dress back to her.

As he walked down the drive to the manor, he met with Sarah coming from the gardens.

'Well this is a very unexpected, but lovely surprise, Guy. It fills my heart with joy to see you are quite recovered from your terrible accident.'

Guy took off his hat and bowed his head in greeting.

'My husband is out at the moment, though I know not where. Was he expecting you?'

'No, my lady. I've come begging a favour.'

'Is it for Ellie? I understand from James Blackwell that the Tea Room is in a terrible mess and you've been helping her.'

He nodded, as he pulled the sodden dress from his bag. 'Ellie lost all her lace in the storm. Some of it has washed up, but I know this is what she's looking for, more than anything. I found it this morning and I dearly want it restored and returned to her.' He looked downcast. 'It's the wedding dress she made for herself. I wondered perhaps if Issy could launder it.'

Sarah took the dress and held it up. 'Goodness, it is a mess. Issy is good but I'm unsure she can do anything about this.'

Guy's shoulders drooped.

'Leave it with me. I'll send it off to a specialist cleaner. It will be as good as new.'

'Would you?' He said thankfully. 'I'll pay.'

'No payment necessary. I saw this in its former glory. It will be a pleasure to restore it. Would you like me to let her know you arranged for it to be cleaned?'

Guy shook his head. 'In the circumstances, it might be a little insensitive. I'm to be married myself next Saturday.'

Sarah reached out to Guy. 'I had hoped to bring you two together, but life it seems has other ideas. Ellie told me what had happened.'

Guy nodded sadly.

'She also told me about the fire, my condolences for the loss of your mother. I did wonder if you would postpone the wedding.'

'It crossed my mind, but with Ma gone, I cannot live under the same roof as Clara until we're married – it wouldn't be proper, so the sooner we're married the better.'

'I see. Are you to return to Poldhu before your wedding?'

'Yes. I'll be there helping for a few more days. James has employed me to help rebuild, so I'm not losing a wage.'

'Well I shall visit in a few days. I have something I would like to give Ellie. As for this…' She held up the damp bundle. 'Rest assured I'll sort everything out. Let me wish you and your future bride many years of happiness, Guy.'

'Thank you,' Guy said, unable to keep the sigh from his voice.

31

For the past eight years, Ruby Sanders had made a home for herself in a tiny cottage at Ruan Minor on the Lizard. She'd moved as far away from Bochym as she could, after being dismissed for a misdemeanour she had not done. The accusation lay heavy on her conscience, and she'd kept herself to herself since the dismissal, for risk of anyone finding out about it. She'd found employment at The Cadgwith Arms as a barmaid, and told a fib that her name was Jane and that she'd moved from Penzance to look for work, so when the Earl de Bochym knocked on Ruby's door that day, her world crashed around her ears.

She bobbed a curtsy, wiped her hands down her apron and promptly burst into tears.

'I didn't take that necklace, my lord. I promise. I know Albert Lanfear said I did, but I swear I didn't.'

Peter stood back in shock at this unexpected outburst. 'Please, Ruby, I just want to speak with you.'

'But I didn't do anything wrong!' she wailed, turning her head to the corner of the room to hide her distress.

'Ruby, I don't for one minute think you did.'

Ruby turned her distraught face towards him.

'May I?' He gestured to the comfy looking chair by the fireside.

Ruby swallowed the lump in her throat and nodded.

'I remember you, Ruby. Do you mind if I call you Ruby?'

She shrugged her shoulders.

'I remember you, when you were in my father's employment.'

Ruby shuddered at the mention of the old earl.

'I can see by your reaction that you do not care to hear his name mentioned.'

Ruby lowered her eyes.

'I understand you left the same week he died. When I was called home from university to deal with his death, I found you too had gone!'

'I'm sorry for your loss,' she answered flatly. *Though good riddance to him!*

Peter smiled. *It was no loss - he was a domineering, cantankerous old bugger, not to mention a bully, but then it wouldn't do to voice that opinion to anyone.* 'It has since come to my attention that certain misdemeanours happened the week you were dismissed from Bochym. I wondered if you could help me, by shedding some light on them.'

Ruby raised her eyebrows.

'I believe that you were done a great wrong, Ruby.'

'You do?' she said, her shoulders visibly relaxing.

'I do. So, would you like to tell me why you think you were dismissed?'

Ruby flopped down on a chair. 'Albert Lanfear said I had stolen a very valuable necklace – the de Bochym sapphires to be exact.' The very mention of the incident upset her again.

'Why do you really think you were dismissed?'

Ruby regarded him for a moment. 'You won't like it if I tell you.'

The earl relaxed into the chair, crossed his arms and smiled. 'I'm listening, Ruby.'

*

That evening, Albert Lanfear felt the sharp end of the earl's tongue. In his own arrogant way, Lanfear could hardly hide the fact he was affronted.

Peter looked at his valet through the reflection in the mirror. He found it almost intolerable to be in his presence, but for now, he must bide his time. As soon as he had verified what he'd learned today, he would very soon wipe that conceited look off his face once and for all.

*

Every day since the storm, Ellie scoured the shoreline for her belongings. The sea gave up a few fragments of her old life, but it was her wedding dress she wanted back more than anything - not that she would ever have an occasion to wear it now. Guy would be leaving soon and nothing would ever be the same. He'd marry Clara and that would be that. She looked towards the Tea Rooms. This was her life now. Despite Philip's misconception, she was a strong independent woman who could stand on her own two feet, but it would have been nice to have had Guy by her side forever.

She turned to walk slowly back up the beach, only to find that Sarah had arrived with several boxes containing a rather lovely thirty place tea set, decorated with roses.

'Lady Carole bought them, but they were never to my taste - I much prefer to have afternoon tea in a plain cup, but they would be perfect for the Tea Room.'

'Thank you so much, Sarah, they're lovely. Let's try them out.'

As she placed the tea tray down, Ellie asked awkwardly, 'Is the earl back from London yet? You said he promised to look into Lanfear's wrongdoings.'

'He is, and he will, Ellie, he always keeps his promises. He's just been understandably busy since his return, I've hardly seen him.'

*

It was late afternoon, Friday 26th September and Guy left it to the last moment to leave Ellie. Silas too was reluctant to leave, having formed a strong friendship with Jessie, which Guy and Ellie thought bordered on calf love. Silas was still a boy at fourteen, but that seemed not to be an issue to Jessie and there were clearly tears in her eyes when they said their goodbyes.

Many months ago, Guy had purchased a beautiful embroidered shawl for Ellie. This along with an emerald green ribbon for her hair was to have been a Christmas gift to her before he had his accident. It had been in his wagon ever since. That morning he'd taken it from its hiding place to unwrap it. Expecting it to be covered in mildew, due to the damp Cornish air, to his surprise he found the seller had wrapped it carefully many times and the shawl was as pristine as the day he'd bought it. When he was ready to leave, he beckoned Ellie to walk with him down the beach.

'I have a gift for you, Ellie. I bought this for you last Christmas.' He placed the parcel containing the shawl into her hands. 'If I'd have had chance to give it to you then, I would not be leaving you today. Open it when I've gone and remember me whenever you use it.' A lump formed in his throat rendering him unable to speak as she held the parcel to her breast, curling her fingers around the packaging.

'Ellie….I don't want to leave you, you must know that, but I can't break my promise to Clara.'

Ellie nodded tearfully.

'In the circumstances, I know this is very wrong of me to say this, but I love you, Ellie, I love you with every fibre of my body.' Tenderly Guy lifted her free hand to his lips. He kissed her palm, gently folding it over so as to keep the kiss safe. He knew that when he let go of her it would be forever, but let go he must, and let go he did.

Ellie could hardly breathe, as she watched with blurred vision as he walked to his wagon. In the distance, the bubbling trill of the curlew filled the afternoon with its haunting sound. Ellie would forever associate this parting with its song.

'Goodbye my love,' she whispered on the breeze.

*

As Guy and Silas made their way out of Poldhu, Ruby and Peter were in the police station at Helston. At Peter's request she had told her story to the sergeant, word for word as she'd told him.

'We could do with some more evidence to back up these allegations, my lord,' the sergeant said flatly.

'I do understand. Would it be possible for you to accompany me to Cury and then onto Poldhu tomorrow morning - I think I know others who can help?'

*

It was dark when Guy and Silas pulled into Mill Lane, Gweek. They'd spent the journey in relative silence, both missing what they couldn't have.

Guy pulled Mazie to a halt in the field next to the mill and began to un-harness her. They were to camp here overnight. He'd sent word to Clara, that as it was unlucky to see the bride before the wedding, they'd return to Bramble Cottage at nine-thirty on Saturday morning to get ready, by which time Clara would have left to get ready for the wedding at Mabel Laity's cottage. No sooner had he settled Mazie than Harry Yates came upon him.

Guy had heard that Harry's wife had died while he'd been in hospital and whether it was lack of his wife's cooking, or grief, Harry seemed to be wasting away, for Guy hardly recognised him.

'Harry!' Guy couldn't keep the shock from his voice as he ran his eyes over the emaciated body of his neighbour. 'Are you ill?'

'I'm afraid so. Dr Eddy tells me I've some problem here.' He laid his hand on his chest. 'And I've lost my appetite.'

'I did wonder, when I saw you at ma's funeral, but I didn't get a chance to speak to you.'

'I didn't stay long, I just came to pay my respects and then went back home. Your ma was a good woman and is sorely missed by all.'

Guy nodded. 'Nevertheless I should have called on you.'

'Don't fret yourself. You had enough on your plate.'

'Are you still able to work?'

Harry shook his head. 'Not for these last six weeks. That means I'm to lose the cottage. It's tied you see.'

'Surely Goldsworthy won't do that.'

'You'd think not, but Philip is a very different kettle of fish to his father.'

Guy grunted in agreement.

Harry's little terrier snuffled his nose at Blue. He

looked down at his little dog. 'We don't know what we're going to do, do we little chap? My cottage will house another tenant on Monday. I've to move out on Sunday. Philip Goldsworthy always gets what he wants you see.'

'You'll not be homeless Harry. One way or another, I'll make sure you're provided for, that's a promise.'

Harry grasped Guy's arm. 'You're a good man Guy. So you're to be married in the morn?'

'I am, yes. You'll come and share some cheer with us at Bramble Cottage after the nuptials, I hope?'

'That's kind of you Guy, I thank you. I'll try and make it. Tell me, do you see anything of Miss Ellie from Poldhu?'

The mention of Ellie jarred his already aching heart.

'Strangely enough, we've just come from there. Silas and I have been helping her clear up after the storm. The Tea Room was wrecked. I felt awful leaving her, but what with the wedding and all….'

'I don't mean to speak out of turn but, tis a great shame you're not marrying Ellie. *She'd* have made you a good wife.'

Guy nodded. *No truer word could have been spoken.*

Seeing he'd struck a cord, Harry found himself in a dilemma. *Should he tell him? Should he?* 'Guy?' He shifted uneasily.

'What is it Harry? Is something else bothering you?'

'Yes. I'm much troubled about something, but I'm a dying man and I'll not meet my maker, without telling you two things that I know. I've nothing to lose. You might think it sour grapes, but I shall tell you anyway. One will settle your mind the other will unsettle it. I'll thank you not to thump me on hearing the latter.'

Guy laughed out loud.

'Come and sit down,' Harry beckoned.

*

At seven a.m. Mazie made her way slowly past the end of Mill Lane and was brought to a halt a little way up Gweek

Drive. Concealed by the great oaks, which flanked the river valley of Gweek, Guy hobbled Mazie and climbed back into his wagon with Silas to wait. With each moment that passed, Guy felt his heart accelerate. Harry's information last night had been a shocking revelation, but in truth, a relief. He'd laboured all night settling things at Bramble Cottage. First thing this morning, he'd pushed a note under the door of Constantine Church, to settle things there, and on his return he and Harry had called on Constable Treen. Now he'd watch and wait for everything to come to fruition. Then he'd drive back to Poldhu to start the first day of the rest of his life.

*

Clara woke early, yawned and stretched and pushed the sheets away.

'Where are you going?' Philip pulled her back into bed.

Clara giggled. 'I'm getting married today, or had you forgotten?' She eyed the black eye he was sporting and kissed him on the lips.

'Ouch, watch my nose!'

'You really need to be more careful Philip.' She gently tweaked his swollen nose to make sure it wasn't broken. 'It must have been one hell of a fall you took last week.'

He brushed her hand away from his nose. 'Everyone falls occasionally. Come here, I want to be the first to bed you on your wedding day.'

She giggled again and spent another half hour with him.

Philip lay back and sighed. 'You're going to be wasted on him!'

She pulled away. 'Well, you're not going to be able to marry me, *are you*?'

He pulled her back. 'I think you'll find a lover is more fascinating than a husband.'

Clara pouted. 'You might be wrong there. I might find Guy is a far better lover than you!'

'Well, you can come and tell me on Monday night

when he's gone back to work. I take it there'll be no honeymoon?'

'I shouldn't think so.' She gave a dissatisfied sigh. 'Guy seems to be married to his work. In fact I haven't seen him for over a week!'

'Worry not, we'll have a honeymoon here in my bed. Go on then, you little minx. Go and marry your Thatcher and become the respectable Mrs Blackthorn.'

She pulled the sheets with her as she got out of bed, but Philip pulled them back leaving her standing naked before him.

He whistled appreciably. 'As I said, you'll be wasted on him.'

Clara blew a kiss and began to dress.

'You need to hope that Guy didn't come back last night to find you gone. Otherwise there might not be a wedding today,' Philip said, rising from the twisted bed sheets.

'I am confident that he didn't. Guy is a superstitious man. He'd not risk seeing his bride before the wedding.'

Once dressed, he kissed her passionately and whispered, 'Until Monday,'

Draping her arms around his neck she answered, 'I can hardly wait.'

She slipped out of the back door and took a deep breath of fresh air. The sun was rising over the Helford River – hopefully it would stay dry for her wedding. She smiled to herself, marvelling at how far she'd come in the last few months. Soon to be mistress of her *own* home now Guy's batty old ma was out of the way, she had a husband to provide for her and a lover to keep her company, right next door. What more could she want? She skipped merrily up the lane, making a detour around the back of Bramble Cottage to the privy.

*

Philip straightened his cravat in the mirror and pulled on his jacket ready for work. He meticulously scraped under his nails and greased his hair down. The mill never stopped. It worked twenty four hours, seven days a week. He liked to make his presence known most days - it kept everyone on their toes.

When a knock came to the door, he shouted, 'Don't tell me you've changed your mind, Clara.' When no answer came, he opened the door to two policemen. 'What's this? What's happened?' Thinking one of his parents had taken a turn for the worse.

'Mr Goldsworthy, you are under arrest for the attempted murder of Guy Blackthorn on December 23rd last.'

Philip's face drained and then flushed. 'What the devil are you talking about?'

'You're to come with us. Anything you say will be taken down and used in evidence.'

Philip's nostrils flared. 'You're making a terrible mistake. Do you know who I am?'

'If you please, sir.' They beckoned him out of the cottage.

'This is outrageous!' Philip bristled angrily as he stepped out and locked the door behind him, before being escorted down the lane to the waiting police wagon.

*

Clara adjusted her skirts as she emerged from the privy. It was seven-fifteen. She had lots to do, before her wedding at eleven. She'd made a cake yesterday, but there were sandwiches to do and the table to set before she left for Mabel Laity's cottage to get ready. The cottage still smelt of smoke since Nellie had burnt herself to a crisp, so she needed to open the windows to let the air blow through. As she rounded the front of the cottage her eyes fell upon a mound of bags beside the front door – *her* bags! On closer inspection she found they were full of her clothes. Her mouth felt dry - Guy must have come home after all. She cleared her throat, and smoothed her dress down. *Come on girl think, what are you going to say to explain? Say you spent the night at Mabel's house, just in case Guy came home, yes I'll say that. I'll make Guy sorry that he questioned my absence and make him pay dearly for putting my things out in the dew.* She took a deep breath and turned the handle – it was locked. She reached down and lifted the plant pot to retrieve the key, suddenly remembering that Guy had changed the lock the day he scurried off to help some friend in need and took the keys with him. She tried the door again thinking perhaps it was just sticking, being new. She knew she'd left it unlocked last night – around here it was safe to leave doors unlocked, but no, it was definitely locked! She knocked fiercely on the door.

'Guy, it's me. What on earth do you think you are doing leaving my things out here?' she shouted. 'Guy, open the door at once.' She stamped her foot in annoyance and moved to the window to look for signs of life. It was then she saw the notice in the window. LET

LET! Who the hell had Guy let the cottage to? Returning to her bags she noticed a note attached to one of them.

Clara,

From the noises coming from Primrose Cottage, you seemed to be preoccupied with Philip Goldsworthy last night, where, as I have been informed, you are most nights. Here is your fare home to Truro. I suggest you catch the nine a.m. wagon to Helston and onwards by train. The house has been let from today - there is nothing here for you now. Guy.

Clara felt the bottom fall out of her world. She'd thought she'd been so careful. Someone must have seen her and told Guy. Well, she wasn't going anywhere. If Guy knew about Philip, she could happily live in Primrose Cottage now – after all, it was a much better house than Guy's. She gathered up her bags and walked back down the lane. In the distance she noticed three men walking away – two of them were policeman and…...

'Philip!' she shouted, 'What the devil is going on?' She dropped her bags on the front path of Primrose Cottage and ran down the lane in hot pursuit. As she reached the bridge, the police wagon pulled away. Clara stood with her hands on her hips in total confusion.

'Something amiss?' Harry Yates asked, as he walked his dog past her.

'No,' Clara snapped and ran back up the lane. She fumbled in her pocket for the key to Primrose Cottage then remembered she'd left it on the bedside table. There was no other key to get in with, so she moved her bags around the back of Primrose Cottage, pulled a coat from one of them and sat down on a bench out of sight. She shivered, whether it was from the dampness of the morning or the realisation that her world was imploding, she did not know. Eventually she decided to walk up to Mabel Laity's house to wait for Philip's return.

She knocked on the door and pasted on a smile. 'Mabel.' Clara swept her eyes upwards. 'I've locked myself out. Can I come in for a while?'

'Of course you can, my luver, but are you not getting married today?'

'No, no, it's been postponed. After a lot of thought we decided it seemed inappropriate, what with Nellie dying.'

Mabel pulled a face. 'Oh, that's a shame - I was looking forward to a good tea. Anyway come in, come in. Tell me what *you* know about what's happened this morning. Our Jamie came back from work to tell me the news. The mill is buzzing with it!'

'News?'

Mabel nodded excitedly. 'Philip Goldsworthy has been arrested on suspicion of attempted murder of your young man, Guy. You know, when he fell from the ladder. Apparently it wasn't an accident!'

'What?' Clara reached out to steady herself.

'Did you really not know? Has Guy not said anything?' Mabel was astonished, though delighted to be the first person to give this morsel of information to Clara. 'Tis said that Philip swapped the ladder for a rotten one, which made Guy fall from the roof. There were witnesses, apparently.'

Clara's throat constricted.

'The general consensus is that Philip will be hanged for the offence. Are you alright Clara? You've gone very pale.'

*

As Clara waited in devastated silence for the nine a.m. wagon to Helston, Ellie was walking along the edge of the surf. She'd hardly slept a wink last night and believed the sea might ease her troubled soul. She pulled the shawl Guy had given her, tighter around her shoulders. It was the most beautiful thing she had ever owned.

It had been ten days since the storm. The roof was fixed, the walls washed, windows mended and floors swept. All should have been well, but for the fact that this was the day Guy would marry Clara. Her heart was terribly sore.

Brandy was splashing in the surf near her legs when he stopped suddenly and began to whine. Ellie spun around and groaned at the prospect of another visit from Philip. She had no doubt that with Guy now out of the picture, Philip would stop at nothing in his pursuit of her - that man would not take no for an answer. Her shoulders relaxed slightly when she saw the postman riding his bicycle down Poldhu hill.

With Brandy secured indoors, Ellie stepped out to meet the postman.

'Good morning to you, Ellie, I've a parcel for you today.' The postman held out a large oblong box.

'For me?'

Archie looked at the address. 'As it says.' He pushed it closer.

Puzzled she took it. 'Who on earth would send me a parcel?' 'I'm just the delivery man,' he said with a wink. 'See you tomorrow.'

Ellie placed it on the table and stared at it. *Well open it then!* She untied the string, eased the box lid open and gasped.

'What is it?' Jessie peered over her shoulder.

'It's my dress - my beautiful wedding dress!' She held the garment up to herself in disbelief. 'But where has it come from? Haven't I scoured the beach since the storm, hoping and praying the sea would give my precious dress back? Now here it is, in absolute pristine condition. It's just not possible!' Ellie turned to look at Jessie with tears of joy in her eyes. 'I'm going to put it somewhere safe now, in the cottage.'

As she placed it carefully in her bedroom drawer, she couldn't help feeling the return of the dress was a double-edged sword - joyful at being reunited but sad that it would never be worn.

Unable to settle at anything, Ellie said, 'Why don't you take Brandy for a quick walk, Jessie, and then the day will be yours to do what you wish? Everything is ready for us to open tomorrow. There's nothing to do at the moment. I think I'll wander on the beach and comb the tide mark.'

Ellie stood at the water's edge as the sea caressed her feet. The day was lowering. Dark clouds gathered at Land's End. The promised lovely day would soon turn wet. The weather suited Ellie's mood. The initial elation at seeing her dress again had waned. She was sad beyond belief. Guy would always be her friend, but she knew he would not visit so regularly once he was married. It would be inappropriate. There would be no more gifts from the sea waiting for her to discover. They were such small pleasures. She would miss everything about Guy.

The tide had turned and was heading back in. She glanced again at the cold front advancing over the sea. She might have at least five minutes to scour the rocks for sea glass, before they were swallowed up by the sea. With a quick glance behind her to make sure no-one was around, she tucked her skirt into her belt and picked her way across the black rocks. Absorbed as always when she was searching, it was the incoming tide which accelerated her return to the shore. As she made her way carefully across the rocks, her thoughts turned once again to Guy. Would he be happy? She hoped with all her heart that he would be … 'Oh!' she cried. Her foot suddenly slipped, but quick thinking helped her to right herself. Holding her hand to her chest to slow her racing heart, relief washed over her. Moving forward, her foot touched another slimy patch of seaweed and to her disbelief, she fell clumsily into the sea. By impulse, her hands grasped desperately for a crevice to hold on to, but her skirt was caught on something and pulled her underwater. *Oh, no!* To her horror the sea engulfed her, she surfaced briefly, treading water and choking desperately, but the waves swept over her head, dragging her once more down into the swirling waves.

32

It proved to be a long journey back to Poldhu from Gweek. The front wheel on Guy's wagon had started to shake considerably as they turned onto the Lizard road.

As Guy inspected the wheel, his thoughts took him back to Gweek and the fall out he'd left in his wake. He hoped the allegations Harry had made about Philip's attempt at murdering him would hold. He was glad that Clara had taken his sound advice and caught the morning wagon to Helston. He'd waited secretly on Gweek drive, until he saw her safely on board, confident now that Harry Yates would not encounter any problems when he and his little dog moved into Bramble Cottage tomorrow.

He'd felt deeply hurt when he'd sat outside Primrose Cottage last evening listening to Clara's laughter inside. He wasn't sure if he'd ever heard Clara laugh like that before. Were they both laughing at the way they had cuckolded him? Perhaps they weren't laughing now!

If he was honest, he didn't completely blame Clara for the affair. He had no doubt Philip had played his part, preying on her discontent, for she'd clearly been discontented. After all, hadn't he left her all week long to deal with his ailing ma? He shuddered as the dreadful image of Ma's burned body swam in front of his eyes - disgusted to know that Clara had been with Goldsworthy while his ma burned to death. He'd never forgive her for the neglect. If she'd been where she should have been, Ma would have been alive today, of that he was sure.

'Are you alright, Guy?' Silas asked, seeing the consternation on his face.

Guy smiled. 'All will be well soon,' he said. 'But it looks as though we need to take a detour to the Wheelwright in Cury. The iron tyre has moved slightly, that's why the wheel is wobbling.'

*

Peter and the sergeant stood outside the undertaker shop

in Cury The sign read:

Mr Gray – Carpenter & coffin maker. Hand-crafted and traditionally styled

There was a fresh smell of wood shavings, and several coffins stood on end along one side of the wall. Gray was busy planing another as it stood on a cradle. His sleeves were pushed up his pale arms and he was whistling tunelessly. So involved in his work, he clearly had not seen them enter.

Peter cleared his throat to catch his attention.

Gray looked at his visitor over the top of his spectacles and quickly put down his tools. He whipped the sweat stained hat from his head and gave a courteous nod.

'Goodness gracious, my lord, please tell me no one has died at the manor.'

'Not recently no. I need to ask you a delicate question, Mr Gray.'

Gray raised his eyebrows and waited.

'It's regarding an incident, some eight years ago.'

Gray scratched his head. 'Eight years ago! I can barely remember what I had for breakfast, my lord,' he joked.

'Oh I think you will remember this one.'

Gray took the joviality out of his voice and fell silent.

'I understand you took the body of a young woman from the manor, during the night, eight years ago.'

'Yes, I did that,' he said solemnly. 'I remember it well. It was young Pearl Martin.' Gray moistened his lips. 'I was told she'd committed suicide and I was to bury her in unconsecrated ground, without a funeral.' He cast his eyes downward. 'I was told to say nothing about it to anyone, so as not to embroil your family in the scandal of a suicide.'

'Who gave you those instructions?'

'Mr Carrington.'

'Did Carrington say why she'd done it?'

'He said some local lad had used and then spurned her. To be fair, she *was* with child and there was evidence on her night dress that she'd been intimate with someone not long before her death.'

Peter grimaced on hearing this, and unconsciously moved the wood shavings on the floor around with his stick.

'When I inspected her body, she had a broken skull from the fall, her nose was broken too and there was blood in her mouth, but what puzzled me most was that her eyes and mouth were wide open, as though in shock.'

Peter and the sergeant exchanged glances.

'So where did you put her?' Peter asked.

Gray wrung his hands nervously. 'In the church yard, my lord, I couldn't do what Mr Carrington requested. I'd known Pearl's family for years - in fact I'd buried them all. There was a grave dug ready, because I was doing a funeral for old Dan Walker the next day, so I lowered her in and covered her over. I said a few words, but it grieved me that there was no proper service."

Peter nodded. 'Can you remember where she is laid to rest?'

'Yes, my lord. Whenever I go down there, I always put a flower on her grave. She's no headstone, you see. She and Mr Walker are along the back wall of the churchyard. Five headstones along from the right hand corner. You know, to this day I can't believe she ended her own life!'

'Well, I don't believe she did, Mr Gray.'

Gray's mouth fell open, as they bid him good day.

*

Ellie emerged as a bundle of clothing tumbling in the surf. Bedraggled and draped in kelp, she crawled gasping towards the beach. It was a good few seconds before she caught her breath and dragged herself to a standing position. Almost bent double, she rested her hands on her wet skirt, dripping and exhausted. The shock of what had just happened made her knees tremble. She reached her hand up to grasp at the beautiful shawl Guy had given her, but it had gone from her shoulders.

Her heart sank. She pushed her sand encrusted hair from her eyes, to scour the rocks, but it was nowhere to be seen. Ellie stamped on the wet sand in frustration. *How could she be so stupid? Had she learned nothing from when she slipped last time? It was lucky she hadn't been knocked unconscious again, otherwise she would not have been able to swim to safety, but oh…*She stamped her foot again. *And now her beautiful shawl had gone!*

Jessie had just returned with Brandy when Ellie staggered into the cottage dragging ribbons of kelp in her wake. Always a cool head in any situation, Jessie guided Ellie back outside to the water pump, stripped her to her petticoats and swilled her with fresh water, before wrapping her in a towel.

With a cup of sweet tea thrust into her hand, Ellie slowly recovered from her ordeal, while Brandy sat by her feet, his large brown eyes looking upwards to make sure his mistress was alright.

The clock chimed ten a.m. reminding Ellie that Guy would make his vows to Clara in an hour. All in all, this was not turning out to be a very good day.

When Jessie returned to the cottage empty handed after scouring the shore for Ellie's shawl, she brought with her two unexpected visitors.

Despite her trembling knees, Ellie dropped a quick curtsy as the earl stepped into her tiny cottage, swiftly followed by a policeman.

'Welcome, please come in.' She gestured them to sit down.

'I apologise for dropping in unexpectedly, Elise, but Sergeant Wallis and I would like to speak with you on a delicate matter.'

'Of course, my lord,' she said trying to tidy her damp hair. 'Please forgive my appearance, I slipped and fell into the sea earlier. Could you give me a moment to make myself presentable? Jessie, please will you brew us some tea?'

Ellie rushed into her bedroom and pulled her hair into a pony-tail. Was this something to do with Lanfear? she thought with a tingle of anticipation. She glanced in the mirror and gave up on her hair - she would have to do.

Her guests were seated by the fire as Jessie served them tea.

'Thank you, my dear,' Peter said to Jessie taking the saucer from her hand. 'I trust you have settled in nicely here?'

'Yes, my lord, thank you.' Jessie glanced at Ellie as she took a seat.

Peter put down his tea cup. 'I suspect you are wondering what this is about?'

Ellie nodded with baited breath.

'I believe from my wife that you have some information about the death of one of our maids. I wondered if you would recall what you saw for the sergeant.'

Ellie glanced between the two men and cleared her throat. 'I do remember what happened, though I'd put it to the back of my mind for a long, long time. It was the worst week of my life.' Her lip trembled. 'I was only ten at the time, but after visiting Bochym during your garden party last month, I was invited to take refuge in the Stewards Cottage after an altercation with Philip Goldsworthy.'

Peter nodded. 'I am aware of the incident.'

'As you probably remember, my father was the old earl's steward and we lived there, before we were dismissed.' Ellie could not keep the edge from her voice.

Peter nodded again sympathetically.

'The visit opened up all sorts of memories for me, particularly memories of the night Pearl Martin died.' Ellie faltered a moment. 'I was woken at midnight by Pearl, at first nothing seemed unusual, because she used to look after me if my mother was busy, and would sometimes read me bedtime stories. It was only when the clock chimed midnight that I thought it strange that she was in my bedroom so late at night. She didn't say anything to me, but beckoned me out of bed towards the window, which was slightly ajar. From there, Pearl pointed up at the attic window in the manor. There was a candle flickering in the attic and I could see Albert Lanfear. He was pushing a large white bundle of what looked like sheets, out of the window.'

The sergeant leant slightly forward. 'How do you know for certain it was Lanfear?'

'I heard him speak, as he pushed the bundle out, he said, "Good riddance to bad rubbish." I remember the thump as the bundle landed in the courtyard, and then several roof tiles and the guttering came away and landed on the bundle. I remember turning back to Pearl, but she was no longer by my side.' Ellie glanced at the earl to see if he believed her.

'But she was definitely there when you saw the bundle being pushed?'

'Yes, my lord.'

'If, as you say it was Pearl being pushed out of the window, how could she have been by your side?' the sergeant asked.

Ellie regarded him before she spoke. 'I think it was her spirit that came to me that night.'

'A ghost, you mean?'

'Yes.'

The constable cleared his throat.

Peter crossed his arms. 'So you're suggesting that Pearl was already dead when she came to you?'

'I'm sure of it.' She cast a critical eye towards the constable and then looked to the floor. 'I've always been susceptible to the spirit world, Pearl knew that. I think she came to me so I could witness what was happening to her. I admit, at the time I didn't really understand what I'd seen or heard.'

'Did you have anymore *visitations* that night?' the

constable asked mockingly.

'No, but I was woken at three that morning when Mr Gray the undertaker brought his cart to take the bundle away. Perhaps you should speak to him?' She gave the sergeant a hard stare.

Seeing Ellie's uneasiness, Peter said, 'We've spoken to Mr Gray, who confirmed that he did collect Pearl's body from the courtyard that morning.'

Ellie sighed in relief.

'Did you tell anyone what you'd seen?'

'I was about to tell my mother the next morning, but we were all summonsed to the manor kitchen. As we sat down, I saw Pearl, standing behind Mr Lanfear. I recall she looked quite distressed. Mr Carrington came in and told us all to take a seat, and I thought it was strange that Pearl remained standing.

'He then told us that Pearl Martin had done a wicked thing by running away after getting herself in the family way, leaving us without a dairymaid or a bye-your-leave. I was confused, I didn't know what 'in the family way' meant and Pearl was clearly stood there in the kitchen. I turned to my mother and told her that Pearl hadn't gone - she was there, crying, behind Mr Lanfear.'

'Her ghost you mean?' Peter spoke before the constable could ask the same question.

'Well yes, it must have been, because she was standing there as plain as you're sat there. I thought everyone could see her.'

'Then what happened?' Peter asked.

'I told my mother that Pearl was probably crying because I'd seen Mr Lanfear throw her out of the attic window last night!' Ellie paused and looked at Peter. 'I'm afraid I don't remember exactly what happened next, except that Mr Lanfear's face turned as red as a tomato, and an almighty row escalated between him and my mother. I'd never heard my mother raise her voice before, but she was really shouting at Mr Lanfear. I was so frightened I started to cry. It was then my father entered the kitchen. He stopped the argument and told my mother to take me back to the cottage and ……' Ellie felt the memory choke her.

'Are you alright, Elise?' Peter asked quietly.

Ellie nodded. 'That was the last time I saw my father alive. I knew he'd slipped on something in the courtyard shortly afterwards. He hit his head and died instantly. It wasn't until a couple of weeks ago that I learned he'd slipped on blood.' Her lip trembled. 'Pearl's blood, it would appear! We left the manor, the day they buried my father. I never understood why we couldn't go back home. Mother wouldn't discuss it, but I'm assuming now it was because of that argument.' She looked directly at Peter. 'Was it?'

Peter tightened his lips and nodded. Ruby had told him word for word about the allegations Elise's mother had made during that argument. 'I am truly sorry about your dismissal and the sorrow it brought on your family, Elise. I *do* know why you were dismissed, but I'd like to wait until we sort all this out before I tell you. Rest assured I will recompense you. I promise.'

Ellie's eyes watered. *Nothing would bring her mother back.*

'Do you see ghosts all the time?' The sergeant asked with his notebook poised.

Ellie directed her answer to Peter. 'I've only experienced them at the manor. In fact I've seen Pearl several times during my visits there. She's still dreadfully upset.' *There were a few ghosts in the manor actually, but Ellie decided to keep that information to herself.*

Peter nodded slowly.

'I know it sounds fantastical, my lord, but I believe what I see.'

'I admit I'm very sceptical. Having said that, several people have seen things in the manor - my wife included, but I've heard this same story about Pearl from another source. Tell me, Elise, do you know a young woman called

Ruby Sanders?'

Ellie frowned. 'I think she was Pearl's friend wasn't she? She might have worked in the dairy with her, but I'm not sure.'

'So you haven't been in contact with Ruby recently?' the sergeant asked.

Ellie shook her head.

Peter glanced at the constable, who nodded.

'Ruby was interviewed by Sergeant Wallis last night. She gave a very similar and more detailed version of these events. We wondered, could you help us Elise?'

'If it brings Lanfear to task, yes, I'll do whatever you ask, my lord.'

'Could you come with us to the manor now? Ruby is waiting in the Stewards Cottage. I think it's time to confront Lanfear while he is off guard. It should only take an hour of your time.'

'Of course, my lord, do you mind if Jessie comes with us?'

'As long as she stays out of the way.'

*

The earl's carriage entered the tradesmen's entrance at Bochym, and so as not to alert the household, they surreptitiously made their way into the back of the Stewards Cottage. Mr and Mrs Parson had been sworn to secrecy about Ruby and Ellie's visit to their cottage. Unaware of what was going to occur today, as the earl's steward, Parson was just following orders.

Ellie stepped over the threshold of the familiar cottage to find Ruby Sanders waiting for her.

'Hello Ellie.' Ruby grinned as she greeted her. 'My, but you've grown since last I saw you!'

Ellie laughed nervously. 'I was only ten, but I do remember you now. You look just the same, Ruby.'

Peter broke up the conversation. 'If you're ready Elise, I can see from here that Lanfear is in the manor kitchen at the moment. All we need you to do is walk out into the courtyard. Lanfear thinks I am away from home, so I suspect as soon as he sees you, he'll be out to confront you. Don't worry we will be right here.'

'What shall I say, my lord?'

'Tell him that you know what he did to Pearl. He's an arrogant man - I think he will dig his own grave.'

Ellie bit her lip. 'I hope you're right.' She could feel her knees tremble as she made to step outside.

'I'll follow you shortly, Ellie. We'll trap the bastard together,' Ruby said patting her on her back.

*

Mrs Blair tutted loudly as she ran her finger across the blunt blade of her meat knife.

'Betsy, I need you to run this knife up to the scissor grinder man in Cury after luncheon.'

'Yes, Cook,' Betsy answered as she tried to scrub the kitchen table around the shoes Albert Lanfear was polishing.

Cook sighed audibly. 'Mr Lanfear, please would you not do that on my kitchen table, I need it clean to prepare luncheon.'

Lanfear ignored her and carried on polishing.

Carrington regarded him for a moment. 'What's eating you this morning, Albert? You've been sitting there for hours in high dudgeon. Have you not had to see to the earl today?'

'No, if you must know. The earl left first thing this morning without summonsing me to dress him! There's something bloody funny going on in this house, I can feel it in my blood.'

'Nevertheless, let Betsy clean the table properly,' Carrington ordered.

As Betsy scrubbed away, it was she who saw Ellie through the window, walking across the courtyard.

'Oh! Ellie Rosevear is here again!' she said innocently.

Lanfear glanced swiftly at Carrington and Bligh. 'What the devil does *she* want? You would think she'd get the message that she's not welcome.'

'Well clearly not,' Carrington mocked.

'Maybe this will warn her.' Lanfear grabbed the meat knife from the table.

Bligh gasped. Not wanting to become embroiled in any other scandal, she ran from the kitchen to hide.

Wrenching the kitchen door open, Lanfear growled, 'What do you want here?'

Ellie felt her blood chill and stepped back a few paces. 'Maybe some justice for Pearl Martin,' she said with confidence she didn't feel. 'I know what you did to her.'

Lanfear snorted as he pulled the door closed behind him. 'You bloody Rosevears, you never learn, do you? You were told to leave, nine years ago, you're going to be very sorry you didn't heed that warning.' His hand tightened on the meat knife he held out of sight behind his back.

As Lanfear began to advance on Ellie, Peter and the sergeant made ready to intervene.

'You just can't keep your nose out of other people's business, can you?' he snarled. 'Your mother was the same.' He grinned, 'But I had that interfering bitch sorted out good and proper. If you don't bugger off, I'll sort you out too.'

Ellie could feel the adrenalin searing through her veins, but she lifted her chin and said, 'You killed Pearl and you're not going to get away with it.'

Lanfear snorted. 'I already have, missy,' he hissed. 'No one is ever going to listen to the ravings of….' He cocked his head. '…what were you then, a ten year old child? Such a tender age to lose your little friend and then of course your stupid father slipped on Pearl Martin's blood!' Lanfear's laugh echoed around the courtyard. 'It couldn't have turned out better. I was rid of you all in a couple of days! But then *you* just had to crawl out of the woodwork, didn't you?' His lip curled menacingly. 'Well, say what you want missy, no sane person will believe your stupid little ghost story.'

Ruby stepped out to join Ellie. 'But they *will* listen to a living witness,' she said coolly, as Peter and the sergeant joined them.

Lanfear stilled as the smirk fell from his face. Realising he was trapped he lunged forward, hooked his arm around Ellie's neck and dragged her back towards the kitchen door.

Ellie screamed, but Lanfear tightened his grip and held the knife to her throat.

'Let her go,' the earl and the sergeant shouted in unison.

'Keep your bloody distance, or I'll do for her right now.'

Ellie yelped as the cold steel knife cut into her skin, she had no doubt that he'd kill her if he had to.

'We know what you've done - there is no getting away from it, Lanfear. Drop the knife now and give yourself up,' the sergeant said.

Lanfear looked at Ruby and sneered, 'You're going to be very sorry, Ruby Sanders, if you've been telling tales, because you're going to have the death of this interfering little bitch on your conscience forever.' He pressed the knife deeper into Ellie's neck.

Ellie trembled with fear as she felt the trickle of blood run down her cleavage. Every nerve in her body was alerted to the searing hot pain from the wound to her neck. She felt her head spin and her knees buckle, but Lanfear held her up and dug the knife deeper into the wound.

Cook emerged from the scullery on hearing Betsy shriek.

'For goodness sake girl, now what is it?' She peered out of the window and gasped in horror.

Peter panicked when he saw the blood. *How could he have put Elise in so much danger?* 'For god's sake man, let her go,' he pleaded.

Lanfear shook his head slowly. 'It seems I've nothing to lose now. I might as well be hanged for a sheep as a lamb.' Ellie screamed as he dug the knife deeper into her flesh, then a large bang resonated around the courtyard and both Ellie and Lanfear fell to the floor.

Cook was standing with a cast iron pan in her hand, her ample bosoms heaving with the effort of the strike. She looked down at her meat knife, saw the blood dripping from the blade and promptly fainted.

As the sergeant handcuffed Lanfear, Peter scooped Ellie into his arms and carried her through the kitchen and up the stairs, barking orders for the doctor to be summonsed immediately.

*

A roaring fire warmed the drawing room at Bochym Lodge, when Sarah arrived. She took a seat furthest away from the fire and looked quizzically at Carole.

'Whatever is the matter Carole, to summons me so urgently?'

'You'll never guess?' Carole said, pacing the room like a caged tiger.

Sarah frowned - Carole's behaviour was quite out of character. 'Enlighten me, please?'

Carole lent forward and whispered, 'Philip's been arrested this morning - for the attempted murder of Guy Blackthorn!'

'Pardon?' Sarah sat to attention.

'Would you believe it?' Carole stated in wide-eyed disbelief. 'This Blackthorn fellow was Philip's best man at our wedding!'

'I know who Guy is,' Sarah said in astonishment. 'Are you sure?'

Carole nodded confidently. 'The police informed me an hour ago. They came to tell me that Philip is in custody.'

Sarah sat up. 'Gracious. When did this happen? Is Guy alright?'

'Oh, apparently it happened last Christmas.'

Sarah's hand flew to her mouth, remembering the terrible accident which befell Guy. 'Do you think he did it?' she asked incredulously.

Carole shrugged her shoulders. 'I know they fell out of friendship with each other over that silly Rosevear girl.'

Sarah bristled. 'Elise is not silly, Carole! You are very wrong in your assumption of her.'

Carole gave a dismissive wave of her hand. 'Well all I know is that Blackthorn took umbrage at Philip for setting her up in the cottage.'

'As did we all!' Sarah added coolly.

Carole rolled her eyes impatiently.

'But why would Philip attempt to kill him?'

'I have no idea, but whether he did or didn't, I have no doubt that he'll get off. He'll have the best lawyer money can buy, but I shall have to divorce him!' she said deeply affronted. 'I will not have our good name tainted by association with such an allegation.'

Sarah regarded her sister-in-law. *Was that a wry smile on Carole's lips?*

*

As Sarah walked back through the arboretum she could hardly believe what she had heard. Lost in her reverie for a moment, a flash of black and white caught her eye as she saw Betsy running like the wind towards the stables.

As Sarah rounded the stable yard, a groom cantered out, almost knocking her sideways.

'Betsy, what is happening?'

'Oh my lady.' Betsy began to wail.' Mr Lanfear has killed Ellie.'

33

Silas sat up straight and craned his neck to catch a glimpse of Jessie, as the wagon rounded Poldhu hill. Guy watched him and grinned, realising there would be four happy people in the Tea Room this day.

The cold front which had threatened all morning chilled the air. A thick misty rain swathed the cliffs at Poldhu, but as always in Cornwall, it probably wouldn't last long. After hobbling Mazie, they were both disappointed to find everywhere locked and deserted. Brandy, who was locked in the cottage, began to whine on hearing voices.

'They can't be far away. It's hardly weather to be out and about,' Guy said. He ran his fingers under the terrace for the spare key to the Tea Room, knowing Ellie wouldn't mind if they let themselves in.

Inside they shrugged off their damp coats and Guy inspected the range. The dying embers suggested they'd been gone for a while.

'Guy, I'm starving. We've not had breakfast. Do you think Ellie has some cake stowed away?'

'Undoubtedly she has - bring me some too.' Guy stoked and rebuilt the fire and put a kettle on to boil. They passed an hour waiting, by which time the day had cleared and the landmass at Land's End could now be seen.

Brandy's whining and barking increased, clearly agitated at being cooped up in the cottage. It was strange for Ellie to leave Brandy unattended for so long. Guy felt a curl of anxiety form in his stomach - perhaps something had happened!

'I'm going up to the hotel to see if they know where they are, Silas.'

'I'll come too. Blue could do with a walk.'

'Well, why don't you go up to Poldhu Head? Ellie may have been over to visit James and waited for the weather to clear before returning, you might see her coming back.'

Guy passed several minutes at The Poldhu Hotel. He'd become firm friends with several members of the staff whilst working alongside them repairing the Tea Room. None of them seemed to know where Ellie had gone, until Eric, one of the groundsmen, approached.

'Hello Guy.' He slapped him on his back jovially.

'You haven't seen Ellie, have you?'

Eric pulled a face. 'Not since earlier. She was beachcombing about three hours ago, just as the tide turned.'

Guy nodded and stood enjoying the breathtaking view from the hotel before setting off back down the cliff path. In the far distance, the impressive St Michael's Mount stood majestically out in the ocean. After every storm like the one they had just had, the Cornish cliffs suffered. Being only sand and shale in some places the mighty waves could eat great chunks out of the landscape. Thankfully the storm had not damaged these cliffs - they were made of granite and would probably withhold an earthquake.

He peered over the edge of the cliff into the cove below. The tide was in and a line of sea birds and oyster catchers were feeding along the water's edge. He watched for a moment until something caught his attention - a piece of material was flapping against the rocks.

Silas had returned with Blue and was whittling a piece of drift wood, when Guy ran past the terrace in a panic.

He sat up with a start. 'Guy, what is it, what's wrong?'

'I don't know yet.'

As Guy neared the water's edge, his worst fears came to fruition – the material he could see, was the shawl he'd given Ellie. It was a good way out, caught on the rocks. As he stood in the surf, the emerald green ribbon he'd given Ellie curled around his ankle - every nerve in his body prickled a warning. He quickly shed his clothes and plunged naked into the incoming tide.

Not being a swimmer himself, Silas gathered Guy's clothes and pulled them away from the advancing water while watching horrified as the waves tossed Guy about like a cork.

Guy powered through the waves as though his life depended on it. When he reached the rocks he heaved his body out of the water, and pulled the shawl from where it had caught.

He held it to his heart. *Oh god Ellie, please don't be caught on the rocks underwater.*

'Ellie!' he yelled into the abyss, as he dived back in and searched for her underwater. Periodically he surfaced, shook the hair from his face and shouted her name over and over, but he could not find his Ellie.

Guy's tormented shouts drifted in on the wind, chilling Silas to the bone.

The air was thick with the scent of drying seaweed. The great pine trees that fringed the west side of the cove, hung heavy with black rooks cawing assertively from their kingdom. When Guy finally crawled from the surf, battered and beaten, clutching Ellie's shawl, his heart imploded. *This time he feared he'd been too late.*

*

At Bochym, the sergeant, with the help of Joe Treen the footman, had dragged Lanfear into the log store, scuffing the toes of his shiny shoes on the ground. Lanfear moaned incoherently as he regained consciousness. With his hands safely handcuffed behind him, Ruby revelled at his downfall. As the sergeant walked out into the courtyard, rubbing his back from the exertion, Joe Treen gave Lanfear a hefty kick in the kidneys.

'That's from everyone who knows you.'

*

Peter had placed Ellie carefully on the deep feather bed in the Blue Room and pulled his cravat off to stem the blood oozing from her neck. *He'd never forgive himself for this.*

'Oh god, I'm so sorry, Elise.' He panicked. 'I never meant to put you in such danger.'

Sarah burst into the bedroom and rushed to the bed.

'Peter! What has happened?' She searched his face for answers.

'I'm afraid it's my fault, Sarah. I used her to trap Lanfear.'

'What?' She looked aghast. 'My god, Peter, how could you let him kill her?'

'She's not dead!' His voice faltered.

'But…' Sarah glanced at Ellie and saw her eyelids flutter. 'Oh thank the lord.'

Ellie began to shake uncontrollably, her fingers trembling as she reached up to her throat - she felt as though her skin was on fire.

'Sarah,' she whispered desperately.

'Stay calm, Elise, the doctor is coming.' She grabbed the cravat off Peter and began to tend Ellie's wounds. 'I need hot water! Now!'

Peter raked his hand through his hair. 'I'll send a maid up with it and bring the doctor straight up when he arrives,' he said.

Sarah gave him a curt nod. Deeply angry with him, she couldn't trust herself to speak to him at the moment.

*

As Betsy made Mrs Blair a cup of sweet tea, Carrington and Bligh stood in the kitchen in stunned silence.

Visibly concerned at the turn of events, Carrington whispered, 'Stay calm Joan, deny any allegations of misconduct.' But when Ruby stepped into the kitchen with Jessie, they realised they were in deep trouble.

As Peter walked into the kitchen, Mrs Blair, Betsy, Ruby and Jessie dropped a curtsy and Bligh grasped Carrington by the arm.

'Bessie, please take some hot water and towels up to Lady Sarah in the Blue Room. Jessie, could you take a carriage to Poldhu and fetch some overnight things. I suspect Miss Rosevear will need you to stay with her tonight.'

Jessie bobbed a curtsy.

'You and you,' Peter pointed at Carrington and Bligh, 'Wait in the housekeeper's room until I send for you.'

Shocked at the vehemence of the earl's voice, they meekly retreated from the kitchen.

'Treen, please stand in for Carrington.'

Joe stood up straight and pulled his shoulders back. 'Yes, my lord.'

*

As Guy and Silas silently walked back up the beach, a carriage came down Poldhu Hill. A woman alighted and ran towards the cottage, halting in her tracks when she saw Guy and Silas.

'Jessie!' Silas ran towards her.

As they fell into an embrace Jessie sobbed. She lifted her head from Silas's chest and glanced tearfully at Guy's distraught face. 'You've heard then?'

'That Ellie has drowned?' Guy answered, his voice faltering as he held the sodden shawl out to her.

'No, Guy, Ellie hasn't drowned….' Jessie's face crumpled. 'It's much more serious than that!'

*

On hearing what had happened to Ellie, Guy jumped in the carriage with Jessie, leaving Silas to follow in the wagon with the dogs.

The doctor had not long left when Guy arrived at Bochym. Without invitation, Guy burst through the kitchen door, almost giving Mrs Blair a heart attack.

'Ellie, Ellie,' he shouted as he skidded down the corridor, looking for someone to direct him to her. He almost collided with Betsy, who had her arms full of blood soaked sheets and clothes.

'Guy.' Sarah, on hearing his shouts, met him on the stairs.

'Ellie, oh my god, where is she?'

Sarah placed her hands gently on his arms. 'She's upstairs - she's lost a lot of blood. The doctor has stitched her wounds and given her something for the pain.'

A cry of anguish escaped his throat. 'I need to see her, please let me see her.'

'She's very weak, Guy.'

'I *need* to see her, *now*!' his voice raised a few decibels.

Peter stepped out of his study. 'Let him go up to her, Sarah,' he said quietly.

Guy swung around to face Peter, but the urgency to see Ellie surpassed any anger he felt towards him for putting her in such danger.

Sarah nodded. 'Of course, come with me.'

*

Guy stepped into the luxurious bedroom, his dirty, sand encrusted boots leaving a residue as he walked slowly towards the bed in which Ellie was sleeping. Her pale face was coated with a thin film of perspiration, and the white bandage at her throat gave her a deathly appearance.

He fell to his knees. 'Ellie!' He reached for her cool hand and brought it to his lips.

Ellie stirred, someone was holding her hand, soft and gentle was the touch. Oh how she remembered that touch – it was Guy's touch. She could smell the sweet reed thatch. His hair always smelt of it. She parted her lips as her tongue tried to wet her paper dry mouth. She felt dreadfully tired, but forced her eyes to open. Her world stilled. 'It is you,' she whispered.

Guy moved to sit on the bed. 'Oh god, Ellie, hold on my love.' His hands rested gently on her arms, the softness of her borrowed silk nightdress felt unusually strange on fingers used to rough cotton and homespun wool.

Ellie could not decipher how Guy could be beside her, she frowned. 'Your wedding?'

He pulled his lips tight and shook his head.

She swallowed, flinching at the pull on her scars. 'Did you renege on your promise?' Her voice was hardly audible.

He shook his head again. 'Clara did.'

Ellie closed her eyes and sighed. 'I'm so tired, Guy.'

'Then sleep my love, I'm right here by your side,' He leant to whisper in her ear. 'But don't you leave me, Ellie, you hear me. I need you.'

Ellie's eyelids fluttered as she fell into a deep sleep.

*

Sarah left Guy watching over Ellie. When she entered Peter's study, he was stood, hands clasped behind his back, quietly gazing out of the window. He'd been expecting her visit. When he turned she was leant against the door, arms folded.

'If you're here to berate me, Sarah, rest assured, I am doing that without your input.'

Shocked to see the grey pallor of his skin, having seemingly aged in the last hour, Sarah was still determined to have her say.

'First of all, Peter, I do not know what possessed you to put Elise in so much danger. And why on earth did you keep me in the dark about what was going to happen this morning?'

'Well there I must ask your forgiveness, my darling. You see, once I'd heard Ruby's story, I knew I must act fast. I didn't want that man under my roof for a moment longer than was necessary. If I'd have told you his true character, you would have flushed him out of the door immediately and he would have gone to ground. Once Ruby had given her statement to the police, and we'd gathered evidence from Mr Gray the undertaker, the sergeant and I went to see Elise for her side of the story. We knew we needed to catch Lanfear unawares, so we set a trap for him.'

'With Elise as bate!' she said through gritted teeth.

'Yes, if you will,' he answered sheepishly. 'She was quite willing, I might add. We know from old how Lanfear reacts to Elise, so we thought her presence in the courtyard would urge him to come out and confront her. He's an arrogant bastard, if you'll excuse my bad language, and we knew he'd dig his own grave, so to speak.' Peter sat down heavily on his seat and shook his head. 'The sergeant and I were ready to step out and arrest him, but Lanfear was armed with a knife, that was when everything escalated into this dreadful nightmare.' He raked his hands through his hair making it stand on end. 'I'll never forgive myself for this act of stupidity.' He looked up hopefully. 'Will she pull through?'

Sarah's face crumpled. 'With the amount of blood loss, the doctor is doubtful. I haven't told Guy.' Her lip trembled.

'I shall pray for her. If she comes through this I'll do everything to make amends. I promise.'

Sarah sighed and sat down. 'Are you going to tell me the whole story?'

Peter nodded, just as the police wagon trundled down the drive. 'I'll explain everything later, darling, just as soon as we get Lanfear off my land.'

Sarah nodded. 'Before you do that Peter, we need to send a telegram to James Blackwell. He needs to know what has happened.'

34

After giving a lengthy statement to the police and following the removal of Lanfear from Bochym, Peter called for Sarah and Ruby to join him in his study. A few minutes later he sent for Carrington and Bligh.

Carrington wore his usual air of authority while Bligh remained stony-faced as they stood defiantly before the assembled audience.

Peter cleared his throat. 'Albert Lanfear has been arrested for the attempted murder of Elise Rosevear and the murder of Pearl Martin, the latter of which you two are guilty by association.'

Carrington's mouth slackened. 'Well excuse me….' he protested.

'Be *quiet,* man.'

Carrington clamped his mouth shut, but flared his nostrils, unaccustomed to be spoken to in such a manner.

'You both knew what was happening to Pearl, and by all accounts neither of you lifted a finger to help her.'

Bligh stood her ground. 'We were only following your father's orders.'

'You have a duty of care to the staff under you. You were not employed to prime our maids to be taken advantage of by my debauched father!'

'But it's Droit de Seigneur – the Right of the Master to use the maids!' Carrington was affronted. 'Your father would turn in his grave if he heard you speak like that about him.'

'Hold your tongue, Carrington. I've allowed you to take liberties in the way you address me long enough, because of your long service here, but no more will I put up with your insolence.' Peter moved closer to Carrington until they were almost nose to nose. 'After what I've heard from Ruby, the very thought of my father sickens me. I hope he turns in his grave regularly. He should rot in hell for what he did to Pearl Martin, as should anyone who assisted him!'

Bligh took a sharp intake of breath and Peter rounded on her.

'Shame on you, Bligh! Shame on you both! When Lanfear killed that poor girl, you two covered his tracks. You lied to the household, telling them that Pearl had ruined herself and run away, when hours before, you had called the undertaker to take her body away!' He glanced between them with cold anger in his eyes. 'If that wasn't enough, you sullied Pearl's name to the undertaker, saying she'd committed suicide. You told him to drop the poor girl in unconsecrated ground, when you had both taken part in forcing her into immorality!'

Bligh stuck her chin out. 'The girl went willingly to your father's bedchamber. She was nothing but a whore.'

'She *was* not, and *did* not, and *you* know it!' He pointed at her.

Carrington and Bligh visibly swallowed hard.

'When Mr Gray took Pearl's body away to make ready for burial, not only did he find she was three months gone with child, but she'd been suffocated and violated that day! My father, as Ruby informed me, was away from home at the time.'

Both Carrington and Bligh glanced at Ruby and shifted uneasily.

'As I said, Pearl was a whore,' Bligh said haughtily, 'She'd probably been free with some lad from the village. Mr Lanfear, as the earl's valet, had gone to Tehidy with his master so he could not have been involved in the girl's demise.'

Peter's mouth tightened. 'And still you lie for him. You know very well that Lanfear had been left behind. By all accounts there had been some disagreement between Lanfear and another valet the previous time my father visited Tehidy. Lanfear was excluded from accompanying my father and left behind!'

Bligh opened her mouth and shut it again without

speaking.

'I don't want to hear any more of your lies. I know exactly what happened to Pearl that night! I also know that you had Mrs Rosevear, a newly widowed woman and her child, banished from the manor, because she'd found out what was going on here.'

'Rosevear was making allegations that would bring your father's name into disrepute. She was dismissed on his orders,' Carrington said in his defence.

'She was *not* dismissed on his orders! As I have just pointed out my father was away from home while all this happened.'

Carrington lifted his chin in defiance. 'I think I knew your father well enough to know that he would have supported any decision I made to protect his name!'

'Do *you,* Carrington? Damn you for your arrogance. The only things you were protecting were your own necks, and that is why you also dismissed Ruby, wasn't it? You falsely accused her of theft, threatened her that she would be reported to the constable and most probably hanged for the offence if she so much as breathed a word of what she'd seen here at the manor. Well thankfully Ruby did speak out and I now know everything about what happened that week - *everything!*'

'We were just trying to protect your father,' Carrington stood his ground. 'As it turned out the whole incident was too much for him. When he heard what had happened on his return, he died of a heart attack three days later - god rest his soul.'

'Fiddlesticks, it was a life of drink and debauchery that killed him. Now, you will both pack your bags and leave my house within the hour. You will *not* be given references.'

Bligh's face crumpled.

Affronted, Carrington said, 'You….you can't do that!'

'I believe I just did. I hope you will struggle to find a roof over your head, and work to sustain you, just as Ruby and the Rosevears struggled when you instigated their removal from this house with your lies. Now, *get out* of my sight.'

*

A horrified hush had fallen in the study as Peter, Ruby and Sarah glanced at each other.

Presently Peter said, 'Thank you, Ruby for all you've done. I promise faithfully that our family will try to compensate you for all the hurt and worry that has befallen you.'

Ruby nodded. 'Thank you, my lord.'

'Oh Peter.' Sarah buried her face in her hands. 'To think we have been paying those monster's wages since all this happened.'

'I know, my love, but justice has been done now,' Peter answered flatly.

'Yes, but at what price?' Sarah cried.

'Indeed.'

Sarah got up and dabbed her eyes. 'Ruby if you'd like to take a seat in the drawing room, I'll arrange for some refreshments for you. Peter, please excuse me, I need to go and sit with Elise.'

*

Pearl stood in the corner of the drawing room, watching her friend Ruby dab her tears. How she wished she could make her presence known to her. Pearl was so thankful that her story had been told at last, but in truth only she knew the true horrors of what that vile creature, Lanfear did to her. Even though she knew no one could hear her, she wanted to tell her story now:

On that fateful day Lanfear had visited me in the dairy, I was taken weeping from my bed later that night. The corridors were empty, cleared by Carrington and Bligh, but I saw them in the shadows, watching as I was dragged into the old earl's bedchamber. The room was hot and stank of stale sweat and brandy. Although the fire blazed in the hearth I shivered uncontrollably as Lanfear stripped me of my nightdress and led me naked to the earl's bed.

Even though I've been dead these last nine years, my skin still creeps with the memory of Lanfear's sweaty hands molesting every part of my body. The earl was drunk - his stinking breath was hot on my face as he tried unsuccessfully to violate me. Eventually he moved to one side and held me down while Lanfear raped me!

This torture, I endured every subsequent night, except when I had my monthly courses, which of course stopped when his disgusting seed began to grow inside me.

I made a fundamental mistake the day I died. I pleaded with Lanfear for money, so I could get rid of the baby. Knowing his character, I should have been wary when he agreed to bring the money that night.....he entrapped me. He said, "When whores ask for money, they must return the favour," as he wedged the chair against my bedroom door. He stripped from the waist and forced himself on me. I screamed for help, but he covered my face with my pillow. In my struggle to breathe, my nose burst, blood trickled down my throat and I choked violently. Stars burst alarmingly in my head until my world turned white. The transition from searing pain and panic to feeling nothing at all was almost instant. My soul moved from under his pounding body to stand by as an onlooker as he continued to violate my lifeless body. When he realised I was dead, he panicked and scrambled from the bed, shaking in his shirt tails. His eyes were wild as they scanned the room, then his gaze settled on the window. I knew then he meant to throw me out of it. I did the only thing I could think of, I went to the one person who I knew could witness what he was about to do - Ellie. I knew she could see things no one else could – it was her gift.

I deeply regret that Ellie was hurt today, but I fear if she had not been attacked by that vile man, his misdemeanours towards me perhaps would not have led to his arrest. After all, what judge would take the word of a child witness who had seen a ghost, and a girl with a grudge?

My other regret was that it was my blood that Ellie's father, Thomas Rosevear, slipped on and caused his untimely demise. He was a good man and if I'd had the nerve to tell him what was happening to me, he would surely have had it stopped. But I did not, therefore it did not stop.

The one thing I don't regret though, is killing the earl…..Yes, I killed him! It took six days after my own demise, but revenge was so sweet. I had no power to move things or rattle windows then, my haunting skills were and still are, minimal, but my piece de resistance was to chill any room I stood in, and that was how I killed him. No fire could warm his bedchamber. As he slept I blew into his mouth and chilled his very soul. He became ill and shivered constantly. The doctor was brought, but no pill or potion would stop the chill which ran through his veins. As I blew on his face on the sixth night, he opened his eyes and looked straight at me. His heart failure was instant. He would never torment another young girl again.

*

As Ellie drifted in and out of consciousness, she sensed the sombre mood in the room. She was frightened. Everyone spoke in hushed tones, and occasionally someone leant gently towards her, speaking words of love and encouragement. She felt the residue of tears Jessie left on her skin when she kissed her on the cheek. *Are people saying goodbye to me?* She wondered.

With James's arrival, Ellie rallied slightly and she managed to open her eyes when his cool hand encircled hers.

'Come on Ellie, come brave,' he whispered, but Ellie felt too tired to acknowledge the challenge.

Her one constant comfort was Guy's hand in hers, his other, gently mopping her fevered brow. She felt so terribly hot.

Snippets of conversations filtered through the fug in her head. Guy's cancelled wedding, Clara's faithlessness, Philip's arrest - nothing made sense.

Suddenly a wave of pain constricted her throat and Ellie thought she was going to choke. Perspiration drenched her nightgown. The conversation in the room ceased, as hands pulled at her fingers to stop her clawing the bandages on her neck.

'Stay calm, Ellie,' Guy whispered as Sarah pressed a glass of water to her paper dry lips. Ellie shivered uncontrollably, as water trickled down the side of her mouth. Sheer panic ensued as she stared wild-eyed at Sarah and Guy. S*he felt as though she was falling into a white abyss.*

'Oh god! Guy?....... Guy?' Her voice rasped. 'Hold me.'

'I'm here, my love.'

She felt the weight of his strong arm across her body, but she needed more.

'No, Guy. Hold me closer. Don't let me fall, don't let me go.'

Guy scrambled on the bed to lie beside her, his thigh pressing intimately against hers. 'I won't let you go, Ellie, I promise.' Choked with emotion, his hand covered hers - their hearts pounding in unison.

With fear and dread burning in his eyes, Guy looked to Sarah, who swallowed back her own tears and quickly beckoned everyone from the room. The door closed… and they were alone.

'I'm right here, Ellie. I'm holding you my love.' He kissed her tenderly on the mouth and felt her body relax in his hold. *Oh God, please don't take my Ellie.*

Ellie felt a great calmness envelope her. She gazed with love into Guy's tearful eyes. 'I'm so tired,' she whispered.

'Ellie, *don't* leave me.'

A single tear ran down her cheek at his heartfelt plea, but Guy's face faded away. A silky breeze enveloped her body and an ice cold hand cooled her fevered brow. Ellie looked up at Pearl who was smiling down on her.

35

The rain fell like a veil of tears over the assembled gathering in Cury Churchyard as the vicar, new to the parish, finished his funeral sermon.

One by one, the mourners approached with a single rose, procured from the hot-house at Bochym Manor.

As Guy stepped back, the last mourner stepped forward, knelt down by the grave and whispered, 'Rest in peace.'

Her slender fingers traced the words on the headstone.

Here lie the mortal remains of Pearl Martin, aged fifteen.

1878 – 1893

At rest now, under the Cornish Sky

When Ellie had been close to death four weeks ago, Pearl had cooled her fever with her ice-cold touch. It was not time for her to go. It was time for her to live.

'Come, my love.' Guy took Ellie by the hand. 'We have a wedding to prepare for tomorrow.'

*

It was seven-thirty a.m. on Saturday 25th October. Ellie was restless to rise, but was forced to endure breakfast in bed on this, her wedding day. She could hear Jessie preparing a tray in the kitchen and resigned herself to allowing Jessie to pamper her.

Ellie's bedroom, which she would share with Guy this very night, faced east and following the rainy day yesterday, today the autumn sun slanted through the gap in the curtains, highlighting the dust motes in the atmosphere. It was going to be a lovely day all round.

Once Jessie allowed her to rise, Ellie changed the bed and polished the room until it sparkled. She stood back and looked at the tidy room. She loved Guy with all her heart, but as her wedding night neared she felt an uncontrollable tremble in her limbs.

'Hello, Elise. Where are you?'

Sarah's voice brought Ellie back to the present.

As Sarah breezed into the cottage bringing with her a delicate waft of perfume, she kissed Ellie on the cheek and held out a box containing her bouquet and headdress. 'Fresh from our hot house - I do hope you like them.'

'They're lovely.' Ellie buried her nose into the fragrant flowers. 'You are clever, thank you.'

'We have white and red rose buds, gypsophila and of course the customary sprig of myrtle, for luck. Unfortunately the myrtle isn't in flower at the moment, Elise, but the leaves hold the same good fortune as the flowers, I promise.' She paused for a moment and tipped her head. 'Is everything alright?'

'Everything is fine.'

Knowing that look of trepidation, Sarah smiled sympathetically, having experienced it herself only last year, as she made ready for her own wedding day. She reached for Ellie's hands, which were cold, and gave them a comforting squeeze.

'Guy is a kind, gentle man, Elise. *All* of this day will be truly wonderful for you, I promise you that.'

Ellie blushed shyly.

'Now, Elise, Peter is here with me. We want to give you something special for a wedding present.'

Ellie blinked. 'Oh, but you've already done so much Sarah, by hosting our wedding breakfast at Bochym!'

Sarah dismissed the comment with a wave of her hand. 'Think nothing of that. You know how I *love* to entertain. Come, this will only take a moment, I think Peter is taking tea with James. I'm so glad James offered to act in loco parentis to give you away, if he hadn't, Peter would have done it in a heartbeat.'

Peter and James stood to greet Ellie. She kissed James and dropped a small curtsy to Peter, who in turn bowed and kissed her hand gallantly.

'Do join us,' he said, 'Jessie has been looking after us.'

'Jessie has been looking after me all morning too, haven't you?' Ellie grinned at her.

As they sat, Peter handed Ellie a large envelope. 'I don't know if this will go anywhere near compensating for the awful thing that happened to you at Bochym last month, Elise or the great wrong done to your family nine years ago, but Sarah and I would like to gift to you the title deeds of this place as a wedding gift.'

Jessie gasped as Ellie shot a questioning look at James, who nodded happily.

'When I told James that I wanted to do something special for you, he very kindly sold the deeds to me. So my dear, you are now the sole owner of The Poldhu Tea Rooms, the cottage attached and the land they sit on.'

Ellie put her hand to her chest and glanced teary-eyed between them. 'I'm overwhelmed, I….I don't know what to say, except thank you.' She pressed the envelope to her breast and looked up at the Tea Room. All this was hers now. 'It's ironic, that the first thing I do on becoming the owner is to close the place for the day!'

Sarah laughed. 'I'm sure your customers will forgive you, this once.'

'I hope so.' Ellie stared out to sea. Though it was October, Poldhu Hotel was fully booked with visitors and because of the fine weather, they would inevitably make there way down to the beach.

At that moment, Tobias Williams, redundant for the winter months now the beach huts were no longer needed, walked past, dragging his reluctant dog down the beach. He doffed his hat at Earl and Countess de Bochym.

Knowing full well his response, Jessie couldn't resist calling out, 'It's going to be a lovely day, Mr Williams.'

'Humph, it won't last,' he drawled.

*

An hour later, Ellie sat at her dressing table. Still pale and a little tired from the blood loss, she rubbed a little rouge on her cheeks and bit down on her lips to stimulate a rosy hue. Possessing no jewellery of her own, she screwed the small pearl earrings onto her ear lobes, which Sarah had kindly lent her.

'Your borrowed item,' Sarah had told her, as she placed the velvet box in her hands.

Ellie had purchased a length of pale blue ribbon from the haberdashery in Helston to tie her new stockings up with – something new and blue. In her petticoat pocket she placed the very first lace trimmed handkerchief her mother had made. It was something old and a piece of her mother to take to church with her.

With Jessie's help, Ellie's long wavy hair was twisted loosely and pulled back from her face, tied with a long white satin ribbon. A halo of white and red rose buds, intertwined with gypsophila, nestled on the crown of her head.

Jessie helped Ellie to slip on the wedding dress she had so lovingly adorned with delicate lace over the last few years. The dress, like herself, had been through many misfortunes, but had survived. The under slip was a simple empire line, gathered lightly under the bust, and made from the finest Egyptian cotton. Betty had sourced a bolt of it from the Helston haberdashery many years ago to make tablecloths. When Ellie had felt the quality, she'd badgered Betty for some of it to make her wedding slip. As she slipped it on, its silky softness felt like the finest silk to her. The over dress was a waterfall of delicate white lace from the high neck to the ground and had taken Ellie years to make.

As Jessie fastened the delicate buttons up the back of the dress, Ellie glanced in the mirror, thankful the dress hid the angry scars on her throat. Even now, almost four weeks since that awful day, Ellie's nights were disturbed, waking to a cold sweat, feeling the knife to her skin. She gently laid her hand to her neck - from tonight, she would not be alone with her fears. She would be safe in Guy's arms forever and a day.

'Oh Ellie,' Jessie cooed. 'It's more beautiful on than it is off, if that's possible. You look like a queen.'

Ellie's smile broadened. 'You look lovely too, Jessie. That dress suits you perfectly.'

Jessie pulled out her new floral dress and swayed to and fro. 'I've never owned a dress like it.'

Ellie turned again to the mirror, and her eyes glittered with happy tears. 'I can't believe this is happening at last, Jessie.'

'Well I truly believe if you wish hard enough for something, it will happen.'

'What do you wish for, Jessie?'

'I wish that Silas will think I'm pretty in my new dress!"

Ellie grasped her hand. 'Silas would think you're pretty if you were dressed in a sack.'

Jessie tinkled with laughter.

'Besides it's customary for the best man to admire the maid of honour, I'm sure Silas won't be able to take his eyes off you.'

Jessie blushed to the roots of her hair. 'Oh by the way, Archie the postman called when you were getting ready, to wish you good luck.'

'That's strange, I never heard Brandy whine when he came.'

'Well, Brandy was wagging his tail and licking Archie's fingers.'

'You're joking?'

'I'm not. I reckon the dog knows that Archie isn't going to bring you bad news anymore!' Jessie grinned.

'Hear, hear to that.'

'If you're ready, Ellie, I think I have just heard the pony-trap pull up.'

Ellie glanced once more at herself in her lovely dress. Guy had rescued it from the sea and it was Sarah who had had it cleaned.

'I think of it as another gift from the sea,' he'd told her.

'Another? You mean like the sea glass?'

Guy had smiled. 'Yes, but the best gift the sea ever

gave me, was when it let me rescue you.'

Ellie smiled at her reflection. 'I love you Guy,' she whispered, before stepping out of her bedroom to greet James.

He pulled her into a warm embrace. 'This is the happiest of days for me, Ellie. I am truly honoured to be tasked with giving you away to one of the nicest men I know. You look stunning.' He held his arm out for her to take.

So she didn't have to walk over the dunes and fill her shoes with sand, the pony-trap had pulled up behind the cottage. As Ellie neared, she faltered on seeing her driver, it was Harry Yates!

'Harry?'

'Good morning, Miss Ellie, and may I say I've never seen a lovelier bride than you.'

Ellie grinned. 'But Harry you're meant to be my guest today!'

'Ah well, this is one driving job I really wanted to do. I would not have missed it for the world.' He took her by the hand and kissed it.

'Thank you Harry, but are you sure you're alright?'

'How could I be anything but alright? I'm about to see you married to the best of men. Come on, up you get.'

She kissed him gently on his whiskery chin and climbed aboard.

*

The new Mr and Mrs Blackthorn emerged from Cury Church, arm in arm into the autumn sunshine, to a modest peal of bells. Amongst their guests were Betty and her sister, the former had dabbed her eyes continually as she watched her surrogate daughter take her vows. Amelia too was there, travelling from Gweek with Harry. Ruby, who had been offered and accepted the role of housekeeper at Bochym, sat quite content on the same pew as the Earl and Countess de Bochym - although they employed her, Ruby classed them both now as friends.

As the guests milled around the peaceful church yard, chatting in the morning sunshine, Harry whispered to Guy, 'I hear Goldsworthy is out of jail. His parents paid his surety.'

'Oh no!' Guy's face fell.

'Yes but the best news is that he's absconded abroad!'

'Really?'

'If that isn't the action of a guilty man, I don't know what is,' Harry said with a nod of the head. 'He'll not show his face around here again. I understand his parents have disowned him. They've put a manager in charge of the mill and put it up for sale. Bert Laity said they're moving back to Launceston where they originated from.'

Guy smiled with relief – that was a load off his mind.

*

The wedding breakfast had been a fine affair – far outweighing anything they could have ever afforded. Held in the French drawing room, all the Bochym staff had been invited to join them, in between rushing back and forth with wine and food. There had been a few changes in the staff hierarchy. Ruby, in her role as housekeeper, smiled and aided Betsy to keep the glasses filled and tables spread with a beautiful buffet lunch. Joe Treen had been elevated to the role of Butler and had made firm friends with Theo Trevail, the earl's new and very likable valet.

It didn't go unnoticed by Ellie that Lowenna Kernow, Sarah's new lady's maid gazed at the new valet with longing eyes. Ellie smiled - a new love story perhaps? She hoped their journey would be smoother than hers.

Carole, thankfully, was not in attendance. Having relinquished all ties with her errant husband, she and her mother had taken themselves off on a very long Italian tour.

*

As they rode in the carriage, swathed in fluttering ribbons, down the hill to Poldhu in the diminishing daylight, Guy and Ellie were both quiet, fizzing with bubbles from champagne neither was accustomed to.

They had politely refused the offer of a luxurious room at Bochym for their wedding night - both wanting to return to Poldhu to begin their married life, where they had fallen in love.

Jessie was staying at the manor for the night, in her old room in the attic. Silas was bedding down in the wagon on the estate to give Guy and Ellie some privacy on their wedding night. From tomorrow, Silas would use Ellie's old box room adjoining the Tea Room, whenever he and Guy were home from work, and Jessie would of course stay where she belonged, in the cottage.

Primrose Cottage would be sold perhaps, when Harry passed on, though both Guy and Ellie hoped that would not be for a long time. Guy's life was here now, near his Ellie, perhaps they would build out from the cottage when two bedrooms were not sufficient.

When they reached home, the cottage at Poldhu felt a little chilly, so Guy bent down to build a fire as Ellie looked on. The cottage had none of the fine furnishings of the room they had spent the afternoon in, but it was cosy and clean and belonged to her now.

'I can't believe this is ours now, Guy.'

Guy sat back on his haunches. 'It's yours, Ellie.'

Ellie raised her eyebrows inquisitively. 'Are we not one now?'

He smiled. 'We are indeed.'

'Then this is ours, Guy.'

She watched until the flames were licking at the kindling. 'I'll go and change out of my dress.'

'No! Please keep it on a while longer. You look so beautiful in it.' He reached for her hand and pressed a kiss into the cup of her palm.

A frisson ran through her body.

'Are you cold?' he said feeling her tremble. 'The fire should come good soon.'

'No Guy, I'm not cold.'

He gazed upon his new wife, knowing her anxiety of their first night together, but he would be as gentle as a lamb with her. It upset him to think he'd hurt her briefly tonight, but then he would make sure that for the rest of his days he would love her gently.

'I love you, Ellie.' He wrapped his arms around her as though to protect her. 'Come let's take a walk to the shoreline.'

He guarded the fire and handed Ellie her shawl. Issy had done a wonderful job laundering it after its dip in the sea.

The soft breeze blew through the tall marram grass as they walked hand in hand to the sea.

Tobias Williams approached, dragging his little dog up the beach behind him.

'So you're back, are you?'

Ellie glanced at Guy and pulled a face.

'Fancy closing the Tea Room on a Saturday - where's a man supposed to get a drink when he's thirsty?' he grumbled.

'Tobias.' Ellie smiled sweetly. 'Surely you can grant me one day off for my wedding?'

'Huh! So you've gone and got married have you?' he grizzled.

'We have, yes,' Ellie said gaily. 'I brought you some wedding cake and there are a few sandwiches in a bag on the terrace table for you.'

'Oh well.' Tobias pushed his finger under his cap as though to doff it. 'Thank ee, tis a kind thought.' He bid them goodnight and set off to collect his goodies. 'Marriage!' he muttered, shaking his head.

Guy and Ellie waited with bated breath, and sure enough as soon as Tobias thought he was out of ear shot, they heard him drawl, 'It won't last.'

Guy laughed gently. 'Oh yes it will.' He kissed Ellie passionately and they ran hand in hand down to the shoreline.

The sunset at Poldhu was magnificent that evening. Had it been earlier in the summer, the sun would have set over Land's End, but today it dipped its fiery ball into the inky blue sea, right before their eyes.

'You can almost here it hiss,' Ellie said as it disappeared, leaving a red gold slit across the evening sky.

'The end of a perfect day,' Guy said, squeezing her hand.

As the evening slowly began to drift across the cliff tops, Guy squeezed her hand tenderly. 'Shall we go back to the cottage, Mrs Blackthorn, so we can start the rest of our lives?'

'Mrs Blackthorn.' Ellie smiled 'How lovely does that sound?'

'Well, it's music to my ears.'

At the cottage door he scooped her into his arms and carried her over the threshold, kicking the door closed with his foot.

*

After the wedding party had departed Bochym, Sarah and Peter walked happily arm in arm along the corridor towards the great oak staircase. As they made to ascend the stairs, a robust gentleman, dressed in seventeenth century clothing, brushed gently against her.

'Oh!' Sarah turned and watched the figure move down the corridor.

'Oh no, Sarah.' Peter shook his head. 'If you've just seen another ghost, I don't want to know.'

Sarah smiled to herself. *Maybe it was time to research what happened in this house during the English Civil War now - and why this gentleman was still here.*

Epilogue

Albert Lanfear was hanged at Bodmin jail on the 14th October 1902. From that moment, Pearl Martin's soul was freed from the confines of Bochym Manor, much to the relief of Betsy, who never had cause to drop another pot in shock again.

End

ABOUT THE AUTHOR

Ann E Brockbank was born in Yorkshire, but has lived in Cornwall for many years. A Gift from the Sea is Ann's fifth book. Her inspiration comes from holidays and retreats in stunning locations in Greece, Italy, Portugal, France and Cornwall. When she's not travelling, Ann lives with her artist partner on the beautiful banks of the Helford River in Cornwall, which has been an integral setting for all of her novels. Ann is currently writing her sixth novel. Ann loves to chat with her readers so please visit her Facebook Author page and follow her on Twitter and Instagram

Facebook: @AnnEBrockbank.Author
Twitter: @AnnEBrockbank1
Instagram: annebrockbank

Please share the love of this book by writing a short review on Amazon. x

*

Bochym Manor

Please note, Bochym Manor is a private family home and the house is not open to the public. They do however have holiday cottages available via Cornwall Cottages. Bochym Manor Events also hold various art and craft workshop throughout the year.

Take a look at Bochym Manor Events on Facebook and Instagram for more information.

ACKNOWLEDGEMENTS

There is always a long list of people to thank for helping me get this book to publication and here they are. First and foremost, my heartfelt gratitude goes to Sarah and Martin Caton and their lovely family for allowing me to use their beautiful home Bochym Manor as a setting for 'A Gift from the Sea'. Sarah, this book is dedicated to you.

As always I could not have written this book without the editorial help and support of some very special people. My upmost thanks go to Angie, for reining in my creative spelling and for putting the apostrophes and commas in the right place and to Cathy for her sensitive editorial suggestions. I cannot thank you enough for your generous time, friendship and expertise.

To my beloved partner Rob, your love and encouragement has kept me writing, and as always your beautiful artwork adds a special quality to my novels.

To the amazing staff at Poldhu Café - I thank you for your support and for sustaining me with the most wonderful frothy coffee while I wrote this novel about your beautiful cove. Also to the lovely staff at The Boatyard Café, Gweek, for equally lovely frothy coffee and for your continual support.

To my darling late husband Peter – you are forever in my heart.

Last but certainly not least, grateful thanks to all you lovely people who buy and read my books. I so appreciate your lovely comments and your continual support. You are all wonderful.

If you enjoyed this book, please can I ask a huge favour from you to leave a short review on Amazon? You can do this even if you didn't buy the book on Amazon! I can't tell you how important reviews are to authors. If you loved this book, please spread the love and tell your friends, hopefully they too will support me by buying the book.

Printed in Great Britain
by Amazon